Praise for Miner

"Spencer creates characters v̶...
Phoebe's sisters find their own matches next.

-Publishers Weekly

THE BOXING BARONESS

"Swooningly romantic, sizzling sensual…superbly realized."

–Booklist STARRED REVIEW

A *Library Journal* Best Book of 2022

A Publishers Marketplace Buzz Books Romance Selection

"Fans of historical romances with strong female characters in non-traditional roles and the men who aren't afraid to love them won't be disappointed by this series starter."

–Library Journal STARRED REVIEW

"Spencer (*Notorious*) launches her Wicked Women of Whitechapel Regency series with an outstanding romance based in part on a real historical figure. . . This is sure to wow!"

-Publishers Weekly STARRED REVIEW

THE DUELING DUCHESS:

"Another carefully calibrated mix of steamy passion, delectably dry humor, and daringly original characters."

—*Booklist* STARRED REVIEW

VERDICT: Readers who enjoyed *The Boxing Baroness* won't want to miss Spencer's sequel.

–Library Journal STARRED REVIEW

A *Library Journal* Best Book of 2023

THE CUTTHROAT COUNTESS:

VERDICT: For anyone who loves the "Bridgerton" books but wishes its heroines were more adept with close combat and weaponry than the pianoforte, Spencer's novel delivers.

–Library Journal STARRED REVIEW

Praise for Minerva Spencer and S.M. LaViolette:

"[A] pitch perfect Regency …. Readers will be hooked." (THE MUSIC OF LOVE)

★*Publishers Weekly* STARRED REVIEW

"Lovers of historical romance will be hooked on this twisty story of revenge, redemption, and reversal of fortunes."

Publishers Weekly, STARRED review of THE FOOTMAN.

"Fans will be delighted."

Publishers Weekly on THE POSTILION

NOTORIOUS

★A *PopSugar* Best New Romance of November

★A *She Reads* Fall Historical Romance Pick

★A *Bookclubz* Recommended Read

"Brilliantly crafted…an irresistible cocktail of smart characterization, sophisticated sensuality, and sharp wit." ★*Booklist STARRED REVIEW*

"Sparkling…impossible not to love."—Popsugar

INFAMOUS

"Realistically transforming the Regency equivalent of a mean girl into a relatable, all-too-human heroine is no easy feat, but Spencer (Outrageous, 2021) succeeds on every level. Lightly dusted with wintery holiday charm, graced with an absolutely endearing, beetle-obsessed hero and a fully rendered cast of supporting characters and spiked with smoldering sensuality and wry wit, the latest in Spencer's Rebels of the Ton series is sublimely satisfying."

—Booklist STARRED review

"Perfect for fans of Bridgerton, Infamous is also a charming story for Christmas. In fact, I enjoyed Infamous so much that when I was halfway through it, I ordered the author's first novel, Dangerous. I look forward to reading much more of Minerva Spencer's work."

—THE HISTORICAL NOVEL SOCIETY

Praise for S.M. LaViolette's erotic historical romance series
<u>*VICTORIAN DECADENCE*</u>:

"LaViolette keeps the tension high, delivering dark eroticism and emotional depth in equal measure. Readers will be hooked."

-PUBLISHERS WEEKLY on HIS HARLOT

"LaViolette's clever, inventive plot makes room for some kinky erotic scenes as her well-shaded characters explore their sexualities. Fans of erotic romance will find much to love."

-PUBLISHERS WEEKLY on HIS VALET

Praise for Minerva Spencer's *Outcasts* series:

"Minerva Spencer's writing is sophisticated and wickedly witty. Dangerous is a delight from start to finish with swashbuckling action, scorching love scenes, and a coolly arrogant hero to die for. Spencer is my new auto-buy!"

-NYT Bestselling Author Elizabeth Hoyt

"[**SCANDALOUS** is] A standout...Spencer's brilliant and original tale of the high seas bursts with wonderfully real protagonists, plenty of action, and passionate romance."

★*Publishers Weekly STARRED REVIEW*

"Fans of Amanda Quick's early historicals will find much to savor." ★*Booklist* **STARRED REVIEW**

"Sexy, witty, and fiercely entertaining." ★*Kirkus* **STARRED REVIEW**

Selina

The Bellamy Sisters
Book 3

Minerva Spencer

writing as
S.M. LAVIOLETTE

Crooked Sixpence
CSP
Press

CROOKED SIXPENCE BOOKS are published by

CROOKED SIXPENCE PRESS

2 State Road 230

El Prado, NM 87529

Copyright © 2023 SHANTAL M. LaVIOLETTE

All rights reserved. No part of this publication may be reproduced, distributed, or transmitted in any form or by any means, including photocopying, recording, or other electronic or mechanical methods, without the prior written permission of the publisher, except in the case of brief quotations embodied in critical reviews and certain other noncommercial uses permitted by copyright law. For permission requests, write to the publisher, addressed "Attention: Permissions Coordinator," at the address above.

To the extent that the image or images on the cover of this book depict a person or persons, such person or persons are merely models, and are not intended to portray any character or characters featured in the book.

If you purchased this book without a cover you should be aware that this book is stolen property. It was reported as "unsold and destroyed" to the Publisher and neither the Author nor the Publisher has received any payment for this "stripped book."

First printing August 2023

10 9 8 7 6 5 4 3 2 1

Any references to historical events, real people, or real places are used fictitiously. Names, characters, and places are products of the author's imagination.

Printed in the United States of America

Chapter 1

London

"Selina, my dear? There is someone here who wishes for an introduction."

Lady Selina Bellamy turned at the sound of her Aunt Ellen's—Viscountess Fitzroy's—voice and was confronted by the most beautiful man she had ever seen. He was tall and lithe with dark gold hair and mischievous blue eyes. A Greek god made flesh; Apollo come down from Mount Olympus to frolic with unsuspecting maidens.

"Lord Shelton, this is my niece, Lady Selina Bellamy," her aunt said, for once not smiling.

Selina dropped a curtsey. "I'm pleased to make your acquaintance, my lord."

"The pleasure is all mine, my lady." Lord Shelton lifted her hand toward his mouth but was not so louche as to let his lips touch her glove. "I suppose I am too late?"

She cocked her head. "Too late?"

"I fear you have given away all your sets and do not have even a single dance free?" His tragic expression might have been convincing if not for the laughter dancing in his eyes.

"As it happens, I have the supper dance free as my partner was called away on an emergency."

"Ah, yes, that poor, poor man."

Selina frowned. "You know who my partner was and what happened to him?"

"No," he admitted. "But anyone called away from a dance with you is a poor, poor man."

Selina laughed.

"I will count the minutes until the supper set," he said, bowing to both her and her aunt and then gracefully moving off into the crowd.

Her aunt inched closer and murmured, "Well. That was unfortunate."

"It was?" Selina asked, confused.

"That man shouldn't be allowed within a league of a gently bred young woman. The only reason Shelton is received anywhere is out of courtesy to the Duke of Chatham."

Selina, who'd been admiring Lord Shelton's broad, elegant shoulders and narrow waist, turned at her aunt's hostile tone. "But… what do you mean?"

"Shelton is Chatham's heir and might very well become duke if Chatham never remarries—which is a distinct possibility—but the man is not good *ton*."

"What did he do?"

"I do not like to repeat gossip, but you should know the story because the dratted man is simply too beautiful and charming for a female's peace of mind." She leaned even closer. "Several years ago, he dallied with Sir John Creighton's daughter. The girl was very pretty, but the family is not wealthy and her father is a nobody. Shelton took the girl out driving in his carriage—just the two of them—and they were caught by foul weather and stranded. He should have offered her marriage afterward—whether anything happened between them or not—but he did nothing. Perhaps a month later the girl discovered she was with child."

"And it was Lord Shelton's?"

Aunt Ellen shrugged. "That hardly matters, Selina. The point is that Shelton did nothing to repair the damage he'd caused. It was his cousin, the Duke of Chatham, who stepped in and found the girl a suitable husband." She clucked her tongue. "The poor woman now lives tucked away in some dreadful backwater with her hayseed husband and—likely—Shelton's babe."

"But you don't *know* the child is his?"

Her aunt gave her a pained look. "It doesn't matter," she repeated.

Selina thought it *did* matter but kept her opinion to herself. "Why did you introduce me to him if he is such a villain?"

"Because he is Chatham's heir." Aunt Ellen repeated. She patted Selina's hand. "There is no harm in dancing with him, but do not be lured into anything… careless, hmm? By that I mean no strolling on the terrace, stepping into unoccupied rooms—that sort of behavior." Aunt Ellen reached out and smoothed her forefinger between Selina's eyebrows. "Don't look so cross my dear, it makes an unsightly line form. You are simply too beautiful to do anything but smile all the time. Remember, my dear, that is what gentlemen like: lovely, smiling, agreeable ladies."

Selina wasn't annoyed by her aunt's order to smile—she'd heard that same command from her own mother times beyond counting. Rather, it irked her how quickly rumors spread among the *ton*, like the one about Lord Shelton. Her aunt didn't know if the child was Shelton's, but that simply did not matter. Give a dog a bad name and hang him.

She might not be so sympathetic to the gorgeous lord had she not been the target of gossip herself, albeit not because of anything *she* had done, but because of her father's gambling. Everyone who was anyone knew that Selina and her five siblings were as poor as church mice thanks to the Earl of Addiscombe frittering away not only his own wealth but his daughters' dowries. Indeed, church mice were better off because at least they had a roof over their heads, which might not be the case much longer for the earl's offspring.

None of the rumors about your father are baseless, are they, Selina? Perhaps there is some truth in the story about Shelton, as well.

She had to admit that might be true; Lord Shelton did have a rakish look about him.

Not that it mattered a whit if Lord Shelton's reputation was deserved or not. The sad truth was that Shelton was a poor man. If Selina was going to save her family from her father's depredations, then only a wealthy husband would serve her purpose.

Still, Shelton *was* divine and there was nothing wrong with looking, was there?

But she would do as her aunt advised and just dance the one set with him. It was the safe thing to do, and Selina was in no position to put her reputation in any danger by acting recklessly.

***

Selina smiled up at the enormous Scottish baron—Lord Fowler—and tried to think of something else to say that might draw him out.

Already she'd attempted at least half-a-dozen conversational gambits and none of them had dragged more than two or three words from the ginger-haired lord. He was so shy that he didn't even meet her gaze.

She'd had her share of tongue-tied dance partners, but never one as bad as Lord Fowler. Indeed, whenever she spoke to him about anything he turned the color of a beetroot and his entire body stiffened, as if he'd just been shocked.

Selina decided to take pity on the poor man rather than pepper him with any more questions.

Mercifully, the dance was over a few moments later and the baron was escorting her back to her aunt when Lord Shelton popped up in front of them. He grinned, his laughing eyes lingering on Fowler before sliding to Selina.

"This is my set, I believe." He offered her his arm.

Selina removed her hand from Fowler's sleeve, but the big man didn't move away. Instead, he glared at Shelton as if he wanted to pull his head off his shoulders. He was such a huge man that Selina was afraid he could actually do it.

"Thank you, Lord Fowler," Selina said, taking Shelton's arm and nudging him toward the dance floor before the Scotsman acted on the violent impulses that were flickering across his freckled face.

Lord Shelton leaned toward her as they walked away and whispered. "Talked your ear off, did he?"

She choked on a laugh and then felt terrible. "He is a very nice man, just exceedingly shy." She gave him a wry look. "Unlike some people."

Shelton laughed, the infectious sound drawing covetous looks from a group of young ladies. "No, I've never been called shy." He took her hand and settled his other hand on her side.

Selina had to steel herself to keep from shivering under his touch.

"I'll wager you are frequently subjected to mooning looks from men like Fowler."

"That is not kind, my lord."

He pursed his lips. "No, it is not. I apologize."

Selina saw the twinkle in his eyes and shook her head. "You are incorrigible."

He laughed. "I've been told it is part of my charm."

The orchestra struck up the waltz and they began to dance. Naturally, the man moved as divinely as he looked, holding her lightly as they floated around the dance floor.

After a few moments of silence, he said, "Your aunt warned you about me, didn't she?"

Selina blinked at him uncertainly.

"I can tell she did because you are eying me with suspicion now." He gave her a silly, squinty-eyed look, as if to demonstrate, and Selina laughed. "There, that is better," he said, smiling. "It was rude of me to ask you such a question, wasn't it?"

It *had* been rude and so was this question. Selina had no idea how one should answer.

Luckily, Shelton was happy enough to go on without a response from her. "I usually don't mind if I've been tried, judged, and hanged before I even dance with a woman, but I feel it more keenly with you."

"Why am I so different?" Selina asked, but inside she was groaning; he was about to start composing odes to her lips or eyes.

"I have been watching you—for weeks, now."

She lifted an eyebrow. "Indeed?"

Shelton chuckled. "I'm sorry. I daresay I sound a bit like a lunatic."

He sounded like… something, but she wasn't sure what.

Selina smiled slightly and said, "Nothing so extreme, my lord."

"I just meant that I've seen the furor you cause whenever you enter a room. And I've noticed how every man in the *ton*—from newly minted lords like Fowler to hardened sophisticates like Chatham and Moncrieff—follows you with his eyes. And yet—" he broke off and shook his head. "No, I've already said too much."

Selina wanted to roll her eyes. Instead, she said, "Please. Do finish—now that you've started."

He gave her a cheeky grin. "Now you are vexed."

"No, but I am curious as to where you are going with your observations."

"With the exception of Fowler—who is obviously too flummoxed by your beauty to utter so much as a peep—every time I watch you dancing you smile and listen and your partner talks and talks and talks."

Rather like you are doing right now, she thought, but of course didn't say it.

Shelton laughed. "Just like I am doing right now."

Selina smiled and this time it was genuine. His self-deprecating humor really was irresistible.

"Does anyone ever ask you about yourself, my lady? Or how you like to spend your time? Or what you think about being yet another commodity on the Marriage Mart?" This time he wasn't laughing or teasing.

It was so unexpected a question that she was, yet again, struck dumb.

"They don't, do they?" he said, looking quite grim. "They don't look past your perfect face to the person who lives behind it. Not because they don't know how to ask questions, but because they don't want to. They simply don't care."

She cocked her head. "And I suppose you do?"

He gave a bark of rueful laughter. "I deserved that."

They danced in silence for a moment, and it was Selina who broke it this time. "You are correct, my lord. Gentlemen rarely ask me questions—about anything. But then I've noticed that most people feel more comfortable talking about themselves."

"Most *men* you mean. While ladies are taught to keep their thoughts and opinions to themselves and *ooh* and *ahh* at our every pronouncement, as if every man is a profound genius."

His words so perfectly echoed her own thoughts that she was amazed. "Do you—do you speak so candidly to all your dance partners, my lord?"

"No, Lady Selina, I do not."

"So… why are you saying all this to *me*?"

"Because I feel like you might understand my feelings about these functions better than most. Do you?"

"I don't know, my lord. What *are* your feelings on the subject?"

"Just that these sorts of occasions are about as dignified as a horse auction. Everything is about appearance and form. There is no substance here, and none is wanted. If a person is beautiful, that is *what* they are—*all* they are. What is inside their head or heart is irrelevant to the *ton*." He gave her a wry look. "You must forgive me for putting it so bluntly and inelegantly, but how can a person *not* lament that the only way to become acquainted with members of the opposite sex is to engage in some of the most vapid, superficial social commerce known to mankind?"

He shook his head, as if Selina had disagreed, and then went on to say, "Oh, I am fully aware that I should just bite my tongue and be quiet. I should be grateful that I'm even admitted into houses such as this one given my tattered reputation. If not for my family connections and—to a lesser extent—my handsome person, I daresay I'd be on the outside peering in." His eyes glittered and for a moment Selina saw real anger behind his carefree smile. "Now, if I were an *ugly* man... Well, I suspect my reception here would be quite different."

"Do you really believe that?"

"Oh, yes. I'm afraid we live among people who care for nothing but appearances."

It was so shocking to hear her own conclusions given voice that Selina spoke before she could stop herself. "I—I thought I was the only one who felt that way."

"There are not many who feel that way, and those of us who do must hide our thoughts." His eyes flickered over her. "You are an exceptionally beautiful woman and when most men look at you, that is *all* they see: a prize to be won, a trophy to possess and display." He nodded sagely. "I am familiar—to a lesser degree—with that manner of thinking, my lady."

Selina could well imagine he was. Of all the gentlemen she'd met during her first few weeks in London there was nobody to match him in appearance. Or charm, for that matter.

"It is insupportable to be treated as nothing more than an appealing cut of meat—no curiosity as to what we are thinking or feeling," he said in a quiet but forceful tone. "I think that is the gravest of all insults: when a person is not even considered worthy of curiosity."

Selina had never thought about it that way, but it was true.

"And if a person ever dares to say that they would like to be more than merely a pretty face they are considered the worst sort of ungrateful wretch for wanting too much."

Selina nodded vigorously. "*Things are so easy for you,*" she mimicked. "*What could you ever have to worry about.* As if being pretty means the rest of one's life is without trouble or grief or pain. As if one's appearance will save one from getting tossed out of one's home."

Shelton's eyes widened at her last pronouncement and Selina was just beginning to wonder if she'd overstepped when he nodded and exclaimed, "Just so!"

His raised voice drew disapproving glares from an older couple beside them.

Selina

Selina and Shelton looked from the scowling man and woman to each other. And then—once he'd whirled them out of earshot of the frowning pair—they both burst out laughing.

Shelton gave her a rueful smile. "I'm sorry if I became... overly excited."

"Please don't be. You have no idea how much I've needed to talk to somebody who understands."

He nodded sagely. "Are your parents pushing you—telling you how it is your duty to rescue the family fortune?"

Her face heated. "I daresay all of London knows of my family's diminished circumstances and my father's part in it."

Shelton shrugged. "It doesn't matter who your father is—all parents are the same when they have attractive offspring to bring to the auction block." He leaned closer and lowered his voice. "I saw you dancing with Chatham and Moncrieff earlier." He gave her a sly look. "You have been honored above all the other young women who've come out this year—or at least that is what Moncrieff thinks, and probably Chatham, too."

"The Duke of Chatham was actually a very attentive dance partner," she said, wondering if she imagined the flicker of disappointment in Shelton's eyes at her words. "As for Moncrieff... Well, he is not alone in feeling that he has honored me. My aunt has not stopped reminding me that he has not danced at one of these functions in years."

"It is true. Probably not since his first Season, which was longer ago than you have been alive. He is known as a great collector of art. I daresay he is looking for the crown jewel for his collection."

She colored under Shelton's pitying look, fearing he was right. The Earl of Moncrieff, who was easily thirty years her senior, had examined her the way one might study a piece of jewelry or statuary for flaws or defects.

"He will offer for you," Shelton said with certitude.

"That is hardly the sort of comment you should be making to me, my lord." And it was *certainly* not the sort of comment Selina wanted to hear.

"I'm sorry, my lady, but—well, it just rankles to know that a man like Moncrieff can aspire to somebody like you while I"—he broke off and gave a self-deprecating laugh. "Let's just say that the two of us are in a similar bind, Lady Selina."

Selina was no fool. She knew that was Shelton's way of saying that he, too, needed to marry for money. She felt a pang of disappointment at his confession but couldn't say she was surprised.

He gave her a determinedly cheerful smile and said, "Just because our roads are destined to run in different directions does not mean we can't enjoy each other's company for the rest of the Season? I can't tell you how much it would cheer me to know there was at least *one* person who wasn't looking at me as if I were the human equivalent of a pheasant to be hunted, stuffed, and mounted."

Selina laughed at the image. "You are very, very naughty to talk to me so candidly, Lord Shelton. But I must admit it is such a relief to know others feel as I do."

The smile he gave her warmed her though and through.

"I am delighted to have found a kindred spirit, Lady Selina. We must resolve here and now to support each other through the remainder of the Season. Will you promise to be my friend—no matter what others say about me?"

Her aunt's warning flickered through her mind, but Selina brushed it aside like an errant insect.

"Friends?" he prodded, looking so hopeful that she laughed.

"Friends, my lord."

He grinned and quite suddenly, the ballroom was much brighter. Selina had made her first friend in London, somebody who liked her for herself.

***

"Well, my dear," her aunt said as their coach rolled away later that night, "You have taken every bit as marvelously as I knew you would. Not only a dance with Moncrieff, but one with the Duke of Chatham, as well."

And one with Lord Shelton, too, Selina gleefully thought to herself.

"Oh, what a feather in your cap it would be to secure Chatham, my dear. He is the biggest marital prize since that ironmonger's daughter snatched up the Marquess of Shaftsbury a while back." Her aunt made a piqued moue. "Now *there* was a waste of a lovely, charming, and delicious man. It is such a shame when an attractive man must sacrifice himself because his family needs money."

Selina thought that was a rather ironic comment given her own circumstances but kept her opinion to herself. Instead, she said, "Shaftsbury? Didn't he suffer a dreadful accident a short while ago?" She was desperate to lure her aunt away from the subject of Chatham. While she didn't *dislike* the duke, she could not see herself married to such a terrifyingly stern and unsmiling man.

"Yes, he did. And Lady Shaftsbury died in the same accident," her aunt said, her tone musing. "It is almost a year since he was left a widower. I wonder if it is possible…" Aunt Ellen trailed off, leaving her thought unfinished in a way that Selina was becoming accustomed to.

A few moments later her aunt shook herself and said, "But never mind about Shaftsbury, my dear. It is Chatham we must set our minds to." She tapped her finger against her chin, her expression thoughtful. "I will have to discover if he is going to Lady Shield's Venetian breakfast this next week. If he is, you will have to have something new to wear. Something in that shade of rose that so becomes you."

"Oh, Aunt Ellen—you've given me so many gowns already."

"No, no, I am quite determined on something new, my dear."

"Thank you so much for inviting me to London and making my time here so pleasurable, Aunt Ellen."

Selina *was* grateful to her aunt, but as much as she loved the pretty dresses and visiting all the magnificent houses, she couldn't help wishing that she enjoyed the balls and parties more. But the truth was that she found it all a bit... empty.

"Oh, pish-tush. It is my pleasure. I assure you, Selina, it is a joy to launch you." Her aunt's smile faltered slightly and Selina knew she was probably thinking about Hyacinth, Selina's older sister, whom her aunt had briefly attempted to launch before admitting defeat and inviting Selina to take Hy's place.

Hy *loathed* socializing of any sort and had begged Aunt Ellen to allow her to serve as companion to the Dowager Lady Fitzroy, a rather crabby old lady who had the excellent sense to take a liking to Selina's reserved sibling.

While Aunt Ellen had been elated and to have Hy off her hands, she would be scandalized if she ever discovered that after the dowager went to bed every night, Hy dressed in men's clothing and slipped out of the house to play cards at various gambling hells.

Her sister was determined to win enough money to pay the interest on the loan their father had taken on Queen's Bower—their home—before the dunners took the house and tossed their family into the street.

While Hy was doing her best to save them all from disaster—and selflessly risking her life every single night on the streets of London in the process—Selina was determined to do *her* best.

She did not have skills like either Hy or their oldest sister, Aurelia—who was an illustrator—but she did have *one* marketable item: her person.

As much as it hurt to admit it, Lord Shelton had been painfully correct earlier when he'd said that he and Selina were not destined for each other. She had barely three months to do what her mother had groomed her to do all her life: marry well and save her family from destitution.

Was marrying for money mercenary? Absolutely. Would it lead to a grand passion? Probably not. But a marriage of convenience didn't necessarily preclude love—or at the very least, affection, did it?

Selina desperately hoped not, because that would be a grim, unbearable, future, indeed.

Chapter 2

Three Months Later

How in the world could one person *cry* so much?

"Oh my dear Selina!" Aunt Ellen wailed. "I cannot delay the inevitable any longer. I simply *must* write to your poor mother today. We have received *no* word from His Grace of Chatham and it is clear that he has had no luck finding that *wretched* sister of yours." She collapsed into yet another fit of sobbing and Selina knew it would be some time before her aunt would be fit to resume the conversation.

Not that there was anything to say that hadn't already been said on the subject.

It was all really quite simple, if rather shocking: Hy had run off in the middle of the night to live the life of an itinerant gambler, and the Duke of Chatham had run off after Hy, presumably to marry her.

Selina was confident the duke would find Hy and make her see sense. It might take him a while—Hy was nothing if not stubborn—but it had been clear to Selina that the duke cared deeply for her sister.

No, it was not Hy's future that was bothering her.

It was something that her sister had written in the letter she'd left for Selina. Something about Lord Shelton.

Selina glanced down at the crumpled, tear-stained missive on her aunt's writing desk, a silent but potent reminder of how life could be turned on its head in an instant.

She couldn't resist the temptation to read her sister's chicken scratch handwriting yet again, even though she had the letter memorized by now.

One part—as always—leapt off the page at her:

I lied when I told you that nobody recognized me on my nights out gambling, Linny.

The duke discovered my true sex weeks ago. And his cousin, Lord Shelton, is on the brink of discovering my identity and using my clandestine association with Chatham to blackmail him.

While Selina was understandably shocked to discover that her sister had been indulging in nighttime assignations with the Duke of Chatham—the most eligible bachelor in London—what had stunned and shattered her, and continued to do so even a week later, was the fact that Shelton would lower himself to blackmail the duke.

How *could* he do such a thing to a member of his own family?

Selina

She knew that Shelton needed money badly, and she certainly sympathized with his plight. But to blackmail his own cousin—and Selina's sister, by extension—was the behavior of a conscienceless scoundrel.

You knew the rumors of his past behavior, but you allowed him to charm you over the last three months. You also allowed him to charm you into refusing all those offers of marriage…

Selina gritted her teeth. *Oh, just leave me alone,* she silently begged. The last thing she wanted to think about was that—in her own way—she was every bit as despicable as Shelton. She had come to London with the express purpose of marrying to save her family and she'd selfishly rejected offer after offer.

Because you were hoping that a miracle would occur and you could have Shelton, instead. And now you find out that he might not be exactly as he seems…

A knock on the door interrupted her miserable musings and Deacon, her aunt's intimidating butler, entered the room holding a salver with a single letter on it.

"Oh, what is it *now* Deacon?" Aunt Ellen demanded peevishly. "Can't you see we are a family in mourning?"

"I am sorry, my lady, but there is an express for you." Deacon frowned down at the rather bedraggled looking missive. "Evidently the messenger suffered a mishap along the ride or the letter would have arrived here sooner."

"An express!" Aunt Ellen shrieked. "No, I cannot bear even one more piece of awful news." She turned to Selina. "You must be the one to read it, my dear. Or perhaps it would be better to just throw it on the fire now."

Selina laid her hand on her aunt's shoulder and gave her a comforting squeeze. "It doesn't feel right to throw away an express without reading it."

Aunt Ellen moaned. "No, I suppose not. Well, go on, then—open it."

Selina unfolded the letter, which was indeed dirty and torn.

There were only three sentences on the page, and she read them quickly and gasped. "Oh, my goodness."

Her aunt whimpered. "I cannot bear one more thing, Selina. Not one more—"

"It is the *best* news, Aunt Ellen. Hy and Chatham married in a small ceremony in a town just outside York." Selina smiled through happy tears at her aunt's stunned face. "Our dear, dear Hy is now the Duchess of Chatham!"

***

Ten minutes and an orgy of weeping—joyous, this time—later Aunt Ellen was happily composing a letter to Selina's parents to inform them they could now, thanks to her, count a duke among their nearest relations.

Selina couldn't stop smiling; reserved, tomboyish Hy had married the catch of the Season and had saved the family from ruin.

She's done what you should have done—what you <u>could</u> have done if you'd accepted any of those marriage offers you received.

Before Selina could commence arguing with the chiding voice—which sounded distressingly like her mother— the door to the sitting room opened and once again it was Deacon.

"Yes, yes, what is it *now?*" Aunt Ellen asked absently, re-reading what she'd written so far.

Deacon cleared his throat. "Lord Shelton is outside walking his horses or he would have come in himself. He wishes to know if Lady Selina would accompany him for a drive in Hyde Park?"

"Shelton," Aunt Ellen repeated, her eyes wide. "The *nerve* of that scoundrel. I want you to go out there and send the man on his way, Deacon."

"But Aunt Ellen—" Selina broke off when her aunt turned to glare at her.

"Selina! You can't want to see the rogue? He is a *blackmailer.*"

"I know what Hy wrote, Aunt. But doesn't he deserve an opportunity to defend and explain himself?"

Her aunt lifted a skeptical eyebrow at that.

"And it is only a drive in the park, after all," Selina added, embarrassed by the wheedle in her voice.

Her aunt cut her a piercing, narrow-eyed look but then sighed and gave a dismissive wave of her hand. "Oh, I suppose it won't cause any harm." A smug smile spread across her face. "Indeed, *nothing* can harm you now that your sister has married Chatham." She made a shooing motion. "Run along, run along. Just don't let that rogue keep you out over an hour."

"Of course not. Thank you, Aunt Ellen."

Selina hurried upstairs to change into her new carriage dress. Although it took almost twenty minutes, the confidence she felt wearing the lovely coral pink outfit was worth the time and delay.

Once she was suitably accoutered with a matching hat, parasol, gloves, and reticule, she took a deep breath and made her way downstairs, her mind in a whirl, cautious optimism blooming in her breast.

It was a good sign that Shelton had come to call—at least she thought it was. It certainly didn't seem to be the action of a guilty man.

As disappointed as Selina had been when she'd read Hy's comment about Lord Shelton, she couldn't discount the possibility that Hy had been mistaken. After all, her sister had been *terribly* wrong about the Duke of Chatham's feelings and intentions toward *her*, hadn't she?

Selina was determined to give Lord Shelton a chance to explain himself before she passed judgement and condemned him.

A few minutes later one of her aunt's grooms was assisting her into Lord Shelton's phaeton. Even though she had seen Shelton several days a week for months, it still struck her just how classically handsome he was. As always, there was something about his laughing blue eyes and full, smiling lips that made *her* feel like smiling.

"Thank you for joining me, my lady. I feared you and your aunt might have already left town along with the rest of the *ton*. I was so delighted to find you still here."

Selina merely smiled, not wanting to start interrogating him until they were out of earshot of the servants.

"Are you ready?" he asked after she'd tucked the rug around the skirt of her carriage dress.

"Yes, my lord."

He turned to the groom. "Let 'em go."

Selina's heart leapt along with the horses who charged down the street in the direction of Hyde Park.

Lord Shelton turned to her and smiled, his eyes glinting. "I'd ask how you are today but you look blooming." He pushed out his lower lip. "However, I can't help but think you don't look as happy to see me as I had hoped."

"Of course, I am happy to see you, my lord," she said, giving him a smile that matched his own in brilliance.

He heaved a melodramatic sigh. "Thank the saints! You had me worried for a moment."

Selina cleared her throat. "There *are* a few matters I'd like to ask you about, however."

Something that looked disturbingly like apprehension flickered across his face but was gone in an instant. "You may ask me anything, my dear—you should know that by now."

She felt a rush of relief at his words. Clearly, she'd mistaken his expression for something else.

He confirmed her relief when he smiled and said, "Please, don't be shy. Ask me anything."

"It is about my sister," she said.

A look of genuine confusion marred his perfect features. "Your sister? Do I know her?"

"You know her by another name."

"What name is that?" he asked, tooling the carriage right past the gates to the park.

"You just missed the entrance," Selina said.

"We'll take a less busy entrance so we won't get trapped into conversation by every park saunterer who wants to stop and gaze upon your beauty. But what were you saying about your sister?"

"You know her by the name Hiram Bellamy."

Shelton's hands jerked the reins and the horses—still lively and skittish—shied. He turned to Selina, his forehead furrowed. "I'm sorry. Did you just say your sister is Hiram Bellamy?"

"Her name is Hyacinth, but Hiram is the name she uses when she dresses as a boy to play cards."

Shelton's lips parted and he stared at her. After a long moment he gave a bark of laughter. "Good Lord. You're serious."

"I am entirely serious."

"Lady Hyacinth Bellamy is also Hiram Bellamy?"

"Yes."

He blinked rapidly. "And does Chatham know who she is?"

"I believe he only discovered her identity recently."

"Bloody hell." He gave a hoot of laughter. "That's—that—it's fucking astounding, is what it is."

Selina gasped. "Lord Shelton!"

"I beg your pardon," he said, but the words were spoken absently and his mind was clearly elsewhere.

They rode in silence for a few minutes, Selina's mind racing at his odd reaction. Why did he laugh?

Ask him about the blackmail, a voice inside her urged.

Selina turned back to him, prepared to do exactly that, but then she noticed his wicked grin and instead asked, "Why are you smiling like that."

"Because your surprising news means that my cousin is in something of a bind, isn't he?"

Selina didn't like his smirk. Not at all. "You knew that Hiram was a woman."

14

"Yes, of course I did," he said, although it hadn't really been a question. Once again, he looked distracted, as if his thoughts were on something else.

Her stomach started to hurt as if she'd swallowed something rotten.

Or poisonous.

"Did you blackmail the duke and threaten to tell everyone about Hy—Hiram—if he didn't give you money?"

He gave her an irritated look. "Who told you that?"

"Did you?"

He shrugged. "Blackmail is such an ugly word. I might have… hinted that I'd be amenable to keeping such a juicy tidbit to myself if my cousin gave me something to make it worth my while."

"Money, in other words."

His smile slid away and his brow furrowed. "Yes, money."

She shook her head, her lip curling with disgust. "You blackmailed your own cousin."

He scowled. "I don't think I care for your tone, my lady."

Selina flinched at his hard look, stunned that he could look at her so coldly and more than a little shaken by how terribly wrong she'd been about him.

He turned away from her, still scowling.

But it wasn't long before he snorted and another grin spread across his face. "It is stunning that Chatham actually believed your sister's story about being a servant. Lord, but he's in a pickle now, isn't he?"

The sickness she'd been feeling turned to anger—at herself mostly, but also at Shelton whom—she suspected—was every bit as rotten as her aunt had said. "You can wipe that odious expression off your face, my lord, because the duke is not in a *pickle* at all. Quite the reverse, in fact. If you were hoping to get more money out of him, you will be disappointed."

Shelton laughed as he cut her an amused look. "Disappointed? I beg to differ, my lady. Chatham will likely do the right thing by your sister and offer for her—how can he *not* do so? But it is *you* my cousin wants to marry. Everyone noticed. Chatham has not danced more than one dance with any girl during a Season in the ten years since his wife died." His blue eyes glittered with bitterness. "You're the one he wants and now he can't bloody have you."

"You could not be more wrong, my lord. It just so happens that the two of them are in love," Selina said, perhaps stretching the truth a bit, although she dearly hoped that was the case. She held his gaze without flinching.

Shelton's jaw finally dropped and his expression was extremely satisfying. "You can*not* be serious. Chatham in love with that gangly—"

"Have a care, my lord; that is my *sister* you are talking about."

He gave her a startled look and then laughed. "Sorry, kitten. I know she's your sister, but she's hardly you, is she?" His blue eyes flickered over her assessingly. "To own the truth, I'm not convinced that Chatham will marry her. Although I don't see how he can avoid it."

"It just so happens that His Grace doesn't want me and never has. He is clearly able to appreciate a person of value when he meets one, and my sister is a treasure beyond price. As to your assertion that he won't marry her"—Selina gave him a smug look and then delivered the *coup de grâce*— "my sister and your cousin married by special license three days ago, so you are wrong on that score, as well."

He stared, the humor draining from his face. "You're lying."

"I am most certainly *not* lying."

"But… if that is the case, then why haven't I heard about it?"

"I daresay there is an express waiting for you at His Grace's house. The messenger was evidently delayed and my aunt only received word a quarter of an hour before you arrived on her doorstep."

He shook his head, his lips parted in shock.

Selina almost felt sorry for him.

But then she recalled that he'd admitted to blackmailing his own cousin and quashed the feeling.

"This makes no sense," he said. "Sylvester *paid* me to stay away from you. Why would he do that unless—"

Selina gasped. "You took *money* to stay away from me?"

He shrugged and gave her a shamefaced look. "Sorry, sweetheart; but… needs must."

Selina shook her head in disbelief. "These past three months you've taken every opportunity to not-so-subtly hint how much you wished we could be together. The entire time you were just *using* me to thwart your cousin." Even as she made the accusation, she held out a glimmer of hope that she was wrong.

He killed that hope with a casual shrug.

Rather than look remorseful or guilty at being caught, he looked amused. "Oh, kitten, don't be angry. That's how it started off, but naturally—after we spent all that time together—I fell under your spell just like all the other poor sods."

He didn't make even the slightest attempt to sound convincing. Because he truly did not care about her.

Selina

"Stop calling me *kitten*, you vile, despicable, insufferable—"

"But you *are* a kitten," he retorted, flicking her a dismissive, mocking look. "You like to pretend that you want people to look beyond your façade and know the real you. But your fluffy exterior *is* the real you. You're soft and sweet and you love to be petted and stroked and all you ever dreamed about was becoming a pampered little pet on some rich man's lap, didn't you?"

Selina's jaw sagged at the venom in his voice and the nasty, taunting words pouring out of his mouth.

He turned back toward the road. "So, my cousin and your sister," he calmly mused, as if he'd not just spewed bile all over her.

Selina crossed her arms to keep from slapping his snide face. Her cheeks burned with humiliation at the realization of how this man had fooled her—and how *easy* it had been for him to do so.

She squirmed as she remembered how much she'd looked forward to seeing him, how she'd treasured spending those few, precious minutes with him at every *ton* function. What an idiot she'd been to believe they had anything in common. Shelton had played her for the silly fool she was. He was right; she *was* nothing but a kitten.

"I know *what* you've done, my lord, but I still don't understand how manipulating my affections helps you in any way."

Shelton sighed. "My cousin is a very wealthy man and controls the family coffers. If I want some of that money I must either do what he says, or I have to make *him* do what I want."

"How were you going to use *me* to squeeze money out of your cousin?"

"I was going to compromise you so severely"—Shelton gave an amused snort at Selina's horrified gasp— "that one of two things would happen. One, Chatham would offer me money to go away so that he could step in and marry you. Or, two, he'd bribe *me* to marry you. Either way, I'd make him pay a great deal." He turned and gave her the grin she'd once found so charming. "But none of that matters now because it is just me and thee, my fair kitten. And that's what you wanted all along, isn't it sweetling? My handsome, charming person for your husband?"

Selina squirmed under his knowing, mocking stare and the truth struck her with all the force of a mallet to the chest. She gave a snort of disbelief. "You don't even like me, do you? You just used me."

"The truth is, kitten, that I don't know you enough to like you *or* dislike you."

Selina was so angry—and so furious at her own gullible stupidity—that she wanted to fling herself out of the carriage.

Instead, she said, "That other girl, the one who had to leave London in disgrace. That was your b—"

"Tut, tut," he scolded, "I think it's better if we avoid that subject."

"I daresay you do. But I want to know the—"

"You'd do better not to pry into matters you know nothing about." He gave Selina a smile that showed altogether too many teeth and his pretty blue eyes were hard, making him look nothing like the lighthearted charmer she knew.

Selina closed her mouth.

He nodded. "That is wise, my lady."

She turned away from him, bristling with anger.

"Ah, don't be vexed with me, kitten," he cajoled, his voice once again friendly.

Selina ignored him.

He turned the horses down a street that was even narrower than the last. And not familiar in the least.

Selina looked around and frowned. "Where are we going?"

"I thought we might stop and have some refreshment—something to calm your shattered nerves."

"Don't flatter yourself," she retorted. "My nerves are just fine. I want to go home."

"All in good time, darling." His expression had become pensive and almost… shifty.

"I want to go home. Now," she said, her voice climbing an octave.

He transferred the reins to one hand and then grabbed her chin, forcing her to look at him. His eyes were an icy blue. "You just sit tight, keep your mouth shut, and be a good girl." He dropped his hand. "My cousin might have married your sister, but I still need money, kitten, a great deal of it."

For the first time, Selina felt a stab of genuine fear. "Wh-what do you mean?"

His lips curved into a smile, one tinged with regret. "I see no reason to deviate from my original plan just because Chatham is married."

"Your plan? You mean to—"

"Compromise your reputation so thoroughly that my cousin will need to step in? Yes, that plan, darling. He won't be able to marry you himself to hush things up, of course. But he can still pay me to do so. I've got a post chaise reserved at the Swan with Two Necks and I'm taking you to Rosewood, where we will stay until Chatham meets my terms."

Selina

Selina was finding it difficult to breathe. "And what if he doesn't agree to them?"

He gave her an unreadable look. "Let's not think about that yet, hmm, kitten?"

Chapter 3

Caius Graham, the ninth Marquess of Shaftsbury, was trapped in the same miserable nightmare.

It didn't help that part of his brain knew good and well it was only a dream. The feelings—the raw terror and gut-churning helplessness—were real enough.

For the hundredth time Caius was forced to relive the worst four days of his life, paralyzed while his wife slowly died a foot away from him. Powerless to help as Elton, his valet—and yes, his dearest friend—along with two other faithful servants were crushed to death beneath the coach, suffering for hours before expiring.

And all because Caius had been bent on selfish pleasure, taking a journey that none of them—except him—had wanted to take in the first place.

In the dream, Louisa begged Caius to make the pain stop. He could feel her broken, bleeding body beneath his hands. But the world around him was dark. Not the restful blackness of a starless night, but a grim, uneasy darkness distorted by dim, taunting shadows.

He'd pounded on the doors of the coach for hours—days—but nobody answered.

Her weeping had torn at his soul and fueled his shame and guilt until it had almost consumed him.

But the silence after she'd died had been a thousand times worse.

"*Reed! John! Elton!*" Caius had called for his footman, coachman, and valet—all three of whom had been riding outside the coach when it careened off the washed-out road and slid down a steep embankment—until he'd been hoarse.

By the time the rescuers discovered the crushed coach four hellish days later, Caius had screamed so much that he'd lost his voice, unable to do anything but croak when hands pulled him from the wreckage.

He must have appeared demented to those men and to the physician who'd finally ordered him tied to the bed so that he might employ a lancet and cup, bleeding him until he'd been too weak to struggle, sunk in a black, bleak nightmare world until Morris had come for him.

"*Help us!*"

Caius's own voice jerked him awake and his head whipped from side to side as he bolted upright in his bed, his body slicked with sweat and tangled in damp sheets.

His lungs worked like a pair of bellows and still he could not get enough air in his lungs.

He blinked against the darkness.

Dear God… he could not bear another night of this. Enough was enough. It was time to do the manly thing.

He crawled across the bed and reached for the nightstand, knocking something off onto the floor that made a dull clang. He yanked open the drawer and felt around for the pistol, sighing with relief when his palm curved around the familiar butt of the gun.

Yes, do it. Do it, you coward!

"My lord?"

Caius yelped and dropped the pistol back into the drawer at the sound of his butler's voice. "Morris?" he rasped, his ragged voice telling him that he'd yelled more than a few times in his sleep.

"Yes, my lord. It is Morris."

"What the devil are you doing in my chambers? Are you acting as my nurse, now?" He fumbled for the drawer and slammed it shut. Good God! What if the other man had seen what he was doing?

"Er, no, my lord. I heard shouting, so I let myself in."

Caius grunted, too tired to chastise the man for doing what any good servant—or decent person—would do. He closed his eyes and sighed. "What do you want, Morris?"

"Mrs. Nelson is leaving, sir."

"Who is Mrs. Nelson."

Morris cleared his throat. "Your housekeeper, my lord."

"Oh." Caius shrugged. "So, she is leaving. What do you want me to do about it?"

"She said you threw a book at her."

Caius didn't recall that, which meant drinking to forget was working—although not quite as effectively as he'd hoped as he could still remember the *rest* of his dreadful life.

"Did it hit her?" he asked dully. Some distant part of him knew he should be ashamed, but he couldn't find the strength to care.

"Er, no, my lord."

Well, that was something, he supposed.

"What time is it?" he asked, although why he bothered, he wasn't sure. What difference did time make to him anymore?

"It is just after ten o'clock, my lord. In the morning," Morris added after a pause.

"Why are you delivering messages instead of my footmen?"

Morris cleared his throat. "Er, well, that is—"

Caius heaved a sigh and flopped onto his back, not bothering to open his eyes. "Never mind, I can guess: Everyone else is too afraid of me, aren't they." Throw *one* book and get a reputation for being dangerous.

It hadn't been a question, but Morris said, "Erm, not *afraid,* exactly, but…" he trailed off when he couldn't seem to find a suitable word.

"Was that all you wanted?" Caius asked, so weary he could scarcely force the words from his mouth.

"Mrs. Nelson just left sir." There was a long pause, and then, "I might still catch her if I were to hurry—"

"Why?"

"She is an able housekeeper, sir," Morris said, audibly pained, which in itself was exceptional as his dignified butler almost never showed any emotion.

The fact that the old man sounded so frazzled made Caius feel like an ogre.

He should apologize for his childish, rude behavior, but he couldn't make himself say the words. He was ashamed and just wanted his most faithful retainer to leave, hating that anyone was seeing him this way.

Again Morris cleared his throat. "Erm, I'm sure I could convince her to return if—"

"Fine, fine. Go after her," Caius said, squeezing his pounding temples with both hands.

"Shall I send one of the footmen up to help you get dressed, my lord?" Morris asked in a hopeful voice.

"I'm not getting up."

"But, er, it is a new day, sir.

Caius laughed. Yes, it was a new day.

"Just *go* and fetch your damned Mrs. Nelson," he ordered. "I'll ring for somebody if I feel like getting out of bed."

Not bothering to wait for an answer, Caius turned onto his side and surrendered to the velvety darkness.

***

"Oh, come now, Selina darling," Shelton said in a wheedling tone. "It's a long, long journey. You'll need to speak to me at some point."

Selina

Selina stared out the window of the post chaise, pulsing with fury as she considered the events of the last few hours, and engaging in a pointless game of, *"What should I have done to not end up in this predicament?"*

Should she have screamed when he'd pulled into the courtyard of the Swan with Two Necks?

Should she have appealed to the ostler for help when Shelton had put her in the post chaise?

Should she have told the innkeeper that she was being abducted against her will?

Selina had not done any of those things because she had believed Shelton's threat—that causing a fuss would only attract more attention and announce their scandalous behavior to all and sundry.

Well, it was too late to berate herself for inaction. Selina could scream now, but nobody would hear her except the postilion. And Shelton, of course. It was almost worth screaming just to annoy him.

Why give him the satisfaction of knowing he has so profoundly routed you?

Selina snorted. He already *had* that satisfaction and more.

"You couldn't have done anything differently, you know," Shelton said, his condescending tone infuriating her further.

"Oh? And why is that?" Selina retorted. "Because you are such a perfect villain you could not possibly be foiled?"

He laughed.

"I daresay you are rather good at this, aren't you? After all, I'm not the *first* woman whose reputation you've destroyed and life you have ruined."

He stopped laughing and turned away, but not before Selina saw anger glinting in his eyes.

Good. She didn't want to speak to him or hear his voice ever again. Of course that might be a difficult goal to achieve if she actually ended up married to the rotter, which seemed more likely with every hour that passed.

"You need to overcome your anger, my dear. Not only is it pointless, but it will cause unsightly lines on that lovely face of yours."

Selina gritted her teeth to keep from retorting. Instead, she visualized flinging open the door and shoving him out of the swiftly moving carriage. She smiled at the image.

"This might not be the romantic love match that you'd hoped for, my lady, but Chatham will pay me the money I ask for and we *will* marry. And isn't that all that really matters at the end of the day?" He chuckled in a smug manner that made her palm itch to slap him. "If you rail against your fate—or me—all it will do is make matters worse for you, not to mention the shame your family will suffer if you cause ructions at every inn we stop at."

Saving her family further shame was a compelling argument and the same one he'd used to blackmail her into the post chaise hours before. Selina's reputation had been ruined the moment they'd been spotted at the Swan with Two Necks. She'd seen at least four people she knew—one an inveterate gossip—and there was no doubt in her mind that all four had probably run, not walked, to spread the news that they'd seen Lord Shelton and Lady Selina Bellamy together at an inn. Alone.

You wanted him, now you have him, a taunting voice in her head pointed out.

Selina allowed herself a brief glance at the man who was probably going to be her husband and scowled at the thought of ever wanting such a selfish, unprincipled rake.

He saw the glance and grinned at her. "Come now. Let us be friends, hmm? You liked me well enough only a few hours ago—I daresay you even believed you loved me—surely you can summon up some of that emotion again?"

She didn't dignify his response. Instead, she stared out the window.

***

By the time Shelton stopped for a change of horses three hours later Selina needed to use the necessary so badly that she was almost afraid to climb down from the carriage.

"Is aught amiss?" Shelton asked when she winced.

"No." She turned away from him and headed toward the busy inn.

Shelton caught her arm. "Uh, uh, uh," he said in a chiding voice. "Just where do you think you are going, kitten?"

Selina scowled at him. "Surely even you cannot be *that* stupid?"

His face turned a dull brick red at her scathing tone. "You'd better put a curb on that vicious tongue of yours, darling—or I'll have to do it for you."

She glared but didn't speak.

"Good girl," he murmured in a truly infuriating voice. "Now, I'll let you go, but first I want you to promise that you won't do anything foolish—like try to escape."

"And where would I go with no money?"

He hesitated, but then nodded. "Fine, you can go—but don't dawdle. We won't be stopping here long."

She yanked her arm free and hurried toward the building.

Five minutes later she was feeling more herself and able to consider her situation with a clearer head. She suddenly realized that she was rushing back to Shelton—like an obedient dog—and stopped in the corridor outside the coffee room. What was she doing going back to him? Yes, she'd promised that she wouldn't try to escape, but why should she worry about keeping her word to such a scoundrel? What was stopping her from—

"*Where is she you bastard?*" a male voice roared.

The bellow originated from inside the coffee room. Curious, Selina opened the door a sliver and her jaw sagged. It was the enormous ginger-haired baron she'd danced with a few times during the Season—the tongue-tied one. Selina struggled to recall his name. It was something to do with birds… Henly? Swanson? Fowler? Yes, that was it! Baron Fowler.

He might help her!

"This is none of your affair, Fowler," Shelton shot back, not looking at all worried that the huge Scotsman was bearing down on him.

"As it happens, I spoke to Lady Fitzroy—whose affair it most certainly is—and *she* begged me to save Lady Selina from your vile machinations, you bloody bounder." Fowler's voice shook the room and Selina suspected he could be heard all the way out on the road.

It was midday, so the coffee shop was doing a brisk trade and there were people at half the tables. Most looked like humble working folk, but—even so—the details of this sort of juicy exchange would soon be known on the edges of the Empire.

And *her* name would be associated with these two fools and their idiotic bellowing.

Selina gave an irritated huff and strode up to the two men. "What is going on here?"

Fowler's head swiveled toward her and his eyes widened. "I've come to rescue you, my lady."

"That is very kind of you, my lord. But perhaps you could do so more *quietly?*" she hissed.

His bright green eyes darted around the room and his freckled face darkened when he noticed his rapt audience. "Oh."

Selina went a step closer, so she could lower her voice. "We need not stand here in this room arguing with Lord Shelton. If you will return me to my aunt's house then I am prepared to depart with you right now."

"I will take you back." Fowler's gaze slid back toward Shelton. "But first I need to teach this cad a few manners, my lady."

"No, you really don't, my lord," Selina forced the words through clenched teeth. "We should just *leave*."

Fowler didn't seem to hear her. "This is no place for a pretty, delicate young lady like you, Lady Selina. I've already talked to the innkeeper, and he has a private parlor set aside. You run along now and wait for me there."

Selina bit her lip to keep from screaming.

"I've engaged a carriage, as well," Fowler went on, "and I will accompany you alongside it back to London"—he glared at Shelton— "like a proper gentleman."

She tried one more time. "Couldn't we just leave now and—"

"*You're* going to teach me manners, eh?" Shelton demanded, talking right over Selina as if she hadn't been speaking. "Why, what an excellent idea. I believe you could stand to learn a few manners yourself, Fowler." He grinned tightly as he unbuttoned his coat and proceeded to peel it off his person.

Selina gasped as she realized what was about to happen. "You don't need to do this, Lord Fowler. I will be—"

"This rascal has ruined your reputation and soiled your honor, my lady," Fowler retorted hotly, shrugging out of his coat. "But fear not, you won't have to marry him to salvage it. You have possessed my heart for months now, Lady Selina."

"Possessed your heart?" she repeated blankly.

"I would be honored to take you as my wife," Fowler said.

"Your wife?" She shook her head vigorously. "Oh, no, my lord, you cannot sacrifice yourself for me, I can't—"

"It would be no sacrifice. I—I love you, my lady."

Shelton hooted rudely, but Fowler ignored him.

Selina stared. "You—you *love* me? But you don't even *know* me, my lord. We've danced a handful of times and you've scarcely said three words to me these past months."

Fowler blushed and opened his mouth.

"That doesn't matter to his sort, Lady Selina," Shelton cut in, smirking at the bigger man. "Fowler doesn't need to know you—doesn't care who you are, at all. He's just another jumped up cit who wants to add you to his collection of pretty baubles."

The baron whipped around and snarled, "You shut your mouth before I shut it for you."

Selina

Shelton laughed and gave the other man a scathing look. "As if marriage to a buffoon such as you would save her reputation. I'm heir to a bloody dukedom, you insolent fool. I think we both know which of us will make her a better husband."

"My lords," Selina said firmly, "I don't want to marry either of you. What I want is to go back to—"

"Hold this." Shelton tossed Selina his coat, his attention riveted on Fowler.

Selina caught it without thinking and then gritted her teeth, squeezing the fabric so tightly it would be badly wrinkled. "Please, my lords, I don't—"

"Take mine, too." Fowler didn't move his gaze from Shelton as he threw his far more expensive coat in Selina's direction, hitting her in the head with it.

"I don't suppose a back-alley brawler like you is familiar with Queensberry Rules?" Shelton demanded, whipping off his neckcloth and hurling it at Selina, his blue eyes sparking as he sneered at the big Scotsman.

Fowler's chest rumbled with an actual growl and he, too, tossed his cravat and waistcoat at Selina, who now held half a tailor's shop in her arms. "I can thrash you under any damned rules you want, Shelton."

Selina raised her voice. "Lord Fowler, Lord Shelton. I beg of—"

Shelton's fist shot out and struck the bigger man in the chin, driving him backward.

Selina yelped and stumbled out of the way.

The Scotsman staggered past her and slammed into a table where three men were eating pastries and drinking coffee. The impact scattered crockery and drove the men to their feet as the table shattered beneath Fowler's weight and his back struck the wall.

The Scotsman found his feet and dropped into a crouch. "You want to fight dirty, do ye?" He roared and then charged at Shelton like an enraged bull.

Selina stared in horror as the two men grappled and the observers—not just the people who'd already been in the coffee room, but more pouring in from the corridor every second—shouted and began placing wagers.

Men jostled all around her, pushing and shoving her farther away from the fray.

"Fightin' over ye, are they lass?" an older woman dressed in the rough garb of a farm laborer asked from beside her. She was standing on her toes to see over the assembled heads, but she darted a quick, appraising look at Selina. "Ain't you a pretty one." She clucked her tongue. "That's too bad."

Selina frowned. "Why? What do you mean?"

"You pretty ones learn to get by on a smile and not to use what's inside your heads."

Selina cut the woman an irritated look. "My head works just fine, thank you. And for your information, they aren't fighting over me. I'm just their convenient excuse; they're fighting each other for their own stupid reasons."

The woman laughed, unperturbed by Selina's sharp retort. "Well, that's men for ye, eh?" She winced as Fowler delivered a particularly vicious hit that sent Shelton careening into a table that had a full tea service on it. The din of pots, cups, and saucers shattering was deafening.

More people shoved into the room and Selina found herself pinned against the back wall by a group of three men dressed like carters who were shouting encouragement.

"What are they fightin' about?" a fourth man asked.

One of the carters shrugged. "Some fancy piece o' muslin'—what else do toff's fight over?"

Selina's jaw dropped. *Fancy piece of muslin?*

Why are you so shocked? Don't you know that is how people will view you? You will have to marry one of these idiots. You know that, don't you?

Selina shook her head violently at the repellant thought. "No!" Her shout was swallowed up by all the other yelling and cheering. "No," she said again, louder this time. "I won't do it."

She was about to throw their garments on the floor when she noticed a fat black leather purse about to fall out of the pocket of Lord Fowler's coat. She grabbed it and hefted it in her palm. It was heavy—full of money.

Selina caught her breath at the bold idea that leapt into her head.

With trembling fingers, she searched the pockets in both garments, coming up with a second purse, a small pistol, a gold chased case that held a quill and fancy penknife, and a silver cigar holder.

Selina stared at the items for a long moment, almost afraid of the idea that was forming her head.

You cannot really be considering such an action, Selina? I forbid it.

It was her mother's voice, as loud as if she were standing beside her.

One of the men screamed—it sounded like Shelton—and the loud *crack* of wood splintering filled the room.

The noise snapped Selina from her fugue and she dropped the clothing over the back of a nearby chair tucked all the items into her reticule until it was bulging at the seams, and then pushed through the throng of bodies, not stopping until she was in the courtyard.

A big hand grabbed her arm and she yelped and spun around. "What's goin' on in there?" a man dressed in a coachman's uniform asked.

"Two idiots fighting."

He frowned. "Over what?"

"Some fancy piece of muslin."

His eyes widened at her vulgar words. Behind him was a coach with men and bags on top and faces peering out the windows.

"Is this your coach?" Selina asked.

"Aye."

"Is there any room left?"

His gaze trailed over her expensive pink taffeta carriage ensemble and the fat reticule hanging from her wrist and he raised an eyebrow. "Er, yes."

"I'd like to buy a seat on it."

"Don't you want to know where it's headed?"

Selina smiled tightly. "I don't care where it is going. Anywhere is better than here."

Chapter 4

The first coach Selina took—the one from the inn where the two fools had been fighting—traveled for more than six hours. By then, her temper had cooled, but her resolution had—surprisingly—only strengthened.

Six hours away from the two men was not nearly far enough. And so she'd taken the next available coach at the busy posting inn.

Unlike the first carriage, where she'd been crammed in along with seven others—this one had been almost empty. It had soon become apparent *why* the coach was so sparsely occupied. There'd been a husband and wife in the coach who had bickered and argued non-stop from the moment the wheels had started to roll. Selina had fled the coach at the next busy posting inn, even though she'd paid for a through seat.

That had been a mistake, but for a different reason. Evidently a woman dressed in an expensive salmon pink carriage ensemble—which was looking a little bedraggled by then—without any luggage or servants to attend her was not well-regarded.

Although she had only needed to wait two hours before she could purchase a seat on another stage, it had been the longest two hours of her life as she'd squirmed under the censorious gaze of the innkeeper's wife. If she was going to continue her adventure, she'd need plain clothing—such as a servant might wear—and a valise to lend her a modicum of respectability.

The carriage had travelled all night, albeit slowly, stopping several times to change horses at inns with no sizeable townships around them.

Selina hadn't given much thought to where she was going. Indeed, she'd briefly considered merely traveling around the country until the money was gone, but that would be quite some time given that Lord Fowler's purse held more money than Selina had ever seen in her life.

Lord Shelton's purse, on the other hand, had contained only a few shillings.

In any event, she had enough money to last for weeks. And she was also free from the duty that had weighed on her for her entire adult life: the expectation that she would make a brilliant marriage.

Hyacinth had lifted that burden from her shoulders by marrying the Duke of Chatham, a man whom countless women had tried to snare for almost a decade. Her reserved, tomboyish sister was now a duchess. Who would have thought it possible that Hy—who didn't even believe in love—had fallen to its arrow? While Selina, who'd always dreamed of marrying for love, had fallen to a scoundrel's lies.

Every time she thought about Shelton's duplicity her belly boiled with fury.

And shame.

Apparently, she was every bit as fluff-brained as many people seemed to think she was, a pretty face with nothing of substance behind it. Her only saving grace—that she might contract a grand marriage and save her siblings—was now impossible given the trail of scandal in her wake. So, what was Selina's purpose *now*?

Those were the thoughts she was pondering as the coach slowed.

"Look, love," the well-dressed woman across from Selina whispered to her darling little girl, pointing to the village outside the window. "We're almost home."

"Is this Market Deeping?" Selina asked the woman, who'd been kind and shared bread and cheese with her when she'd seen that Selina hadn't brought any food.

"Indeed, it is."

"Do you know where this coach goes next?"

"The driver will stop for a change of horses and then he will head back the way he came."

Selina frowned; she did not want to go back the same way. "Do you know if there is another coach today?"

"You are in luck. On Tuesdays a second coach leaves at a quarter to three."

That meant more hours spent sitting in a coffee room and avoiding the nasty looks of some innkeeper or his wife.

The woman's eyes crinkled with concern as she took in Selina's obviously expensive, albeit grubby and wrinkled, pink carriage ensemble. "My name is Mrs. Cooper and my father is Reverend Charles Sayers, the vicar here. If you are… lost, or need help, you could come along to the vicarage with Cora and me. We could help you while you reached out to your family—or friends?"

Selina's eyes burned at the other woman's generosity. "That is *very* kind of you, Mrs. Cooper. But I am fine," she lied. "I just lost my luggage yesterday and have been out of sorts ever since."

"I can imagine. We would not like that at all, would we Cora?" Mrs. Cooper asked her daughter.

"No, mama. I should hate to lose my new frock."

Selina and Mrs. Cooper laughed.

"And you would not like to lose grandpapa's birthday gift, either, hmm?" she teased the little girl.

"No, I wouldn't like to lose that," Cora agreed with less conviction.

Mrs. Cooper smiled at Selina. "It is my father's sixtieth birthday next week and Cora and I took a brief holiday to buy him a special present."

"A mother and daughter trip… how lovely," Selina said, with perhaps a bit too much envy in her voice. She hurriedly added, "I hope his birthday is a happy one."

Mrs. Cooper was charming, and Selina was struck by an almost irresistible urge to take her up on her kind offer and follow her to the vicarage to avail herself of the comfort and care the other woman emanated.

But that was foolish. Here she was, barely a day on her own and already looking for somebody to take care of her!

The coach jolted to a stop and her thoughts with it. The entire equipage bounced and shuddered as people began leaping off the back and top. Inside it, the quiet elderly couple, spinster schoolteacher, and Mrs. Cooper and Cora all hurried to collect their possessions.

Selina had nothing to gather thanks to her hasty escape. If she'd been smart, she would have stolen Shelton's valise, which the scheming dog had slyly hidden in the box on the back of his phaeton when he'd collected her from her aunt's house.

And what would you have done with his things? a dry voice in her head asked.

She could have sold them. Or—she thought with a smirk—worn them. And why not? Her sister Hy had been dressing as a boy for years.

It might be difficult to pass for a boy with hair down to your big bottom and that oversized bosom of yours.

Selina scowled at the *big bottom* and *oversized bosom* comments and raised her hand to her blond curls. It was shallow and vain of her, but she *loved* her hair and would hate to cut it.

Why are you worrying about that now? You don't even have *Shelton's clothing.*

She knew the chiding voice was right. Rather than pointlessly lamenting what she *hadn't* done, she should use the next few hours to acquire a valise and some proper clothing so she wouldn't draw so many harsh looks at whatever town she stopped in next.

Buoyed by that thought, Selina turned to Mrs. Cooper, smiled, and asked, "Could you point me in the direction of a modiste shop in Much Deeping?"

***

Two hours later Selina was clothed in a simple brown dress, plain brown cloak, brown ankle boots, and a straw bonnet adorned with a narrow brown ribbon. She'd thought that brown seemed like a better color if a person wished to go unnoticed. However, judging by the stares she was garnering as she walked down the street with her valise, she'd been wrong. It was a small market town, and a stranger would attract attention no matter *what* color they wore.

Selina

Well, she'd soon be on her way and a great deal more comfortably clothed and shod, too.

As she approached the entrance to the posting inn a distinguished but flustered voice caught her attention and Selina slowed her pace. The voice belonged to an older man who was arguing rather heatedly with a harsh-faced woman wearing an expression of rigid disdain.

"*No*, Mr. Morris, I will not go back. It doesn't matter how much he offered to increase my wages. I've tolerated his tantrums and vile abuse for almost two months and that is two months longer than I should have borne it."

"But Mrs. Nelson, you will leave here without any recommendation if you don't give the marquess proper notice."

"I don't care. I have recommendations from my prior employers. And if I cannot find work then I will go and live on my sister's charity. Anything would be better than working for the Marquess of Shaftsbury."

Selina's ears perked up: the Marquess of Shaftsbury? She'd heard of him—who hadn't—even in the remote village of Little Sissingdon, where Selina had grown up, they'd read of his exploits in the newspapers. Her brother Doddy worshipped the man, holding him up as the ultimate Corinthian and all that was admirable in a man.

And her Aunt Ellen was so enamored of the marquess that she'd shared several risqué stories with Selina. Evidently, Shaftsbury had given the Duke of Chatham competition when it came to driving all the matchmaking mamas into a frenzy. But rather than choose a daughter of the *ton*, Shaftsbury had married a screamingly wealthy iron heiress, thus putting an end to the hopes and dreams of dozens of young women.

He'd not returned to London since the death of his wife in a carriage accident the year before. And now this angry woman—an upper servant, by the look of it—had just claimed that *anything* was better than working for the marquess.

How intriguing…

Rather than enter the inn, Selina stepped aside to allow other customers to pass, pretending to look for something in her reticule while shamelessly eavesdropping on the increasingly noisy argument.

"His lordship has suffered a difficult few months, ma'am. He is not normally this way. I'm sure if you came back and—"

"*A difficult few months?*" the woman repeated in disbelief. "His accident was almost a year ago. While I am deeply sorry for what he has endured, his lordship is behaving like a lunatic, Mr. Morris. It is not *normal* for a man to do nothing but sleep, drink, and box. You are not doing him any favors by pandering to him or concealing his condition. You should notify his next of kin—he has a younger brother, does he not—and his lordship should be put in an institution where he can receive the proper care. The man is simply not in possession of his faculties."

Selina sucked in a shocked breath. An institution? What in the world could be wrong with the marquess? Why did nobody in London know about this?

Mr. Morris—a butler, Selina surmised—drew himself up to his full height and gave the woman a withering look. "His lordship is perfectly in control of his faculties. I must warn you against spreading rumors of that sort, ma'am, or you could find yourself the subject of a defamation action."

Mrs. Nelson rolled her eyes and snatched up the valise that had been sitting beside her feet. "Find somebody else to serve as a target for his lordship, Mr. Morris, because I am not coming back, no matter what inducement you offer."

Mr. Morris's expression remained haughty until the woman had stormed off. Only when she was gone did he allow his despair to show.

Selina's heart pounded so loudly in her ears that at first she thought it was the thundering hooves of approaching horses.

But no, it was the sudden, mad idea that was leaping up and down inside her head, demanding her attention.

The Marquess of Shaftsbury needed a housekeeper—desperately?

If there was one thing Selina knew plenty about, it was managing a household. While she wasn't as efficient as her younger sister Phoebe—who'd handled most of the housekeeping chores for their family—Selina had always been far better at soothing the ruffled feathers of their servants or placating irate tradesmen who'd haunted their house demanding to be paid. And she also had a practical turn of mind that lent itself to solving minor domestic problems. She did not have Phoebe's experience or skill with ledgers, but their mother had insisted that all her daughters learn how to review a housekeeper's accounts to check for pilferage or waste.

That is all true, but do you really want to be a servant? This was not her mother's voice, but that of Nanny Fletcher, one of Selina's favorite people in the world.

The position of housekeeper is hardly that of a scullery maid. In many ways, it is like being mistress, but without the bother of having a husband to flatter and appease and pander to.

I'm not so sure it is as easy as all that, my dear.

Selina shrugged away Nanny's concerns. The more she thought about it, the more she liked the idea. Indeed, this was a positively serendipitous turn of events. Here was work that she could do and might even be good at.

Not to mention it would be very interesting to see what was so wrong with Shaftsbury that a servant had refused to return, even for more pay.

Why not go home to Queen's Bower and begin adjusting to your new role as social leper?

Selina

Selina scowled at the return of her mother's voice. She didn't justify that snide comment with a response.

Instead, before she could lose her nerve, she picked up her valise and stepped toward the butler, who was still staring mournfully after Mrs. Nelson, as if he hoped she'd have a change of heart.

She cleared her throat delicately. "Sir? *Sir?*" she repeated.

Mr. Morris turned toward her slowly, his vague gaze taking a moment to sharpen. "Er, yes, miss?"

"I do hope you'll forgive me, but I couldn't help overhearing your conversation with your former housekeeper."

When the old man just blinked, Selina gave him her most potent smile. As it had done countless times in the past—regardless of a man's age or situation—the expression cast a spell over Mr. Morris and his proud features softened as he took in her person. "I'm sorry, my dear, but what did you say?"

"I understand you are in need of a housekeeper."

Mr. Morris frowned. "Er—"

"It just so happens that I am recently available and seeking a new position."

Morris's eyes bulged. "*You* are a housekeeper?"

"Indeed, I am," she lied without shame.

An emotion—too complicated for Selina to decipher—flickered across his distinguished face. He gave her a kindly, slightly condescending smile, "This position is for the Marquess of Shaftsbury, miss. Your references would need to be, er, quite impressive."

Selina opened her mouth and a whale of a lie surged out of it. "Until quite recently I worked for the Duke of Chatham."

Morris's jaw sagged. "*You* were Chatham's housekeeper?"

Selina told herself not to be offended by his obvious disbelief. "I left his employ a short while ago and for the past few months I've been on holiday. I was just returning to my sister's house when I overheard your conversation. Although it is hardly conventional, it sounded as if your need might be a bit... urgent."

Morris's shoulders stiffened. "It is true that his lordship has recently found himself rather, er, short of staff, but we are hardly *desperate*."

Selina's first impulse was to persist and reemphasize her faux credentials. But then she thought about Hy and wondered what her clever, canny sister would do.

Bluff. That was the term she was looking for.

She gave Morris a cool smile and said, "Ah, I see. Well, it seems I am mistaken. I am sorry to have intruded. Good day to you, sir." Selina bent to pick up her valise and didn't even have to take a step before Morris pounced on her like a starving fish going after a baited hook.

"Er, no, no—don't leave just yet."

It took a herculean effort not to grin.

Morris's faded blue eyes moved up and down Selina's person—not in a lascivious way, but with perplexity. "If I might be so bold as to say, miss—"

"It's *Mrs.* Lanyon." That had been the name of their housekeeper at Wych House. "I've been a widow these past three years," she added, more than a little amazed at her newfound ability to lie so quickly and easily and without so much as a twinge of conscience.

"My deepest condolences." He gave a respectful pause and then said, "You must have married *very* young."

Selina knew that she should have bought some mobcaps when she was shopping. There was nothing like a primly covered head to make a woman look older.

"I have the fortune to look younger than I am, sir," Selina said, her mind racing. Just how much she could embellish upon her one-and-twenty years before people suspected she was lying?

Morris lifted an eyebrow, clearly skeptical.

"I am one-and-thirty," she blurted, and then had to bite back a groan when his second eyebrow joined the first.

He stared, and, for just a moment, Selina thought he was going to accuse her of lying.

Thankfully he did no such thing. Instead, he nodded slowly and said, "And you say you worked for Chatham?"

"That is correct."

"Er, you can provide proof of that, I hope?"

This was one area in which she could speak with utter confidence. "I can promise you a *glowing* recommendation from Her Grace of Chatham."

A letter was the least Hy could do to make up for her recent escapades. After all, her sister had planned to run off and live the life of an itinerant gambler, certainly she could have no issue with Selina doing something as mild as taking a housekeeping position?

Besides, her sister loved her and would do anything for her.

Morris's brow furrowed more deeply the longer he studied her, rather like a man faced with a complicated mathematical problem. Selina could practically *feel* the position slipping from her grasp the longer the old man had time to look at her and think.

She needed to act. *Now.* "Rather than stay and begin today, I could always return home to, er, Penzance," she said, choosing the farthest flung town she could think of. "I could send you the letter of—"

"No, no—you needn't wait until you can offer proof of your experience." A look of pure panic leapt into Morris's eyes. "You seem a very well-spoken and intelligent woman, albeit a trifle young to possess such an impressive work history." He gave a forced laugh. "But why would anyone lie about such credentials if they did not possess proof?"

Selina laughed along with him. "Why, indeed? A person would need to be mad to do such a thing." Or at least bored, reckless, and depressed about her own lackluster existence.

Morris began to look more pleased as the notion had time to sink in. "His Grace of Chatham's own housekeeper," he repeated with a smile. "What a windfall that you happened to be passing through at the exact moment I should be in search of a new housekeeper." A notch appeared between his eyes. "I must say this seems extremely, er—"

"Fortuitous." Selina assaulted him with the full force of her smile.

Morris looked momentarily poleaxed and then shook himself and said, "Yes, yes, most fortuitous." He paused and then said, "Er, how much of my conversation with Mrs. Nelson did you chance to overhear?"

Selina blushed, as well she should, but decided to tell the truth for a change. "I heard her say that his lordship threw something at her."

He pursed his lips. "I'm afraid that is true."

"Is that something he does often, Mr. Morris?"

"To my knowledge that is the only time he has ever done such a thing."

Selina held his gaze; the man was hiding something. She struggled to recall everything she'd heard. The housekeeper had said something about the marquess's *condition.* What had she meant by that?

"His lordship has not been himself these past months," Morris said quickly, as if reading her thoughts.

"Oh?"

"He suffered a terrible accident."

"And was he badly injured?"

"He is not… the same," Morris prevaricated, his pale cheeks darkening.

"What do you mean?"

"His traveling coach went off the road and the marchioness and three servants were also with him. None of the others survived."

"That is indeed terrible," Selina said, the words woefully inadequate.

Morris's handsome old face suddenly looked ancient. "I'm afraid it is even worse than that."

Selina felt a sudden chill, even though the day was overly warm. "Wh-what do you mean?"

"His lordship was trapped inside the coach with his wife's body, unable to get out."

She sucked in a breath. "For how long?"

"Four days."

"*Four days?*" she repeated, appalled. "Why… a person could go mad in such a situation."

Morris's lips tightened; his expression frigid. "Does this change matters, Mrs. Lanyon?"

Did it? Selina stared at the old butler as her mind raced. She could not imagine the horror the marquess had endured, but it was clear the man needed help if he was offending servants and throwing things—and drinking and boxing, too, according to the last housekeeper. Selina frowned. Although what boxing had to do with any of it, she couldn't quite unders—

Mr. Morris cleared his throat.

Selina shook off her thoughts and met the butler's apprehensive gaze. "No, Mr. Morris, it does not change matters." She smiled up at him. "I am ready to leave when you are."

Chapter 5

The day had been very long—as had the one before it—and there was nothing Selina wanted to do more than fall into bed, but her work was not finished yet.

When she'd arrived at Courtland—the marquess's country house—that afternoon Mr. Morris had called together the servants and introduced her. She'd seen the startled looks and knew most of them would be wondering if the butler had gone mad to hire such a young woman to fill such a responsible position.

Fortunately, their expressions of concern had eased when Mr. Morris mentioned her tenure as housekeeper for the Duke of Chatham.

Selina herself had bolstered their good impression by behaving with the cool confidence that her mother had drummed into her all her life, a confidence the countess had insisted Selina would need when she finally found herself mistress of some lord's grand establishment.

Oh, how her mother would gape in horror to see just how Selina was employing all those lessons now.

Selina found it interesting that she'd never actually *felt* coolly confident before today. Something about this new position had infused her with a sense of self-assurance that was as intoxicating as any wine or spirits.

Mr. Morris had given her a tour of the house and had also introduced her, individually, to the other senior staff.

The only person Selina had *not* met was the marquess.

"Is his lordship away from home?" she'd asked, when it was apparent there would be no introduction to the master of the house.

A cagey expression had flickered over the old man's face. "Er, his lordship is here, but he has been… under the weather."

Selina wondered what sort of illness caused symptoms like throwing things.

All she could think of was dipsomania.

Of all the dozens of rumors she'd heard about the infamous Marquess of Shaftsbury—that he was an audaciously reckless, womanizing, sporting-mad Corinthian sought after by women and emulated by men—she'd never heard of him drinking to excess. But perhaps that was a result of his wife's death and the horrible accident.

Well, whatever the reason, Selina could hardly bull her way into his lordship's chambers and introduce herself, could she? She would just have to wait and see what happened tomorrow.

She'd eaten dinner in the servant's hall that night—taking her rightful place at the foot of the table—and had needed to pinch herself more than a few times to prove that this day was real and not just a fever dream, and that she was actually the Marquess of Shaftsbury's housekeeper.

True, she'd exaggerated her experience—fine, she'd outright *lied*—in order to get the job, but who would ever believe that she, Selina Bellamy—raised to be nothing but a rich man's ornament—could lie like a champion?

Even her siblings—who loved her dearly—viewed her more as a gentle, innocent pet that needed care and protection rather than a woman who was capable of taking care of herself.

Everyone in her life thought she was pretty, delicate, fluff-headed Selina whose only purpose was matrimony. Nothing but a sweet, harmless little *kitten* with tiny little *kitten* claws that couldn't hurt anybody.

Of course, that accusation wasn't without teeth. Marriage *had* been her *raison d'être* for as long as she could remember. But her first London Season—something she'd always dreamed about—had profoundly changed her way of thinking. Three months of being fawned over by men who didn't know the first thing about her—nor did they care to know—had been enough to drive the desire for marriage right out of her head.

Are you sure it wasn't Shelton's deception that did the driving?

Selina scowled at the unwanted thought. She'd be happy if she never thought about Lord Shelton for as long as she lived.

Unfortunately, that would be impossible now that Hy had married Shelton's cousin. Selina knew Shelton had lived at the duke's house in London during the Season, even though the men seemed to despise each other. She suspected the duke's support of his cousin wouldn't change even after Chatham learned about the abduction.

One way to avoid seeing Shelton for the foreseeable future was to keep this position.

Which reminded Selina that she needed to write a letter to Hy and wheedle a letter of recommendation for Mr. Morris.

Selina yawned. Perhaps she would leave the letter until tomorrow. She was exhausted and still needed to do the nightly walk-through of the house, a job she had gladly taken from Mr. Morris's fragile shoulders.

It was well after eleven o'clock; surely the house would be asleep by now and she could get this done and go to bed.

Selina

Armed with a hand candle, Selina made her way through the servant section of the house. It was amazing how quiet everything was. A person would never guess that forty plus human beings were asleep all around her.

She knew the marquess must be terribly wealthy to keep such an enormous staff. Her own family had been poor for so long that they'd not had more than three servants for years—and even those were more than her father could afford and often had to wait months for their wages. It would be a relief to live in a household that did not constantly hurt for money and to no longer need to pinch every penny.

Selina decided to start her walk-through in the foyer and try to retrace today's tour from memory. It wasn't as easy as she'd thought. The house was an enormous, sprawling series of interconnected corridors and staircases and she ended up lost and turned around several times.

Selina was almost finished—having discovered one unlocked door and two unattended candles that somebody would get a scolding for tomorrow—when she recognized the magnificent double doors that led to the library. She'd not had time to examine the room that afternoon; now would be an excellent opportunity to see what the marquess kept on his shelves.

She opened the door and was contemplating lighting more candles when an angry voice boomed from the darkness, "Who the hell is that?"

Selina screamed and peered into the gloom.

"Answer me!" the same voice bellowed.

Selina took a few steps into the room, until a desk materialized, with a man seated behind it.

"Damn you. Tell me who you—"

"I am Mrs. Lanyon, my lord. Your housekeeper." At least she assumed the disheveled man in shirtsleeves was the marquess.

"I thought your name was Nelson?"

"Er, no, she was my predecessor." Selina moved closer so they didn't need to shout. "Mr. Morris hired me today." She stopped in front of the desk, trying not to gawk at the striking man behind it.

When Selina had first met Shelton, he'd brought to mind a sunny god descended from Mount Olympus. This man—with a cold sneer marring his starkly beautiful features—was Shelton's underworld counterpart. His blue-black curls, ghostly pale skin, and piercing gray eyes combined with a chiseled jaw and high-bridged aristocratic nose to create cold, almost Satanic, perfection.

He glared fiercely at the candle in Selina's hand rather than meeting her gaze. "Morris hired you? *Today?*"

"Er, yes, my lord. It was a fortuitous event that—"

"Fortuitous?" he barked.

"Yes, I was in between positions and—"

"You sound like a child." His sneer deepened and he didn't bother to take his gaze from the candle, the arrogance in his pose telling her that a mere housekeeper wasn't even worth a glance.

Selina bristled. "I assure you that I most certainly am *not* a child."

"What are your credentials? Where did you work before?" He fired the questions at her in a rude, imperious tone that made her face heat.

"I worked for the Duke of Chatham, my lord."

His eyebrows shot up at that. "Impossible. I know Chatham's housekeeper and the woman is a marvel. He would never get rid of Mrs. Mercer." His lips pulled into an even more unpleasant smirk. "But if Chatham *did* give her the sack, then I'll be sure to tell Morris that she is now available for hire. The woman is a gem above all others."

Irrationally, Selina was irked at being compared to some faceless *gem* of a stranger and found wanting. "Well, she is not a gem now, my lord, because she is dead."

The marquess looked shaken by that news, but not as shaken and shamed as Selina felt for giving vent to such a horrendous lie. What had got into her? She wasn't a cruel or devious person and rarely told falsehoods if she could avoid it—especially not viciously and for no reason—and yet she'd been lying all day long.

She opened her mouth to apologize, but he spoke first.

"Dead," he repeated, and then dropped his gaze to the desktop, which was, she suddenly noticed, completely bare.

Selina frowned when she saw the floor around the desk was littered with various objects; one of them an inkwell tipped on its side.

"Oh dear," she said. "I'm afraid some things have fallen from your desk, my lord. There looks to be ink all over the carpet." She hurried forward. "Let me just—"

His head whipped up. "Just leave it alone and get out."

Selina recoiled at his anger. "But the ink will stain—"

"I said to leave it be and get the hell out."

Selina gawped. "But my lord—"

"Christ, woman—what is so difficult to understand? I said *get out!*" He lurched to his feet, shoved his chair back hard enough to topple it, and then came charging around the desk.

Selina

Or at least he tried to. Instead, he bumped into the sharp corner of the slab of wood, gave a pained grunt, and then doubled over at the force of the collision.

Selina instinctively took a step toward him to offer aid. "My lord, are you—"

He straightened up slowly, his face contorted into a snarl. "Out! Out! *Out!*" Once again, he started toward her but stepped on the inkwell, turned his ankle, and staggered into a wingchair.

"Goddammit!" he raged, shoving the chair hard enough to send it skittering across the room. He'd barely taken two steps when he ran into yet another chair and took a rather nasty spill onto an end table.

Selina distinctly heard the cracking of wood but did not attempt to help him. Instead, she backed toward the door. Was he *mad?* Drunk?

He struggled to his feet, pointed an accusing finger at the fireplace, rather than in Selina's direction, and shouted. "You heard me, *get out!*"

Selina stared in shock.

Lord Shaftsbury wasn't drunk.

He was blind.

Chapter 6

The next morning Selina wondered if there was any point in writing a letter to Hy. Surely the marquess would sack her after last night?

She decided to wait until after breakfast—in case he summoned her early—before deciding what to do.

Selina ate her meal with the rest of the servants and then set about her day, the entire time waiting for a summons.

But... nothing happened.

She waited again that night. After all, the marquess seemed to be nocturnal in his habits.

But no summons ever came, and the house was silent when she did her evening walk-through that night.

And there was no angry summons the next day, either.

By the third evening after their confrontation, Selina decided she could safely assume that she still had a job and sat down to write to her sister.

My Dearest Duchess,

Before I explain the purpose of this letter, I wish to say **CONGRATULATIONS** *dear sister! Aunt Ellen received His Grace's exciting missive right before Lord Shelton tricked me into a carriage and commenced our (botched) elopement. But more on that subject shortly.*

How I laughed with glee when I heard that I must now address you as Her Grace. It makes me smile to think of you presiding over a grand ducal estate, wielding a scepter, wearing a coronet, and draped in an ermine robe. I want to hear all about it when you respond to my letter, which I hope you will do with all haste.

As to my situation at present...

If you are reading this, then you will have heard about Lords Fowler and Shelton and their ridiculous fisticuffs at one of the busiest posting inns on the North Road. While they both wanted me—and everyone else in the vicinity—to think the fight was over my honor, I am perfectly aware it was for their own masculine edification and enjoyment.

You must think I am truly a featherbrain to believe anything Shelton said to me after what you wrote in your letter. I have nothing to offer in my defense.

I allowed Lord Shelton to lure me into his carriage under false pretenses and then was (foolishly) surprised to discover that he planned to spirit me to the border.

I was, at first, delighted when Lord Fowler arrived at the inn. Unfortunately, he promptly insisted that he would be the one to save my reputation by marrying me.

Selina

Neither one of the muttonheads cared a jot what I wanted, Hy. Neither one of them bothered to ask.

Well, I don't care a jot how shredded my reputation is. With you married to Chatham, my reputation is no longer of any consequence. Thanks to you, dear sister, it is no longer my duty to marry a wealthy man.

Indeed, I needn't marry at all. To be frank, I am no longer sure that I even wish to.

For once I can do what *I* would like to do.

The only problem is that I don't know *what* I want to do. For so long—all my life, in fact—I've thought about nothing but marriage. Without that goal to occupy my mind, I find myself both liberated and at loose ends.

Which leads me to my current situation.

I have taken a position as housekeeper in the Marquess of Shaftsbury's country house.

Is your jaw sagging? Are you flummoxed?

Well, I suppose you have a right to be flummoxed and more.

Why did I do such a thing? I suppose I did it because I did not want to go home to Queen's Bower and resume my mundane life, with Mama disappointed (and haranguing me constantly) that I didn't make a grand marriage and Papa slinking off to gamble now that your new husband can pay off all his debts.

And before you even offer, I *know* you would give me a home with you and His Grace. I know I could live off your bounty for the rest of my days and be a doting aunt to your children. I still might do both those things, dearest Hy.

But not just yet.

I would think that you, of all my sisters, would understand the desire to stand on my own two feet for once.

I have no special skill to get by on like your genius with cards, or Aurelia's wonderful artistic abilities. I am not efficient and organized like Phoebe. Nor am I passionate and fascinating like Katie is.

I am the pretty and sweet sister. The useless sister now that I've failed to even do the one thing I was supposed to be good at.

In any case, I've spent my entire life being groomed to run the household of a powerful, wealthy, and titled man.

And so here I am, doing exactly that, albeit in the position of housekeeper rather than wife. It has only been three days but already I can tell that I am *good* at it.

Are you smiling? I think you are. I hope you are happy for me and approve of my adventure because I need your help. It seems I may have told the butler, Mr. Morris, that I was the Duke of Chatham's housekeeper for a time.

You see? You've not even been married a week and already I am using your new position to my advantage.

But there is nothing for it, my dear sister, I need a letter of recommendation from His Grace of Chatham.

Selina paused, brushing the quill back and forth against her chin, wracking her memory to recall just what she'd told Morris about her time as Chatham's housekeeper... Had she said she'd *just* left that position? Or that she'd been gone several months?

She shrugged. If she didn't recall what she'd said, it was unlikely that Mr. Morris would.

Selina turned back to the letter.

I'm sure your husband is a <u>very</u> busy man, so maybe you could write the recommendation saying that I was an exemplary employee in every way for three years, until we amicably parted ways six months ago.

I think I'd much rather the letter come from you, dearest Hy. It doesn't matter that you weren't married six months ago—nobody will care or know. Certainly not the butler here, who is truly an old dear and desperate for somebody to take the weight of running the household off his shoulders.

I know you cannot keep my situation a secret from your new husband, and I want you to set his mind at ease about me so the two of you can commence your marital bliss rather than tearing about Britain searching for your errant sister.

Please tell him that I am well and that he needn't thrash Shelton. At least not too much. But—if you would not hate it—could you keep my location a secret? I'm just afraid that if such information were to be made known (to Mama, for example) that my adventure would be very brief indeed.

I don't know how long I will stay. It is possible his lordship will sack me when he learns there is a young housekeeper managing his grand estate. But regardless of the duration of my adventure, I need the letter and also some clothing. Oh, and could you please purchase some mobcaps for me? Something very plain and ugly—no lace for me now. If you could send the most practical of my clothes, along with your letter of recommendation, I would think you the best sister in the world.

I <u>do</u> hope that you haven't only married the duke to rescue your family, Hy. Have you? I pray it is a love match for you. His Grace certainly behaved as if he cared a great deal for you when he came seeking you at Aunt Ellen's house.

I hope to hear from you soon.

Your affectionate sister,

Linny

***

Selina

Selina took the letter to the post office in Much Deeping herself the following morning rather than mail it from Courtland. After all, it wouldn't do for Morris to see that she'd addressed a missive directly to the Duchess of Chatham.

Over the next week life quickly took on a predictable rhythm at Courtland and Selina enjoyed the challenge of learning the layout of the truly magnificent, sprawling house as well as familiarizing herself with the almost sixty servants who were employed by the marquess.

At the back of her mind that first week was a faint expectation of ... *something*. If not a summons from the marquess himself, then surely some admonition from Morris about disturbing his lordship in the library that night.

But there wasn't so much as a peep from either the butler or master of the house.

Selina quickly discovered that the man rarely left his rooms during the daylight hours. Not for meals, not to go into the village, not to go anywhere.

But at night? Well, that was another matter entirely.

Truly, he roamed the house like a wraith, drifting through the corridors and leaving a swath of destruction in his path. Not that she saw him again after that first night. He seemed to do his haunting after she'd done the evening walk-through.

Even so, Selina dreaded opening any doors on her nightly inspection, but it was her duty to check for candles that might have been left burning or windows or doors had been left open, so she gritted her teeth and entered every single room.

Except for his lordship's chambers, of course. Or the room at the end of the hall, diagonal from the marquess's spacious apartment.

Judging by the noises she heard emanating from that room almost every night, Lord Shaftsbury spent a great many hours in there. She'd even gone outside the house to look up at the windows, but the drapes were always pulled tight.

The sounds she heard were violent ones—slaps and groans and thuds—and she'd hovered outside the door more than once, chewing her lip ragged, wondering if she should go inside and see if he needed help.

But the memory of their one and only exchange prudently held her back.

Selina was not normally a pessimist, but something about the rage that had flowed off the marquess like rain sheeting off a roof had frightened her. He was a man walking on an edge so fine that he would eventually topple over or be sliced right in half.

***

On the eighth morning of her new job, Selina had finally had enough. She waited until after breakfast, when it was only her and Mr. Morris left in the servant hall and fixed the butler with the sort of stern look that she'd seen her Aunt Fitzroy's housekeeper use on the male staff at Fitzroy House.

"Lord Shaftsbury has not come out of his rooms since my arrival, Mr. Morris." She decided not to tell him about the bizarre confrontation in the library that first night. "You must know that is not normal."

The dignified old man cringed at her softly spoken, but undeniable, criticism of the situation.

"He comes out at night, Mrs. Lanyon."

"I hardly think that qualifies, Mr. Morris."

"He has been a bit worse of late," Morris reluctantly admitted, "but I have hopes he will soon come about."

"I overheard your conversation with that farmer who came to call on his lordship two days ago—Mr. Devlin, I think his name was."

Morris's face fell. "Oh."

The farmer had come, hat in hand, to request an audience with the master of Courtland. It appeared a tree had fallen through his roof during a recent summer storm. He was a tenant farmer and relied on the marquess to maintain the property. Morris had promised to promptly relay the man's message to his lordship.

Selina strongly suspected that had not happened.

While she felt sympathy for Morris, she also sympathized with Lord Shaftsbury's people, who depended on him and hadn't had any help since Selina had moved to Courtland—and probably for some time before that.

She stared at the old man while she pondered her next words. Although the marquess was clearly wealthy, the estate was rapidly falling into a state of disrepair without guidance. The house itself had been rather grubby and disorganized when she'd arrived. Likely because Morris had been stretched to his limits and the last housekeeper clearly unable to cope with the master of the house. It had taken Selina the first five days to impose order on the maids. None of the servants were *bad*, they just lacked discipline. The household was beginning to come back into proper shape, but the estate was still suffering. Without its master, matters would only become worse.

There were likely many more repairs than Mr. Devlin's roof, and autumn was rapidly approaching. Mr. Morris—a family retainer who'd probably dandled the marquess on his knee as an infant—was simply too close to the situation to do what was necessary.

That only left Selina.

"I can't help noticing that no valet has joined us for meals. Does he dine with the master?"

"No. His lordship's valet—Mr. Elton—died in the same accident as Lady Shaftsbury."

That might explain Lord Shaftsbury's disheveled appearance.

Morris hesitated and then added, "Mr. Elton came to work for the marquess when his lordship was only fifteen. They were very… close. It is too painful for his lordship to consider hiring somebody new just yet."

Selina did not point out that it had been almost a year. Instead, she said, "Surely somebody must do for him? One of the footmen?"

"I see to his lordship." Selina stared until Morris cleared his throat and added, "But only if he summons me."

"And how often does that happen?"

Mr. Morris didn't answer.

Selina clucked her tongue. "Oh, Mr. Morris. How long will you allow this to go on?"

"I don't know what to do," he confessed, a quaver in his normally firm baritone voice, his stiff shoulders slumping.

Selina thought about what Lord Shaftsbury must be suffering. Not only had he lost his sight and his wife, but he'd evidently lost a loyal servant. She'd grown up with long-term retainers and knew they could often be closer to one than one's family. Her own childhood nurse, Nanny Fletcher, was more beloved by Selina and her sisters than their own mother.

But the man she'd seen the other night in the library had looked more than just sad; he had looked demented by grief.

"Can his lordship see at all?"

Morris's eyes widened. "How do you know about that?" he demanded, his surprise quickly turning anger. "Did one of the servants tell you?"

"No, they haven't said a peep—which is quite a miracle, by the way. I found out when I accidentally encountered his lordship in the library one evening. And before you ask, he was not happy to see me."

Morris opened his mouth, as if to ask what had happened, but then seemed to give up. He slumped in his chair, lost in his own thoughts.

"Mr. Morris?"

"Hmm?"

"Can his lordship see at all?"

"He hasn't mentioned anything. But then… Well, he hasn't said anything *at all* about it."

"What does he do all day?"

"He sleeps."

"And then roams the house at night."

It wasn't a question, but Morris nodded.

"And what about that room down the corridor from his?"

"It is his private gymnasium."

"Gym—what?"

"Gymnasium. It is a Greek word. Perhaps you've heard of Gentleman Jackson's Saloon in London?"

Selina pulled a face. "Ah, boxing."

"Yes, just so." Morris's faded blue eyes gleamed with humor at her feminine disgust of the violent sport that men appeared to love so much.

"But… if he is boxing, that means there is somebody in there with him?"

"No, he is conditioning himself."

Whatever that meant. But at least it explained all the alarming sounds she'd heard.

"His rooms have not been cleaned in the eight days I've been here, Mr. Morris."

"No, his lordship does not permit anyone to enter them."

"Does he have a secretary? A steward? Somebody we could apply to for help? Some… some male relation or acquaintance he is close to?" Because—in Selina's experience—men only listened to other men, and then only if they respected their opinions. Men never listened to women. At least no man had ever sought *her* opinion or listened to her when it came to any matter of importance.

"He sacked his steward a few months after his accident."

"Did the man take advantage of his blindness?" she asked, sickened by the thought of such abuse.

"Oh no, not at all. Mr. Spivey was his lordship's father's steward." He coughed delicately. "He, erm, well, he tried to argue with his lordship about leaving his room and… it did not go well for him." His look was significant, as if to say: if the marquess sacked an old family retainer, there wouldn't be much hope for Selina or even Morris, if either of them pushed the issue.

She chewed at the inside of her cheek. "Is there *nobody* else we could ask for help."

Morris's face puckered into an expression Selina could not decipher.

"What is it, Mr. Morris?"

"There is his younger brother—Lord Victor. But... well, they were never close. Lord Victor is eight years younger than his lordship and they rarely spent any time together. When they did..." he trailed off and shrugged.

"You mean they don't get along?"

Morris nodded. "I believe the last time they spoke to each other they had a rather terrible row."

"Are you saying they *dislike* each other, or just that they argue?" In Selina's experience that was an important distinction. Her parents disliked—or even hated—each other. Her sister Katie and her brother Doddy—the two youngest—fought like cats and dogs, but they loved each other fiercely.

"Er, no, I wouldn't go so far as to say *dislike*. But they are very, very different."

"Different how?"

"Lord Victor was a somber, quiet young man who was very close to their mother. Lady Shaftsbury was an intensely religious woman. After the old marquess died she lived out her remaining years in a convent."

Selina had no response for that.

Morris lowered his voice and said, "I'm afraid that neither her ladyship nor Lord Victor ever approved of his lordship."

"What do you mean?"

Morris hesitated and she could see he was considering his words carefully. "His lordship has always been, er, gregarious and um, popular. Both with his peers and with, erm"—he recalled to whom he was speaking, and his mouth snapped shut.

"Ladies?" Selina guessed, amused by his prudery. "You won't shock me. I know about some of Lord Shaftsbury's more infamous exploits."

Morris's eyebrows arched high, reminding Selina that she was supposed to be a servant and not privy to *ton* gossip.

"His name has been mentioned more than once in society columns and scandal sheets," she pointed out.

"Ah, yes," Morris said, nodding. "Well, his lordship's mother and brother never approved of his lifestyle."

"But he married. Surely he was no longer as wild as he'd been in his youth?"

Morris opened his mouth, hesitated, and then said, "The marriage was of a very recent vintage and the new Lady Shaftsbury was not precisely... happy here. His lordship spent a great deal of his time elsewhere."

Which probably meant the marquess had lived in London and kept a mistress. Selina wanted to ask more, but it seemed wrong to pry into her employer's marriage. But his brother—that was a subject worth pursuing.

"Even if Lord Victor disapproved of his lordship, surely he would see that his brother needs his help now?" Selina frowned. "Has he not come here and witnessed the state of things for himself?"

"Lord Victor is... Well, he is a monk."

"A *what?*"

"A monk."

Selina had never met a monk or even heard of one—at least not outside of fiction. "A monk," she repeated at a loss for anything more intelligent.

Morris nodded. "He lives in a monastery just outside Rabat." At Selina's blank look he explained. "That is a city in the Kingdom of Morocco."

"His lordship's brother lives in *Africa?*"

"Yes. He has been there—goodness, it must be eight years now."

"I thought Morocco was a Muslim country?"

"There is a Christian monastery there, that is all I know."

"And he didn't come home when he heard of his lordship's accident and the death of his wife?"

Guilt bloomed on the old man's face and twin spots of color darkened his cheeks. "Er, no."

"Oh, Mr. Morris." Selina clucked her tongue. "Are you telling me that Lord Victor doesn't know about his lordship's blindness?"

"Mr. Spivey wrote to inform him of her ladyship's death."

"But nobody told him that his lordship is blind?"

Morris winced, as if *blind* was a vulgar word. "His lordship specifically forbade Spivey from summoning Master Victor home—or even mentioning his... affliction. When I suggested the matter to the marquess a few months after Mr. Spivey left, his lordship became angry. He—he threatened to sack me, Mrs. Lanyon." Morris hurried on, as if a damn had shattered within him. "He warned me against doing anything of the sort—of telling anyone. He'd already made it clear the servants were never to speak of his condition outside of this house, or even gossip about it to each other."

Selina held his guilty gaze. "I think you know that we must write to Lord Victor, Mr. Morris."

"I *cannot* go against his lordship's explicit instructions, Mrs. Lanyon."

"No, I can understand that." Her mouth firmed into a grim line. "But *I* wasn't forbidden to write to him."

Morris's eyes widened. "You mean—"

"I will write a letter to his lordship's brother."

"You will?"

"Yes."

"What will you say?"

"I won't mention his blindness," she quickly assured him. "Just that his lordship has need of him."

Morris's face puckered. "Oh, I don't know, Mrs. Lanyon. It will make his lordship *very* angry when he finds out."

"Matters cannot continue this way, Mr. Morris. Surely you must see that? Not only is there his lordship's health to consider, but what of the estate and all his dependents? Is anyone paying bills? Seeing to repairs? Who is taking care of things? That poor farmer's roof cannot be the only matter that needs attention?"

"I have been paying the most pressing bills—at his lordship's direction, of course," he hastily added at Selina's no doubt surprised expression.

"I'm afraid that is not enough, Mr. Morris."

"Oh, I know you are right—I do. It's just—" he broke off, his eyes dangerously glassy. "It hurts to see him this way, Mrs. Lanyon. His lordship has always been such a vibrant, active man, always so strong and capable and in command. Even as a little boy he was brimming with life and mischief. Always into this or that. I keep hoping…"

"You're hoping that he comes back to himself—that he regains his vision."

"Yes. Even though I know that is foolish."

"We *must* do something or the estate and people will suffer. Do you think his lordship—the man you *used* to know before this horrible accident—would want that?"

"No—he would hate that. He has always been an exceedingly conscientious master and landlord."

"Then we must take matters into our own hands until he is well again—at least until he is ready to resume his duty."

"Yes, you are right."

"I will write the letter, if you will provide Lord Victor's direction."

Morris gave her a look of weary gratitude. "You are correct, of course." His pale lips curved up slightly. "This is painful, but I am relieved you've taken a stand. And I must say I am pleased I happened on you that day."

Selina's face heated with pleasure. "Why, thank you, Mr. Morris. I am pleased you did, too."

He looked away, clearly discomfited by too much emotion. "Oh," he said, suddenly. "This came for you in the morning post." He slid a thick letter across the table toward her.

A quick glance at the sender's name showed that Hy had used Mary Fletcher, which was their nanny's name. Clever, clever Hy.

She smiled at Mr. Morris. "Ah, this is from my sister—Mrs. Fletcher. I *do* hope she was able to locate the Duchess's recommendation."

Selina unfolded the letter and saw there were two sheets. One contained only a few sentences from Hy, saying she would send a proper letter, along with some clothing, in a day or two.

The other letter had all the pomp of a ducal decree. A speedy reading assured Selina that Hy had done exactly as she'd asked.

She met the butler's curious gaze. "Here is my letter of reference."

Morris took it, his eyes moving quickly over the page before he turned back to her. "Her Grace speaks *very* highly of you. I'm sure his lordship will be more than satisfied with this, Mrs. Lanyon."

Selina thought about the marquess's reaction to her that first night and doubted Morris's optimism. She also doubted that the butler would even show Lord Shaftsbury the letter.

"Perhaps I should take it to him?" she offered.

The look of horror on Morris's face almost made her laugh. "Er, no, no, that won't be necessary. I will tell him."

"Soon? I should hate to stay on here if he doesn't wish to have me. I'm sure you understand, Mr. Morris."

"Yes, of course. I will tell him soon."

Selina hesitated, and then said, "Even though I am writing to Lord Victor I still think we should see if we can encourage his lordship to leave his chambers and apply himself to some of his business. At the very least we should be allowed into his rooms to do some cleaning."

"But—"

"I daresay Lord Victor would be angry if he arrived and found his brother living in filth and the estate floundering."

The old butler capitulated without much of a struggle. "Very well. But—not today, please. Can we not wait until tomorrow?"

Selina wanted to ask what possible difference another day would make, but she had badgered the poor old dear enough already. "Very well," she said, echoing his words. "But we will go to him tomorrow."

Chapter 7

Tap... tap... tap.

Tap... tap... tap.

The annoying noise slowly nagged Caius from a deep, dreamless sleep.

He forced his eyes open and blinked into the darkness. What the devil had woken him?

Tap... tap... tap. The sound came from the door.

"What?" he shouted.

"It is Morris, my lord. Er, may I come in?"

Caius blinked and rubbed his eyes before glancing at his nightstand.

And then remembering that he was blind.

As it did every single day, that recollection crushed him anew, squashing the breath out of him like a giant fist squeezing his chest.

"My lord?" Morris called out.

"What do you want, Morris?" he asked wearily. "And why can't you just leave me alone?" he added under his breath.

"I need to speak with you, my lord. If you have a moment."

If he had a moment? Caius almost laughed. That's *all* he had: moments and hours and years, his life yawning before him like one endless, pointless nightmare.

He closed his eyes and let his heavy limbs relax. Maybe if he just ignored the man, he would go awa—

Tap... tap... tap....

His eyelids flew open. "Bloody hell. Come in, dammit!"

The door opened.

"Well, what is it?" he demanded when the old servant didn't speak.

"I thought you should know that Mrs. Nelson did not return, my lord."

"Fine."

"I engaged a new housekeeper, my lord."

Caius's lips twisted and he knew the expression would be unpleasant. "Yes, I know. She claims to have worked for Chatham."

The door shut and he heard feet approaching the bed. "Yes, my lord. I have a letter of reference from the Duchess of Chatham."

"Indeed? The dowager wrote to you about the new housekeeper?" Caius recalled Chatham's mother from years before, when he'd gone to stay at his house during several school holidays. He distinctly recalled Chatham's mother as being even more distant and reserved than his own. It was difficult to imagine her lowering herself to write a letter of recommendation for a servant.

"Er, no, my lord. The letter is from the duke's new wife."

"Chatham remarried?" he asked stupidly. Obviously he'd remarried if there was a new duchess.

"Yes, my lord."

"When was that?"

"I don't know, sir. I must confess I've read no announcement in any of the newspapers."

Caius grunted, already losing interest in an old friend's new marriage.

He flicked a hand dismissively, and then wondered if he'd made the gesture in the right direction. Oh well, who cared? Certainly not Morris.

"Was that all?" he asked.

Again, there was a long pause.

"Good God, Morris, just *speak* would you?"

"Are you going to come out of your chambers today, sir?"

Caius scowled. "Why?"

"I, er, well there are some letters and—"

"Letters," Caius repeated flatly.

"Yes, my lord. And bills."

"And you think I can read those, do you?" Caius shouted, and then immediately felt like a self-pitying arse. "Never mind," he added, in a slightly more civil tone. "Just pull out the ones that are the most urgent and prepare the drafts for me to sign." Then they could go through the embarrassing process of Morris guiding the quill for him.

"Of course, sir."

"Was there something else?" he asked when the man didn't leave.

"I—er, are you hungry, sir? Or—"

"No. I want nothing. You may leave."

"Very good, sir."

The door shut and Caius was so exhausted that his body felt like it was hewn out of stone.

Sleep. That's what he needed.

Sleep.

As always, his eyelids slid shut the moment his head hit the pillow. Caius wrinkled his nose at the odor of stale sweat; it was probably time to have the bedding changed. When had he last summoned a maid?

The thought made him tired, and he yawned.

He'd just fallen into a comfortable doze when he was again woken from his slumber. This time not with a gentle tap but with a window-rattling pounding.

Thud. Thud. Thud.

Caius jerked bolt upright. "Good God! What in the name of all that is holy do you need *now*, Morris?"

"My lord?" said a voice he'd heard only once before but hadn't forgotten. It was a clear, crisp, and mellifluous voice that he might have found pleasant if not for the fact that it belonged to an interloper—an unwanted witness to his pathetic life.

Caius ground his teeth. "I've just spoken to Morris. What in the world could you need now?"

"Morris?" she repeated.

"Yes, my butler," he shot back snidely.

"Er, that was yesterday, my lord."

Caius opened his mouth, but no words came. Surely he had not slept through an entire day? "What time is it?"

"Ten o'clock. In the morning, my lord."

No. That was impossible.

"My lord?" she prodded. "Are you... confused, sir? Do you need—"

It suddenly occurred to him that the woman was inside his bloody *bed*chamber. "What in the name of God do you think you are doing in here? Get out immediately."

The door shut.

Caius was more than a little surprised at how easy that had been.

He was about to lower his head to the pillow when he heard light, distinctly female, footsteps.

The *audacity* of the woman. "I told you to get out."

"I thought it best to stay and speak to you, my lord."

"Just who in the—"

"I know of your loss—"

"My *loss*?" he shouted at her, his voice so loud it made his head pound. "Who do you think you are? You don't know the first fucking thing about me!"

"I hardly think that sort of language is necessary, sir."

"Did you just *chide* me? In my own damned bedchamber? You—you *interfering*—"

"Your people need you, my lord—the hundreds who did not die that day."

Caius's jaw sagged and an undignified gasp slipped out.

"Your tenants are in distress—their cottages in need of repair before winter sets in. One gentleman has a tree through his roof. There are leaks in the south wing and one is so bad that the priceless marquetry flooring has been all but ruined. There are—"

Caius reached for the first thing he could find on his nightstand—a book, for God's sake. There was a bloody book sitting on his nightstand when he'd not been able to read for almost a damned year. He snatched it up and hurled it across the room, taking care to throw it *away* from the sound of her voice.

The satisfying sound of glass shattering filled the room. "Get out!" he bellowed.

He heard footsteps again and then a soft sigh. "Oh, what a shame. This is a lovely old book and you have cracked the spine. And this vase is quite destroyed."

She'd not left; she was *deliberately* disobeying him.

His head buzzed with fury, as if hornets had taken up residence in his skull. Caius needed to raise his voice to hear himself speak. "You are no longer needed here. I am *sacking* you if you need me to spell it out."

"If you want to sack me, then you will have to make me leave, my lord."

A bark of startled—and yes, slightly hysterical—laughter slipped from his mouth. "You think I won't? By God, I'll summon the constable and have you dragged from the house by your hair."

"You would need to get up to do that."

He sneered. "I may be blind, but I still recall where the servant pull is."

"I disconnected it before I came up from the kitchen. You can yank on it all you want; nobody will come."

Caius's jaw sagged and an honest-to-God shiver of fear crawled down his spine.

"You're mad," he said, his voice far too breathy for his pride.

"You have a beautiful house, and the grounds are lovely. Your people adore you, but everything is suffering without your attention. I've seen what happens when a lord neglects his people, and if matters are allowed to go unchecked for much longer there will be no coming back."

Dozens of words—some crude and vulgar—leapt to mind. Strangely, the words his mouth chose to release were, "You have *seen* such a thing? Are you telling me that Chatham has ever neglected his duties?"

For once, she didn't respond instantly.

"Well?" he goaded.

"No, I'm not speaking of Chatham. I'm talking about the very first position I held." She suddenly sounded hesitant—not so bloody self-righteously confident. "I was too young and diffident to know what to do back then."

"You don't sound exactly ancient now," he said dryly.

"I've been working as a housekeeper for years. Mr. Morris has my letter of recommendation from the Duke of Chatham, sir."

"From Chatham's *wife*," he corrected.

"Yes, that is true."

"His marriage must be of a recent vintage."

Once again there was a slight pause before she answered. "They've been married almost six months, sir."

Caius swore he could hear the lie in her voice. "Six months?"

"Yes."

"Morris said it wasn't in the papers."

"They married in Scotland—by special license."

For the first time in longer than he could remember, Caius felt a spark of something. It was so foreign that he didn't recognize it at first.

Curiosity.

There was a tone in her voice—a hesitancy—that was… off. Just what was the woman up to?

"Who did you work for before Chatham?" he asked, strangely reluctant to let go of the conversation now that it had started, uncaring of how he must appear to this woman—sprawled on his wrinkled, filthy bed, shirtless and—he hastily felt his hips and breathed a sigh of relief when he realized he was at least wearing drawers—unwashed and unshaved. He could see himself clearly in his mind's eye, and what he saw mortified him.

"Lord Addiscombe."

"What?" he demanded rudely.

"You asked me who I worked for before His Grace of Chatham and I said Lord Addiscombe."

He snorted. "Addiscombe?"

"You know of him?"

"Of course I know of him. The man is a fiend for cards. I'm surprised he can even afford servants. I thought he'd lost everything."

"He did lose everything, or almost everything," she admitted, an almost unhappy edge in her voice. "That is why I left."

"Hmmph. Well, my situation is hardly like Addiscombe's," he said, irked that she'd even compare him to a man who'd gambled away every farthing he could lay his hands on.

"Neglect is neglect, my lord."

He gritted his teeth at her prim, chastising tone. "And just what do you propose I do, Miss—what the devil is your name again?"

"Mrs. Lanyon."

"And just what do you suggest I do, Mrs. Lanyon? Ride about my estate and inspect the tenant farms for damage? Read the letters that Morris says are piling up? Hmm? What?"

"You had a steward you could have directed to do those things."

Caius scowled. She was talking about Spivey, the same man who'd been his father's steward. Spivey, who'd been so horrified by Caius's blindness that he'd wept quietly every single bloody time they had been in the same room together.

But he was hardly going to tell this pushy upstart that.

"Mr. Morris says that he has been managing the most pressing issues, but he said that Mr. Spivey has inquired about coming back to work. You could—"

"Morris has a big bloody mouth. Perhaps I should sack him as well as you when I get out of this bed and stagger downstairs—which I will do, mark my words."

"Mr. Morris didn't want to tell me anything. I pressed him on the issue."

"Ha! Now *that* I can believe."

"If you don't want to rehire Mr. Spivey, I could contact the employment agency and—"

"*No.*"

"Why not?"

"Because I don't want strangers seeing me this way!" Caius bit his tongue, *furious* that he'd allowed such a pitiful collection of words to leave his mouth. He couldn't see her face, but her silence spoke volumes.

The thought of this stranger—this nosy, interfering harpy—pitying *him* goaded Caius into a black rage. "Damn you to hell, woman!" he roared. "None of this is any concern of yours."

"I am your housekeeper, my lord."

"No, you are not. I bloody well sacked you."

"You are in need of help, my lord."

"Good God." Caius gave a laugh of disbelief. "You *still* refuse to leave."

"Let me help. I've already seen you—I know you are blind—so you wouldn't need to bring in any... strangers."

Caius could only gape in disbelief.

She took his stupefaction for consent and pressed on.

"I can manage household accounts, read and respond to letters, and—and generally follow directions."

"Here's a direction for you to follow: Get. Out. Of. My. House."

Her sigh was audible. "You need *somebody*, my lord."

Caius's head pounded and he couldn't even recall how they'd *begun* this conversation. How had this aggressive female even been allowed to enter his private chambers? Where the hell was Morris and why had he permitted this to happen?

How in the name of God would Caius ever get this damned nagging female *out* of his rooms?"

Chapter 8

Selina was behaving abominably to invade the marquess's private sanctum and refuse to leave, but she knew that the only way to chivvy a person out of despair was to give them something else to turn their mind to.

Anger—which she'd certainly managed to elicit—was a far better emotion than apathy. It was healthier, in moderation, and could motivate a person. Hopefully it wouldn't motivate him to throw more things, although the book certainly hadn't come anywhere near her.

She knew she should leave, that she shouldn't have entered his bedchamber to begin with. But now that she was there, she couldn't give up. Nor could she stop staring at his mostly nude body.

His torso was hard sculpted muscle without so much as a trace of fat. It wasn't normal to have skin stretched so taut and Selina knew from speaking to the servants that he rarely ate very much of the food that was delivered to his room. Even wearing little more than a scowl, he was exceedingly handsome, if gaunt-faced and dark-eyed with exhaustion.

He'd obviously not shaved for days, but his facial hair could not conceal the exquisite bone structure of his face. And his eyes? Well, they were his crowning glory, an unusual silvery gray with thick, dark lashes and heavy lids that gave him a perpetually sleepy look, even when he was seething with rage. Which he'd been doing almost since the moment she'd barged into his chambers.

"*You* want to be my secretary?" Before she could reply, he scoffed and said, "Don't you have enough work to keep you busy, Mrs. Lanyon?"

"I have plenty to do, but not so much that I could not help you with your correspondence for a few hours every day, my lord."

"Help me?" he repeated, as if she were speaking in a foreign language. Emotions flickered across his face: fury, disbelief, loathing, confusion, and more.

The man was the human equivalent of a vigorously steaming pot, his emotions slopping over the sides like boiling water. Anyone who ventured near risked painful burns.

Selina knew the wiser path would be to leave him to his misery and let him boil until there was nothing left in the pot, until he was truly a shell of his former self.

Or she could take a chance—risk getting scalded—and finally do something worthwhile with her life.

He awkwardly swung his feet off the bed and stood, exposing the full length of his magnificent, scantily clad body.

Selina swallowed, and then did it again. Even though he was underweight, he had a powerful build and was easily six or more inches taller than her own five-feet-three. He should have intimidated her, but all she felt was pity and regret that such a glorious creature had been brought so low.

"Fine," the marquess shouted, spittle spraying from his lips. "You want to read my letters, poke around in my affairs—you want to *help*?" He sneered and flung his arms out in a vaguely Christlike gesture, the movement doing enticing things to his shoulders, chest, and abdomen. "You can *help* me bathe and dress. How about that, Mrs. Lanyon?"

She couldn't stop her eyes from wandering over every inch of him.

And he was showing a great many inches.

"Well?" he demanded, lowering his fists to rest on his narrow hips. "I'm waiting."

"Wouldn't you rather I summon Morris or one of the footmen to—"

"I want nobody *helping* me except *you*, Mrs. Lanyon. As you were so gracious to point out how deficient I am and *insist* on helping me, you can now serve me in all ways." He dropped his hands to his sides and then—with a nasty smirk twisting his beautifully sculpted lips—he deliberately scratched his crotch.

He barked an ugly laugh when Selina wasn't quick enough to catch the gasp that escaped her. "Now, you can either obey my order or get the hell out of my house, Mrs. Lanyon. If you don't, I *will* leave this room—I don't care if I have to crawl all the way to Much Deeping on bloody knees in my current state of undress—and I *will* bring the constable to haul you out kicking and screaming if need be." He raised one eyebrow, smirked, and then pulled the tape that held up his drawers.

Selina watched in open-mouthed shock as the fine but badly wrinkled muslin slid to the ground.

"Fetch me my robe," he ordered.

She squeezed her eyes shut and was about to turn away when a voice in her head stopped her.

Why should you turn away? It was her sister Hy's voice.

It's immodest, that is why, another voice retorted—one that sounded remarkably like Nanny Fletcher.

Why should Linny bother protecting his lordship's modesty when he has no interest in doing so? Hy demanded.

Nanny had no answer for that.

Selina

Go on, Linny, Hy ordered. *You wanted an adventure. Don't let this opportunity pass you by.*

And so Selina opened her eyes and turned around.

And took a nice long look.

Long being the operative word.

The marquess wasn't the first naked male she'd seen. Indeed, she'd observed dozens of men in various stages of undress when she and her sisters had volunteered at the temporary hospital the army had set up in Little Sissingdon.

Selina's mother had been scandalized at the thought of her daughters waiting on male commoners in a filthy hospital and had forbidden them to go anywhere near the establishment.

But their father had, for once, put his foot down. "You are obviously unaware that there is a long, venerable, tradition of service among the women on my side of the family, my dear." The earl's gently condescending tone and snide smirk had made Selina squirm for their mother, who was, in general, undeserving of anyone's sympathy. The Countess of Addiscombe was a selfish, superficial, cold, and judgmental woman who'd made all her children's lives hellish over the years. But the earl was hardly any better. After all, it had been Selina's father who'd gambled away his daughters' dowries and his son's patrimony.

In any case, their father's intervention had meant that Selina and her sisters had witnessed not only a great deal of human suffering, but also a great deal of male anatomy.

But she had to admit she'd never seen one as fine as Lord Shaftsbury's. Unlike most of the men she'd helped bathe, feed, and nurse, his lordship's pale skin was flawless and unmarked by scars. He had obviously led a very active life and continued to do so in that private room of his just down the corridor.

He shifted from one foot to another, the action drawing her attention to his legs. And to what hung between them.

Goodness, but he was well-formed all around.

"Well?" he taunted. "Are you going to fetch my robe, or just stand and stare?"

Selina wrenched her gaze from his breeding organ and glanced around the cluttered room, her eyes settling on a crumpled pile of silk brocade. She snatched it up, shook it out, and approached him. "I'm behind you, my lord. If you raise you right arm waist-high, you will find the sleeve of your robe."

For a moment she thought he would resist her overture, but he surprised her by docilely allowing her to sheathe him in thick, wrinkled silk.

Her gaze lit upon the clock on the nightstand and she frowned. Why was it still there? He had no need of it.

She shook the pointless thought away and noticed it was only a little bit after ten o'clock.

Good Lord. It felt like she'd been in his chambers for hours.

"I shall ring for a bath," she murmured, hurrying across to the servant bellpull.

He turned, facing directly at her for once. "I thought you disconnected the pull?"

"I lied, my lord."

A look of genuine surprise rearranged his handsome features before it was replaced by a scowl. "You *do* like to live dangerously, don't you, Mrs. Lanyon?" He didn't wait for an answer, which was just as well. Instead, he turned away, fumbling and tripping his way through the cluttered room toward an open doorway that probably led to his bathing chamber, not that she could see in the gloom.

The moment he slammed the door behind him Selina slumped against the wall with a shaky sigh. What in the world had she been thinking to tackle a problem like the Marquess of Shaftsbury?

***

A surprisingly short time later Caius found himself sitting in a steaming tub of water.

Although the door to the bedchamber was closed, he could hear what sounded like an army of elves busily at work.

He felt a faint flicker of shame at the filthy mess the servants were currently coping with. And then he quickly quashed the feeling; if they wanted to blame somebody for today's nasty job, they should look no further than his newest employee.

A mean-spirited little smile tugged at Caius's mouth when he recalled the breathy gasp that had slipped out of her when he'd dropped his drawers. He didn't feel guilty—why should he? He'd not invited her into his chambers. Besides, she was a widow, so a naked male body wasn't anything she'd not seen before, was it?

Even so, Caius felt an irksome twinge of guilt; he really was behaving like an arse. Why was he resisting her overture of assistance so vigorously? If the woman wanted to thrust her way into his room and insist that he use her as his secretary, so be it. There were always bills and letters to be dealt with and poor Morris didn't deserve the extra work. Caius would tolerate the woman and use her services for a few days and *then* he'd sack her.

A loud knock on the door interrupted his thoughts. "My lord?" an annoying female voice said. "Are you finished yet?"

"No, damnit, I'm not. When I want you, I'll bloody well call for you," he snapped irritably, even though he'd been on the verge of getting out of the tub. But he'd be damned if he allowed her to push him around any more than she was already doing.

Caius snorted with disgust—mainly at himself and what he'd become—and closed his eyes and laid back against the gentle slope of the tub, his mind more active than it had been in days—months, even.

Yet another thing that was *her* fault.

He had worked damned hard to bury any and all thoughts these past months and she had wrecked all his hard labor in less than an hour. While his combination of drunken nights interspersed with brutal evenings spent in his gymnasium was not perfect, it *had* allowed him to escape his grim reality for hours at a stretch.

You might be able to outrun the day, but you've had no luck escaping your nightmares, have you?

No, he hadn't. It amazed him that he could drink himself into a stupor and still dream. How was that even possible? What, exactly, would it take to muffle everything, all the time?

I think you know the answer to that.

Caius's thoughts slid inexorably to at least one solution to all his problems—the one that called to him from the drawer of his nightstand. Blowing his brains out had become a dangerously attractive option the longer he went without a decent night's sleep.

And now here he was, stone sober and clear eyed—so to speak—with nothing to buffer him against the world.

Caius realized he was gritting his jaw—*again*—and forced himself to loosen the tight muscles. Instead, he thought about what he'd do once he was out of the damned tub. Answer letters? Deal with bills and tenant requests? Neither of which he could see.

The thought left him heavy with weariness. It also left him with sickening, gut-churning shame. He could not deny that he'd been heaping his responsibilities onto the frail shoulders of his oldest and most faithful servant. Poor Morris. The man wasn't a steward and didn't deserve the tasks that had been thrust upon him.

It wasn't like Caius to shirk his duties. Yes, he'd been reckless and foolish as a younger man, but he had never in his life behaved so reprehensibly when it came to management of his estates.

But then he'd never been struck blind before, either.

At first, when he'd come home after those four nightmare days in the coach, Caius had tried to adjust. After all, what was the alternative? There was nobody else to take over his duties.

Victor—his heir—hated him and had chosen to hide away from the world in his bloody monastery.

Even if Caius could stomach summoning his younger brother after what had occurred between the two of them all those years ago, he doubted Victor would come. And if he *did* come, Caius couldn't rule out the possibility that his brother would seize the opportunity to extract his pound of flesh now that Caius was vulnerable.

Bloody hell. His life was a disaster.

Despair, guilt, and shame washed over him when he recalled the housekeeper's chiding words about Morris. Expecting the old man to manage Caius's vast estate—not to mention the rest of his properties—hadn't just been irresponsible, it had been cruel. How could one person manage all those hundreds of tasks when it had always taken Caius, a steward, and a personal secretary in the past?

And of course he'd had Elton's help, too, because his valet had managed more of Caius's personal business than most valets. He'd been more than just a servant; he'd also been Caius's best friend; a fact had irritated the hell out of both his father *and* his mother. He smirked. Their united disapproval of his friendship with his servant had been the one and only time his parents had ever agreed on any subject.

Elton. Just thinking the name caused a gnawing ache in his chest. God but he missed the man. Maybe, if Elton had survived, Caius would give a damn and want to get through this nightmare that was now his life.

But Elton was dead, and Caius was a useless blind lump.

His bed, comfortable and safe, called to him with the lure of a mythical siren. With a stronger lure, because Caius wanted sleep far more than he had ever wanted to fuck any woman.

He couldn't recall anymore why he'd ever chased after females or wanted to bed them so badly. He'd lost all desire for sex. That was probably a damned good thing, because what woman would want a worthless, fumbling fool who could barely make it from his bed to his chamber pot without hurting himself?

Yes, bed.

Caius sighed with relief at the thought. The bills had waited this long, what was one more day? When he got out of this damned tub he'd crawl into his bed—which now had fresh sheets—and he'd—

You can't go back to bed, my lord, an unwanted voice harangued. *This farce has gone on long enough already. It is time to assume your duties.*

Caius winced; good God, the Lanyon woman had somehow got inside his head.

You know I'm right.

"*Aargh.*" Caius squeezed his temples, as if that would somehow shut her up.

A loud knock on the door made him jolt. "My lord? I heard a noise. Is everything—"

"*Hell and damnation woman!*" He lurched to his feet so fast he became lightheaded. He stood naked and dripping in the cool air, his fury keeping him plenty hot. "Well?" he shouted when silence was his only answer. "What are you waiting for, Mrs. Lanyon? Get in here and give me something to dry myself with."

The door opened and feet—not small, by the sound of them—hurried across the floor and a towel draped over his shoulders.

"Mrs. Lanyon?" Caius asked, already knowing the answer.

"Er, no, my lord," his footman James admitted in a voice that radiated anxiety.

"Where the hell is she?" Caius demanded, lowering the large flannel to his hips and wrapping it around his waist.

"Mrs. Lanyon had to nip downstairs for a moment."

Caius barked a laugh. "I'll just bet she did. Put your shoulder under my hand, James."

The man obeyed and Caius climbed out of the tub without falling on his face. "Where is my robe?"

"Right here, my lord," James said.

Caius waited for more information, but apparently James wasn't as prescient as the presumptuous Mrs. Lanyon.

"Hold up the right arm first," Caius ordered.

"Er, my right arm, my lord, or—"

"Mine." Caius struggled to keep his temper as his footman hurried to stand behind him. After all, it wasn't James's fault that he didn't know how to dress a blind man. He rarely used any of the footmen to valet him, choosing to rely on Morris on those rare occasions when he didn't simply ransack his dressing room for buckskins and a shirt.

Morris again. Christ, but he'd leaned on the poor man.

The old butler had known Caius ever since he'd been born. He'd administered more than a few swats to Caius's bottom when he'd been a lad. Caius's mother and father had trusted their upper servants implicitly when it came to disciplining their two sons—an unusual approach for aristocratic parents. Both Caius and Victor had been raised to respect their elders, regardless of the person's status.

But Caius had not been a little boy for a very long time and Morris had deliberately disobeyed him by allowing the Lanyon woman to harass him.

He couldn't help smirking at the thought of his aged butler facing off against the virago he'd hired. *That* should teach the old man to employ managing females. Morris was probably hiding in a cupboard somewhere after having unleashed Mrs. Lanyon on him, hoping to wait out Caius's temper tantrum before resurfacing.

"Er, shall I shave you, my lord?" James asked.

"Yes, yes, you might as well," he muttered.

As Caius and James moved through his toilet, he discovered that James was quite good at valeting. He was intuitive and efficient and didn't chatter. He also didn't emanate profound sadness, which is what Morris did whenever he was around Caius, as if it broke the old man's heart to see the pitiful state of his employer.

Caius recalled hearing, at some point in his life, that people who lost one sense often developed their other senses to compensate. He'd thought that meant hearing and touch, not the sort of emotional sensitivity that now seemed heightened whenever he was around other people.

Spivey, his ancient steward, hadn't just emanated sadness whenever he saw Caius, the man had openly wept. And he'd *kept on* weeping, day after day. He'd finally had to sack the man. It had been that, or throttle him.

James neither wept nor radiated grief. Instead, he came across as a man who was desperately eager to please and careful not to offend. Like a good servant, in other words.

The exact opposite of Mrs. Lanyon, in other words.

Caius's lips twitched. The woman was cloaked in an aura of ruthless determination, clearly willing to sacrifice the individual—in this case *him*—without a second thought if she believed doing so was for the greater good.

It was odd how young her voice sounded considering that she had the confidence of a far older woman. She was exactly the sort of domineering female Caius had always avoided. And now here he was, dancing to her tune after a mere few hours.

Outrageous!

He tried to construct a picture of what she looked like in his mind's eye. After a few attempts he gave up; all he could imagine was his old nurse—Mrs. Emory—a woman who'd given him more beatings than all the other servants combined. Not that Caius hadn't deserved every single one of them as he'd been a savage little brat.

Mrs. Emory had been a tall, raw-boned woman with eyes that had been all-seeing. At least it had seemed that way to six-year-old Caius.

It would be just his luck if Morris had hired Mrs. Emory's much younger sister.

Selina

By the time Caius was breeched, coated, and booted, he was exhausted. How had he done all this every single day of his life? How had he gone to Jackson's three afternoons a week and spent every night out at various entertainments, not coming home until dawn most days?

Just... *how?*

James cleared his throat, making Caius realize that he was standing still like a statue.

He sighed; it was time to face his tormentor.

"Lead me down to the library and then go and fetch Mrs. Lanyon."

Chapter 9

Selina wasn't sure what to expect when she entered the library—shouting? Scowling? A shower of books aimed at her head?

But Lord Shaftsbury merely sat at his desk, face forward, his hands motionless atop the surface.

He didn't make any sign that he'd heard her enter, so she cleared her throat.

His lips, so attractive and shapely, tightened and then curved into a sneer. "Ah, my persecutrix has arrived."

Selina couldn't help smiling at the word, even though she knew he wasn't jesting.

"I've brought today's mail with me." When he merely stared at her—or so it seemed—she added, "Shall I open the letters and read them to you?"

"They aren't going to read themselves, are they?"

She sighed. "What I meant to ask is whether there was something else you wanted to do first?"

He shrugged. "All this was your idea, Mrs. Lanyon. I will let you tell me what to do as you are so good at it."

Her face heated at his accusation, but she refused to feel bad for invading his privacy and badgering him. It wouldn't be right to leave him to wallow in his misery; too many people depended on him. And he had too much to live for, although she suspected he would hurl something at her if she said that.

"I will start with today's mail and work back in time. I shall sit across from you at the desk and take notes as you instruct me on what actions you wish to take."

When he didn't respond, she pulled a chair toward the front of his desk, unfolded the letter on the top of the pile, and began to read.

***

Caius didn't know when he stopped being annoyed at Mrs. Lanyon and began being interested in the information she relayed. His mind felt like a leviathan rising slowly from the depths.

The longer she read, the more fully he understood his sheer neglect.

And the longer she read, the more anger and shame he felt at himself.

Mrs. Lanyon, with her prim, brisk, and unemotional approach to the wreckage of his life only irked him more. He knew his reaction wasn't just irrational; it was downright ungrateful. But that didn't matter. He still couldn't bring himself to speak to her with anything but curt civility.

Selina

As they waded through bill after bill—and upwards of two dozen repair requests from various tenants—he struggled with the agonizing realization that he would no longer be able to direct any of these repairs himself.

He couldn't even ride out to his tenant farms. Hell, he couldn't find the damned stables or mount a bloody horse or see to guide it anywhere even if he could.

The enormity of everything that he *could not do* threatened to overwhelm him and suddenly his skin was prickly and hot and it was difficult to get enough air in his lungs. Was he asleep? Was this yet another nightmare he would wake up from in a cold sweat?

"My lord? *My lord?*"

"What?" he barked.

"I can't help noticing that you appear to be… distressed. Is something wrong?" Her quiet voice pierced his inner havoc like a bolt of lightning illuminating a black, seemingly impenetrable storm.

Caius's mind swarmed with emotions, none of which he wanted to admit to.

"I daresay it all seems overwhelming, but this is a first step, my lord. Once you have taken this step, we will take a second step. And so forth. Think only of one step at a time."

"We?" he wheezed, his fists so tightly clenched the bones ached. "*We?*"

"Yes, I am here to help. I know you think this is insurmountable, but—"

"But *what*? Just *what* do you think you know?" His arms and legs shook as if a fever rolled through his limbs. "How could you *possibly* know what I am thinking?" His shout echoed in the room, his body vibrating with rage.

The silence was louder than his yelling; it filled the room, bearing down on him like the atmospheric pressure before a storm. He could actually *hear* the movement of blood and the pounding of his heart.

Thud… whoosh.

Thud… whoosh.

Thud… whoosh.

A knock on the door made him jump, even though he knew the sound hadn't been loud.

"What is it now?" he demanded, his voice raw, but not as raw as his emotions.

"It is the tea tray, my lord."

Tea.

His body responded like a faithful hound to a familiar command. His mouth watered, he swallowed convulsively, and his stomach growled, reminding him that he'd not had breakfast.

You've not shown enough of yourself to her? You want her to watch you eat and drink, too?

Caius stiffened at the unpalatable mental images—him fumbling with delicate crockery and breaking it; food on his face; tea spilled on his clothing—and scowled.

"No tea," he barked.

The room was strangely silent even though he knew there had to be at least two other people just a few feet away—*her* and a servant with a tray.

"You can set the tray down right there, Mary. Thank you."

Caius was frozen with disbelief as the door closed again.

"My lord," Mrs. Lanyon began. "Perhaps—"

"Did you just contradict my order in front of one of my servants?"

A long pause and then, "Yes."

He laughed but it held no amusement. This woman would harry him to the ends of the earth unless he put an end to it, badgering and bossing him until he was nothing but a shrinking, squeaking rodent in a corner.

Caius pushed to his feet. "You dare to treat me with disrespect—to *dismiss* my orders—in my own home. Your behavior is insupportable, Mrs. Lanyon. Consider yourself discharged. Write out a letter of recommendation for yourself—say whatever you want—and pay yourself three months' worth of wages. Have Morris bring both the letter and draft to me and I will sign both, and you will leave. *Today*."

It was so quiet for a moment that he thought she'd gone.

It appalled him that his first reaction wasn't relief, but… disappointment. Was she really routed so easily?

Of course he should have known better.

"I have a proposition, my lord."

He shook his head. "That is not how this works, Mrs. Lanyon. I am the master and you are the—"

"Yes, yes, yes, I heard you before," she said, employing a dismissive tone that no servant had ever used on Caius in his life. In fact, he couldn't recall *anyone* speaking to him in such a tone. "If I don't scurry from the room you will summon the authorities to throw me out. I understand all that. However…"

"However?" he snapped when the annoying woman stopped.

Selina

"It would be embarrassing for you to do that. Would it not? For the entire village to hear that you had to summon a constable to rid yourself of one small woman?"

Caius hands clenched so hard that he felt something pop in his thumb, as if he'd pulled the finger out of joint.

He ignored the pain and glowered in her direction. "Are you threatening me, Mrs. Lanyon?"

"No, only making an offer."

"*What* offer? The offer to drive me to madness with your incessant nagging?"

The bitch *laughed*!

"My family tells me that I am adept at managing people. It is a kinder word than *nag*."

Caius was torn between fury at her careless dismissal of his threat and an odd, pinching ache in his chest. He'd not heard anyone laugh for *months*. The sound was... it was...

You're not only blind; you've also mentally defective if you are beginning to find her bullying appealing.

The internal voice—which he generally ignored—scored a direct hit with that comment.

"I don't give a damn what your family calls you, Mrs. Lanyon. I just want you to *leave*."

If Caius hadn't learned how to listen more closely, he might have missed the sharp inhalation that told him that his words had finally got through to her.

And yet *still* she was not beaten.

"I'll make you an offer, my lord," she said. Although she still sounded bustling and confident, Caius could hear hints of weariness and resignation. He should have felt triumph at putting her in her place. Instead, he felt something unpleasantly like guilt.

He immediately slapped away the unwanted emotion, bolstered his resolve, and said, "Unless your offer includes you leaving my house, I'm not interested."

"It does include that."

He blinked.

"But only if you give me a chance, first."

"A chance?"

"I've been thinking about your situation."

"My *situation*?" he repeated, sounding like a bloody parrot.

75

"Yes, your blindness."

Blindness.

The word wasn't any louder than any other she'd spoken and yet it sliced through him as sharply as any blade.

He was blind.

Blind.

Nobody had said that word aloud before—not the doctor, not Morris or Spivey. No one.

Yet again, she had robbed him of speech.

Mrs. Lanyon either didn't notice the effect on him, or—more likely—didn't care, and barreled on without any encouragement from Caius. "In the village where I grew up the cobbler's son was born blind. My siblings and I played with him when we were children. His mother and father always treated him the same as their other children. Oh, they didn't just throw him into things," she said, as if Caius had denied her claim. "But they had expectations of him."

He didn't like where she was going with this. Not at all.

He sneered. "Is there a point to this wholesome tale of country life, Mrs. Lanyon?"

Once again, she laughed. As it had before, the unexpectedly squawky sound—so at odds with her well-modulated speaking voice—curled around him like an elusive, enticing melody. Before he could ponder his idiotic reaction, the woman resumed her yammering.

"Nicholas Allen is his name, and he works with his father in his shop. Nick's shoes and boots are every bit as well-made as Mr. Allen's. He is married and has a baby. He makes his way to and from his father's shop every day under his own locomotion." Her tone shifted, becoming accusatory. "And Nick is a poor, uneducated village cobbler, my lord."

"Are you *scolding* me, Mrs. Lanyon?"

"I'm not scolding you, my lord. Well, maybe I am a little," she admitted, having the stones to chortle. "I'm just saying it is possible for you to have a life—a *good* life. It won't be the same as the life you had before, but surely anything is better than hiding away in your bed for the rest of your days?"

Never in his entire thirty-seven years had Caius wanted to strike a female. He shook with impotent rage, his empty hands clenching on nothing but air when he wanted to smash and tear and rend.

She nattered on heedless of the fury about to erupt in front of her. "I—I don't mean to be rude or insulting, my lord."

Selina

"Please don't flatter yourself that I could be insulted by anything *you* said, Mrs. Lanyon."

"You *are* angry. I'm terribly sor—"

"I don't want your bloody apology. You compare me to some country cobbler and find me wanting? And then you have the *audacity* to tell me I can still be happy and have a wife and children? As if you can understand *anything* about my situation or what this—this *travesty* of a life is like?"

"I didn't mean—"

"I want you *gone*, Mrs. Lanyon—by the end of the day. And if you don't leave under your own—"

"Please, my lord"—her voice broke on the last word.

For a long moment the only sound in the room was the echo of her plea and Caius's ragged breathing.

"Please, don't make me leave," she said, her voice low and almost… desperate. "I—I don't have anywhere else to go."

Yet again she'd robbed him of speech. This time it was her weary, dejected tone rather than her words that froze him. Who would have believed the bold, relentless Mrs. Lanyon—who'd been haranguing him *all morning long*—could even feel such emotions?

Some ugly, twisted part of him wanted to punish her—to attack the tender underbelly she'd just exposed—and make her as miserable and hopeless as he was. It would be easy to do. He might be a pitiful wreck, but he was still a powerful man—a lord—while she was a mere servant and a female one, at that. He could yank the rug from beneath her feet—take away this job and wreak havoc on her towering self-assurance. Caius could drag her down into despair with him.

At least for a little while.

But she was a competent and—except for this brief lapse—confident woman who would soon find another position, with or without his help or hindrance, and Caius knew she would flourish.

While he would still be a miserable, cowardly shell of a man hiding in a dark room, just as she'd accused.

"I like it here, my lord," she said, her quiet voice jolting him from his unpleasant thoughts. "I—I like this job." She sounded more than a little amazed by that. "I like the other servants and your home is lovely. I suppose I could simply do my job and not interfere"—he snorted rudely, but she soldiered on. "But it seems wrong to bear witness and do nothing. Can you not just give me a chance? Not forever, only for thirty days—and if you still want me to leave after that, then I will go without a struggle."

A wave of exhaustion washed over him. "Why don't you just take the money I'm offering and go now?" he asked, ashamed by the plea in his voice.

"Because I am good at my job, my lord. For the first time in my life I—"

"You what, Mrs. Lanyon?" he asked, momentarily diverted from his path by the fact that she almost sounded as lost as Caius felt.

"For the first time in my life I feel like I could really be... of value."

For some reason, Caius didn't think that was what she'd been going to say.

"Please," she said. "Why don't you let me help you?"

Any sympathy he'd been feeling toward her evaporated at the pity in her voice. "I don't need your bloody pity or your damned help!"

"You need somebody's help!" she shouted back.

Caius's blood thudded in his ears, the violence of his emotions—and the constant bouncing from one extreme to another—left him dizzy. He dropped his hands to the desk, struggling to steady himself.

"Just what are you afraid of, my lord? Can anything be worse than lying in bed all day? Or—or drinking yourself into a stupor and wandering the hallways of your home like a ghost? Or spending your nights alone in that room of yours doing who knows what, until you are so exhausted you can barely stagger back to your chambers?"

"You've been spying on me?" he demanded in disbelief.

"It's hardly spying when I'm doing my job. Besides, I haven't seen *you*, but I've seen the wreckage you leave in your wake. Meanwhile," her voice rose, "your home and people languish while they wait for you to do *your* job." Her voice rang out in the cavernous room. "What can it possibly hurt to give me thirty days? At the end of that time, if you are not happy with the way things are, then you can go back to doing whatever it is you've *been* doing, which is—well, quite frankly, I'm not exactly sure what that is. So, I ask you: why not accept my offer? Could things possibly be any worse?"

"You—you interfering, impudent *saucebox*. You have the gall—the sheer effrontery—to ask me how matters could possibly be worse in a month?" Caius's head pounded and his nerves felt like they were on fire beneath his skin. "I'll tell you *how*. Because right now I only suspect that there is nothing to live for. What happens when I make a bloody effort only to discover that what I suspect is actually the truth?" Caius squeezed his eyes shut. Never had he wanted to take words back as desperately as he did at that moment. But it was too late, and the room echoed with his pathetic admission. He wanted to crawl into the deepest, darkest crack in the earth and never show his scalding face again.

Of course he'd have to ask for help to *find* the fucking crack, first.

Selina

He dropped back into his chair and massaged his aching temples.

Caius had almost forgotten he wasn't alone when she said, "But what if the opposite is true? What if you discover there *is* something to live for, my lord?"

***

The raw misery on Lord Shaftsbury's face was too painful and Selina had to look away.

Unfortunately, the moment she didn't have *him* and *his* problems to think about, her own unenviable life came rushing at her like an especially vicious riptide.

Her chance to do something—to be something other than the ornamental sister who couldn't even do *that* right—would be over. She would have to tuck her tail between her legs and—

"Why should I trust that you'll do anything helpful? How do I know you have anything more to offer than a competent secretary or steward? In other words, *why you*, Mrs. Lanyon."

Selina quashed the hope that leapt in her chest at his question. She swallowed, cleared her throat, and summoned a controlled, cool tone of voice—the sort that didn't set men's teeth on edge. She knew at least that much—how to please and placate a man, didn't she?

Or you could just try and be the woman you want to be, instead of the woman everyone else expects. If not now, then when?

Selina paused at the silent question. What if she didn't know who that woman was?

She looked up into the marquess's eyes. His pupils constantly flickered back and forth and she knew he must feel at a disadvantage not knowing exactly where to look.

The grief that surrounded him—oozed out of him—created an almost palpable haze. He was so... profoundly damaged, and not just the loss of his sight. Whatever had happened over the course of those terrible four days, he had not even begun to move past it. Perhaps he never would. Could she truly help such a man?

"Well?" he prodded when she remained silent.

"That is a good question, my lord."

"And do you have a good answer?"

She hesitated, and then forced herself to say, "I don't see anyone else offering."

His nostrils flared and for a moment she thought he'd start shouting again. Instead, he snorted. "You are, if nothing else, direct, ma'am."

"I'm sorry, that was—"

"Fortunately for me," he said, raising his voice to speak over her, "I don't need to rely on your charitable impulses." He gave her a frosty smile. "I can always hire a steward or secretary to *help* with correspondence and estate matters. Why should I keep an insolent, presumptuous, and argumentative housekeeper to do those tasks?"

"Because I've also got... ideas."

One of his jet-black eyebrows cocked. "Ideas, hmm? I suppose you mean more impertinent suggestions spawned by your cobbler friend?"

"Yes. And some of my own." He opened his mouth, but Selina did not let him speak. "Besides, aren't you—" she caught herself. She really needed to remember that the marquess wasn't one of her siblings whom she could argue with or manipulate. He was her employer. He was a *man*, and the little she knew about men was that they liked to be in charge. Or at least they liked to believe they were in charge and give that impression.

"Aren't I *what*?" he demanded. "Go on, Mrs. Lanyon, don't become craven now, after you've pulled me out of my chambers like a terrier yanking a badger from its burrow."

She laughed and his expressive eyebrows drew down over the bridge of his nose until they formed a rather intimidating V.

"I'm sorry for laughing, my lord, but that was a very diverting image."

"You are stalling, Mrs. Lanyon. What impertinence was about to slip out of your mouth before you stopped it?"

She sighed. "I was going to say: Aren't you bored?"

He blinked at that.

"If nothing else," Selina rushed on, emboldened by his momentarily muteness, "wouldn't thirty days of accepting my assistance and considering my ideas be a diversion from boredom?"

His jaw flexed, as if he were chewing on her words. Rather than look pleased by what he was mulling over, his expression just grew darker.

Selina closed her eyes and sighed, quite suddenly enervated. It was impossible to convince a man like Shaftsbury if he didn't want convincing.

Well, at least she did not have much to pack. She would go home to Queen's Bower and face her mother's wrath. How bad could it be? Thanks to Hy, she no longer needed to worry about being tossed onto the street and—

"Thirty days."

Her eyes flew open at the quiet words and she looked into his beautiful gray gaze. She knew he was blind, but his pupils seemed so fixed on her that her skin prickled.

"You—you mean you'll try things my way?" Selina cringed at the disbelief in her voice.

"I will *consider* your suggestions," he corrected. "If I do not approve of something you suggest, you will not plague me on the subject. Nor will you contradict my orders. Ever. Understood?"

Selina began to smile. "Yes, I understand."

"And no meddling in my affairs without my permission."

Selina thought about the letter she'd just sent to his brother and caught her lower lip. His lordship meant from *this day* forward, didn't he? Surely he couldn't expect her to promise about things that she'd *already* done?

"I will have your word on that, Mrs. Lanyon," Lord Shaftsbury said.

"Yes, my lord, I promise I shan't meddle without your permission."

He snorted. "Why don't I believe you?"

Because he was smart.

He went on, "After thirty days have passed you will leave. *Without* me needing to summon the constable to drag you out."

The words were like a slap and her face burned. For a moment, she was tempted to make *him* hurt, to tell him that she would leave that very moment and he could stew in his own misery for the rest of his days.

But there was a brittleness about his prideful stance—a tension in his face and eyes that told her how much it cost him to stand firm. And *that* stopped her from lashing out and doing something rash and childish.

Besides, Selina had won; she'd got what she wanted from him. She could afford to be magnanimous.

And then there was the fact that she'd probably be running for the door and eager to go home after a month at Lord Crabby's beck and call.

"Well?" he barked, making her jump and reinforcing that last thought.

"Agreed, my lord. Thirty days, and then I'll leave without a fuss."

Chapter 10

The air was thick with tension when Selina left the library, as if everyone in the house was holding their breath.

She glanced at her hands as she strode down the corridor; they were shaking. They'd *been* shaking.

What am I doing? I can't mend this man—he is too broken, too angry, too... hopeless.

What else do you have to do? You are now such an object of derision that you can't show your face in London and do the one thing you've been groomed to do. You are of no use to anyone else, anywhere.

She snorted at the cruel, but accurate, accusation.

If she fled Courtland, she would go home and be a source of disappointment to her mother. Or she could go and live off the bounty of her sister.

Neither option had much appeal.

He was hostile today, but he will be less resistant once we've begun to work together and make his life easier and more pleasant. Won't he? she all but begged.

But the voice in her head had no clever response to that.

A cracked plinth with a nose-less bust perched on it—yet another casualty of Lord Shaftsbury's late night wanderings—caught Selina's attention as she strode down the corridor. The sight of such wanton, pointless destruction firmed her resolve: There was *one* bit of foolishness she could take care of today.

Selina found Morris where she expected to find him—hiding in the pantry.

He gave her a fearful look when she opened the door. "Did he—"

"He did not sack me."

"Oh, thank God," he murmured.

At least one person wanted her here.

She did not see the point of telling the old man that her time at Courtland was limited. Instead, she said, "As soon as his lordship returns to his chambers today, I want the servants to remove all the obstructions from the corridors. Not in places like the long gallery, of course, but in the hallways in the family wing."

"Er—what?"

"Come now, Mr. Morris. We've all noticed the broken vases, tipped columns, and other destruction. We need to move everything that is breakable."

"Move it where?"

"The house has one hundred and thirty-six rooms, sir; pick one." He just stared, so she went on. "Oh, and I'll want all the carpets taken up, as well."

He looked at her aghast. "You want to remove *all* the carpets?"

"Yes. All of them. They can be taken outside, thoroughly beaten, and checked for signs of damage before they are put away."

"But… why?"

"They muffle sound, Mr. Morris, which is something his lordship is in dire need of to navigate. Also, I've seen him trip over them."

The old man looked stricken. "Oh. I'd not even though about that."

Selina patted his shoulder. "I didn't either until I did a few… experiments."

"Experiments?"

"Yes. Last night I didn't light a candle and navigated the house only by touch; it took ages. Naturally I went through a second time with my eyes open," she assured him with a smile. "But I wanted to see what it was like *not* to be able to see. I wanted to know what made a person's progress more difficult. I must admit that it helped me understand—a very little—what it is like to be without sight. It's not the same—there is always still moon and starlight and such—so I was still at an advantage, but I learned what some of the worst impediments were, and those were clutter and carpet."

"That was very clever of you."

She flushed at his praise. "I should have thought of it sooner—" Selina broke off as she saw a pained look spasm across the old man's face. "Oh! I didn't mean that you—"

"I know you were not trying to make me feel deficient, Mrs. Lanyon. I am castigating myself for letting his lordship just sit in his rooms and rot. I—I… well, I'm afraid I've taken the marquess's accident and condition rather hard."

"You've known him all his life while I just met him. It is easier to see a problem when one is at a remove or viewing it with fresh eyes."

His own eyes became dangerously watery. "Yes," he murmured. "Yes, I suppose so."

Selina hurried on. "I realized quickly—especially in my own chambers—that it is critical to put everything back in *exactly* the same place if I was to move about without crashing into things. Not even a few inches off. So, from now on, we need to make sure all the maids put items back in the exact same place. We can use chalk to mark the floors and it will not damage them. "

"That—that is a very good idea." Mr. Morris sounded bemused, but he nodded.

"Perhaps you might go and direct the footmen to begin with the removal of the carpets and such? I am going to gather the maids."

Rather than look annoyed at being ordered about by a mere housekeeper, Morris appeared relieved to have some direction.

"Oh, I almost forgot," Morris said as he opened the door, "I had one of the maids take a package up to your quarters."

"A package?"

"Yes, it looks to be from Mrs. Mary Fletcher—your sister, isn't it?"

"Indeed, it is." Hy must have sent her clothing. Perhaps there was a letter inside the package, too? Selina was torn; she really did need to gather the maids, but she was dying of curiosity—

"Why don't you take a few minutes to go and see what it is," Mr. Morris said, reading her eager expression correctly. "I'll get everyone moving in the proper direction. By the time you've had a look we'll be ready for you."

"Thank you, Mr. Morris."

It was a struggle to recall her dignity and not sprint up to her chambers, where she found a very large brown paper wrapped parcel on her bed.

She tore open the heavy paper and grinned when she saw the letter tucked in between two very plain—and brand new—gowns.

Selina hastily unfolded the letter and dropped into a chair to read.

Dear Linny,

Imagine my surprise upon reading your letter. Where to start?

I suppose I should first confirm that yes, I am married to Chatham. Although I never thought to have a husband, I find that marriage to him suits me exceedingly well.

Selina had to laugh out loud at her sister's temperate description of marital bliss.

Your letter caught up to us in London, which is where we returned after meeting up with Fowler and Shelton and then following your trail until it disappeared into thin air.

Selina couldn't resist a smile at that. So, her method had worked. She wasn't as witless and clueless as everyone believed.

The two men thrashed each other—there was no clear winner—and only after they were both bleeding and broken did they notice that you'd absconded. Apparently with their money and—according to Shelton—with his prized pistol?

I must admit I vexed Chatham by laughing at that part. Still, who would not be amused that two idiots both bent on saving an innocent, witless female are the ones who ended up penniless and in need of rescuing? Because that is exactly what happened, Linny. They needed to wait there to be rescued by Chatham and me.

Selina grinned at her serious sister's twisted sense of humor.

Yes, we were out looking for you, too, Linny. If you'd waited but an hour we could have taken you back to London with us. Evidently Fowler neglected to tell you that part...

Selina scowled; he certainly had. Not that she would change what had happened—not yet, at least.

But I digress.

Regarding your request for confidentiality. Of course, I won't tell anyone where you are, Linny.

Well, except Chatham. We do not keep secrets from each other—at least not anymore—so he had to be told. Don't worry, I extracted a promise from him <u>before</u> telling him where you were. The promise was that he would not interfere or try to bring you home.

While he isn't sanguine about leaving you in the role of a domestic, he did mention that he was close friends with Lord Shaftsbury when they were in school. He said he'd not seen his lordship since the accident, but insists the man is honorable and hardly the sort to molest his servants, even one who looks like you.

I chortled at that part, Linny. Because I cannot imagine how you pass for a housekeeper. Not that housekeepers are required to be ugly, but you must admit you've never seen a housekeeper who looked like <u>you</u> before.

Selina smiled absently at her sister's compliment, her thoughts on something else entirely. The Duke of Chatham, who counted himself a friend of Shaftsbury, didn't know the man was blind. How had the marquess managed to keep his condition such a secret—even in the village nobody seemed to know. Shaking her head, she turned back to the letter.

Despite being so pretty that you will probably have all the male servants in love with you, I suspect that you will be excellent at your job. I know we all teased you horribly—calling you the Gentle General—and remarking on your "managerial impulses" when we were younger, but that sort of skill will make you an invaluable housekeeper.

I have taken the liberty of contacting both our aunt and our parents and telling them you have reached out to me and are fine. Naturally they both tried to get your whereabouts from me. Aunt by begging piteously and Mama by attempting to browbeat and hector me.

I must confess that outranking her is probably more pleasurable than it ought to be.

Selina laughed at the thought of her quiet, unassuming sibling pulling rank on their domineering mother.

Fortunately—or unfortunately, depending on how you view it—I didn't have to say much to her because Chatham stepped in and informed her that nobody would speak that way to his wife, not even a parent.

Oh, Linny. I wish you could have seen how neatly and quickly he put Mama in her place. For the first time in my life, I didn't have to worry that she could lock me away or punish me somehow.

Selina felt a sharp stab of anger toward her mother at Hy's admission. For years their mother had threatened Hy with one punishment or another if she did not obey her wishes. It saddened Selina that she didn't love either of her parents, but they had done very little to deserve either affection or loyalty from any of their children.

Ah, but once again I've wandered far off the topic.

Aunt Ellen returned all your things to Queen's Bower so I just purchased new clothing for you—things that would be suitable for a housekeeper—rather than send for yours. Before your jaw drops with amazement, I must confess that I didn't choose them myself; I brought my maid with me to shop and she did the selecting. Yes, I have a maid, if you can believe it.

Hy was many things, but a woman with sartorial taste was not among them.

Chatham said that any of my siblings who wanted to live with us were more than welcome. He mentioned specifically that I should extend that offer to you. When you are done adventuring and ready to come home, please know that we would love to be your home.

"Aww, Hy," Selina murmured, her eyes burning.

So, now that I've finished your business, I suppose I can tell you about what happened since you've been gone.

If you are wondering about our siblings—which I certainly was thanks to Mama's meddling with our letters while we were in London—here are the latest details.

Phoebe married Paul "Iron Mad" Needham.

Selina gave a startled yelp. "*What?*"

I'm sure you recall Needham.

Indeed, she did. The wealthy industrialist had called on her Aunt Ellen twice during the first few weeks that Selina had been in London. Her aunt had indicated that the Earl of Addiscombe had been behind those visits. They'd had a few uncomfortable drives in Hyde Park and then she had never seen him again.

Evidently because he'd been courting Phoebe!

Well, the man showed excellent sense.

So, our sister is now a Viscountess. I've not had a chance to see her yet, but Chatham and I both wrote to extend invitations, so I hope they might visit soon.

I know you won't be surprised to learn that Mama kept Phoebe's marriage a secret from everyone—especially ton gossips—for fear that such a connection to a man of business would harm your marital prospects.

Selina

I was especially ashamed to learn of her behavior because Needham has been exceedingly generous toward not only Phoebe, but the entire family. Doddy will be starting at Eton this autumn and is currently cramming with a tutor to prepare.

"Good for you, Doddy," Selina said, relieved that her dear little brother was getting away from their controlling mother and careless father.

Mama has an establishment in Bath and Papa has, not surprisingly, taken up residence in Brighton so he can be close to his old cronies for the summer. And Needham financed all that, in addition to paying off all Papa's debts.

Selina squirmed at the thought of how much money Phoebe's new husband must have laid out. Needham had rescued them all and their mother had treated him as if he were a filthy secret.

She shook her head in disgust. Just when she thought the Countess of Addiscombe could not behave any worse, her mother surprised her.

And part of Selina was just as selfish because her thoughts immediately went to their home—Queen's Bower. Now that her mother and father lived elsewhere the family home was uninhabited. At the end of her thirty days at Courtland she could move home without having to worry about living with her mother.

Not that the countess wouldn't fuss about a young unmarried woman living alone, but Selina knew the last thing her mother wanted was to have her in Bath, disturbing whatever happy, self-indulgent life she'd obviously made for herself.

She turned back to the letter.

Mama sent Katie off to live with Aunt Agatha after Phoebe's wedding.

"Oh, no," Selina cried. Their Aunt Agatha was almost worse than her sister, the countess.

I've already received a frantic letter from our aunt—and three from Katie—begging us to take Katie off her hands as soon as possible. She says our youngest sister is 'man-mad' and cannot be controlled.

Selina chortled at the thought of a *man-mad* Katie. No doubt that would be a force to be reckoned with.

It was Chatham who suggested she come to us. While seventeen is a bit young for a Season, Katie will turn eighteen next May, so it is not too terribly soon. Chatham pointed out that his Aunt Lenora—who will be helping me through my first Season as duchess—could easily manage Katie's come out, as well.

And so I'll have our man-mad little sister here with us in less than a week. I am delighted to have her, and I know Chatham will enjoy her company.

As for my mother-in-law... well, the Dowager Duchess of Chatham (that is what she has asked me to call her) is a topic for another letter. Already I have rambled too long.

Be careful and be happy, my gentle, loving sister. I am so delighted that you are out in the world having an adventure. If Shaftsbury doesn't treat you well, you must come live with us immediately.

Love,

Hy

Selina's heart overflowed at her reserved sister's affectionate words.

And if her eyes might have overflowed a little, too—well, there was nobody there to notice. She folded up the precious missive and tucked it in the pocket of her petticoat.

The letter had lifted her spirits and given her a fresh infusion of optimism.

She would keep it on her person for the next few days. That way she could take it out and re-read it if she required motivation.

Somehow, she suspected she would be reading it often.

Chapter 11

The next morning Selina scarcely opened the library door before the marquess started speaking. "What has happened to all my carpets, Mrs. Lanyon?"

"How did you know it was me?" she asked.

His scowl deepened and he opened his mouth—no doubt to threaten to sack her—but Selina didn't give him a chance.

"I removed the carpets because I thought it would help you identify people by their tread. Also, they were so overlapped in several of the rooms that I tripped more than once, so I thought it might be prudent." The part about tripping was a fib, but what could it hurt?

His nostrils flared, as if he were sniffing the air and trying to smell something else to complain about.

"I also removed a good many of the, er, *objets d'art* from the corridors and a few pieces of furniture from this room and some others."

"Yes, I noticed," he said in a quiet, menacing tone that left her chilled. "Who gave you the authority to do such things?"

"You did—when you said I had thirty-days to do as I wanted."

"I *never* said those words," he shot back.

"If you don't like it then you can have the servants put everything back in thirty days."

"Twenty-nine-and-a-half, now."

Selina laughed. "Was that a joke, my lord?"

He grunted.

"I was thinking back to Nick—the cobbler I told you about?"

He sighed. "I'm blind, not mentally incompetent, Mrs. Lanyon. You only mentioned the man yesterday. Of course, I recall *Nick* the peerless cobbler, a shining beacon of masculine perfection to blind men the world over."

"No need to be nasty, my lord."

He bared his teeth and Selina hastily continued. "One of the things I noticed about Nick's parents' home was how it was uncluttered. And his shop is likewise spartan. All his tools have their particular place. And as he shares a bench with several others, he and his father have clearly marked the spots for everything. If somebody uses something, they put it back *exactly* where it should be."

He made a dismissive gesture to the desk he sat behind. "I hardly need to know where my quill and pen knife are, do I? I won't be jotting anything down or writing any letters."

Selina took a deep breath and told herself to be patient—she had another twenty-nine-and-a-half days. "No, that is true. But there are other items you might wish to access with ease and consistency. And there is also the room itself."

"I don't exactly have any use for a library anymore, do I?"

Selina sighed and couldn't help noticing the tiny smile that twitched his lips at the sound. Oh. So, his lordship liked to get a reaction out of her, did he? The wretch.

She was sorely tempted to get a reaction out of *him* by smacking down the item in her hand, but she knew that was childish. And right now, having one child in the room was plenty.

Instead, she said, "I've brought you something."

"What is it?" He sounded wary and wore an expression to match.

"It is not a live asp, if that is what you are worried about."

He snorted. "I am not *worried*."

Liar. She strode to his side. "Hold out your right hand."

His hand tightened into a fist where it lay on top of the desk. "Why do I think that is not a wise move, Mrs. Lanyon?"

"Don't worry. It's nothing awful or disgusting."

He gave her a pained look and held out his hand.

Selina watched while his long, sensitive-looking fingers explored the head of the cane.

"This is my silver-handled walking stick," he said his brow furrowed.

"Nick uses a cane and is able to make his way around our village without any assistance."

"Ah, the inestimable *Nick*. Again."

She ignored his sneer. "I think it would be better than barking your shins and running into walls," she said, allowing a bit of a taunt into her voice.

His lips tightened, but—for once—he didn't lose his temper or threaten to sack her.

So... progress.

"I've had the servants clear the clutter out of the rooms you might wish to use. If you consent, I will have them do your chambers, as well."

"You mean I have a choice?" he retorted, but it lacked the heat of his usual grousing. Instead, he was idly spinning the walking stick, the absent-minded gesture practiced and graceful.

Selina walked to the bellpull and gave it a tug. "While we wait for a servant, allow me to walk the room with you."

He frowned. "Walk it?"

"Yes, so that you can get a sense of it and pace off the distances."

His frown deepened.

"Unless you'd prefer me to summon James or Mr. Morris to walk it with you?"

He scowled and flapped a dismissive hand. "No, no, you will do."

Ah, such graciousness.

***

"Not out to the side, "Mrs. Lanyon said—for the fourth or fifth time. "Hold it out in front of your body and tap it, my lord, don't slide it."

"You think I need your directions on how to use a walking stick?" Caius snarled. He seemed to do that a great deal—snarl—when he was around Mrs. Lanyon.

"Your fingers are digging into my arm," she replied in the mild voice that, quite unreasonably, irked him.

He gritted his teeth and loosened his grip. Also, he lightly tapped the stick in front of him, rather than off to the side, as she led him around the room for the dozenth time.

"Are you counting?" she nagged.

"*Yes*, I'm counting." That was a lie; he'd forgotten to count, but he did so now.

She stopped after their next round. "I'm going to stand by your desk. You walk the loop without me."

"You like to give orders, don't you?"

She gave a sudden, startled laugh, the sound girlish. "Yes. My younger siblings used to tease my about my *managerial* impulses and call me the *Gentle General* when we were younger."

"Only when you were younger?"

"They don't listen as much to me now," she admitted, unruffled.

"The General. Yes, that fits."

"I said the *Gentle General.*"

"Think of it as a promotion, General Lanyon." He shuffled his feet, not really wanting to make the loop by himself, mainly because he'd not paid attention and had forgotten how many steps there were until he needed to turn. But how could he tell the blasted nagging woman that she smelled too damned attractive and kept distracting him? And who would have believed that Caius Graham, a man whose nickname had been *The Libertine* even when he'd been a green lad, would now be flustered by the mere scent of a woman? And a servant at that.

And then there was the *feel* of her. For all that she possessed a huge, tyrannical personality, her arm was delicate, her height clearly well below his. Until he'd touched the fragile bones Caius had all but forgotten she was a female.

Touching her had reminded him that he'd not had a woman in over a year because he'd been at Courtland for two months before the accident. And when he'd been at home—in the same house as his wife—he'd not gone to a woman's bed. Not her bed, nor anyone else's.

He hadn't missed it. Indeed, today was the first time he'd even thought about women or sex or physical pleasure.

Not that he was thinking of having sex with General Lanyon. God forbid. He might be a desperate, pitiful—

"My lord? Are you going to—"

"I'm going, I'm going," he muttered, and then proceeded to walk right into the corner of the desk. "Dammit!" The walking stick clattered to the floor as Caius cupped his jewels. There would be bruises later—he'd feel them, even if he couldn't see them—and it was nobody's fault but his own.

A strangled coughing sound invaded his haze of pain.

"Are you... *laughing* at me, Mrs. Lanyon?"

"No," she said, her voice clearly choked with mirth.

"I'm glad you find it acceptable to laugh at a blind man."

"I'm sorry," she said, sounding anything but. "Here; I've fetched your walking stick."

He rudely snatched the cane from her and used the desk to orient himself before setting off.

"Remember to hold the stick out to the front rather than—"

"*Ooff!*" Caius gritted his teeth to hold back the gasp of pain as he yet again rammed into something hard—the back of a chair—with his groin. *Zeus*! He'd not taken so many hits to his balls in a year of rugby.

"If you hold the cane out to the front you will find the obstacle with *it* rather than your body."

"I know that," he snapped.

"Turn in a quarter circle and then take six steps before you turn right," she said, sounding unperturbed by his bad behavior.

That only made him angrier.

Caius contemplated throwing his stick to the floor and engaging in a full-blown tantrum, but he suspected Mrs. Lanyon would refuse to fetch it for him a second time and he'd need to grope his way around the room on his hands and knees to find it. So he obeyed her directions.

"Good," she said, her voice nearby and to his right when he came to a halt a moment later. "You are two steps away from where you started. Why don't you close the distance and try the same loop again. Count out loud if it helps."

"Not bloody likely," he said beneath his breath, but did another turn. This time he made the loop without banging his crotch into anything painful.

"Excellent, my lord."

He felt his lips curve into a smile and hastily caught it.

"The door is ten or eleven paces straight ahead. I will meet you there."

Caius began walking without questioning her, and then wanted to slap himself. Since when did he blindly follow a woman's orders? Or *anyone's* orders, for that matter?

Blindly. Ha.

When he'd counted off ten paces, he extended the stick a little further and it tapped the door. She was right; holding the cane out in front certainly made walking easier. And less painful. He'd used a cane for years, but as a fashion statement rather than walking aid. He'd not expected to *need* a walking stick until he was old and gray.

"The door handle is to your left about six inches."

Caius smirked at her subtle hint. "Ah, thank you for reminding me that I'm supposed to be a gentleman."

"It is past time," she muttered.

"I heard that," he said, earning one of her squawks of amusement and feeling a stab of pride at having made her laugh again.

Argh. He was pitiful.

After he'd closed the door, he turned to her and held out his arm. "Where to now, ma'am?" he asked once she'd set her hand lightly on his sleeve.

"I thought we might visit the orangery."

"The orangery?"

"Yes, it is a large room that is filled with—"

"I *know* what an orangery is." He turned to her, making sure to tilt his face down to account for the height difference. "You are exceedingly droll, Mrs. Lanyon. Dangerously so, one might say."

"For a servant."

Caius snorted. He was about to tell her she was unlike any servant he'd ever met when he recalled Elton. His valet had been more polished about making mock of Caius, but he'd not held back.

And you killed him.

"Is anything wrong, my lord?"

Caius realized he'd stopped. "No," he barked. "Why are we going to the orangery, Mrs. Lanyon? Are you going to have me on my knees in the dirt gardening? Harvesting vegetables?"

"No, it is a lovely place to sit and relax."

"Have you been lounging, Mrs. Lanyon? You really do have too much time on your hands."

"I was *not* lounging in the orangery; it was merely speculation on my part," she shot back. "I do, however, walk through it every evening on my rounds. It is an exceedingly lovely place. The population of finches is especially charming and right now there are a profusion of flowers in bloom.

"I know all that, Mrs. Lanyon. After all, it is *my* orangery."

"When was the last time you were in it, my lord?"

He scowled. "Oddly enough I've had other matters on my mind these last twelve-months."

She sniffed—it was soft, but he heard it.

"What?" he demanded. "You might as well just speak up if you are going to make that annoying *sniffing* sound."

"I did *not* sniff."

"You did. And like any woman worth her salt, you are skilled at packing a wealth of meaning into a mere sniff. My own mother, may the Lord rest her soul, was a champion sniffer."

Once again, she laughed.

That was what Caius had wanted from her, although God knew that his mother was hardly a subject for levity.

"Are you counting your steps, my lord?"

"Yes, of course I am," he lied.

"How many thus far?"

"Oh, is there to be a quiz, Mrs. Lanyon? Pardon me, I wasn't aware or I would have brought my slate and chalk with me."

She laughed and Caius's hand tightened around the head of the walking stick.

"Twenty-seven, twenty-eight, and twenty-nine," she said, coming to a halt. "Make a quarter turn to your right you will find the stairs." She hesitated. "If you—"

"I hope you are not going to ask me if I am capable of walking down stairs."

"No, of course I wasn't."

He clucked his tongue as he released her arm and grasped the thick wooden stair railing. "Lying to your employer, Mrs. Lanyon? What can I expect next? Pilfering the sugar? Selling the silver?"

She chuckled and Caius forced his feet to begin the descent. He wouldn't have admitted it for a thousand pounds, but he'd not been to the ground floor of his own house in almost a year

Stairs were a much different proposition when one could not see them and he was bloody exhausted by the time he reached the landing, where he turned without instruction, the memory obviously sunk deep into his muscles.

Mrs. Lanyon gave a hum of approval and he experienced such a warm rush of achievement that he immediately felt like a fool. Maybe he *had* suffered some damage to his brain in that accident.

Once he reached the ground floor she said, "Did you—"

"Nineteen," he said, and then turned to the right again, but waited for her to take his arm.

"I was surprised by the great number of finches that live in the orangery," she said as they walked at a sedate, but not too elderly, pace.

"There have been finches for hundreds of years," he said. "If you look closely at my family's escutcheon you will see a finch incorporated. The story is that one of my distant ancestors was saved by a finch's song. There is a book of family history in the library if you are interested."

"How was he saved by a finch?"

"The Graham in question was fighting in some battle—don't ask me which war, for there has been an endless parade of them, with Grahams taking part in most of them with bloodthirsty zeal—and a finch sang out just as a man was about to leap out at him. The birdsong alerted my ancestor, and that minor advantage saved his life."

"That is an interesting story."

"I doubt it's true."

"Why not?" She sounded affronted by his skepticism.

Caius shrugged and felt her hand shift on his sleeve. "Maybe there was a finch—I'm *sure* there was a battle—but it seems unlikely that a man would notice birdsong in the middle of a skirmish with all that clanging and banging and shouting."

"Were you in the war, my lord?"

"No, but I have heard stories of what it is like in the heat of battle." Not stories that were fit for a woman's ears, not even a servant's.

Like all young bloods Caius had wanted to join the army, but his father—who'd rarely denied Caius anything—had put his foot down. His motivation hadn't been so much affection for Caius as a concern that Victor might inherit. His father had never liked his youngest son, believing him to be a weakling because of Victor's religious devotion.

Yet another story not fit for a servant.

They walked in silence for a while.

When Mrs. Lanyon stopped, she said, "We are at a turning point—do you recall which way we—"

Caius huffed. "Of course I recall. It's my own damned house, isn't it?" He turned left without waiting for an answer.

They walked down the corridor side-by-side without touching this time.

"I apologize for that," he said abruptly. "What?" he demanded, when she inhaled sharply. "You don't think a marquess knows how to apologize to a servant? Ha!" he went on before she could speak, "My parents didn't agree on very much, but one of the things they *did* find common ground on was that their children respect their elders, regardless of the person's social class." He snorted. "Mr. Morris tanned my hide more than a few times when I was a lad."

She laughed. "It is hard to imagine him doing such a thing so violent."

"Oh, trust me, I was a little right little bas—er, savage—and I brought it out in people."

"That isn't difficult to believe."

"I suppose I walked right into that one, didn't I?"

"Rather."

Caius suddenly realized the tapping not only sounded different, it felt different. "There used to be a runner here," he said, his cane making a staccato *tap tap tap* as they went.

"They needed cleaning, but we can return them if you don't find the hard floors helpful. Naturally all the other items can be returned to their places, as well."

Caius just grunted. He'd be damned before he admitted that the idea had been a good one. He'd racked his bollocks more times than he wanted to count running into the furniture and bric-a-brac that filled his bloody house. Several months ago, he'd tripped and fallen over one of the many shadowbox tables that one of his ancestors had been so fond of, smashing the table to bits and jamming a finger so badly that it had swollen to twice its size. He'd been more careful after that, but he'd still barked his shins and bruised his hips countless times.

Not only did the carpets mute the sound of footsteps, but they muffled the sounds that helped him orient himself in a room or hallway. It was a damned good idea, and he knew he should thank her.

You would if you weren't such an arrogant sod. Sir.

Caius smirked. The voice sounded like Elton, but his proper valet would never have called him a *sod*. At least not out loud.

"We are here," she said. "Did you count your steps, my lord?"

Caius growled.

"I'll remind you when we go back."

Caius turned in a quarter of a circle and groped for the door handle. Once he'd opened it, he waited to hear her enter before following her into the humid, warm, and fragrant room.

It had been a while since he'd entered the orangery; mainly because it had been Louisa's sanctuary and she would have exuded enough chill to cause frostbite and kill the plants if he'd intruded.

"Shall we walk the rectangle?"

"Yes. Tell me what you see," he ordered after a moment.

"There are the orange and lemon trees, of course, but they are not in blossom right now. I also see pineapples, leeks, chrysanthemums, begonias, calendula, ranunculus—"

"Those are all flowers, I take it?" he asked, impressed that she knew so many varieties.

"Well, not the pineapples and leeks."

Caius laughed, the sound startling him. It was, he realized, his first genuine laugh in a year. Perhaps even longer.

"Ooh, and here are some peonies." She stopped, so did Caius. "Come closer so you can smell them, my lord."

Caius sighed but did as she bade.

"No, you'll need to lean closer—more, a little more—"

Caius found his nose surrounded by unspeakable softness and the familiar scent of his mother, who'd had something of a mania for peonies and had dried the flowers and stored her clothing in the sachets.

He pulled a face and straightened.

"You don't like peonies?"

"I find the scent cloying." Not to mention it was tied to unpleasant memories of his mother's grim face—always disappointed in Caius for some infraction or other. It was a good thing she'd had Victor; he'd been the perfect son for her.

They resumed walking and a moment later she said, "I see Mr. Russell and he is feeding the finches. May we go closer to watch?"

Caius nodded. The birds were almost shockingly loud the nearer they got. "Noisy little beggars, aren't they?"

"They sound beautiful. Good afternoon, Mr. Russell."

"Good afternoon, my lord, Mrs. Lanyon."

"Russell," Caius said by way of greeting. The old man had worked at Courtland for at least fifty years. He was head gardener but had a staff of eight to do the actual work. He was a genius with plants and Courtland would mourn when he eventually retired.

"If I might be so bold, my lord, it is good to see you up and about," Russell said, emotion roiling beneath his normally calm voice.

Caius grunted and turned to Mrs. Lanyon. "Mr. Russell is another one who warmed my breeches."

Russell gave a surprised laugh. "Only the one time, I believe."

"Once was enough. You have a hand like a shovel if I recall correctly."

Russell chuckled.

"What did you do to deserve a spanking, my lord?" Mrs. Lanyon asked.

"Do you remember, Russell?"

"Indeed, I do. His lordship had just got a new ball and was playing with some of the estate children. I warned him to take his game away from the orangery."

"But I did not listen," Caius admitted.

"I believe it was that pane of glass there"—he must have pointed— "that the ball came through."

"My mother was furious. She was the one who insisted on the beating."

Caius thought the silence was rather strained.

Russell cleared his throat. "By and large his lordship was a very good lad," his gardener offered valiantly, but not very truthfully.

Caius laughed. "Your memory is kinder to me than I deserve, Russell. Carry on."

"Good day to you, my lord, Mrs. Lanyon."

Caius walked on, Mrs. Lanyon quiet beside him.

Once they'd gone some distance, she said, "Mr. Russell mentioned that he's worked for your family since he was nine."

"I am not surprised. His father was head gardener before him."

"Your people are very loyal—not just here, but in the village, as well. There—well, there wasn't a soul who spoke of your injury when I arrived."

"I am a fortunate man when it comes to my people," he said after a long pause. It astounded him that nobody had let his blindness slip. Part of him was proud to inspire such loyalty. Another part wondered if he'd have languished in his own self-pity for so long if the truth had been known.

Well, the cat was out of the bag, so no use in thinking about it now.

He stopped. "If I am oriented correctly there should be a bench not far from where we are standing. It is on the right, facing the largest of the orange trees."

"You are correct, my lord, it is just a few steps ahead."

"Let's sit for a moment."

Once he was seated, he heard Mrs. Lanyon shifting beside him, clearly nervous to be doing nothing but sitting in the middle of the day.

If she wanted work, he could give her some. "I have been thinking, Mrs. Lanyon."

"You won't want to make a habit of that, my lord."

Caius turned slowly to face her; his lips parted in shock. "I beg your pardon?"

She gasped, as if only then realizing what she'd said. And to whom she'd said it. "I'm sorry, my lord. I don't know why I said that. It—it just... slipped out."

Caius's lips wanted to twitch, but he controlled them. The last thing he wanted was for her to know he found her cheeky comments amusing. "Is this the sort of thing that *slipped out* when you worked for Chatham, Mrs. Lanyon?"

"Er, no. It won't happen again, my lord."

They both knew that for a lie, but he let the matter be. "I want you to go through the correspondence and collect all the tenant requests. Ask Morris if he knows of any that we've not addressed. When you have them all together, we will put them in order of immediacy and I will start calling them in to discuss it."

"You will?"

"You sound shocked. Am I really such an unpresentable cripple? I needn't walk, you know—or drink tea or eat—in front of them. You can sit me behind my desk like a potted plant."

"I'm not worried about you, my lord. I'm just surprised that, er…"

"That I have capitulated without a fuss?" he suggested, amused by her sudden reticence. After all, this was the same woman who'd stormed into his chambers and held her own when he'd dropped his drawers. Behavior for which he was more ashamed than he liked to admit.

"Well… yes."

"I would no more try to go against your will than I would shake my fist at the tide, Mrs. Lanyon."

She laughed. "I really wish I was as fearsome as you like to imply, but I suspect you are mocking me."

"Not a bit. I know you have the staff well in hand and you've been here less than two weeks."

"How do you know that?"

"Beeswax."

"I beg your pardon?"

"The corridors and rooms were redolent with beeswax polish. I believe I noticed it the same day I met you for the first time. Until then, I'd not smelled it since my last housekeeper—not the Nelson woman."

"I don't like to speak ill of another servant, but my predecessor didn't seem terribly fond of dusting."

Caius had often smelled gin on the woman's breath. Not only that, but Mrs. Nelson's voice had carried strong undertones of disgust whenever he'd had any dealings with her. She'd been an unpleasant woman, but he'd still not had the right to hurl items at her.

Which reminded him of how he'd hurled a book, if not *at* Mrs. Lanyon, then certainly in her presence.

"To be fair to Mrs. Nelson, she had good reason to leave," he said.

"Did she?"

Caius couldn't help snorting at her arch tone. "You think I should apologize for my appalling behavior, don't you?"

"Oh, was it appalling?"

He smirked. "I am sorry. I was very rude."

"And when was that, my lord?"

He laughed. "When I threw a book in your presence."

"And?"

Now he was openly grinning. "When I, er, disrobed in front of you."

"Hmph. Yes, you were appallingly rude."

"I said *very rude*."

She sighed.

"But I take your point," Caius said, amazed at his own admission. This woman certainly had an ability to bend him to her will.

He waited. And waited. And finally said, "So?"

"My lord?"

"Aren't you going to accept my apology?"

"I'm not sure."

Caius threw back his head and laughed. "You must surely be the most unusual housekeeper in England, Mrs. Lanyon. Whyever did Chatham let you go?" he asked, the question a serious one.

"I, er, had to go and nurse my sister."

That was another lie—he could practically *smell* it. The woman was the worst liar he'd ever heard.

"And Chatham wouldn't hold your position for you? That does not sound like him."

"I wasn't sure how long I would be away, so I wouldn't have been comfortable asking him to wait."

"I hope it wasn't terribly serious?"

"What do you mean?"

"Your sister's illness," he reminded her.

"Um, no. It wasn't serious. She is well."

Caius smiled. *Oh, Mrs. Lanyon, how nice it is to discover that you do at least <u>one</u> thing poorly. Just what are you lying about?*

Chapter 12

"I've three more for you to sign, my lord," Selina said, sliding the first letter in front of him and then swallowing before reaching out to move his hand—his *gloveless* hand—to the right spot over the parchment. She knew it was just his hand, and it was only a brisk touch, but something about feeling his warm skin caused a distracting sensation in her belly. And lower.

If Lord Shaftsbury even noticed that they were touching, he certainly didn't show it. He quickly signed all three letters she positioned for him and then pulled off his signet and handed it to her.

"Here you are." He snorted softly. "I don't know why I bother wearing it; you should probably keep it."

Selina didn't know what to say. He was prone to making these odd pronouncements that left her confused. And worried.

In the days since their walk in the orangery she had accompanied him all over the house. Until yesterday, when he'd sent James to tell her he'd not be meeting her. Selina knew that he'd had a late night because she'd had a late night and had not done her walk-through until after one o'clock, when she'd caught sight of him just closing the door to his gymnasium.

Around two-thirty, unable to sleep and too restless to write the letter she owed Hy, she'd put on her dressing gown and slippers and had tiptoed up to listen at the gymnasium door. He'd been in there, the rhythmic *thud, thud, thud* loud enough to shake the door.

He was politer than usual this morning, but he looked dead-eyed and gaunt.

Selina had the oddest feeling that he was slipping away from her.

"That is all of the letters for today," she said. "Shall I read you some of the newspaper, my lord?"

He hesitated a moment and then nodded. "Please."

But ten minutes into her reading she could tell he wasn't paying attention to the story on tariffs he'd asked for. When she finished the article, she skipped to the back section where the notices were. He rarely wanted to hear any of those, but she thought they might amuse him.

"Yesterday, a landau drawn by a pair of zebras made its appearance in Hyde Park and—"

The marquess barked a laugh. "You just made that up."

Selina chuckled. "No, I didn't—I couldn't. I'm actually not sure I know what a *zebra* is. Are they the striped horses?"

"They look like a horse but are considerably smaller. I don't suppose the paper says what fool was driving them?"

"That would be Lord Hendrix."

"Ah, that fool. Why am I not surprised," he muttered.

Selina had danced more than a few sets with Lord Hendrix and had to concur with her employer.

"What next?" she asked. "Do you want to hear more about the mountain that exploded in Java?"

"No."

"How about the plague currently raging in Algiers?"

"Ach," he waved a hand. "I think that is enough of the newspaper for today. What time is it?"

"Almost three o'clock, my lord."

"Good Lord, but I've kept you working late. Go on—you may leave. Tell James I shall want him in an hour."

"Of course, my lord."

Selina stood and made her way to the door. Just as she set her hand on the doorknob, she remembered the letters, which needed to go out with today's mail. She turned around to fetch them and stopped.

The marquess was sitting at his desk, just as she'd left him. His hands were resting on top of it, and he was staring straight ahead. Except she knew he wasn't staring; he was just... sitting.

He was in a room with thousands of books, sitting behind a desk that was piled with letters—some from his friends—and he could not look at or enjoy any of it. At least not unless somebody helped him.

His expression was bleak—lifeless—and her throat tightened and tears stung her eyes, welling over so quickly she didn't have a chance to stop them before one rolled down her cheek.

She hadn't made a sound, but he turned toward her. "Oh. Are you still here, Mrs. Lanyon? Did you need something else?"

She had to swallow down the lump in her throat that threatened to choke her. "No, my lord," she said in a hoarse voice, opening the door with a hand that shook and closing it with a definitive click so he'd at least know that he was now alone.

Selina nodded at Timothy—the footman whose job it was to wait outside any room his lordship was in, should the marquess need help—and she hurried toward the linen closet at the very end of the hall. Once she was inside it, she leaned against the door, slapped a hand over her mouth, and let the tears fall, muffling her sobs.

For days he'd shown up for their morning meetings perfectly garbed and ready to work through the backlog of mail. He had been so different from those first few days that she'd believed he was on the path to his new life.

They never had tea—he had that alone in his room—and she knew that he made his own way back and forth to his chambers and that he'd even gone down to the orangery twice to sit.

But it was such a *lonely* existence; one where he was dependent on somebody else for every little bit of mental stimulation.

It was wearing on him—she could see that. Every day that passed she knew he was more aware of how his life was forever changed, and not for the better. Yes, he could now navigate his house, or at least part of it, and he would soon have his first meeting with one of his tenants. But that would be here at Courtland, not out at the man's farm. He'd been nowhere for a year. Surely he must be feeling caged, no matter how luxurious and beautiful Courtland was.

He was doing the things she'd suggested—the correspondence, the repairs, and she read to him for an hour from several newspapers—but all that only took three, maybe four, hours. And they were rapidly making their way through the backlog. Soon, there would only be the daily business which would not take more than an hour.

What did he do the rest of the day? What did he do when he went back to his room and disappeared inside it until the next day? James, whom she'd pulled aside and privately queried, said his lordship dismissed him every afternoon and only summoned him about an hour before he came to his daily meeting with Selina.

What in the world could occupy all that other time—from two o'clock most afternoons until ten the next day? Why hadn't Selina thought about that sooner? Almost a third of her thirty days gone and she'd done nothing other than the barest minimum.

Her tears subsided and she dried her face; she would need to go to her room to rinse off the evidence of this orgy of crying before she could go down to the kitchen.

And then she would need to come up with a plan for the less than three weeks she had left.

***

Caius's urge to stay in bed was strong, as if a huge weight was pressed against his body.

What did it matter if he got up, dressed, and dragged himself to the library? Thanks to Mrs. Lanyon's efficiency he was rapidly coming to the end of his correspondence. He had meetings with tenants, but what was there other than that?

Caius closed his eyes. He would go back to sleep; he could miss today.

You've already missed one day this week. The voice was Elton's. More and more his dead valet appeared in his head, horning his way in with an aggressiveness that he'd never have employed in real life.

I was a servant then; now I am just your imaginary companion.

Caius could hear the subtle humor in the voice. He wasn't so far gone as to believe Elton was really talking to him, but that didn't make what he had to say any less persuasive.

He *had* missed one day this week. To miss another… Well, there was always the possibility that Mrs. Lanyon would come and pull him out of his bed.

His lips twitched at the amusing thought, but he sighed, swung his feet to the floor and rang the servant bell. By the time he was bathed, shaved, and clothed he was almost glad that he'd gotten out of bed.

When he reached the library, Mrs. Lanyon was already there.

"Good morning, my lord. Before you sit, I thought we might try something a little different today."

Caius felt a mild spark of interest. "Oh?"

"I thought we might go to the music room."

"Why?"

"It's a room you might like to visit on occasion."

"Why?"

She heaved a frustrated sigh. "Because I could play for you, if you like."

His eyebrows lifted. "*You* play the piano?"

"And the harp," she retorted testily. "Why are you smirking? Do you believe a housekeeper cannot have such accomplishments?"

"I never said that."

"You implied it."

"How prickly you are, Mrs. Lanyon."

"You mean how prickly for a *servant*."

Caius meant exactly that, but she was sounding increasingly huffy and while prodding her was entertaining, he was very interested in listening to some music. Please God let her skills be at least adequate. He was not a music afficionado, by any stretch, but he'd had to tolerate more than his fair share of talentless *plinking* while he'd been hunting a wife in *ton* sitting rooms.

They walked to the music room side-by-side, but not touching. He'd already come this direction many times since the corridors had been purged of their clutter, but he'd not bothered to enter the music room.

He stopped when he thought he was close to the door.

"Very good," she praised. "You are only about two steps off."

He tried not to preen too much and opened the door for her.

"There are not many obstacles to learn in the room," she said, once they were inside. "The piano is about fifteen paces ahead. To the right are three chairs and a settee in front of the fireplace. The servants shifted the piano so that it is closer to the windows. The drapes are open and the day is cloudless. You will be able to feel the sun on your face when you sit on the bench."

"Why would I sit on the bench? I thought you were going to play?"

"Have you ever played a piano?"

He barked a laugh. "I'm a man."

She sighed.

"Those heavy sighs of yours are annoying, Mrs. Lanyon."

"Have you heard of Bach, Beethoven, and Mozart?" she asked in the prim, chiding, distinctly un-servantly voice she often employed with him. The tone that made him feel… feisty.

"Thank you for the brief lesson in music history, Mrs. Lanyon. But I don't play, so why should I sit on the bench?"

"I thought you might enjoy getting a feel for the instrument."

"Why?"

"Oh, for pity's sake! It won't hurt you to sit there for a moment."

He snorted, amused by her annoyance and fire.

"You know what you remind me of, my lord?" she demanded, clearly nettled.

"I'm afraid to ask."

It turned out he didn't need to. "A rat that is stuck in a trap. That happened once in our pantry when I was younger. When we tried to capture it—to release it from the trap—it just kept snapping. Even though we wanted to help, it tried to bite us."

Caius's eyebrows shot up. "Did you just compare me to a verminous rodent, Mrs. Lanyon?"

"I beg your pardon, my lord, but the similarity is really quite striking."

He snorted. When had any of his employees ever spoken to him in such a fashion?

Elton never allowed you to get away with anything, a cool voice said.

Caius ignored the unwanted reminder of his dead valet.

A man you as good as executed, the voice persisted.

Bile rose at the accusation, just as it always did. Caius swallowed it down. His hands were shaking, so he fisted them.

"My lord? Is something amiss?" Mrs. Lanyon asked in a gentle, very un-Mrs.Lanyon-like voice.

Caius ignored her question and snapped, "Fine. I will sit on the damned bench."

"Good," she said, sounding unruffled by his rudeness. "It is ahead of you—"

"I recall—fifteen paces," he retorted, and stormed ahead until his cane struck wood. He leaned forward and felt the bench. Once again, a rush of achievement flooded him at merely walking across a room. He dropped down hard enough to jar his tailbone and grimaced. "There. Are you happy?" he demanded, propping his walking stick between his knees.

"I've lifted the lid," she said, ignoring his baiting. "You can reach out and feel the keys."

Caius opened his mouth to ask *why*, but she didn't let him speak.

"Just humor me, my lord."

He snorted and set his hands on the keys, wincing at the clangor he made. He gentled his touch, suddenly curious to explore the smooth, cool ivory and perhaps coax a less jarring sound out of the instrument. There was something about touching the keys and instantly making a sound that was strangely rewarding.

Only when he realized that he'd been fumbling about for several minutes did he stop and glare in her general direction.

"Well, what do you think?" she asked.

"About what?"

"Would you like to learn how to play?"

"*What?*"

"I could teach you."

"What the devil for?"

She didn't answer immediately, and when she did, it was with a question. "May I make an observation?"

"I suspect I could not stop you, Mrs. Lanyon."

"You don't seem happy, my lord."

His anger, which was never far from the surface these days, spiked. "How astute of you, Mrs. Lanyon," he all but snarled.

"So, why not try some new things and see if you can *be* happy?"

"You think learning to play the piano will make me *happy*? You think it will make up for everything I have lost?" he demanded in open disbelief.

Once again, she hesitated—a tentativeness that was unlike her, or at least unlike the sides she'd shown to him thus far, which were overbearing, dictatorial, and implacable. Why was she curbing her tongue *now*?

"Just say what you are thinking," he ordered, pained at the thought of her choosing her words around him. Already everyone in the house treated him like a fragile piece of glass, handling him with kid gloves.

"What did you do before your accident? What sorts of activities did you enjoy?"

"What do you think I did?" he asked hotly. "I was a *man* then, and I did the things that *men* do. I rode and I hunted and I boxed and went to my clubs and gambling hells and I read my own goddamned letters and visited my tenant's farms and a hundred other things that I can no longer do." And he'd gone to his lovers' beds while in London, or—for the year before his accident—he'd bedded his new wife the few times she'd allowed him into her chambers.

Caius kept those last activities to himself. No matter how much Mrs. Lanyon might annoy him, she was still a female and deserving of respect.

"Why *can't* you still do some of those things, my lord? You cannot see, but your limbs all function and you are healthy and have the financial means to explore… options."

Anger flared fast and hot at her words. "Everything is just so easy for me because I have money, isn't it Mrs. Lanyon? Why can't I make an effort and be like the sainted cobbler *Nick*?"

"I'm not saying that."

"Then what the hell are you saying?"

"I know your life will never be the same. And I know many of the activities you once enjoyed are no longer possible. But perhaps you might still do some of those things with a little adjustment? Not read letters, of course, but you can pay a visit to a tenant's farm—you can go in a carriage," she hurriedly added when he opened his mouth to scoff. "You might even ride at some point, although you won't be able to hunt. Naturally both those activities now necessitate having a companion along. As for boxing—you already practice that alone, do you not?"

Selina

Caius's mind was flooded with the images she painted with her words. The yearning she evoked inside him was stunning—and infuriating. How dare she dangle such hope in front of him?

When he didn't—couldn't—bring himself to answer, she went on.

"And there are many, many other ways to entertain yourself. Ways that will reward your other senses—hearing and touch, for example," her voice faltered and she suddenly sounded… young and uncertain.

Very young.

Caius realized he didn't know a damned thing about her other than she'd once worked for Chatham. Morris had tried to read him the letter of recommendation but he'd not been interested.

He was now.

"How old are you?" he demanded.

She hesitated, clearly surprised by the change in subject. "I am one-and-thirty."

Caius laughed. "You are not."

"Yes, my lord, I *am*."

Caius could feel her feathers fluffing up at his accusation. He smirked. "You sound much younger."

"Well, I'm not."

He was beginning to recognize what he thought of as her *falsehood voice*. Mrs. Lanyon had just told him a bouncer; he was sure of it.

Caius tucked away his suspicion; he would consider the matter more closely when he was alone.

He pulled the conversation back on course. "Why the devil do you care so much about me being happy, Mrs. Lanyon?"

She didn't answer right away. Finally, she said, "When I was younger my sisters and I volunteered to help in a temporary hospital in our village."

"You mean a hospital for soldiers."

Caius wanted to groan; he could already guess where this was going.

"The men who came to that hospital had all been badly injured. Most were missing limbs; some had lost their reason. There were several who'd been blinded or deafened. One man had suffered both losses."

God. Caius couldn't even imagine such a nightmare.

"Most of them no longer needed a doctor's care, but they were still not"—she broke off and cleared her throat, as if the words had become stuck. "They were—"

"They were living in the wreckage of what their lives once were," he finished.

She drew in an audible breath before saying, "Yes, that is a painfully accurate description. As volunteers, we could only do so much for them. It—it never seemed like nearly enough."

Caius had not stepped foot in an army hospital, but he had an imagination, and knew that what she'd seen would not have been pleasant.

"Many of them didn't have family to care for them and were eventually taken off to—well, I don't really know where they went. Nowhere good, I suppose."

"Poor houses, workhouses, or almshouses—if they were fortunate." Many would have ended up living on the street and begging for pennies.

"I suspected as much," she said, sounding miserable and something else— guilty? "It—it didn't seem right that they'd given up so much for England and then came back to a lonely life of dependence and poverty."

No, it didn't. Caius had seen those men with his own eyes before he'd lost the use of them. He'd sat in Lords among those wealthy, privileged few who made the laws for everyone else. He had argued for decent pensions and more services for returning soldiers, but he had never helped anyone with his own hands or spared a single injured soldier so much as a moment of his time.

Not like the woman beside him had.

Her words shamed him, and—for once—he didn't know how to respond. He was suddenly weary. Weary of his anger and suspicion and hopelessness, and, yes, weary of his unhappiness.

Caius heard her inhale, as if to speak, but she must have decided to hold her words in.

"If you have something to say, then say it, Mrs. Lanyon."

"It's just… you are now taking charge of the estate matters, you can move around your house with confidence and are venturing out into more parts of it every day—"

"Yes, yes, yes—I know all that. What is your point with all this, Mrs. Lanyon? Do you see me as one of those soldiers? A poor damaged creature with nowhere to go? I assure you that I am not."

"I know that my lord—of course I do. It's just that I think it is time for you to do something that makes your life worth living. It is not enough to simply exist."

Simply exist?

Caius's temper soared and he had to fight to keep from shouting at her—from confessing that *simply existing* was taking every single ounce of energy that he possessed. But he was already an object of pity for her and he refused to make the situation even worse.

So instead, he lashed out. "What would you have me do, Mrs. Lanyon?" he asked in a silky voice that did little to conceal his anger. "Have I not completed the tasks you've set for me? Are there more hoops I must leap through for your approval?"

"That isn't what I mean."

"Then what the hell *do* you mean?" he thundered.

"You are right that you are not an impoverished soldier who is alone in the world. But you *are* a human being who is in need of kindness, if only you would allow people to help you, to—"

"You *have* helped me, ma'am." He frowned and shook his head. "Why are you saying all this? Because I don't wish to play the piano?"

"No. I—it's something I've been thinking about." She made a noise of frustration. "Please, just—just give me a moment to collect my thoughts, I'm trying to explain."

Caius bit his tongue and forced himself to sit and wait. He'd asked her to speak, after all. The least he could do was listen.

"What I meant to say is that I think your life needs more in it or you will"—she broke off and swallowed audibly.

"I'll *what?*"

"I think your interest in living will fade if you do not have something more."

Caius wanted to tell her that it had *already* faded, but—for once—he managed to keep the mortifying declaration of his own weakness behind his teeth.

"You said I needed *more*, Mrs. Lanyon. More what?"

"I'm not sure—that is why I'm rambling so badly. But I think you need something that makes your life worth living. Every day you seem just a bit… grimmer. Every day there is a little less of a spring in your step. I'm—I'm afraid you will give up, my lord, and I don't know how to stop that. That is all I am trying to say—very badly: that I don't want to see you give up on life as so many of those soldiers did. You just… *can't.*"

"I have no intention of giving up, dammit!"

"Then why do you keep that loaded pistol in your nightstand, my lord?"

***

Lord Shaftsbury's eyes widened at her impertinent question, and he inhaled deeply, the action filling out his chest in a way that made Selina realize just how much bigger than her he was.

She steeled herself against his fury and prepared for another sacking. She would deserve it, too. After all, who was she to pry into his privacy and demand explanations from him? Her behavior was obnoxious and he was quite justified in being angry.

The marquess scowled for so long he seemed to have frozen. After several agonizing minutes had ticked past, he gave one of his bitter barks of laughter. "Why am I not surprised that you looked in a drawer in my nightstand? I suppose the drawer was quite dirty and required dusting?"

Her face scalded at his rightfully sneering look and tone. "No, I was just—"

"I know exactly what you were doing, ma'am." His nostrils flared with each breath, his jaw flexing as if he were struggling to hold something back.

But his words, when they came, couldn't have shocked her more: "You have humbled me, Mrs. Lanyon."

Selina blinked. "*Wh-what?*"

"I'm not talking about the pistol," he said, his lips tightening. "We shall discuss your propensity to poke around where you should not be poking at some later date. In depth. But what I do agree with is that I do not get to take the easy way out of my situation. I do not get to give up." He turned toward his hands, which were lying palm up on his knees. "It is..." He paused, and the silence dragged on. Finally, he said, "It is daunting to think of all the things I will never do again."

Tears sprang to her eyes at his quiet admission. Selina could not imagine what it must be like to suddenly be blind, but she suspected it was much more than daunting. It must be demoralizing and debilitating and terrifying.

The marquess sighed. "You are right that I have advantages those soldiers couldn't even dream of." He gave her a wry look, his face no longer taut with anger and bitterness. "I appreciate your concern for my welfare—if not your prying—but I'm not sure I feel ready to take on playing an instrument. I have my hands full learning the lay of the house and my estate. However, I think you may be correct that I should take the gig out to visit one of the tenant farms. There is no use hiding away. My people might as well become accustomed to me the way I am now. I'm sure the first time will be awkward, but it will pass."

Selina bit her lower lip at the desolation that flickered across his handsome face. But then he visibly shook himself and his mouth curved so slightly she couldn't really call it a smile, but it was still beautiful, like glimpsing sunlight peeking through the clouds after a storm, just a flash of straight white teeth between his lips. "If I am to jaunter about the countryside in a dogcart then I will need somebody to handle the ribbons. Are you good for such a task, Mrs. Lanyon?"

She wiped a stray tear from her cheek and said in a husky voice. "I will never be a member of the Four in Hand Club, but I am adequate."

Selina

He snorted, but then his good humor fled, replaced by a look of grim determination. "I just want to make one point clear, Mrs. Lanyon."

"Yes, my lord?"

"I'll accept your help, but I don't want your pity."

"I understand, my lord. And just let me add that I don't think you need it. You are a strong, intelligent man who is facing an exceptionally trying situation. You've been bruised by what happened, my lord. But you are not broken."

"Strong?" He gave a bitter laugh. "I don't think so. If you'd not come along, who knows how long I would have wallowed."

His gratitude warmed her, but she didn't like the bitterness and self-loathing that were creeping back into his voice. "How long has that pistol been in your nightstand, my lord?"

His mouth tightened and Selina thought she might have finally pushed him too far, but then he snorted and said, "Point taken, Mrs. Lanyon."

"As for why your faithful servants like Mr. Russell or Mr. Morris never intervened, I think they worried they'd cause you more harm. They have known you all your life and love you. They want to protect and shelter you."

He gave her a wry smile. "I take it you don't share their opinion."

"I don't think coddling is good for you and I certainly don't think you need it. I will always speak my mind, my lord."

"Yes, I believe you will, Mrs. Lanyon. I am grateful for that. And also your… enthusiasm, which has been a breath of fresh air and proved a distraction."

"I am pleased to hear it, my lord."

"I didn't say it was a *good* distraction."

Selina huffed. "But, what—"

He chuckled. "Don't fly into a pucker. I am teasing you, Mrs. Lanyon. These past few weeks have not been comfortable, but I suspect they have been… necessary. So," he said, shaking himself. "We are in agreement on the issue of no coddling or pity, at least."

Selina felt better—lighter—than she'd felt in days. "Absolutely no coddling or pity. Now, may I play for you, my lord?"

"I would like that, Mrs. Lanyon. I would like it very much." He stood and tapped his way over to the chair nearest the piano, the one facing her.

Selina started off with *Moonlight Sonata*, which was her favorite piece of music. She'd played it so many hundreds of times that the notes were part of her. But even after hearing the sonata so often, the first movement—the *adagio sostenuto*—made her throat tighten with emotion and she had to squeeze her eyes shut to keep from weeping while she played it.

When she reached the *allegretto*, and it was safe to open them again, the first thing that met her gaze was the marquess.

Selina's fingers stumbled slightly at the expression on his face. His lips were parted, his pale cheeks flushed, and he looked... transported.

And there was a wet sheen on his cheeks that looked very much like tears.

Chapter 13

Selina woke with a start and it took her a moment to recall why she was sitting in a chair with a candle burning. And then she saw the book in her lap and realized she must have fallen asleep while reading.

A quick glance at the clock showed she'd been sleeping for hours; it was close to two o'clock and she'd not done the nightly walk-through. She sighed, heaved herself out of the chair, and briefly considered stuffing her feet back into her ankle boots. Why bother? Who would be around at this time of night to be offended by her soft wool slippers?

Selina picked up her hand candle and set off. Although the day had been stressful, it had also been a relief to reach some sort of accord with the marquess that afternoon. At least that is what it had felt like to Selina. But who really knew? Tomorrow morning, she might show up to the library and find the same bitter, unhappy, obstinate man waiting for her. It wasn't that she expected a miraculous change, but she hoped Lord Shaftsbury at least retained some of the optimism she'd glimpsed today.

When Selina reached the landing in the family wing, she saw that the large sash window at the end of the corridor was open. The day had been scorching, so one of the servants must have opened it and then forgotten to close it.

She was about to shut it when she heard a noise behind her. The door at the other end of the corridor—the one that led to the suite of rooms that held his lordship's boxing gymnasium—was wide open. His lordship must have opened it to cool down his room.

For a moment she was confused why there was no light coming from the room, and then cursed herself for a ninny. The marquess would hardly light a candle when he didn't need one.

She had been in the gymnasium before—there wasn't a corner of the house that she'd not explored—and had even supervised a quartet of maids while they'd quickly and thoroughly cleaned the grubby, dusty room just a few mornings earlier, even though the marquess had grumbled and snarled when she'd suggested it.

"Is there anywhere in this house you *won't* force your way into, Mrs. Lanyon?"

"I understand nobody has entered the room except for you and Morris for months, my lord. Mr. Morris has done his best to clean it, but he is eighty-three years old and it is hard on his knees to crawl around on the floor and clean corners."

He'd scowled at her unsubtle chiding. "You have the most astounding way of scolding me while keeping a respectful tone, Mrs. Lanyon."

"Thank you, my lord."

"That wasn't meant to be a compliment, Mrs. Lanyon."

"I'm sorry, my lord."

His eyebrows had drawn down, his expression suspicious—as he'd been right to do, since she'd been biting her lip to hold back a smile. It was interesting that she did that: hid her expressions even though he couldn't see them. Yet somehow, he seemed to sense when she smiled, almost as if he could hear it.

"Fine! Clean the damned room. But if you move anything so much as a quarter of an inch there will be hell to pay."

"Of course, my lord."

Selina grinned even now thinking of his scowl.

The methodical *thwap, thwap, thwap* grew louder the closer Selina crept to the open door. His lordship must be striking the large, boiled leather bag which hung from the ceiling. Apparently, that was the bag's sole purpose: to be punched.

Selina held up her candle and peeked around the door frame into the room.

She sucked in a noisy breath. The marquess was indeed pounding the bag with punches that rocked the heavy thing on its chain. But he abruptly stopped and turned until he was facing the door.

"Who is there?" he demanded in a voice breathless from exertion.

Selina opened her mouth to speak, but nothing came out. All she could do was gawk at his sweaty, muscular, hard, glorious, mostly nude body.

Lord Shaftsbury's coal black eyebrows drew down until they formed a V over his striking eyes, which looked like opals in the dim light of her hand-candle. He remained motionless for what felt like an eternity and then huffed out a breath as he turned back to the swaying bag. Rather than resume pummeling it, he reached out and set his hands on either side of it, stopping it from swaying.

He released the bag and began to unwrap the strips of material that covered his hands. Once both hands were bare, he strode directly toward Selina, his eyes boring through her—like a hawk sighting its prey.

She was just about to beg his pardon—to apologize for sneaking and spying—when he abruptly stopped and reached out to his side, his fingers seeking the ugly bucket that sat on the rough-hewn table. Once he found it, he dropped the fabric strips into it and then did a precise half turn and walked back across the room, his gait so confident that Selina knew he'd done this same series of actions hundreds of times.

He stopped at a metal rod that had been embedded into the frame of one of the floor-to-ceiling casement windows, made another precise turn, until he was again facing Selina, and then lifted his arms and stood on his toes, his fingers stretching until the tips touched the metal rod. He gave a small hop, clasped the bar, and then proceeded to pull himself up slowly, until his chin was just above the bar.

Over and over he performed the same movement.

It was... mesmerizing.

The marquess wore only a pair of buckskin breeches—no boots, stockings, shirt, or coats. The old leathers looked soft and were worn thin, hanging low on his lean hips, exposing a taut V of muscle that looked a great deal like the wooden board the washerwoman used to do the weekly laundry.

Selina exhaled slowly and shakily as her eyes roamed from the tips of his toes to the damp, tousled dark brown curls on his head.

His eyes were closed and his expression was one of absolute concentration as he lifted and lowered his body in slow, controlled movements that caused the muscles of his torso to ripple so enticingly that her mouth flooded with moisture in a way that usually only happened when she was confronted with her favorite desserts.

And then her gaze snagged on something that momentarily confused her. The fabric at the front of his breeches was strangely contorted. Almost as if—

This time she caught her gasp before it could slip out, biting her lower lip so hard she tasted blood.

His breeding organ was erect!

Or at least she thought that's what it was.

Selina had never seen a man's breeches distorted in such a way. Not that she ogled that part of men's bodies. At least not terribly often. However, there were some men—like Shelton, for example—who wore their pantaloons and evening breeches *so* snug that it was difficult not to steal a look or two. Or ten.

And not once had she seen such a ridge. A *thick* ridge.

Although Selina was a maiden with only a few kisses to her credit, she knew plenty about sexual intercourse. Her oldest sister Aurelia was an illustrator for scientific journals. Over the years Aurelia had, under a male nom de plume, drawn all sorts of fascinating subjects.

Because she was a female in a man's world, Aurelia had needed to be stealthy about finding examples to study in order to hone her skills, especially when it came to subjects that society deemed unfit for a woman to look at, like the human body.

Her sister had used her time volunteering at the soldiers' hospital to learn as much as she could about male anatomy.

Selina, Aurelia, and Hy—the three oldest siblings—had engaged in several frank discussions about intercourse and sexuality over the years.

"I feel I should be the one to make sure you know what awaits you in the marriage bed," Aurelia had admitted when she'd presented Selina and Hy with some rather explicit drawings of male and female anatomy. "Because I know Mama will not bother telling any of us anything useful." Even Hy had laughed at the image of their cold, starchy mother talking to them on such an earthy subject.

But gazing at the vigorous, vibrant man currently on display before her was exceedingly different than looking at cold, lifeless anatomical sketches.

Selina suddenly noticed that his lips were moving, as if he were counting, and that his movements became stiffer and jerkier with each lift.

"*Forty*," he hissed, and then dropped to his feet. He bent over, his hands on his knees, his breathing heavy.

Selina was just about to turn and tiptoe away when he spoke.

"Why now? Why after almost a bloody year?"

His tone was so normal that Selina almost said, *why what?*

Thankfully she regained her wits in time.

A bare second later the marquess gave a laugh filled with bitter self-loathing and said, "You're pathetic, Caius. But then who really gives a damn?" That last part was muttered under his breath as he pushed upright, made another of his precise quarter turns and strode confidently toward the scuffed and battered leather sofa that sat along one wall.

The marquess dropped onto it with a tired sigh and stared sightlessly ahead.

And did… nothing.

Yet again Selina was about to sneak away when he suddenly scowled and unhooked the catches that held his placket closed.

Selina stopped breathing.

He gave a negligent tug on the five buttons and exposed the fine muslin of his drawers beneath.

If you don't leave now, you are a depraved, sneaking pervert, her mother's voice chided.

If you do leave right now, then you are a chicken-livered dunce, a coolly amused voice countered, this one sounding a great deal like Hy.

Selina agreed with the second voice and quietly inhaled, filling her burning lungs as the marquess lifted his hips and shoved down his drawers and breeches, exposing the cause of the ridge beneath the soft leather.

She knew she was spending a great deal of her time with her mouth open, but it seemed the only reasonable response to something so… momentous.

Selina

The marquess slid a hand around the thick, ruddy shaft and groaned, his head falling against the back of the settee as his fingers tightened and began to move.

Selina's thighs clenched reflexively and an exquisite wash of pleasure rippled from her sex to her belly and breasts.

Oh, my.

Her eyelids had just fluttered shut when his voice, guttural and thick, jerked her from her bliss.

"Just leave me alone, Louisa."

Chapter 14

Caius was perfectly aware of what a pitiful creature he was at that moment. He might not be able to see, but he could still visualize how he must look. Sweaty, exhausted, and hollow-eyed from his inability to sleep, garbed only in worn-out old rags, sitting alone in the middle of the night, fisting his own cock because nobody else was likely to ever want to touch him again.

At least not unless he *paid* a woman to pleasure him.

Ever since he'd taken his first lover at the age of fifteen—a widowed friend of his mother—Caius had avoided prostitutes. He'd gone into brothels twice with his mates and both times the pungent smell of unwashed, over-perfumed bodies and human desperation had shriveled his cock in his breeches. His friends had mocked him for his fastidiousness, but he hadn't cared. If all he had to look forward to was a future with whores in it, then he'd rather fuck his own hand.

And so here he was, doing exactly that.

Oh, poor, poor Lord Shaftsbury. Still alive and able to toss one off.

Caius's lip twitched slightly at the sound of his dead valet's voice. He'd much rather listen to Elton mock and scold him than listen to Louisa's cries and recriminations.

Shut up and get on with it, phantom Elton ordered.

Caius obeyed. He had to admit that his own hand felt pretty damned enjoyable tonight. For almost a year he'd not touched himself. Oh, he'd woken up with the obligatory cockstand every morning, but he'd felt no trace of desire.

He had always heard that a brush with death caused people to want to embrace life with a vengeance, especially when it came to sexual congress.

But then Caius's exposure to death had been significantly more than a *brush*. It had taken Louisa hours—perhaps as long as a day—to die in the confines of that wretched coach.

"Caius... please... just make it stop..."

He gritted his teeth as thoughts of his dead wife tried to intrude on this brief oasis of pleasure. "Just leave me alone, Louisa," he begged, immediately feeling like a fool. Thank God he was the only one who'd heard.

It usually took only the thought of his dead wife to throttle his desire, but tonight there was another woman who intruded and delayed the inevitable downward spiral into darkness and misery.

May I play for you, my lord?

Mrs. Lanyon's velvety, almost prim, voice shot straight to his balls, just the way it had that afternoon when he'd sat beside her on the piano bench.

The great Shaftsbury boxing the Jesuit while fantasizing about his housekeeper, Elton taunted. *I'll remind you that is your <u>servant</u> you're tossing one off to, my lord.*

I don't bloody care, Elton. Caius tightened his grip and groaned; by God it felt good to feel something other than hopelessness and self-loathing.

I daresay that second feeling will return shortly after you spend all over your belly, sir.

Caius had no doubt of that. But, again, he couldn't bring himself to care.

May I play for you, my lord?

He smiled as his shaft pulsed in his fist. It was damned strange that just the memory of her voice could get him so hard. Indeed, he couldn't recall being aroused by a woman's voice before.

Caius snorted. He didn't have a whole lot else to cling to now, did he?

Of course, there was her scent, too: lavender.

If somebody had asked him what he thought about lavender, he would have said it was too sharp and astringent. But something about the way the harsh botanical smell mingled with Mrs. Lanyon's own clean, womanly scent combined to create an aroma that didn't just contribute to his masturbatory fantasies, it also infused him with the most tranquilizing sense of calm.

Arousal and serenity together. Who would have believed that combination of emotions was even possible?

Caius could summon her voice quite easily and he could even imagine her saying words that she had likely never said in her life and never would.

Let me stroke that for you, my lord.

His lips twitched into a satisfied smile as he fisted himself from root to tip, slicking his palm with the copious liquid leaking from his cock.

What did the woman look like? She certainly didn't sound like any servant he'd ever known. He told himself that was why he didn't feel guilty using her voice for his own depraved pleasure—because she spoke just like a woman of his class, the words as crisp as freshly starched linen.

Her accent? Are you really going to use that as an excuse?

It was indeed pitiful, and he would have scoffed if anyone else had tried to use it to justify their behavior.

And yet… Caius didn't feel as if he were preying on an uneducated woman with no ability to defend herself.

In truth, he was not preying on her at all. Surely a man was allowed to do whatever he wished in the privacy of his own mind—and his own damned house—no matter how improper?

May I play for you, my lord?

Caius groaned. *Yes.* She could bloody well play for him. It had been the best half hour of the past year; thirty minutes of pure escape from his thoughts.

She was good—*exceptionally* good—and possessed the sort of skill that only came from hours and hours of practice. Perhaps she was the daughter of some impoverished Oxford don. Or maybe the eleventh child of a country squire and she'd been forced into service because the family coffers had run dry. That would certainly explain the accent.

Whoever the hell she was, Caius had finally found a reason to get hard again. He felt alive for the first time in ages.

And you owe it all to the woman you are currently masturbating over.

So what? What I'm doing doesn't hurt Mrs. Lanyon.

This would never go beyond mere fantasy, and nobody would ever know about it except *Caius.*

***

Go now you wicked girl!

Selina didn't move. Why should she? Nobody would ever know that she had stayed to watch.

God will know, a voice boomed in her head.

She bit her lip. *But… surely there is nothing wrong with merely watching?*

It is a sin.

So what if it was? Chances were very good that Selina had so destroyed her reputation—thanks to Shelton and that fool Fowler—that she would never marry. This moment—watching this exceedingly sensual and private, er… activity—was probably the closest she'd ever come to a truly erotic experience.

You can't leave now, Linny; you will be able to re-live and enjoy this episode for years to come. Hy's voice drowned out poor Nanny.

Selina didn't need her phantom sister's encouragement; she knew this was something she'd never forget. Besides, surely what happened in a person's head was their own business and—

His lordship gave another guttural groan and then lifted his hips up off the settee, his fist moving faster, the wet sounds filthy and erotic in the silence of the room. His chin suddenly jerked down and his eyes opened, his breeding organ a blur in his fist.

Selina

"Yes," he grunted, the word shredded by his clenched teeth. "*Fuck!*" he shouted as his body jerked and—shockingly—liquid jetted from the fat crown, propelled with enough force that some of it landed all the way up near one of his tiny brown nipples.

Every muscle in his body flexed over and over again, the savage tension delineating the exquisite details of his torso.

It was painful to wrench her gaze away—Selina could have stared at him for hours—but she needed to go before he came back to himself. She slid a foot backward and a board creaked beneath her slipper.

His head whipped up. "Who's there?" he demanded hoarsely, his gaze seeming to burn right through her.

Selina pressed her palm against her mouth and froze.

His nostrils flared slightly, as if he was scenting something. "Mrs. Lanyon?"

She gasped, whirled around, and ran, her ancient wool slippers skidding and sliding over the freshly polished wooden floor.

Chapter 15

Selina laid in bed and stared at the ceiling until five the following morning, not getting so much as a wink of sleep. All night she had tossed and turned, foolishly waiting for a summons from the marquess, as if the man would ring for her in the middle of the night.

But he would undoubtedly do so today.

Selina washed and dressed and went down to the kitchen to await the end of her first and only job.

She wasn't surprised that the marquess didn't ring before breakfast as he rarely rose before ten o'clock. But as eleven o'clock loomed—the time they usually met to go through the prior day's correspondence—she began to believe he was waiting for her to arrive in the library to lower the axe.

Well.

He might want her to suffer on pins and needles all night and morning, but she would put an end to her worrying right now.

She strode toward the library even though it was five minutes before the appointed hour. But when Selina flung open the door, saw immediately that his lordship wasn't at his desk.

Had she beat him to their daily meeting?

"Mrs. Lanyon?"

Selina squawked like a startled hen and spun around.

"I'm sorry," he said, amusement coloring his tone. "I didn't mean to startle you." The marquess was sitting in front of the fireplace at a small table. On it was a chessboard. "I wondered if you played chess, Mrs. Lanyon?"

Selina stared, a hand over her racing heart. He didn't look angry, or disappointed, or—

"Mrs. Lanyon?"

"Yes, my lord?"

"I asked if you play chess?"

"Er, yes, my lord, I play. Not well," she hastily added. Indeed, of all her siblings—even her young brother Doddy—she was the least accomplished at the game.

The marquess nodded and turned to the board. "My father taught me how to play when I was very young." Something flickered across his expressive face too quickly for her to understand.

She stared, her crushing worry and mortification slowly turning to relief, her heart gradually slowing to a bearable rhythm. He did not look like a man who was about to sack a servant. Was it possible that he didn't know that it had been Selina spying on him last night? He'd said her name, but—

"My father was not normally the sort to sit still," Lord Shaftsbury continued, his tone thoughtful. "He preferred hunting, riding, shooting—things of that sort."

"He was a man of action." Her voice was a bit too breathy, but otherwise she sounded almost… normal.

"Yes. I am—or I was, rather—cut from the same cloth. I rarely even played cards, only indulging to be sociable. But this"—he gestured toward the board in front of him, knocking several pieces over in the process. He pulled a face. "Blast."

Selina hurried over and knelt, picking up the five pieces and replacing them.

His face tilted toward her and he gave her a wry look. "I was going to say that chess was something I wouldn't mind playing. But I suppose what I just did was a sign."

"You mean that knocking them over was a sign that you can't play?"

"Yes."

Selina turned to look at the board as her thoughts—which had been fixated on being dismissed for spying on her employer while he masturbated—slowly changed direction.

When his brow furrowed, she realized that he must be wondering what she was doing.

"I'm sorry, my lord—I'm still here. I was just thinking…"

"About?"

"About how the problem could be solved."

"I'm not sure it can be solved." He snorted, his expression becoming bitter. "Unless I regain my sight."

Selina was not going to touch *that* subject with a barge pole. Instead, she picked up a pawn and said, "Hold out your hand. Er, please," she added when his eyebrows arched haughtily.

He extended a hand and Selina placed the piece in his palm. "Can you tell what that is?"

As he explored the ivory pawn with his elegant, tapered fingers Selina had a sudden flashback to the night before—to when those fingers had been wrapped around something else entirely.

"Mrs. Lanyon?"

She wrenched her gaze up from his hand. "I'm sorry, my lord?"

"Is aught amiss? You suddenly... gasped."

"Oh. I twisted my foot the wrong way," she lied.

"It is remiss of me not to have offered you a seat." He jerked his chin toward the chair across from him.

It wasn't remiss at all for a master to keep a servant standing—even an upper servant—but she wasn't going to argue. Instead, she sat.

He lifted the game piece he still held. "It's a pawn."

"Let me give you another one."

They went through all the pieces, and he quickly and easily identified them all.

"So," she said, when he'd finished. "You can clearly tell the pieces without any problem. That leaves the board and their position on it."

"And the fact that I'll knock them all off if I start groping them."

Selina nodded, pensively staring at the board. "I'm just thinking," she said absently after a moment of silence had passed.

"About?"

Selina glanced up and saw that he looked curious—almost eager—about what she might say. All her life her mother had instructed her to be quiet around men.

"Men don't care for babblers. They want a woman to listen to them, not talk. You don't need to *really* listen," the countess had amended with a sour look. "You just need to do a convincing job of appearing to do so."

Selina thought this might be an instance where her mother was wrong.

"Do you mind if I just, er, talk through my ideas?" Selina asked.

His lips curved faintly. "I would prefer it. When it is too quiet, I wonder what is happening."

That made sense to her, and she should have thought of it before. "I'm thinking there are three issues you are facing."

He sat back, rested his hands on the arms of his chair, and then nodded. "Go on."

"First, you need to be able to handle the pieces to know what they are. Second, you need to know what square you are on. And last, you need to be able to tell your pieces from your opponent's. Can you think of anything I missed?"

He sat quietly for a moment, considering her words, and then shook his head. "No, I think that covers everything important."

Selina

"Surely a woodworker could make you chess pieces out of wood instead of ivory?"

"I'm sure they could, but why use wood as opposed to ivory?"

"I thought it might be more durable," she said, and then winced. "I'm sorry, I didn't mean to imply that you would be dropping them a great deal."

He chuckled, the rare, warm sound causing a mild flutter in her belly. "Don't worry that you offended me, Mrs. Lanyon. You are correct that wood is more durable. But that doesn't solve the other problems."

"Ah, but it is part of the solution. Have you ever seen a wooden spool with thread on it?"

"No, I don't think so."

"It is something seamstresses use. They get the thread from the mill and once it is empty, they return the spool to be refilled. Of course, they need thread for all sorts of colored fabrics, so they have many spools. They keep a wooden board with holes in it and wooden dowels fit into the holes and each dowel holds a spool. I was thinking if there were holes in the squares and then short dowels in the bottom of the pieces that they could be slotted in and kept stationary."

A smile—the genuine one—slowly spread across his face. "How very, very clever you are Mrs. Lanyon. Are you sure you aren't secretly an inventor?"

His expression made him too gorgeous for Selina's comfort. And his praise—a rare gift indeed, at least from a man—caused her to give an embarrassed laugh. "It is nothing, just a practical way of thinking, my lord."

His pale gray eyes gleamed with humor and something else: admiration. Not because she had a pretty face or generous bosom. But because he liked the way her mind worked.

"You say the word *practical* as if it were a bad thing, Mrs. Lanyon."

"My mother always said that men didn't care for women who were too clever."

"She was wrong at least once, wasn't she?"

Selina blinked. "I don't understand?"

"Mister Lanyon married you, so at least *one* man must have liked your practical mind."

She felt like a fool. "Oh, yes. Mr. Lanyon was very fond of my, er, common sense."

He shocked her by grinning. "Well, there you have it."

Selina had never seen a more handsome man than the marquess when he smiled.

***

Caius honestly couldn't recall ever having such a *practical* conversation with a woman. Nor could he believe how much he was enjoying it. He hated to admit it, but what Mrs. Lanyon's mother had told her was correct: most men didn't want to listen to a woman. It shamed him even more to admit that he would have agreed with her assessment until recently, when humility had been forced upon him.

He doubted that he could have come up with the ideas she'd already thought up so quickly and easily. Either because he was simply too close to his own impairment to think clearly or because she was cleverer than he was, or both.

What Caius did know is that he was a beneficiary of her agile mind and would do everything in his power to encourage her.

"You've solved one of the problems, Mrs. Lanyon," he prodded. "What about the board and differentiating the black from the white pieces?"

"Wellll," she drawled after a moment. "What if the game pieces were different shapes for each side? There is no rule saying they must be the same, is there? Couldn't a woodworker carve two entirely different sets?"

"You aren't practical, Mrs. Lanyon."

"I'm not?" she said.

She sounded so forlorn that Caius felt as if he'd just kicked a puppy. "I should have said that you aren't *just* practical. You are something of a practical *genius*."

She gave one of her squawky laughs. "Thank you, my lord."

"It is my pleasure. Now, you have only one more problem to solve: the board."

"Hmmm. I will need to give that some thought. I shall also need to find a woodworker."

"You might ask Morris if old Jem Bascum is still around. He's quite a craftsman and carved one of those griffins on the main staircase, which my father had to have replaced when I was a boy."

"Those are lovely—I never would have guessed they weren't made by the same craftsman."

"Two craftsmen separated by at least three hundred years." Caius smirked. "I will always be grateful to Jem for his clever work."

"Oh?"

"I'm the one who broke the griffin. Some friends and I decided to slide down the bannisters and my foot caught at the end and snapped the griffin's head right off." He grimaced. "It was not a good day."

She laughed. "My sisters and I were caught doing something similar, although there were no griffins involved, only—" she stopped abruptly.

"Only what, Mrs. Lanyon?"

"I was just going to say it was a far less grand staircase."

Caius was certain that his plain-speaking housekeeper had just fibbed. About what, he didn't know.

"Where did you grow up, Mrs. Lanyon?"

It wasn't his imagination that there was a longer than average pause before she said, "Hampshire, my lord."

"And what did your father do in Hampshire?" She was quiet for so long that he felt compelled to add, "I only ask because you are quite accomplished."

"Accomplished?"

Just what was making her so nervous?

He let her stew a moment before answering. "On the piano, for example."

"Oh, that. Yes, I had lessons when I was younger, and my family could still afford a tutor. My father was a freeholder, but our family fell on hard times, and so I went into service."

That would explain both her accent and her less-than servant-like demeanor at times.

"You met your husband after you'd been working?"

"Yes."

Again, he heard that hesitation in her voice.

"Was that while you worked for Chatham or Addiscombe—or was there somebody else?" Caius gave her an apologetic smile. "I'm afraid I didn't ask Morris for your references or I would already know all this."

"Oh, yes."

"So, where did you meet Mr. Lanyon?" he persisted.

A long pause, and then, "When I worked for His Grace."

"Your husband worked for Chatham, too?"

An even longer pause.

"Only temporarily. He was a painter."

"A house painter?"

"Um, no."

"A portrait painter?"

"Yes."

"He must have been of some renown to paint Chatham."

"No, he didn't paint the duke," she said, sounding a bit... harried. "He, erm, cleaned his pictures."

"So... not a portrait painter, but a portrait cleaner, then?"

"That was how he earned his living, but he was a painter, as well," she said, distinctly testy.

"Is it difficult for you to speak about him? Have you been a widow long?"

"No, it is not painful. It has been some time."

Caius allowed the silence to stretch. And stretch. And stretch.

"It has been five years," she admitted, the words sounding as if they'd been squeezed from her lungs.

Caius could practically *smell* the lie this time.

He didn't speak, choosing to let her stew a bit, his thoughts drifting back to earlier, to when she had arrived in the library. She had seemed very... skittish.

Why?

He could think of only one thing that might have shaken his housekeeper's normal stoicism. *Had* Mrs. Lanyon been peeking into his gymnasium last night? Had she watched him? Heard him?

Caius had thought he'd heard a sound come from the open doorway at the time, but once he'd emerged from his post-orgasmic stupor, he'd decided that he'd imagined the noise—or at least he'd imagined its source—and that it must have been the creaking of the old house.

But now... for some reason he was beginning to question that assumption.

Surely his prim housekeeper would have declared herself if she'd come upon him engaging in such an activity?

***

Selina wanted to scream. How had they gone from talking about chessboards to discussing her imaginary dead husband?

And why was his lordship just sitting there and wearing that uncomfortably knowing smile?

Foolishly, Selina had not concocted a story about being a widow. She'd simply not believed that she would ever need it. After all, his lordship had shown no interest in her past or her credentials.

Until today.

And now she had babbled a ridiculous tale about having a painting *cleaner* for a dead husband and had further claimed that she'd been widowed five years when she was almost positive that she'd told Mr. Morris it had been *two*. Or perhaps three?

Selina

Aargh! She was *such* a featherbrain.

On the bright side, she'd not thought about what had happened last night for the past five minutes.

But she was thinking of it now as she sat across the chessboard from him.

She swallowed hard as she studied his handsome, well-groomed person. He bore so little resemblance to the sweaty, naked, animalistic creature she'd watched last night that Selina might have believed she'd imagined the entire episode.

But then a vivid image of his slick, pulsing breeding organ flickered through her mind. No, she couldn't have imagined something she'd never seen before, could she?

Oh, God. Why couldn't she control her willful thoughts?

"Mrs. Lanyon?"

Selina jolted. "Yes, my lord?"

He stood and nodded toward the desk—getting the direction perfect today. "Shall we commence with the morning's business?"

Selina stared at him. His voice and expression were so mild—so... normal.

Could she dare to hope that he'd not guessed it was her, after all?

***

It had definitely been Mrs. Lanyon who'd listened—and probably watched—as Caius had tossed one off in his *supposedly* private boxing parlor last night.

And he was positive that she was lying about her dead husband, too—or lying about how she'd met him or where.

A *painting cleaner*? His lips twitched as he absently listened to Mrs. Lanyon read a letter from Mr. Biggle, the caretaker of his London house. He'd already decided on his reply to Biggle, but he enjoyed the sound of Mrs. Lanyon's voice, so he let her finish reading.

He'd not been entirely certain that she'd seen him last night until she'd brought several letters for him to sign a few moments ago.

She usually just picked up his hand—as if it wasn't attached to his person—and matter-of-factly positioned it over the letter. But today she'd gone to ridiculous lengths to push and shove the letters in such a way that it hadn't required her to touch him. And when he'd accidentally touched her palm with the tip of his fingers when handing her the signet, she'd jolted, causing the ring to bounce off the desk onto the floor.

Caius might be misreading those signs of extreme nervousness, but he didn't think so.

He should be ashamed if his suspicion was true, but he simply couldn't make himself regret it. After all, nobody had forced her to look, had they? He'd left the door open to get some sort of breeze—he didn't like opening his windows because people outside could see in, so he'd opened a window at the opposite end of the corridor.

Doubtless she would have heard him either counting or punching or... grunting. Or even talking to himself like a lunatic. In any event, it should have been clear to her that the room was occupied. If she'd come closer and peeked inside then—

"My lord?"

"Hmm?"

"I said the letter from Mr. Biggle was the last for today. How shall I reply?"

"Please tell him that I've authorized both the work on the roof and the new chimney stack, but that I wish to wait to replace the cookstove."

"Very good, my lord."

Caius heard papers being shuffled.

It was time to speak on the subject he'd been mulling over.

"I have decided that I would like you to read to me each day, Mrs. Lanyon."

The paper shuffling quieted. "You mean you want me to read something other than the newspaper?"

"I would like to continue with the newspapers, but I'd also like to listen to a novel. I was never much for reading fiction, but now..." he trailed off rather than state the obvious.

"I see."

Her voice was so toneless that he couldn't tell if she was annoyed, startled, or pleased by his request.

"If you are over-burdened with your duties, you may engage more help," he said, irked by how defensive his own voice sounded.

"You mean I should hire somebody to read to you?"

"No," he said immediately. "I have learned to tolerate you"—Caius stopped and scowled at her bark of laughter.

"I'm sorry, my lord," she said, not sounding the least bit remorseful.

"Laugh all you want," he snapped, "but I don't want an army of strangers parading through my house and gawking at me."

"No, of course not, my lord."

Was that mockery he heard in her voice? It had better not be.

"I don't want to become accustomed to anyone else, Mrs. Lanyon. At least not yet. So if you need help, hire somebody to do the household tasks."

The pause lengthened and he was about to demand to know what she was thinking when she spoke.

"What book would you like me to read, my lord?"

There. That was the tone he'd wanted: pleasure. She didn't view reading to him as a burden; she sounded as if she would enjoy it. The thought eased the uncomfortable tightness in his chest. She was a servant, paid to do as he bade her, but for some reason Caius didn't want her to consider time spent in his company a nuisance.

"I will leave the choice of novel up to you, Mrs. Lanyon."

"And I may select anything?"

He pursed his lips. "Yes, but don't make me regret placing my trust in you."

"Don't worry, my lord, I promise I won't choose a gothic novel," she said, once again sounding amused. "What time of day would you like me to read to you?"

"I think after dinner."

"Oh."

He bristled at the sound of her flat, monosyllabic response. "I hope that is not an imposition, Mrs. Lanyon?"

"No, of course not, my lord."

He grunted. "Good. Well, that is settled, then. We are done here for now. You may go."

You sound like an autocratic, pompous arse. The woman is giving up her evenings for you. The least you could do is sound grateful.

The real Elton would <u>never</u> have said such a thing, Caius retorted.

Imaginary Elton had no response, but Caius sighed, and said, "Mrs. Lanyon?"

"Yes, my lord?"

"I look forward to whatever book you choose."

Chapter 16

D*ear Linny,*

In vain have I waited for a letter from you. Clearly you are too busy enjoying your exciting new life to write to your poor sister.

Selina chewed her lip, ashamed. Every night—after she finished her far too pleasurable hour with the marquess in the library, reading to him, she came up to her room and sat down to write to Hy. But every night she couldn't seem to decide what to *say*. Lord Shaftsbury was an intensely private man and it just seemed wrong to tell anyone—even her dear sister—too much about him.

But she would have to send *something*, and soon.

She turned back to the letter.

I hope you are enjoying your new wage slavery/freedom.

Selina laughed out loud. Hy was the quietest of her siblings but had a sense of humor that was delightfully dry.

Chatham wants me to say thank you *(there is heavy irony on those words) for leaving him to cope with your two lovelorn swains.*

He expected Fowler to visit him at some point, but Shelton's arrival was quite a surprise.

Given that Fowler and Shelton were punching each other in the face the last time they were in the same room we worried there would be more fisticuffs. But they've been exceptionally well-behaved, although I'd not go so far as to say they like *each other, both of them are bonding in their evasion of Katie.*

Did I mention that Chatham issued an invitation for any and all of our siblings to stay with us for as long as they would like? Am I being terribly obvious about dropping such a hint to you?

Selina chuckled. Her sister had sent three letters in the brief time Selina had been at Shaftsbury's house and all three had not-so-subtly hinted that Selina should go and live with Hy and her brand-new husband.

She might accept their offer at some point, but they should both be able to spend some time alone together before family started to descend on them. Although it sounded like they weren't getting much time alone together right now.

Although it has only been a scant four months since we've last seen our youngest sister, Katie appears to have aged at least five years. Gone is the sixteen-year-old with skinned knees, torn skirts, and flyaway hair. Our aunt has worked something of a miracle on our sister. I'm not sure it is a good *miracle—I think she is too young to be this "man-mad"—but the horse is already out of the barn.*

Selina

Since her arrival Katie has been stalking both Fowler and Shelton with all the predatory skill of an Amazonian warrior. It is quite amusing, and Chatham has laughed until he cried more than once as Fowler—and to a lesser degree—Shelton both try to come up with polite, but firm, ways to dissuade our sister's interest and attention.

Finally, after a rather unfortunate incident involving Shelton and Katie and an afternoon stuck in the weapons room, Chatham summoned his father's spinster sister—the redoubtable Lady Constance—to stay with us. She is ostensibly with us to help me ease into my new role next Season—and she will assist with that, I'm sure—but the real reason for her presence is to chaperone Katie. And probably me, too, although Chatham denies it.

Selina laughed aloud at that. She didn't envy poor Lady Constance; Hy might appear oblivious to most things, but she could be resistant if she felt as if somebody was trying to manage her.

I will end this letter with a plea. May I <u>please</u> give your address to our siblings? I'm sorry to ask, but I'm not sure how much longer I can hold out against the badgering and threats. It isn't just our younger siblings who miss their gentle, loving Linny, but Aurelia, too, has begged me to pass along her desire for correspondence. I'm sure it is no surprise to you that you are everyone's favorite sister. All our lives are a little less bright and cheerful without you in them.

So, may I allow them to write?

Take care of yourself and <u>do</u> write to me soon.

Your loving sister,

Hy

Selina wiped away a few happy tears that had slid out before she could stop them. She knew she wasn't *really* the favorite sibling, but it was lovely of Hy to say that.

She re-read the letter twice more and then stared at the paltry response that she'd started days ago and had not added to since.

Dearest Hy,

First off, I deeply apologize for neglecting you these past weeks. It is no exaggeration to say that I am busy from the moment I wake up in the morning until I fall into bed at night. I don't tell you that so you will feel bad for me, Hy. The amazing thing is that I absolutely love my job.

That was the truth and Selina still couldn't believe how much she enjoyed overseeing the marquess's household. Normally a housekeeper would share the burden with a butler or house steward, but Mr. Morris was tired and weary from dealing with Lord Shaftsbury for almost a year and he'd been grateful to hand over most of the household responsibility to Selina.

The staff was enormous and well-trained and she'd never enjoyed such luxury. The servants were good, hard-working people who knew their jobs well and did them with only a modicum of direction on Selina's part.

She turned back to the letter and wrote:

I know you will scarcely believe it, but I am good at running the marquess's house.

All those years when Mama told me my only duty was to sit quietly, look pretty, and wait for wealthy suitors to flock, it appears I can do something else.

I am going to confide several matters to you that should go no further than Chatham and our siblings—and yes, you may tell them my address and remind them to direct any correspondence to Mrs. S. Lanyon and to use the surname Fletcher for their own name.

Here is the secret you must keep: the marquess suffered the loss of his vision in the accident that killed his wife and three treasured servants. He has, naturally, had a difficult year.

I am pleased to report that he is adjusting to his new circumstances. With time, I believe he will be able to do many of the activities that he used to do.

You know me, Hy, I could not keep my opinion and ideas to myself and forced the poor marquess to listen to tales of our own dear Nick and how he lives and thrives.

Everyone in the marquess's household was too intimidated to suggest changes to his routine, so my first two weeks here were rather an uphill battle, but he is gradually incorporating many of Nick's tools into his life.

I have taken on several non-housekeeping duties like reading to his lordship and helping with his correspondence until such time as he can engage a new steward.

Oh, Hy—how you will laugh to hear that I am reading Pride and Prejudice *to him. I daresay Doddy would weep to learn that his Corinthian hero is enjoying a comedy of manners.*

In a few days his lordship will venture out to one of his tenant properties and I shall serve as his driver and secretary on the journey.

You can see that my days are very full.

I expected this to be an adventure, Hy, but I never expected to enjoy myself so much.

As to the subject of Fowler and Shelton, please apologize to the baron for me. He had a great deal of money and several nice valuables in his pockets. I will return his personal possessions and what remains of the money at some point.

Shelton, not surprisingly, had only a few shillings in his pocket. Oh, and the pistol. I have not yet decided whether to give that back. Lord Shelton is not in my good books, Hy, and you may feel free to tell him as much.

You might also mention to Lord Fowler that the next time he proposes to a female he might try to engage in a few conversations with her beforehand.

Is that terribly cattish of me? Well, they have both earned it. That afternoon at the posting inn was the most mortifying of my life.

But that is enough of that.

Indeed, I am going to end this letter now so that I may send it along tomorrow.

Selina

Take care and do pass along my love to Katie.
Your useful sister,
Selina

***

Selina took a sip of tea to soothe her throat and continued reading:

"May I ask to what these questions tend?" Mr. Darcy asked.

"Merely to the illustration of your character," said Elizabeth, endeavoring to shake off her gravity. "I am trying to make it out."

"And what is your success?"

She shook her head. "I do not get on at all. I hear such different accounts of you as puzzle me exceedingly."

"I can readily believe," answered he, gravely, "that reports may vary greatly with respect to me; and I could wish, Miss Bennett, that you were not to sketch my character at the present moment, as there is reason to fear that the performance would reflect no credit on either."

"But if I do not take your likeness now, I may never have another opportunity."

"I would by no means suspend any pleasure of yours," Mr. Darcy coldly replied—"

Lord Shaftsbury laughed out loud and slapped his knee. "By God I am beginning to like this Darcy fellow."

Selina smirked, secretly delighted that he was enjoying the story so much. When she'd shown up with a copy of the novel—which he had in his very own library—he'd made masculine noises about not caring for *maudlin sorts of melodramas*, but she had reminded him that he'd allowed her to choose.

"Are you sure you wish me to keep reading this story, my lord?" Selina couldn't resist asking now. "Or shall I find something else?"

He gave her the sort of open grin that seemed to come more easily of late, a smile that caused her heart to gallop.

"Are you gloating, Mrs. Lanyon?" He went on before she could answer. "And well you might gloat; this is an exceedingly diverting story."

"Thank you, my lord."

"The author paints no pretty picture of the male of the species. Indeed, he seems determined to depict aristocrats as either toweringly arrogant or featherbrained twits."

"A woman wrote the novel my lord."

"Is that so?"

"Yes. You do not look very surprised at that."

"Why should I be? *Tsk, tsk.* You cannot have a very high opinion of me if you think I'd be surprised to hear a woman is capable of writing a diverting story."

Selina flushed at his accusation because it was exactly what she had thought.

"Ha! I knew it," he said, even though she'd not spoken a word. "Just because I was an adherent of sport does not mean I'm an unlettered ape, you know."

"I don't think that. It's just—"

"I know, I know. We men like to behave as if we are the only ones in possession of any brains. You have proven over and over again that is most emphatically untrue, Mrs. Lanyon."

Selina flushed again, this time with pleasure. "Thank you, my lord. That is very kind."

"No, it's not bloody kind. It's the truth. Er, beg your pardon," he said, giving her a slightly sheepish look.

Lately he'd cursed far less in her presence and had taken to apologizing for his rather colorful language.

"Oh," she said, recalling a piece of good news. "I wanted to tell you that Mr. Bascum has come up with a very clever idea for your chessboard."

"Did he? What is it?"

"He is making the white squares all raised slightly above the black."

Lord Shaftsbury's lips parted. "Why, it's rather obvious now that he has come up with it, isn't it?"

She laughed. "Yes, that is what I thought, too. He should have the board and pieces ready in another two weeks."

"That is good news, indeed."

Selina didn't remind him that her thirty days would be up just before then.

Instead, she said, "Who is your favorite character in the book, my lord?"

"Lord, I don't know. Am I meant to have a favorite?"

"It is permissible," she said, smiling when he laughed.

Selina

"Well, then, I suppose if I had to choose, it would be Darcy. I would not mind meeting such a man. Who is yours?"

As little as two weeks ago she would have said Mr. Darcy without hesitation. Indeed, every young woman Selina knew who'd read the novel was more than half in love with him.

But looking at the flesh and blood man across from her, she now found the fictional creation quite lacking in comparison.

"I would like to meet Elizabeth," she said. "I like how decisive she is, how confident."

"You are also a very strong-minded woman, Mrs. Lanyon. I shudder to think what *two* of you would get up to together."

Selina was strangely flattered, even though she knew she was not at all like the confident, independent woman in the novel. After all, Elizabeth Bennett refused to hide her true self or marry for anything less than love while Selina had *sat quietly and looked pretty* for years while planning to sell herself to the wealthiest suitor.

"I know the book is meant to be a satire or comedy of manners," Lord Shaftsbury said, "but I'm hoping that the tale takes a dark turn and ends with Mr. Bennett throttling his wife and shifting blame for the murder onto the shoulders of that idiot clergyman."

Selina laughed. "I'm afraid you are destined to be disappointed, my lord."

"Ah, as I feared. Well, I already know what the ending will be," he said, a smug look on his handsome face. "Miss Elizabeth Bennett will bring the prideful Mr. Darcy to his knees and her sister—the rather colorless, mealy-mouthed lass whose name is slipping my mind just now—will marry that fool Bingley, although why anyone would want him is beyond me."

"Because he's worth *five thousand pounds a year*," Selina said, affecting the high-pitched, grating voice she used for Mrs. Bennett.

The marquess shuddered. "Good Lord but you do a terrifying impression of that woman."

"It's not hard to guess that those two couples will end up together," Selina pointed out.

"Perhaps not. But I also predict that Mr. Bennett will put Lydia over his knee and finally give her the walloping she so richly deserves."

She laughed again.

"I don't really believe that last bit will happen," Lord Shaftsbury admitted after they'd both had a chuckle. "But I'm sure about the rest of it."

"Why are you so certain about the ending? Have you heard others discussing the book?" Selina had heard countless discussions in the various London drawing rooms where she'd spent a good part of three months.

"Me discussing a book? Lord no. My friends are not the bookish sort and if they were, they'd hardly admit to reading a melodrama."

"I thought perhaps your wife might have mentioned reading it."

Selina knew the words were a mistake the moment they were out of her mouth and silently cursed her infernal curiosity.

His expression cooled in an instant. "If my wife had read it, the last person she would have discussed it with was me."

Selina could see by his pinched expression that he regretted his words almost as much as she had just regretted her question.

He abruptly stood. "That is enough for this evening, Mrs. Lanyon," he said, and then strode confidently toward the decanters that held the spirits he preferred.

It made her heart glad to see how far he'd come in only three weeks.

Which made her remember there was only one week remaining in their bargain. Would he enforce the agreement? She feared he might. He'd certainly made no noises about wanting her to stay on.

Selina sighed, replaced the marker in the book and set it on the side table before standing. "Do you need anything else, my lord?"

"No. I shall see you in the morning," he added, his voice slightly less grim than it had been only a moment earlier. "Recall that you will be taking the reins tomorrow and serving as coachman—or gigs*woman*, as the case may be." He barked a laugh at his own jest. "Good night, Mrs. Lanyon."

"Good night, my lord."

Selina was sorry she'd brought up his wife. It wasn't just cruel—even after a year—but it was also something a real housekeeper would never do.

Truth be told, she'd developed a bit of a mania for learning about the marquess's wife and the sort of marriage he'd had.

Lady Shaftsbury's rooms were still filled with her things. A piece of needlework sat in its tambor, forever awaiting her return, an improving religious tome on the nightstand, and the feminine scent of roses still lingering in the air.

Something about knowing the former marchioness favored that particular flower made the woman more real to Selina.

She had spent more time than she should staring at the full-length portrait in the long gallery. Lady Shaftsbury had been a handsome woman rather than pretty, her most striking feature a pair of large, chocolate brown eyes that were generously fringed. Although she wore a placid expression there was a tightness about her mouth that spoke of deep unhappiness, no matter the painter's facility with the brush.

Beside her hung an excellent likeness of the marquess. It had surprised Selina at first that he'd chosen to be painted in his hunting toggery. The garments were exquisitely tailored but obviously worn and comfortable. He casually cradled a fowling piece while a hound and brace of partridges rested at his feet. His dark curls were windswept, his gaze directed at the viewer, and his thin, mobile lips pulled into a faintly mocking smile, as if he found the entire process of being painted amusing.

It was a portrait that oozed confidence, power, and masculinity. The man in the picture had life at his feet—that was the undeniable message. The man she'd just left upstairs would present a different subject for an artist. No less masculine, but the smile lines had deepened into grooves that spoke of disappointment and suffering.

The marquess might believe himself diminished, but Selina thought he was a far more interesting and complex person now than the carefree sportsman depicted in the portrait.

It was too bad that Selina, a mere servant, could never tell him such a thing.

Chapter 17

"There are some clouds," Selina admitted when Lord Shaftsbury asked her to describe the weather. "But they seem far off—nothing that will bother us until later in the day, long after we have returned to Courtland."

At least she hoped so; Selina positively *loathed* storms, unlike Aurelia and Hy, who used to creep up to the attic on stormy nights and crawl out to the miniscule belvedere that crowned their family home, Queen's Bower. They'd cackle like Shakespeare's witches and let the wind and rain lash them until their hair was wild and their nightgowns were soaked.

Selina had gone up there once at their urging. Vertigo and a crushing terror of lightening had paralyzed her with fear so that Hy had needed to carry her back inside.

That had been the one and only time she'd been so foolish.

"The ride to the Tanner farm will take at least an hour." The marquess's mouth pulled down at the corners. "If you think we will be caught in foul weather, then—" He stopped and swallowed, his normally pale face even paler.

Selina knew why he was agitated; his carriage accident had been caused by bad weather. But that had been while traversing one of those dreadful passes in the Lake District, Hardknott or Kirkstone or some such. Still, if the storm was what he remembered…

"We don't need to go today," Selina said quietly.

His eyebrows snapped down in the center, giving his face a vaguely satanic cast, and he scowled. "You promised me no pity, Mrs. Lanyon."

"Yes, sir. I apologize."

"Ring for the gig—tell Thomas to make sure the hood is in working order as the thing is so rarely used. And then go fetch your cloak and bonnet. I will meet you outside."

Selina hesitated, still not sure this was the best idea.

"Go!" he barked.

"Yes, my lord." Selina swallowed down her worries as she hurried from the room. If he wanted to go, then they would go.

When she got down to the foyer a scant ten minutes later Lord Shaftsbury wasn't there, so she opened the door and then paused on the threshold.

Edgar, one of the grooms, held the gig horse's head while his lordship walked around the small conveyance. His expression was thoughtful, and she knew he was pacing off distances. Even though Selina closed the door quietly he must have heard her because he turned.

"Mrs. Lanyon?"

"Yes, I'm here."

He walked toward the front of the carriage, using his cane with one hand, and held out the other toward her. "Come, let's be off."

Selina smiled—proud of him—and took his hand to climb up. "Thank you, my lord," she murmured, picking up the reins while the marquess passed back behind the gig and then climbed up. If his movements were less than graceful, she knew they'd get better the next time, and the next.

She nodded to the groom—who was watching the marquess with curious eyes—and then clucked her tongue and they were rolling away from Courtland.

"You will turn right when we reach the end of the drive," the marquess said after a moment of silence.

Selina had driven small carts and carriages all her life, but her father's household was poor and the gig they'd used these past few years had been around since the time of the first George. Their one remaining horse—Minnie—was gray-muzzled, phlegmatic, and prone to expelling gas at the most embarrassing moments.

This was an entirely different experience and Selina held the reins lightly, pleased that the horse was neither spavined nor overly frisky.

Lord Shaftsbury sat face forward, his top hat casting a shadow and obscuring his expression. At first glance, he looked relaxed and calm, but his fisted hands—which rested on his thighs—told another story. She wanted to say something comforting, but suspected the kindest thing she could do was pretend she didn't notice.

Once she had turned onto the main road he spoke again. "You'll go three-quarters of a mile and take another right just past the mile post. I'm afraid the road to Tanner's farm isn't the smoothest. It's more of a cart track, truth be told, and it will be a bumpy journey from there on."

"This is an exceptionally well-sprung gig." And the seat was generously padded and comfortable.

His mouth pulled down at the corners. "It was my wife's. Her father had it specially made for her as a wedding gift."

She grimaced, wishing she'd not mentioned the carriage.

He turned to her, his pupils mere pinpricks, his silvery gray eyes even paler in the sunlight. "You needn't flog yourself for bringing up a subject that touches on my dead wife, Mrs. Lanyon."

Selina felt a bit flustered that he'd known what she was thinking. "Are you a mind reader, then, my lord?" she asked tartly, even though a real servant wouldn't take such a tone or ask such a question.

He smiled wryly. "It doesn't take a mind reader to notice how everyone clams up whenever I mention my wife—or how people go to great pains not to say her name."

"It is called common courtesy, my lord. Perhaps—being a peer and uncommon—you weren't aware of it?"

The grin he flashed her squeezed the breath from her lungs: *this* was the Lord Shaftsbury she'd heard about—the charming, handsome heartbreaker. "Touché, Mrs. Lanyon."

"You wife must have loved the country for her father to have given her such a gift."

"She loathed it. Not once did she use it—at least not to my knowledge."

Selina frowned. "Then—then why did he buy it for her? Did he know her so little?"

"I daresay he hoped that she would come to love living in the country."

"Do you think she would have?" Selina couldn't help asking.

He shrugged, the gesture emphasizing the breadth of his shoulders and the perfect fit of his black clawhammer coat, which covered his body so sleekly it moved with his slightest gesture. He seemed larger out of doors than he did in his house, which she thought was odd. Perhaps it was because this was his natural milieu.

"She didn't like Courtland and she didn't like London," the marquess said.

"Was there some place she did like?"

"Bristol." His chin dipped and he turned his hands palm up, as if he were studying them. "Her father owned shipyards, mines, munitions manufactories—all sorts of different businesses. He was something of a financial genius. She'd spent her entire life in Bristol." He pursed his lips. "He made her go to London and she hated it. She hated the people—who looked down on her—and the parties. She hated me," he said in a toneless voice.

Selina's lips parted, but she could not think of a single thing to say. His wife had *hated* him?

The marquess continued without a response. "Her father and I arranged the wedding between us. Louisa said *yes* to my proposal, not because she wanted to, but because it was her duty. The same reason I asked her to be my wife: duty. It turned out that our obedience to duty was the only thing we had in common." He cleared his throat and looked up from his hands, staring straight ahead. "Let me tell you about the Tanner farm so that you will know what to look for when we arrive," he said, obviously finished with the acutely personal subject.

***

Caius was relieved when they reached his tenant farmer's house, even though it meant more staring and awkwardness. But nothing could be as awkward as the atmosphere in the gig after he'd poured out the depressing details of his marriage to Mrs. Lanyon. Not only was the story of how he'd met and married Louisa dismal, but—in hindsight—there was something mercenary and distasteful about reducing marriage to such a commercial transaction.

He'd also felt like a damned sack of turnips just sitting on the bench, letting a woman drive—something that had never happened in his adult life. Indeed, the last time he'd been driven by a female was when he'd been a boy—maybe six or seven—and his mother had made him come along when she'd delivered the obligatory calf's foot jelly, old clothing, and improving religious tracts to Courtland's poorer tenants.

"These people are your responsibility, Caius, not just their physical well-being, but their eternal salvation. You must remain vigilant and root out any diseases of the spirit as well as the flesh."

Caius had forgotten that lesson until his new housekeeper had reminded him of his duty toward his people—albeit omitting the part about saving their souls from hellfire.

When they reached Tanner house, Mrs. Lanyon stopped the carriage and then waited for Caius to help her down. It was a small thing—disembarking from a gig and walking around it to help a woman—but it made him feel marginally less pathetic.

"Welcome, my lord," Tanner said in the over-bright tone that people tended to use with Caius these days, as if he'd lost his wits *and* his hearing in addition to his sight.

"You do us great honor, my lord," Mrs. Tanner chimed in while Caius stood beside his housekeeper and stared—he hoped—in the right direction.

He could feel the Tanner family's eyes—a good eleven or twelve pairs of them, counting their assembled children—crawling all over his person.

"This is my housekeeper, Mrs. Lanyon. She is here to make note of the damage," he said, not sure why he bothered to explain her presence. Caius wasn't accustomed to caring about what his servants and tenants thought or wondered and he found it irksome. He suspected his newfound concern could only be due to his unconventional housekeeper.

He shoved aside the useless thought and said, "Perhaps you might show us around, Tanner."

"Of course, my lord."

For the next hour or so the farmer and his wife led them around the farm, house, and outbuildings, Mrs. Tanner talking ten to the dozen while her husband only added the occasional comment.

Caius asked questions—something that was actually easier than he'd dared to hope—and Mrs. Lanyon wrote down the pertinent details. While it was true that he couldn't see the current condition of the property, he recalled it well enough from memory that he could visualize the repairs that were needed.

Once they'd toured everything that needed to be looked at—and more—Mrs. Tanner invited them into the house to have some refreshment.

Caius didn't know why he hadn't expected the invitation, but it temporarily robbed him of words.

Thankfully, Mrs. Lanyon was prepared. "Thank you so much, Mrs. Tanner, but his lordship has two other appointments today," she lied.

Regrets were expressed all around and they took their leave. Soon they were rumbling along on the rutted, pitted, rocky road, Caius's back jolting painfully.

"I thought that went… well," Mrs. Lanyon said once they were well out of earshot of the Tanners.

Caius grunted.

She chuckled. "Was that a *yes*, my lord?"

It was hard not to smile at her infectious laughter and teasing tone, but Caius managed. "It was fine," he admitted grudgingly. "But there are another ten or fifteen journeys to make just like this one before the summer is through."

"That is true," she said. "Which is why I wanted to talk to you about hiring a new steward and secretary.

Caius frowned. "Why? You did well enough today." She'd done better than well enough, and he knew he should say so, but something held him back. Was it just because she was a woman? Could he really be that big of a pigheaded arse?

Yes, Elton's dry voice answered.

"My thirty days are almost over, my lord. It would be best to hire somebody sooner rather than later."

Dammit! He'd forgotten about that blasted thirty-day agreement.

"You've taken another position?" he asked.

"Not yet."

"Then you can stay longer," he declared.

Silence met his arrogant declaration.

Why don't you try <u>asking</u>. Nicely.

Caius cleared his throat. "I will naturally increase your wages," he said, hoping she didn't hear the desperation beneath his words.

But before she could answer, a deafening crack of thunder shook the humid air.

"Damnation," he muttered, gripping the railing beside the bench seat. "Why didn't you tell me the storm had come our way?" he asked.

"It—I didn't—"

Another crack, this one louder than the last, cut off her words.

Caius scowled, furious at the way his heart had started to pound at the sound of a little thunder. "Did you get a chance to count?" he asked.

"Yes. It was seven seconds between the lightning and thunder." Her voice shook and she didn't sound like the same woman as a mere moment earlier.

"Is something amiss, Mrs. Lanyon?"

"Er, I'm not exactly fond of—"

More thunder blotted out her last words.

"Good Lord," he muttered. "That was fast."

"Five," she said, her voice shaking.

"That sounded closer."

"Yes."

"We need shelter. Where are we?"

"I—I don't know—I'm not—"

"I know you are frightened, Mrs. Lanyon, but you must help me. I need you to be my eyes. What do you see around us?"

"A—a field of barley on the right and a stream on the left."

"Do you see a bridge?"

"No."

"Do you remember the last mile post?"

"Uhm, I think it was seven, or maybe six."

Caius closed his eyes, which seemed necessary to imagine a map in his mind's eye.

"Do you see trees up ahead—a great many of them?"

"Yes, on the right-hand side."

"Good. We will head for those trees. There is a gamekeeper shack not too far off the road. You will need to go faster, Mrs. Lanyon," he said quietly but firmly when more thunder rumbled.

There was only a brief hesitation before she clucked her tongue and snapped the reins. Caius was glad he was already clutching the railing when the cart bolted, and he braced his feet and tugged down the brim of his hat when he felt it lifting off of his head.

Beside him, she laughed, the sound giddy and slightly hysterical. "I'm sorry," she said in a breathless voice. "I've never gone this fast before."

Although Caius couldn't see, he could feel and hear, and he doubted they were going above three miles an hour. Memories of reckless races in his curricle bombarded him as the wind kicked up. It was a far cry from a mad dash to Brighton like the time he'd beaten the Duke of Westmoreland, but it was exhilarating, all the same.

His lips twisted into a self-deprecating smile. *This* is what he'd been reduced to: enjoying a dash in a gig down a country lane, driven by a woman. Strangely, the thought didn't depress him as much as he would have expected.

"I see a turn ahead," she said, her shrill voice interrupting his thoughts. "It is right before an exceptionally large elm."

"That's the one, ma'am. You might want to slow down just a bit before you turn," he added, just as a fat drop of rain struck his nose.

She slowed the gig but still took the turn fast enough that Caius had to lean against it.

Yet again she laughed, but this time there was more pleasure than fear in the sound.

Caius didn't realize he was smiling like an idiot until he reached up to wipe the rain from his face.

Chapter 18

The rain was coming down in sheets by the time they reached the gamekeeper's cottage. His lordship had not been jesting, it really *was* a shack, perhaps the size of Selina's bedchamber, shutters rather than glass covering the single window.

"I don't suppose you know how to release the horse from the carriage?" Lord Shaftsbury asked, needing to raise his voice to be heard above the rain.

"I'm sorry, my lord, but I've not seen a set-up such as this one before."

He nodded, his wet face expressionless. "Bring the gig as close as you can to the lean-to just off the back of the shack."

Selina did as he bade her. When she brought the horse to a halt Caius hopped down, made his way around the back of the gig, and held out a hand for her. Even a week ago he'd not have been able to navigate such a simple task so efficiently.

Once she was beside him, he said, "I'm afraid you'll need to hold my walking stick and wait for me to unhook Bessie, so that you can guide her into the stall."

"Of course," she said, clutching his cane and watching as he felt his way to the rather bewildering looking array of straps and buckles on Bessie's harness, which looked nothing like the simple gig attachments she was familiar with.

His fingers were surprisingly deft as he methodically unhooked the gig shaft.

A bolt of lightning illuminated the slate sky and Selina jolted as she whispered the seconds.

Only three. It was close. They needed to hide—to get out of the storm before—

"*Mrs. Lanyon.*"

His emphatic tone told her that wasn't the first time he'd spoken her name.

"Yes, my lord?"

"The horse is skittish. Go stand by her head—talk to her, tell her everything will be fine and not to be scared," he said, giving her a faint smile. Drops of rain clung to his thick eyelashes, and his pupils were the same gray as the sky. "All will be well, Mrs. Lanyon," he added when she couldn't seem to move. "We are almost finished."

Selina nodded jerkily, recalled that he couldn't see, and said, "Yes, my lord." She moved to the horse's head. "You're a good girl, Bessie. His lordship is taking care of you. All will be well," she murmured, stroking the nervous horse's soft nose while more lightning lit up the sky, the charge in the air raising the small hairs on her neck. "G-good girl. We'll be—" she broke off when something brushed her arm.

The marquess was beside her. He lightly grasped her elbow and smiled down at her. "Hand me my cane." Selina did so. "Good, now lead Bessie into the stall, Mrs. Lanyon. Go ahead," he gently urged when she just stared.

Selina nodded, exhaled shakily, and guided the jittery horse into the narrow stall with calming words. Once she'd shut the low gate, she turned to find his lordship standing right where she'd left him.

Stop being such a terrified ninny, she mentally chastised. *He needs your help; he has no idea where he is right now.*

Calmed by the thought, she raised her voice to be heard over the wind and rain and said, "I'm going to take your right arm."

He nodded and they left the meager protection of the overhang and made their way toward the shack. Selina needed to push the door all the way open to cast enough light before she could recognize the outline of a table, two chairs and a cot within the small structure.

"I need to leave the door open as it's so dark I can't see," she said once they'd stepped inside out of the rain.

"The gamekeeper usually leaves a hand-candle and tinderbox on the windowsill."

"Yes, I see it." Selina glanced toward the table and chairs. "Go four steps forward and you will encounter a small wooden table with two chairs."

He nodded and followed her directions.

Once he'd seated himself, Selina took a few minutes to light the candle and then closed the door just as a bolt of lightning struck close enough that light flashed through the gaps in the rude wooden shutter.

She squeezed her eyes shut when the thunder struck. This time, the sound was different—a violent *pop* and *woosh* followed the rumble.

"Did it strike the horse shed?" the marquess asked, getting to his feet.

Selina opened the door a crack and gasped. "No, it hit a tree. My goodness, it's flaming like an enormous torch. I can't believe how much of it is burning, even in all this rain."

He came to stand beside her, his eyes staring in the direction of the tree, almost as if he could see the bright fire beyond.

"Can you see anything at all, my lord?" she couldn't help asking.

"I can see shadows," he said his nostrils flaring slightly as smoke drifted toward them. He turned toward her. "I *think* I can see you—am I looking at you?"

"Yes, you are," she said. "What do you see?"

"Not much, you're just a dark smudge." He hesitated and then said, "It's like looking through very, very murky water." He turned back to the tree. "Sometimes—like now—I can see faint flickers of color—red and yellow."

"The fire."

"Yes, fire is often visible. But not all the time."

"Is—do you think it is getting better over time?"

His lips tightened and he shook his head. "No. I have not noticed an improvement."

"Did the doctor—"

"He didn't know. He said it might get a little better or it might always be this way. He cautioned against any... expectations." He returned to his chair without waiting for a response.

Selina shut the door and studied him for a moment, chewing her lip. For the first time it occurred to her that she—an unmarried maiden—was utterly alone with a man. And not just any man, but with her handsome, incredibly appealing, employer.

A shiver wracked her, and she noticed that her light summer cloak was soaking wet. A quick look at his lordship showed the same was true for his clawhammer, although his leather breeches might have repelled the rain.

"I'm going to build a fire," she said.

He nodded, his expression blank, as if he'd gone somewhere else.

Selina pulled her gaze from him and bustled about. The fire had already been laid in the hearth so all she'd needed to do was get it started. There was a tripod and a kettle and a quick look through the only two cupboards yielded a dented tin of tea.

She stared at the small wooden bucket she'd found. Doubtless there was a well or stream nearby, but she hardly wanted to go running around looking for water with lightning setting trees on fire. Instead, she opened the door and glanced around; rain was pouring off the roof in sheets.

"Where are you going?" the marquess asked, a hint of anxiety in his voice.

"I thought I'd make some tea—I just needed some water."

"The stream is behind the horse shed, but you shouldn't go out there now."

"No, I'll just collect some rainwater that's running off the roof. I know it is not ideal, but—"

"It will be fine. And it's better than wandering about."

Selina hurriedly set out the bucket and then closed the door. "Your coat is soaked, my lord. If you remove it, I can dry it in front of the fire."

He stood and hesitated. "I shall need some assistance getting it off."

"Oh, of course." Selina moved to stand behind him and helped him ease the tightly tailored shoulders and sleeves off once he'd unbuttoned it. The garment molded to his muscular form like oil on water, the expensive wool damp beneath her fingers. He smelled so good—like rain, leather, and a hint of spicy cologne—that a powerful, aching need flooded her. She leaned forward to press her face to his back and fill her lungs with his scent and—

"Mrs. Lanyon?"

Selina startled, her nose barely an inch from his silk waistcoat, and jerked back. "Oh, er, sorry," she muttered.

Once she was a safe distance from his intoxicating person, she shook out his coat and hung it over the back of the other chair.

Her own garments were soaked through and clammy on her skin, the little building so damp and cool that her teeth chattered.

"What is that sound?" he asked.

"Er, that is my teeth."

"Good Lord, woman. Go stand close to the fire."

"I am, but my cloak was not enough to keep me dry."

"Take it off."

"I did. My dress is wet, too."

"Take it off, as well."

"My lord!"

"What?" His lips twitched. "It's not as if I can see you. Why should you freeze if you don't have to? If I recall, there is a cot in here—is there a blanket on it?"

"Yes."

"Take off your wet things and wrap up in a blanket if you are concerned about modesty."

Selina stared at him, her heart pounding faster and sending a rush of blood pulsing through her that warmed her.

He smirked. "I'll even close my eyes if you like."

She gave a choked laugh. "I suppose it is foolish to freeze."

"Very."

She slowly stripped down to her stays, chemise, stockings. She deliberated taking off her ankle boots—which were wet as well—but decided they were warmer than bare feet.

Lord Shaftsbury kept his eyes dutifully closed as she wrapped the blanket around her body, fashioning it like a toga, of which she'd seen many at the masquerade balls she'd attended this past Season.

"There; I am garbed like a Roman. You may open your eyes now."

His gray eyes were a dark silver in the low light, his expression stern and unsmiling as he stared straight at her.

Foolishly, Selina's face heated. "I'll—I'll just check the water." She hurried outside.

The bucket was nowhere near full but had enough in it to yield a few cups of tea. Once she'd set the kettle to boil and added a few more pieces of wood to the fire she sat down on the cot, causing the ancient ropes to squeak.

The marquess's head whipped around. "What was that?"

"It's the cot," she explained. "I'm using the other chair to dry our things."

He stood. "Take my chair."

"I'm fine here, my lord. Really, I am quite comfortable."

He hesitated, as if he might argue, but then nodded and sat.

Another crack of thunder shook the shack and Selina yelped before she could help it.

"I'm so sorry," she said when he jolted at the sound. "I don't like thunder, even though I know it's the lightning that is dangerous."

"You needn't worry; we will be safe in here."

"You don't think the lightning will hit the building like it did that tree?"

"No."

Selina raised her eyebrows at his confident answer. "Whyever not?"

"Lightning rarely strikes structures."

"Really?"

"Yes."

"Are you just saying that to make me feel better?"

"Yes."

She laughed, the sound slightly hysterical.

"Tell me about your family," he said. "I know you mentioned sisters and a brother."

"Are you trying to distract me, my lord?"

"Yes."

She chuckled and this time it sounded more normal.

"But I'd also like to hear about them," he said.

His interest warmed her; masters rarely took a personal interest in their servants. "What do you want to know?"

"How many are you? Are you the oldest? Youngest? Are your siblings married? Do they work? Where do they live? Do you have nieces and nephews? Anything."

"Goodness," she murmured at the barrage of questions. "There are six of us. I am the third eldest. Only two of us are married and both of them married recently." *Very recently.*

"Other than you."

Selina blinked in confusion. "I'm sorry?"

"Only two are married other than you."

Selina bit back a groan. What a *fool* she was. "Yes, of course—that is what I meant: except me."

His lids lowered slightly and she dreaded his next question, but he merely sat and waited for her to speak.

"The ones who married are closest in age to me." She paused and then added, "Nobody ever thought either of them would marry."

"Oh, why is that?"

"Well, my next oldest sister never evinced any interest in men at all." Selina still couldn't believe that Hy had married the catch of the decade—and that it was a love match. "The only thing she seemed to like was playing cards—or so we'd believed."

Lord Shaftsbury laughed. "Indeed?"

"Yes, when we were growing up, she often dressed as a boy and sneaked out of our parents' house to go and gamble."

The marquess was openly grinning now. "Is she any good?"

"Very. I didn't know *how* good she was until we were living in London and she won hundreds of pounds. She met her husband in a gambling hell. He thought she was a young man at first."

He laughed. "What a story they will have to tell their children. She sounds like an interesting woman."

"She is. We always thought she was brilliant—and warm and funny, too—but… Well, she is not classically pretty and she is *very* reserved and that combination meant that most men didn't bother to see beyond either of those things until her husband."

"When did you live in London?"

"I beg your pardon?"

"You just mentioned living in London," he reminded her. "It mustn't have been long ago as you said she only married recently."

Selina cursed herself, scrambling to come up with something convincing. "Oh, I didn't live there, I was just visiting my sister. My older sister." There was another lie she would have to remember. Drat!

"This was after you left Chatham's?"

Selina's mind whirled as she tried to recall what she'd told him. "Um, oh, the water is boiling." She leapt up and hurried to the kettle. "There is a knob of sugar left—would you like some?"

When he didn't answer, she paused in her bustling to look at his face. He wore the strangest expression. Selina couldn't decide what it meant.

Chapter 19

Why did Mrs. Lanyon keep lying to him—and she *was* lying, even somebody who didn't know her well could hear it. What was that business about living in London and then *not* living in London?

Caius felt the air move, smelled a hint of lavender, and then heard a soft *thunk* on the table.

"The mug is at three o'clock, my lord."

"Thank you." Caius now recalled that he had not eaten or drunk tea in front of her before. Well, he was parched and he could hardly send her outside while he consumed his cup, could he?

He gingerly extended his hand, pleased when the mug was exactly where she'd said.

A moment later the cot creaked and they sipped in silence.

"Go on," he ordered, when it was clear that she wasn't going to resume her lying without some prodding. "You'd told me about one sister, what about the other one who just married?"

"Oh, yes. Erm, well, I've not met her husband yet. I was—I was working and couldn't get away for her wedding. But he is quite a successful merchant and will be able to help our parents."

"Your mother and father are still alive?"

"Yes."

"And is she a card sharp, as well?"

Her enticing laughter filled the room. "Phoebe? Oh, no, not in the least. She is the practical one among us."

"More practical than *you*?"

"Yes, far more. Indeed, she is so efficient that my skills were hardly necessary when we were growing up. Phoebe has managed the household since she was scarcely more than a child."

"Why is that? Is your mother ill?"

"No, not ill, but… well, my mother was the only daughter of a wealthy merchant, and she was raised with… expectations."

"Ah," he said, the picture becoming clearer. So that must have been why his housekeeper was uncharacteristically forthright in her manner and knew how to play the piano so exquisitely. Although her accent wasn't that of a Cit. "Did you go to school?"

"No, there wasn't money enough for that. My, er, my father was not a prudent manager of my mother's inheritance."

She sounded too grim for him to pry any more in that direction. Instead, he asked, "What about your other siblings? The one who was ill?"

"Ill?"

Caius almost laughed. "Yes, you remember—the reason you no longer work for Chatham?"

"Oh! Yes, that was my oldest sister, who earns her crust in a most unconventional manner."

Her words fired Caius's imagination. "Indeed?"

"She is an illustrator for scientific journals and articles."

Hmph. That wasn't at all what he'd expected. It also didn't sound like a lie. How interesting…

"She must be very good at what she does."

"Aurelia is very skilled, but she has to disguise her sex in order to sell her work."

"Aurelia. That's a pretty name. One called Phoebe, one Aurelia—and the cardsharp, what is her name?"

"Um, Hyacinth."

There was that tentative note, again.

"Another pretty and usual name. What is your name, Mrs. Lanyon—if I may be so bold?"

She cleared her throat. "Selina."

"Selina Lanyon—that quite twists one's tongue."

She gave a startled laugh "It does, a bit," she said, as if it had never occurred to her before. "What is *your* Christian name, my lord? Er—if I may be so bold," she said her words a mocking echo of his.

"You've read all my correspondence and you've paid all my bills and you still don't know my first name?"

"I don't recall an instance of it coming up. You always just sign with *Shaftsbury*."

"I suppose you are correct. My name is Caius."

"That is unusual—how do you spell it?"

"You've probably heard it pronounced the more traditional way, which sounds like *Guy-us* but my mother was from Cambridge and there it is more commonly pronounced *Keys*, so that is how she said it."

"Keys," she repeated. The sound of his name on her tongue caused goose pimples to rise on his cool, damp skin.

Outside the wind picked up and the rain drummed more heavily on the flimsy roof of the shack.

"The rain seems to be getting worse," she said, concern coloring her words.

"I haven't heard any thunder in a while—have you seen any hint of lightning?"

"No," she admitted, still tentative.

"Then it will be moving away from us," he assured her. "Where did you live when you were married?" he asked. If nothing else, making up lies would keep her thoughts off the weather.

"When I was married?" she repeated, clearly stalling for time.

Caius smirked. "Yes, when you were married. To Mr. Lanyon, the painting cleaner," he reminded her.

"Of course I recall who I was married to," she snapped. "We lived in Hampshire."

Before he could ask if that was before or after treating her ill sister, a vicious gust of wind shook the shack and Mrs. Lanyon yelped.

Caius heard the bed ropes squeak and the sound of hurried footsteps. He stood. "What is wrong?"

"I forgot to put the fender back and the wind came down the chimney and blew the coals out of the hearth. It snuffed out the candle, too—but I can see bits of red all over the wood floor," she added in a breathy voice, the sound of scuffling and hurried movements filled the air.

Caius stood, struck with a familiar, gut-wrenching powerlessness. The house could burn down around their ears, and he couldn't do a damned thing to help her.

Anger and frustration built inside him, and it was a struggle to swallow it down. Just when he began to feel that he might adjust and find a new way to live, he was forced to admit how useless he was, and how dependent he would always be on others. He could memorize his way around his house, or around the back of a carriage, but doing anything impromptu or responding to emergencies would forever be beyond his ability.

An abyss of despair yawned before him, and Caius had to force himself to turn away from it. Instead, he said, "Can you extinguish all the embers, or should we leave?"

"I've kicked most of the big pieces into the hearth, I'm just making sure there aren't any hiding under the cot or table." After a few moments she said, "There, I think I got them all. But it is very dark now and the few remaining coals don't cast much light. I'm coming toward you, my lord. I left the candle and tinder box on the table across from you," she explained.

Caius heard shuffling steps and then the table jolted, followed by a soft, pained, feminine grunt.

Without thinking, he reached out. It was fortunate that his hand encountered an arm—a *bare* arm—rather than some other, more private, part of her body. "Did you hurt yourself?"

"I just hit the edge of the table with my hip."

"It is really that dark?" he asked, loath to release her, although he did loosen his grip.

"Yes, the fire is just a few dying coals."

Caius was painfully aware of the fact that she hadn't moved away from his hand.

"You could not see the fire when it was still burning?" she suddenly asked.

"No. It must be a roarer before anything gets through."

They stood there, neither of them moving. The soft skin of her inner arm was like the finest silk against the pads of his fingers.

"Tell me what you see," he said gruffly, his heart pounding.

"A few lumps of red in the hearth, faint hints of gray between the slats of the shutters, and you." He heard her swallow. "Although you're just a shadowy lump."

He smiled. "Ah… shadowy lumps. Yes, I'm familiar with those." He lowered his voice. "Then we are almost even, for a change."

"Yes," she said, the word so soft he could barely hear it. Her voice was breathless, and he heard something that sounded like… anticipation.

Caius felt it, too—his skin so sensitive it was almost painful, his breathing roughening, as if every lungful was a labor.

When was the last time he'd felt this alive?

This… reckless?

"You were out in the corridor that night—it was you watching me, wasn't it?" Caius didn't explain what he meant. Either she would admit it, or she wouldn't.

It might have been a few seconds or several minutes, time seemed to change shape as he waited in the darkness—but not alone, this time.

"Yes."

Blood roared in his ears and, although it was cool and damp, Caius was sweating as if he'd spent an hour in his gymnasium. "What did you see, Mrs. Lanyon?" he asked in a raspy voice.

"I saw... everything."

Caius was hard—painfully so. The desire he felt for this woman—whom he'd only known a few weeks and had never even seen—baffled and excited him. Why did he want her so damned badly? Why was he asking her about his shameless behavior that night?

Just what was it about her?

For first time in his life, he'd wanted the woman herself, rather than her face or body.

It was... terrifying.

And exhilarating.

His hand tightened on her arm, and he heard her breath catch. "You must have lingered if you saw *everything*."

"Yes."

"Why?"

This time he heard her swallow before she said, "Because it was... exciting." She hesitated and then added in a voice that shook, "And it was beautiful."

Her words left him flushed with ridiculous pride, as if stroking his cock was something to be proud of and not an activity that every adolescent boy in Britain did three times a day.

"How did you know it was me?" She sounded embarrassed but also curious.

"I don't know." He paused, threw common sense and caution to the winds, and said, "I just hoped it was."

Caius heard a gulping sound and then, "W-why?"

"Because I liked the thought of your eyes on me." His face was so bloody hot that it was probably glowing. He knew he should be ashamed that he was confessing such feelings, but he couldn't regret feeling so alive.

"Mrs. Lanyon?"

"Yes, my lord."

"I find that I am teetering on a precipice."

"Oh?"

"If you step away from me right now, we can forget this conversation ever happened and I will never mention that night again."

"Or?" She'd come closer, so close that he felt hot breath on his chin and smelled black tea and lavender.

"I want to kiss you."

She didn't hesitate. "Yes... please."

He smiled like an idiot. "I need to feel you—" he stopped and chuckled. "That sounded naughtier than I meant. I just—"

"I know what you mean. It is how you see me—with your fingers and hands."

Caius took that as permission and slid his hand from her forearm, where it still rested, up to her bare shoulder. "You really did strip down to your underthings," he said, his voice embarrassingly hoarse.

"Did you doubt me?"

"I wondered," he admitted.

Her shoulder was delicately boned and gently sloped toward a neck that felt elegant and swanlike.

Her breathing quickened when his fingers gently traced the curve of her jaw. She had sleek, velvety eyebrows, a small, upturned nose, and a determined little chin—her face heart-shaped.

He lifted his other hand and let the pads of his fingers graze her silky hair, which was plaited and coiled into a crown.

Caius saved the best for last, his lungs wheezing as if he were running while he caressed the incredible plushness of a lower lip that was surely a work of art.

She felt...

"Beautiful," Caius whispered, and then he lowered his mouth over hers.

**

Beautiful.

Selina had heard the word applied to her countless times over the course of her life, but never with such reverence or wonder.

Or desire.

There were hints of surprise and even a faint whiff of relief beneath those other emotions. Selina had to smile at the latter reaction: the marquess had wanted to kiss her even before he'd known how she looked. He'd wanted *her*—the person who inhabited her body, not her blue eyes or blond hair or dimples.

Why did he want her? Because he liked being badgered and argued with? Because she cared about him and whether he got out of bed and found a life worth living? Or was it just a matter of convenience: because she was right in front of him? Could she have been any woman?

Those thoughts and more raced through her mind, her heart beating nineteen to the dozen as he explored her with light touches that sent delicious shivers through her body.

He was big and warm, towering over her in the darkness, but his fingers were so gentle he might have been touching a work of spun glass. He took his time, his caresses careful yet thorough, as if she were something rare and worth savoring.

Selina forgot about the howling wind and pouring rain that battered the building and felt only *him*. She moaned softly as satin lips brushed against hers, swaying toward him. His chest was hard and warm against her aching breasts and her nipples were suddenly so sensitive they chafed against the fine muslin of her chemise.

Her fingers slid over the warm buckskin covering his narrow hips and he gave an approving growl, his head tilting and his lips pressing harder as they opened, the hot slick caress of his tongue causing flutters in her belly and lower.

Selina had kissed with tongues once before—years ago—but it had been sloppy and rather… disgusting.

This was a masterful, erotic invasion, the tip of his clever tongue stroking and teasing—luring her own tongue out until she was boldly, if clumsily, exploring. She grabbed him harder, her fingers digging into the taut flesh of his waist.

He lightly skimmed up and down her spine, venturing lower with each sweep of his hand, until he was grazing her bottom, pulling her tighter against him, the hard ridge she'd spied that night digging into her belly.

He groaned and cradled her head with one hand, holding her close with the other and deepening his sensual invasion.

Selina couldn't get near enough—she wanted to climb him, to taste and squeeze and investigate every inch of him with her mouth, hands, and body. A whimper of frustration rose above the wind and rain, and she was vaguely aware that it had come from her.

His lordship must have heard it, too, because he slowly raised his head. "Oh, Mrs. Lanyon, how can such a very, very bad idea feel so damned good?"

***

The words slipped out of Caius's mouth before he'd thought them and he stiffened at the sound of her name—Mrs. Lanyon—a stark reminder of what he had momentarily forgotten: they were master and servant, and Caius was a bloody dog bent on debauching his own housekeeper.

It took an inhuman amount of effort to step away from her—to release her lush curves when every fiber of his being wanted to throw her onto the cot and bury himself so deeply inside her that they became one.

It would be ecstasy.

For a while.

But afterward it would be unbearably awkward. He might even lose her if she was too embarrassed to continue working for him.

He allowed himself one last caress of her sweetly curved jaw before pulling completely away. "I apologize, Mrs. Lanyon."

The was a long pause before she moved away.

"It was just a kiss, my lord. There is no harm done."

She didn't *sound* angry…

Caius didn't know whether to feel relieved or insulted by her easy dismissal. What he did know was that he should be bloody grateful for her mature acceptance.

"You are correct, Mrs. Lanyon. And you have my word it won't happen again," he promised her. "And—and I hope it will not influence your decision about what I asked you earlier today." When she didn't answer, he reminded her, "About staying after the thirty days are over."

"Oh, yes, that. Well, I have no other position as of now, so I suppose I could stay. Just a little while longer, until you have a secretary you trust."

It wasn't the answer he'd hoped for, but at least he had time to earn her forgiveness—to make her believe that he really could, and would, control himself—and persuade her to stay. "Thank you."

"Do you hear that, my lord?"

It took him a moment before he knew what she meant. "Ah, the rain has stopped."

It appeared their brief holiday from reality was over.

Chapter 20

It took twice as long to get home—or at least it felt that way to Selina.

She felt strangely wooden as she sat beside his lordship and guided Bessie through the mud, her senses... muffled.

The marquess must have sensed her mood—or perhaps he also felt emotionally detached—because he barely spoke on the drive.

Selina didn't understand what had just happened—or why Lord Shaftsbury had suddenly stopped. She'd not wanted to stop. She'd wanted more of... *something*... so much more. Indeed, it had been the most glorious ten minutes in her life. Never had she felt so alive and aware.

Evidently the marquess had not felt similarly moved.

She knew she would have to sit down and think about what had happened at some point.

But not now. Not while sitting beside his big, warm, distracting body.

Although the rain had stopped and the wind had settled, the rutted path became two small rivers. They had to proceed with painstaking caution until they connected to the larger road that led to Courtland.

The sky was gray, but the sun didn't set until late at this time of year, so they approached the house just as darkness began to fall.

A groom trotted out to take the gig and they weren't even to the door before it opened, divulging a rather wide-eyed Morris.

"Ah, here you are, my lord, Mrs. Lanyon," the old butler said, a tremor in his normally calm voice, as they stepped inside the foyer.

"What is wrong, Morris?" Lord Shaftsbury asked, obviously sensing the old man's mood.

"Ah..." Morris's pale blue eyes slid to Selina and he grimaced and mouthed something at her.

Selina squinted, unable to read his lips.

"Morris?" the marquess prodded, holding out his hat and gloves.

"Well, er—"

"Hello, Caius."

The marquess made a noise of surprise and turned toward the staircase where a stranger was descending.

Selina

"Victor?" the marquess said, his voice unnaturally high. "What in the world are you doing here?"

That's why he looked familiar; it was Lord Victor, the marquess's brother. Selina had seen his portrait among all the others in the gallery.

Lord Victor didn't speak, his eyes—gray, like his brother's, but darker and colder—flickered over the marquess's person. "You are looking well, Caius. Far better than I expected," he said in a crisp, unsentimental tone that Selina found jarring considering that he'd not seen his sibling in nearly a decade.

"What did you expect?" the marquess asked coolly, his momentary surprise replaced by haughty wariness.

"The letter I received had me prepared for the worst."

"You received my letter *already*?" Selina blurted.

Both the marquess and Lord Victor turned to her and spoke at once.

"You wrote to my brother?"

"*Your* letter? Who are you?"

Selina wrenched her gaze from her employer, answering his brother's question—the easier one, by far. "I am Mrs. Lanyon, his lordship's housekeeper."

Lord Victor's eyebrows rose, his eyes flickering over her face. "Housekeeper?" he repeated, visibly stunned.

"You wrote to my brother?" the marquess repeated, sounding less than pleased.

Selina opened her mouth to confess.

"She did so at my urging, my lord," Morris said, before she could speak.

If the old servant believed that would appease their employer, he was wrong.

"*What* did you write, Mrs. Lanyon?" Lord Shaftsbury demanded in an icy voice he'd not used on her since her first week.

"I—I just wrote to say you needed, erm, some assistance."

Shaftsbury's eyebrows drew down in a way that made Selina take a step back. "What made you think you had the right?"

She felt pinioned by his freezing gaze. It didn't matter that he couldn't *see* her. At that moment, she felt flayed to the bone.

"It scarcely matters what she wrote as I haven't seen it," Lord Victor interrupted in a dismissive tone. "The letter I am talking about came from Squire Henley. And I received it four months ago. He mentioned the state of the affairs here at Courtland, and also told me you'd not been seen in public, nor were you at home to visitors." He paused and then added, "He did not mention anything about a new housekeeper."

The marquess's jaw flexed and he turned slowly away from Selina to face his brother. "I don't wish to discuss my affairs in the foyer, Victor." He handed Morris his gloves and held his hand out for the cane the old man had been holding for him. "Let us go up to the library."

For the first time since he'd come down the stairs, Lord Victor looked hesitant. "Er, do you need my arm, Caius?"

"No."

"At two o'clock, my lord," Selina murmured, unable to allow him to start walking without knowing where the stairs were.

He scowled at her before pivoting in the direction she'd given and tapped his way toward the stairs.

Selina waited for him to bark a command that she should follow, but it never came.

Only when the two men had disappeared did Morris turn to her, his face ashen. "I wanted to warn you—to tell you that Lord Victor hadn't come in response to your letter, but…"

Morris trailed off and Selina gave him a smile she wasn't feeling. "Thank you for trying to rescue me."

"I believe we are both in a great deal of trouble, Mrs. Lanyon."

Selina sighed. "I daresay you are correct."

It appeared her job here would end even before her thirty days had passed.

***

Caius told himself there was no point in getting angry or losing his temper, and to look on the brighter side of things. He'd not seen Victor in almost a decade and now would be a good time to mend the breach between them. Their last argument had been ugly and emotional, and it had pained him to think about some of the things he'd said.

That's what he told himself.

But he *was* angry and not just at his brother for his condescending attitude. He was furious at Mrs. Lanyon. What she'd done smacked of betrayal. Worse, her actions told him that she thought he wasn't capable on his own. All her words—all her assurances—had been lies.

But he would have to think about *her* defection later, because he suspected he'd have his hands full dealing with Victor.

Caius opened the door to the library and tap-tapped his way to his desk—he needed the security of a large chunk of wood in front of him—and leaned his walking stick against his thigh once he'd sat.

"Why don't you pour us both a whiskey, Victor." He hesitated and then added, "Or is that against your, erm, whatever?"

His brother sighed audibly.

Caius raised his hands in a placating gesture. "I wasn't being sarcastic. I truly do not know what sort of, er, ethos you have embraced. It's not as if you ever told me," he couldn't resist adding.

"Yes, Caius, I can drink spirits."

He waited for more, but it appeared that was it.

Caius sat in silence. Listening to the clink of crystal and then footsteps as his brother approached the desk. He silently thanked Mrs. Lanyon for removing the carpets.

Then he recalled that he was currently *very* angry with his housekeeper.

"I am holding the glass directly in front of you," Victor said.

Caius lifted his hand, and his brother slid the cool crystal between his fingers. "Thank you."

He took a drink—a large one—and set the glass on the desk. He was about to ask his brother where he was sitting—so he'd know where to position his body—when Victor spoke.

"How long has that woman been your housekeeper?"

It was hardly the question he'd expected. "A little over a month. Why?" Caius didn't mention that he'd not spoken to her for the first week of that time.

"What sort of credentials did she come with?"

Caius frowned. "Why are you so curious about her?"

His brother surprised him by chuckling, the sound dusty, as if from disuse.

"What is so amusing?"

"I was going to ask if you were blind, but then I realized that is exactly the case."

Caius's face heated. "Forgive me if I don't see the humor in that."

"I'm not amused by your condition, Caius. I do wish that you'd *told* me about it, however."

"Why? So you could rush here and take charge—that is why you are here, isn't it? I suppose Henley told you about my... *affliction?*"

"No, actually—he didn't know what was wrong with you. I didn't find out what was going on until I spoke to Morris, just a few hours before you arrived."

Caius couldn't help being impressed that his employees had kept his secret so well, he wouldn't have expected it to last as long as it had.

"Fine, so now you know I am blind. I fail to see what this has to do with Mrs. Lanyon and why you appear to be so suspicious of her, even though you've only just met."

Again, his brother surprised him by laughing. "If you could see her, you would know why I am asking."

"Why? What is wrong with her?" He could hardly tell his brother that he'd felt up the woman earlier that day and had found her to be perfectly delightful.

"There is *nothing* wrong with her."

Caius gave an irritated huff. "Good God, Victor. What are you getting at?"

"I mean that she is the most beautiful creature I have ever seen."

Caius's mouth opened, but he wasn't sure what to say. She *had* felt nice—pretty, even—but it truly hadn't occurred to him that she was *that* attractive.

He shrugged. "What of it? There is no law saying that servants cannot be beautiful, Victor."

"No, that is true. But she is also exceedingly young, Caius. You must know how hiring such a woman will appear to all our neighbors?"

"She is one-and-thirty, Victor. And I refuse to justify your second comment with an answer."

Victor gave a disbelieving snort. "If she is more than twenty-three, then I will eat my hat."

Caius was annoyed because he had thought the same thing—not about eating a hat, but that she sounded very young.

Again, he wasn't going to tell his brother that.

Instead, he said, "I hope you have a good appetite because she has a glowing letter of recommendation from the Duchess of Chatham. In any case," he said, raising his voice to talk over his brother, "she is an excellent employee and I don't really care what her age is. Also, who I hire as a housekeeper is scarcely any business of yours—nor of anyone else's. I'm more interested in what Henley said in his letter to have you haring back here. I thought you were never coming back," he added pettishly. "At least those were the words you hurled at me when you left."

His brother chose to take the high ground and ignore Caius's childish taunt. "Henley mentioned you'd not been seen in months—by anyone—and that your tenants' needs were going unmet. He went on to give several specific instances."

Caius gritted his teeth, furious—not at Henley for poking his nose where it didn't belong, but at himself for deserving such criticism.

"It is true that things have been awkward for some time. But I've just returned from inspecting the Tanner farm today and—"

"With your housekeeper."

Caius bristled. "Yes, with Mrs. Lanyon. What of it?"

"It is very unusual to take one's housekeeper out to one's tenant farm."

"You are now the arbiter of my business affairs?"

"Is that all it is—a *business* affair?"

"It's none of your damned *business,* is what it is, Victor."

His brother's laughter—bitter and unamused—filled the room. "That is rich, coming from you, Caius."

"You cannot still be angry that I wouldn't allow you to throw yourself away on a vicar's daughter almost nine years ago. Or is that why you've come back, Victor? To lord my infirmity over me and extract your pound of flesh?"

"This is *our* family's estate, Caius. It matters to me if you are driving it into the dirt through neglect or incompetence."

"While I am still alive, it is *my* estate."

"Not if you cannot—"

Caius raised his fist and slammed it on the desk. Only at the very last instant, when his hand struck crystal, did he recall the damned glass of whiskey.

Chapter 21

The library bell jangled loudly and repeatedly, causing Morris and Selina, who'd been sitting in glum silence drinking tea, to startle.

"That sounds… angry," Selina said, getting to her feet as the bell continued to ring.

Morris began to struggle to his feet and she laid a hand on his shoulder. "No, allow me, Mr. Morris. Please, you've put up with all this for hours, it is my turn. It is late; why don't you go to bed."

"Are you sure, Mrs. Lanyon?" he asked. It was a measure of his exhaustion that he didn't protest.

"Absolutely," she said, already striding toward the door. "Don't worry. If you are needed, I won't hesitate to disturb you," she lied. The poor old dear had dark smudges beneath his eyes and was dead on his feet.

The instant she was out of the kitchen her mind resumed its racing. Her main concern was the letter she'd written and what his lordship would say to her. Selina growled, frustrated beyond belief. She had only *just* begun to establish a civil relationship with the marquess, and now *this* had to happen.

Today at that shack was rather more than <u>civil</u>.

Her heart skipped a beat at the memory of that kiss and the way he'd explored her. None of his touches had been offensive or pushing, just sensual and tender.

And arousing.

How she wished that it hadn't been so dark and that she'd been able to see his face.

Selina immediately felt ashamed of her thought. That was how his life was every day: dark and sightless. Hadn't she learned yet just how much she had? Why did she always expect more?

She arrived at the library in what had to be record time and paused a second to calm her breathing before knocking.

"Come in."

Lord Shaftsbury sat with his bloody hand raised over his desk, Lord Victor hovering beside him.

"Oh, my goodness. What happened?" she demanded rushing toward his lordship.

The marquess scowled. "I told him not to ring for you—it's just a small cut."

"It's *not* a small cut," Lord Victor said, looking distinctly green.

Selina

Selina guessed he was one of those people who hated the sight of blood.

"Let me see, my lord."

The marquess heaved a sigh and held out his hand.

Selina clucked her tongue as she examined the wound. "It is certainly *not* a small cut." She frowned. "I think it might need a few stitches."

"I can summon a doctor," Lord Victor said, clearly eager to get away from the blood.

"Absolutely not," the marquess said, his face turned toward Selina. "You spent time at that hospital—surely you can slip in a few stitches."

Selina laughed. "*Slip in* a few stitches? You *do* realize stitches involve needles? Needles jabbing into your flesh."

Lord Victor moaned and lifted a hand to his mouth.

Selina cut him a look of amused exasperation. "My lord, if you are going to faint or vomit, please go sit down—one patient at a time."

The younger man no longer wore the superior expression she'd seen earlier. "I'm not fond of blood."

Was anyone?

Luckily, she didn't say that. Instead, she said, "Mr. Morris has gone to bed and all the other servants are settled. Will you help me, my lord? Or do I need to ring for somebody?" That was yet another of those questions a true servant would never ask, but Selina had the feeling it scarcely mattered since her days at Courtland were probably numbered.

"Er, I don't know," Lord Victor said. "What did you have in mind?" he asked, turning toward her but averting his gaze from his brother's bloody hand.

"Nothing that will require you to get close to any blood," she assured him. "Would you mind fetching my mending basket from my quarters? It is in the parlor beside the wingchair."

"Are you in the same rooms the housekeeper has always occupied?"

"Yes," she said. "And would you also please bring a jug of water and some towels from your chambers, if you do not mind—I'm sure Morris will have sent a maid up when you arrived."

Lord Victor nodded and left without another word.

Selina looked down at Lord Shaftsbury's hand, which was still resting on her palm, and said, "There is always a little water in the pitcher near the decanters. I'm going to get that—keep your hand raised up."

Before she could turn away his hand—the uninjured one—closed around her wrist. "Tell me what you said in the letter to my brother, Mrs. Lanyon."

Selina grimaced. "It wasn't Mr. Morris's fault that I wrote. I badgered him, so please don't—"

"I'm not going to punish Morris. I want to know what you wrote."

"I said that you could use a bit of assistance in the wake of your accident. I didn't say anything specific. I'm sorry, I know what I did was—"

"Wise," he said, surprising her. "I was angry at first," he admitted with a wry smile. "But…" He shook his head. "Go get the water," he ordered quietly, releasing her.

Selina paused for a moment, studying his face. Were his cheeks darker? Was the marquess… blushing?

***

Caius felt like an idiot. What the hell difference did it make that he now knew Mrs. Lanyon was so beautiful that she'd rendered his brother speechless? Why in the world would that knowledge make him blush like a virginal schoolgirl?

Quite suddenly, Caius wondered what Mrs. Lanyon made of *him*. How was it that he'd not thought about that before?

Because you are the master and she is the servant and, therefore she would naturally find you appealing?

Caius winced at the thought. Surely he could not be so contemptibly vain?

He heard her footsteps approach and composed his face, praying he didn't look as flustered as he felt.

"I'm going to light several more candles so I can check for glass in the wound," she said, setting something—a candelabrum, he assumed—on the desk. "There, that is better," she murmured after a moment. "May I see the cut, please?"

He held out his hand and she took it in her much smaller, cooler hands. "Are you in pain?" she asked after pouring water over his palm.

"No."

"You can tell me if you are, you know. I won't think less of your manliness."

Caius snorted. "I assure you; it doesn't hurt."

After a moment she said, "I don't see any glass. But I do think I should give you two—maybe three—stitches."

"You've done that before?"

"No, but I've watched plenty of times."

He smiled.

"What?" she asked.

"You really are fearless, aren't you?"

She gave one of her squawky chuckles. "I'm very much *not* fearless—or don't you recall all my yelping and gasping during the stor"—she broke off, as if suddenly recalling exactly what had happened between them during the storm in question. She cleared her throat and said, "In any case, I hardly think stitching up a wound counts as *fearless*." She lowered her voice and asked, "Are you angry that your brother is here?"

It was a sign of how accustomed Caius was to her very un-housekeeper-like behavior that he didn't bristle at the question. Before he could muster up an answer the door opened and the man in question entered.

"Here you are," Victor said.

"Thank you, my lord."

"Er, do you need me to do anything else?"

"You could pour his lordship another glass of whiskey—and perhaps one for yourself as well."

Caius smiled at the amusement he heard in her voice. He'd forgotten how green his brother got at the sight of blood. Caius himself didn't care to look at a bleeding wound, but it didn't make him ill like poor Victor.

"Are you ready, my lord?" she asked him after Victor had given him the glass and he'd thrown back the contents in one gulp.

"Yes."

"This will sting," she warned.

It *burned* like the very devil, but Caius bit his tongue and held still.

"Just two more," she murmured, subjecting him to the same torment twice more. Once she'd finished, she washed the wound and tied a cloth around his hand. "Is that too tight?"

He flexed his hand. "No, it's fine. Thank you."

"Are you hungry, my lord?"

He was, but he was too bloody exhausted to eat. "No, thank you, Mrs. Lanyon. Victor, are you—"

"Morris already fed me," his brother said.

"Then you'll have to excuse me, because I'm ready for bed." He hated to admit it, but it was suddenly difficult to keep his eyes open.

"Should I ring for James?" Mrs. Lanyon asked.

"No, I can see to myself."

"May I do anything else for you, my lord?"

"No, thank you, Mrs. Lanyon. Why don't you take yourself off to bed."

"Of course. Good night, my lord. Good night, Lord Victor."

His brother barely waited for the door to close before saying, "She is not a housekeeper, Caius—or at least not *only* a housekeeper. She sounds as if she is one of us."

He knew his brother was right. Her accent was even more noticeable now that Victor was there; the two of them could have been brother and sister.

"We need to find out who she really is," Victor said.

"No, we don't."

"What?"

"She has been an exemplary employee, Victor." Beyond exemplary, but he hardly wanted to confess just how much she'd done to pull him from his slump. "Her past is immaterial to me. If she is hiding something, that is her concern."

Caius would have cause to remember those words barely two weeks later.

Chapter 22

The marquess had apparently decided not to sack Selina for her impertinence in writing to his brother. At least he didn't summon her to the library to tell her that she was sacked.

He didn't summon her to the library at all. Indeed, he scarcely said a word to her over the next ten days.

Selina hadn't realized how much of her day she spent with Lord Shaftsbury—and how much she'd looked forward to that time—until the arrival of his lordship's brother.

All the matters that she'd assisted the marquess with, Lord Victor now took in hand.

Well, except for the daily reading sessions and the private piano concerts. Those just stopped entirely.

Three days in a row she'd gone to the music room at their usual time, but his lordship never came.

As for the evening readings, she discovered those were over when she'd shown up in the library after dinner the night after Lord Victor arrived.

The two men had been conversing when she'd entered the room and Lord Victor had given her a startled look, shot to his feet, and said, "Yes, Mrs. Lanyon? Did you need something?"

Before she could respond the marquess spoke, "Mrs. Lanyon often reads to me after dinner." He smiled stiffly. "Perhaps we might postpone the reading for a while."

"Of course, my lord."

And that had been that.

The two men spent most of every day either closeted together in the library or—after the first few days of Lord Victor's visit—they went out in the carriage and returned calls. Evidently his lordship had simply stopped receiving his visitors after his accident and now he needed to make amends.

Selina was pleased that the marquess was confident enough to leave the house and venture out into the world—without her help—and she told herself that she was happy for him.

But that was a lie. Who would have guessed that she was so mean-spirited as to begrudge a man who'd lost his sight an opportunity to socialize? She'd never had such selfish, unworthy thoughts about another person in her life.

It didn't take much reflection to realize that she was jealous. That she'd begun to think of the marquess as *her* project, rather than a living, breathing person who deserved to have a fulfilling life. She'd begun to think of caring for him as *her* fulfilling life.

It was painfully clear that he no longer needed her. For anything except keeping his house in order.

Sometimes, late at night when she tossed and turned and sleep eluded her, she wondered if that kiss in the gamekeeper's shack had even happened.

Despite the loss of all her time with Lord Shaftsbury, Selina found that she was busier than ever. Especially after Lord Victor decided that the entire house needed to be thoroughly cleaned from top to bottom. Once she'd overcome her irritation at his imputation that the house was *dirty*, she embraced the chore as it kept her working from dawn until well past dark every day and gave her something to think about other than the marquess and how much she missed him.

Ten days after Lord Victor's arrival at Courtland—and just as Selina was congratulating herself on only pining for Lord Shaftsbury's company five or six times an hour, as opposed to every other minute—the marquess's younger brother sent for her.

She was sitting with Morris in the kitchen, the two of them polishing silver—a never-ending task that she found soothing—when Timothy delivered the message.

"Lord Victor wants to see me right now?"

"He said at your earliest convenience, Mrs. Lanyon."

Which meant right now.

"Thank you, Timothy." Once he'd gone Selina removed the apron she'd donned and checked her face for smudges, finding a large smear of gray on her jaw.

"What do you think he wants?" Morris asked as she wet her thumb and wiped off the smut.

Selina shrugged, tucked a stray curl back into place, and turned to him. "Who knows? Perhaps he wants us to start cleaning and organizing the shrubbery now that the house is sparkling?"

Morris gave a startled laugh, and then looked guilty that he was mocking a member of the family. Selina was a bad influence.

"I'll hold dinner for you," he said as she strode toward the door.

"I'm sure this won't take long." At least she couldn't imagine the grim-faced Lord Victor wasting too much of his time on a mere servant. Indeed, he seemed to avoid Selina, preferring to deliver orders through footmen or speak directly to Morris. This summons was unusual, and her mind raced as to what he could possibly want as she made her way to his study.

"Come in," he called out when she knocked. "Ah, Mrs. Lanyon," he said, glancing up from something he was writing. "I shall be with you in a moment."

He didn't offer her a seat, so Selina stood in front of his desk and was reminded of the few times she'd been sent to her father's study for some infraction she'd committed. The Earl of Addiscombe was not an intimidating figure and Selina and her sisters had much preferred his lenient punishments to the ones their mother had meted out.

Unlike her father, Lord Victor made an excellent disciplinarian. He radiated the sort of stern severity that sent shivers of apprehension through her body even though she was an adult and not a little girl.

After at least five minutes, he replaced his quill in the standish, sanded the document, and then pushed it aside before turning to her.

For someone who was probably only six or so years older than Selina, he possessed the dignity of a far older man, his gray eyes cold and assessing as they swept over her person.

He gestured to the chair in front of his desk. "Have a seat… Lady Selina."

Selina's bottom was in the chair before she realized what he'd just said. Her jaw dropped. "How—"

He gave her an exasperated look. "Surely you didn't expect this masquerade to go on forever?"

Selina wanted to ask him why it was so difficult to believe she was a housekeeper, but decided now was not the time. "How did you find out, my lord?"

He sat back, his elbows resting on the arms of his chair, his narrow-eyed gaze making her feel very young. "My first clue was your face."

Selina blinked. "That makes no sense. There are plenty of attractive servants in the world."

He snorted. "I think we both know you are not merely *attractive*." He waved a dismissive hand when she opened her mouth. "There is also your accent and the manner in which you comport yourself—neither of which are of the servant class. But that is neither here nor there. What *is* important is what we are going to do now."

"You mean… I can stay here and continue working?"

He laughed, and for the first time, she heard actual amusement. "In a manner of speaking."

"Why don't you say what you mean and quit toying with me, my lord."

"You've not only made a fool of Shaftsbury by taking this position, but you've also been seen out and about with him, so it's only a matter of time before the truth of who you are is known."

"I haven't made a *fool* of him. I've—"

Lord Victor raised his hand.

Selina *hated* that she responded to masculine authority like a dog trained to heel, but it seemed that twenty-some years of conditioning were difficult to ignore.

"You are an earl's daughter," Lord Victor said in a cool voice. "You know what you must do to make this situation right."

"If you are worried about this ruining my reputation then you should know I am already beyond the pale."

"It is not *your* reputation I'm worried about; it is my brother's good name that concerns me. I know about your ill-advised trip with Shelton, and I know how it ended in a brawl with Baron Fowler." He frowned. "I'm sure all of London knows. Indeed, the news has probably spread to the Outer Hebrides. My brother's reputation, on the other hand, was relatively untarnished until *your* arrival in his life."

Selina hated Lord Victor at that moment, all the more so because everything he said was true.

Lord Shaftsbury would already face an uphill battle when it came to returning to society as a blind man. When it became known that he'd *blindly* hired an earl's daughter as a servant he would be laughed at as well as pitied.

Just because she agreed with Lord Victor didn't mean she appreciated the way he was talking to her. The man could give her mother lessons in how to deliver a humiliating scold.

"What are you suggesting, my lord? Should I put a period to my existence? Would that make you happy?"

"What would make me *happy* is if you would cease dramatizing your situation and take responsibility for your actions."

"Fine. What do you propose, my lord?"

"There is only one solution, and you know it. You must marry my brother."

Even though she'd been expecting it, his words drove the air from her lungs, robbing her of the ability to give a clever retort—not that she had one.

"I know how you helped him," Lord Victor went on when she didn't speak, his tone only slightly less abrasive. "And I also know how unconventional that help has been. No, my brother didn't tell me about the musical afternoons or the hours spent together—*alone*—with him in his library. I had to all but torture that information out of Morris."

"I'm sure you were up to the task of abusing a sweet old man," she retorted.

"Yes, well, that *sweet old man*, should have written to me before I had to hear the humiliating news about my brother from our neighbor," he snapped, his cold eyes sparking with fury. He stood, came around the desk, and leaned against it, crossing his arms as he stared down at her. "Are you going to be difficult, my lady, or are you going to do the proper thing?"

She ignored his question and asked one of her own. "Have you told his lordship who I am?"

"No." He gestured to a piece of paper on his desk. "I only received the news in today's mail." He sighed and his stern expression suddenly softened. "Lady Selina, let us not be adversaries—I know I've been harsh, and I apologize. I"—he broke off and ran his fingers through his hair. "I need to say something to you that does not make me very happy."

Selina shuddered to think what this man might have held back, but said, "Please, speak freely."

"I cannot leave my brother here at Courtland unattended."

Her brow furrowed. "I don't understand?"

"I wish to return home—to *my* home—but until the marquess is in capable hands, I don't feel that I can do that. At least not in good conscience."

"He is not a crippled, my lord. Yes, his blindness presents obstacles, but they are not insurmountable and in the past few weeks he has made great strides toward independence."

"Because of you."

"I was the catalyst," she admitted. "But that was all he needed—a slight push in the right direction. I was able to share some ideas with him because I grew up with a boy who is blind. Anyone with such knowledge could have shared those insights."

"But nobody did, my lady. Not until you."

She flung up her hands. "Fine, I accept credit for starting him on the road to self-sufficiency, but the majority of it is all his hard work."

"He will never be self-sufficient, and you know it."

"He is a wealthy man who can engage any number of servants to aid him."

"He needs *constant* assistance, my lady. I know that because I've spent the last ten days with him. You might think I displaced you out of pique"—he cut her a knowing look, and Selina had the grace to blush— "but that is not so. I wanted to spend time with him to assess his abilities. You are right that he can move about his home with some degree of confidence. And a steward could do a great deal of the work that you and I have done. But what about the rest of his life? You read to him, play the piano for him, and have even taken the brilliant step of engineering a chessboard—yes, he told me about that—so that he might enjoy a game he has always loved."

Selina tried to ignore the pleasure his praise gave her but failed miserably.

"Those are not the tasks of a secretary or steward or housekeeper, Lady Selina, they are the responsibilities of a life companion." He paused, and then said, "Of a wife." Lord Victor gave her a long, hard stare. When she didn't speak—what in the world could she possibly say?—he continued, "It took him a good five years to meet his last wife and clearly a London Season is out of the question for him. Even if it wasn't, there is still the issue of this... embarrassment."

"You mean me."

"Yes."

Selina tried to imagine herself married to the Marquess of Shaftsbury. It was surprisingly easy to do after seeing his more human side.

Not to mention that kiss and those caresses.

She shoved that far too stimulating thought to the back of her mind. The last thing she wanted was to shame herself in front of this aloof, insulting man. After a moment, she met his gaze, "And if I don't agree to do what you are saying?"

Lord Victor uncrossed his arms, set his palms on the desk, and leaned forward. His face—which had softened—turned cruel and cold. "If my brother won't marry, then I must stay here. And if I must stay in England, it will not be to serve as my brother's keeper."

Her heart fluttered—and not happily—at his words. "Wh-what do you mean?"

"I mean I will petition the court to have him declared incompetent and I will take control of Courtland and all his other properties."

She gasped and sprang to her feet. "No! You cannot do that—he is not mentally incompetent."

Lord Victor shrugged. "I will be able to find more than a few witnesses who will attest otherwise." He gave her a hard look. "Indeed, I'm sure your testimony—of what condition you found him in when you arrived—would be most compelling to a judge."

"I would never say—"

"You wouldn't have a choice. Your testimony could be compelled."

Selina shook her head. "What sort of brother are you? How could you even threaten such a horrible thing?"

"I am a pragmatist, my lady. I don't want to be master of Courtland, but I know that Caius will not step aside willingly. That means he will have to be removed and put somewhere he can get the assistance he so clearly needs. Likely he will go to a sanitorium that deals with such prob—"

"You *beast*!" For the first time in her life, Selina struck another human being.

Lord Victor's head snapped to the side but—except for the red handprint quickly forming—his expression did not even change.

Selina lifted her hands to her mouth. "Oh, God! I—I don't know why I did that! I am sorry—so very sorry, my lord."

For the first time since she'd met the man, he smiled—and it was genuine. "I'm not sorry."

"Are you *mad*?"

"I wanted proof that you care for my brother, and you just gave it to me."

She gawked.

"Yes," he said, although she'd not argued. "You care for him—enough to go against your nature and hit me. Will you allow him to be displaced from his position and sent to live somewhere else, my lady? Will you?"

Selina didn't know she was crying until a tear splashed onto her hand. "How can you do this?" she whispered. "How can you make such a threat?"

He ignored her questions. "Will you do it? Will you make his life worth living, Lady Selina? Or will you condemn him to a solitary existence?"

Her hand twitched to hit him again, but she caught herself. "If his lordship asks me to marry him, I will give *him* my answer." She turned on her heel and marched toward the door, but his voice stopped her.

"If you do this, you can never let him know what I've said today. You know that, don't you? My brother is an extremely proud man—there are none prouder."

Selina knew that better than anyone.

"If he knew why you accepted his offer it would shame him—unman him and—"

Selina whipped around. "And that is something you know a great deal about, isn't it, my lord—shaming people? Don't bother answering that," she snapped, turning her back to him.

This time when she reached for the door Lord Victor did not stop her.

Chapter 23

"She is Addiscombe's daughter?" Caius knew he'd already asked that question once already, but he couldn't come up with anything better.

"Yes."

"And you discovered this *how?*"

"It wasn't difficult. Morris showed me the letter of recommendation from the Duchess of Chatham and I assumed there must be some connection as Chatham's wedding announcement was only recently in the newspaper and he barely married a month ago. The announcement also mentioned his new wife's name and the names of her siblings. Finding the truth about Chatham's housekeeper wasn't difficult as the woman has worked for his family for thirty years and is something of a legend."

Caius felt a pang of relief; at least Mrs. Mercer wasn't dead. She'd been kind to him when he'd visited, and he knew Chatham was very fond of her.

"By the way, her other sister—Lady Phoebe—just married Viscount Needham."

"Did she indeed?" Well, she'd told Caius she had two sisters who'd married recently. His lips twitched as he recalled how she could never seem to remember very much about her own husband.

Now he knew the reason. Because she'd never been married.

Caius did not want to think about why that thought made him so happy.

"There is something else," Victor said, his tone uncharacteristically tentative. "Something I read in the newspaper."

"What?"

"The reason she is here—and that she took this job—is because she fled London under rather ignominious circumstances. It seems—"

"Stop."

"Don't you want to know?"

"It is her story to tell; not yours." Caius heaved a sigh and leaned back in his chair. "I think I can see where you are headed, Victor."

"I thought you might."

A sudden, unpleasant thought struck him. "I hope you haven't confronted Mrs. Lany—er, Lady Selina—with this?"

"No, of course not. I wanted to speak to you, first."

He gave another sigh, this time one of relief. He was glad Victor hadn't opened his mouth and tried to pressure the poor girl.

Girl.

Caius bit back a groan. "How old is she?"

Please, God, don't let her be an infant.

"I believe she is twenty-one—rather old for her first Season, but the family have had financial troubles."

Caius grunted. Twenty-one was young, but it could have been worse: she could have been eighteen, which was the age of most debutantes. He'd taken pains to avoid marrying a very young woman the first time—Louisa had been twenty-eight, well on the shelf—but it seemed he would not have that choice this time.

Stop behaving as if marrying this woman would be a burden; you are bloody delighted, my lord.

Caius ignored his dead valet's taunting and said, "And you think it is fair to condemn this twenty-one-year-old woman—by all accounts a diamond of the first water—to life with a blind man, Victor?"

His brother gave an exasperated huff. "This is the best solution, Caius—you must know that. People will find out what has been going on here—already she is known in the village and people are talking—and once the news spreads she will not have any future at all."

Caius barked a laugh. "I daresay the life of a social pariah is still better than being wet-nurse to a cripple."

The long pause told him that his brother was struggling to come up with a convincing counter argument.

"Morris told me the two of you got on quite well," Victor finally said. "He said she appeared happy with her life here. He also said—"

"I can see that Morris needs to be reminded who he works for," Caius bit out.

"Don't be angry with him, I had to all but apply thumb screws to get anything out of the man. Caius…"

His normally confident—to the point of arrogance—brother paused.

"Oh, for pity's sake, Victor; just spit it out, already."

"You like her, do you not?"

"What are you trying to say?"

"This solution isn't just for the best; I also think it is one that might suit the both of you."

Caius bristled. "Please tell me you've *not* said anything about this to her?"

"I told you I hadn't—I would never do that. So," he said after a moment, "will you do this?"

"I don't know, Victor. I need to talk to her. There are two people in a marriage, after all."

"But you're going to—"

"I'm not discussing this with you. Just send a servant to ask her to come see me, Victor," he said, cutting off his brother's impertinence, something he probably should have done the moment Victor confessed to looking into his housekeeper's identity.

"Of course," Victor said after a long pause. Caius heard him move toward the door and then stop.

He waited, expecting some further question or advice. Thankfully, Victor must have changed his mind and left without speaking.

Caius took several deep breaths and considered what he was about to do. Before he made any offer, he wanted to hear from her own mouth why she'd engaged in this charade and if she was hiding from something or someone. He'd not take advantage of a woman who needed safe harbor. If she was running, he would help her, not trap her into marriage.

Marriage.

He gave a humorless laugh and shook his head.

Regardless of what his brother said, Caius was not going to marry a second woman who wanted nothing to do with him. At least with Louisa, he'd been a fully functioning man. With Mrs. Lanyon—Lady Selina, he reminded himself—he had nothing to offer but a title, which was unlikely to sway her if she was willing to leave behind life as an earl's daughter and take a service position.

He had money, but with her sisters married to wealthy men she didn't need to worry about that, either. Caius knew Chatham well; the man would take care of his wife's relations. She didn't need to go back to Queen's Bower or face another Season if she didn't want to.

She had choices, she didn't need to be trapped into a life with him.

Far too soon there was a knock on the door.

He took one last deep breath and said, "Come in."

Chapter 24

Selina truly didn't know what reaction she could expect from Lord Shaftsbury. He wasn't humorless like his brother—thank the Lord for that—but it was *his* life that she'd careened into. She might not like Lord Victor, but his assessment of the situation was on point: the marquess's quiet existence would get turned on its head if her identity became known.

She sighed and knocked.

"Come in," a familiar voice called out.

He was standing when she entered. "Lady Selina?" There was a faint twist to his lips and it was difficult to decipher. Was he bitter? Angry? Amused? Resigned.

"Yes, my lord."

"Have a seat."

That was nice, at least he wasn't going to keep her standing like his brother. But then he'd never done that when he'd believed her to be a servant.

Once she'd sat, she said, "Thank you, my lord," to let him know he could resume his own seat. "I assume Lord Victor told you about me."

"He told me your name, but he hasn't told me what drove you to accept a servant position in my household. I thought you might enlighten me, if you don't mind."

Selina *did* mind having to relate her foolish life to this man, but she owed him that much. "Are you familiar with Lord Shelton?"

He blinked in surprise. "Er, he's Chatham's heir—that is unless the duke has a new heir to go along with his new wife?"

"Oh. You know about that?"

"Mmm-hmm. But do go on. What about Shelton?"

"I made the mistake of getting into his carriage, and rather than take me to Hyde Park, he took me on the Great North Road."

"Ah. Well, I can't say I'm terribly surprised. Shelton's been nothing but trouble to the duke for years. Did he relent and return you home?"

"No, I escaped."

He laughed. "I expect that was rather a blow to Shelton's pride. So, how did you manage that?"

"We'd stopped to changed horses at a posting inn when an—an acquaintance arrived and offered me his assistance."

"An acquaintance?"

"It was Lord Fowler," she said. "He is—"

"I've met him. A rather large ginger-haired fellow if I recall correctly. I take it he was another of your suitors?"

"In *his* mind, perhaps, although I'd exchanged no more than half a dozen words with him during the Season." Selina bit her lip. "That was unkind of me. I suspect he offered because he is a friend of Chatham's and heard I was in a post chaise with Shelton."

"How did he—"

"We were seen at the Swan with Two Necks."

Caius winced. "Shelton was not exactly stealthy."

"No. He didn't mean to be. He—he wanted to use the elopement to pressure his cousin for money. He never really wanted to marry me."

The marquess shook his head, his expression one of disgust. "It isn't the first time he's done such a thing; the man is a conscienceless rogue, my lady. You are better off without him."

"I know that. Now."

"So, er, Fowler took you home, then?"

"That was his plan, but the two men started to argue and then began to fight, ostensibly over me." She sighed. "It was more than a little mortifying. While they were entertaining each other"—the marquess laughed— "I stole their purses and used the money to buy a seat on a stagecoach. Too make a long story short, I took several coaches and ended up at Much Deeping."

"I don't understand how you got a job as my housekeeper?"

"I shamelessly eavesdropped on Mr. Morris talking to your former housekeeper. When I realized the position was open, it seemed... providential."

He laughed. "*Providential?* You mean you've always wanted to go into service?"

"No, but it seemed better than going home in disgrace." She hesitated, and then said, "I know you've heard of my father because I recall talking about him once."

He grimaced. "Lord, I can't for the life of me recall what I said. I apologize if it was unkind."

Selina chuckled. "No, you were quite restrained. Several months ago my father managed to gamble away our home, and—"

"Wych House, isn't it?"

Selina

"That is our ancestral house—which is another story entirely. The house I'm talking about is Queen's Bower, a little manor we've called home for years. Father borrowed against it and could not pay back the money. That is the main reason I went to London."

"You were going to marry to save your family," he said.

"Yes. It sounds mercenary, but—"

"You are not the only one in such a position, my lady." He smiled wryly, reminding her he'd married an heiress. "Baron Fowler is an extremely wealthy man—so why did you run from him?"

"Because I'd just learned my sister Hyacinth married the Duke of Chatham. I knew our family's immediate worries would be over."

"Forgive me for being obtuse, but if that was the case, then why run off at all?"

Selina groaned. "I'm doing a terrible job explaining myself."

"Take your time; I'm in no rush."

"It's hard to talk about all this without sounding like a conceited, mercenary, fortune-hunter."

He laughed. "I know you well enough by now not to think any such thing, my lady. Just give me the words with the bark on them—as you always do."

"Very well. Let me start my story in a different place. All my life I believed my duty—my sole purpose—was to marry a wealthy man and replenish the family coffers. When my Aunt Fitzroy invited me to London—which just so happened to coincide with learning about my father's disastrous loan—it seemed like a Godsend. The Season was more successful than I could have hoped. Fowler wasn't the first proposal I received from a wealthy man." She swallowed and said, "There were several others. And I turned them all down."

Rather than look confused, Lord Shaftsbury nodded. "When push came to shove, you didn't much want to sacrifice yourself."

"It was beyond *selfish* to refuse those offers. I despised myself and I was so ashamed that I kept the truth from my sister Hyacinth, who was going out every night and risking life and limb to earn the money we needed. But I just couldn't bring myself to do it."

"I understand you better than you think, my lady."

Selina could see from his expression that he was telling the truth.

"I know Chatham—rather well, in fact—and he'd never let anything happen to his wife's family. Even your father will be able to start over with a clean slate." He scowled. "Although I hope Chatham keeps the leash short. Erm, no offense to you, my lady."

Selina laughed. "No offense taken. Trust me, we have all wished that somebody would take his leash."

"So... if you knew your sister had married a wealthy man then I still don't understand why you wanted to work as a housekeeper?"

"Because making a grand marriage was all I was ever good for and yet I couldn't even do *that* right. I just—I just want to do something else. I know it sounds mad, but I saw this position as a way to make something of myself."

"You mean because you could help me?"

"I didn't even know about your, er, situation when I lied my way into the job," she confessed.

His lordship laughed. "Well, at least you are honest."

"One of the few things I know about is running a household, so I thought a housekeeping position sounded like something I could actually do." She sighed. "I wanted to know what it felt like to be useful for something rather than just being admired as an ornament. Because that is all I've ever been, my lord. And I *know* it sounds ungrateful to resent my appearance when so many young women would give their right arm to be pretty, but it is so... so lowering to be nothing but a—a bauble. But that does not justify me lying to sullying your reputation by association."

He scoffed. "You don't have to worry about my reputation, my lady. First of all, and this might come as news to you, but I've never been a pillar of respectability."

Selina laughed. "I'm aware of your reputation, my lord. We used to read about your antics in the newspapers."

He groaned. "Just so you know—those stories are almost always an exaggeration."

"Naturally."

He grinned at her teasing, but it quickly faded. "Nobody knows you are here except Victor and me, Lady Selina, and neither of us will say anything."

That was so kind of him, especially after how awful his brother had been, that Selina yet again got teary.

It's time for you to make this easier for him, her conscience prodded.

Yes, it was.

Selina cleared her throat and said, "People don't know about what has happened yet, but you know how things are among our set. Word will inevitably get out."

There, that was as much pushing as she could bring herself to do, and even that shamed her. It was bad enough she'd put him in this position, pressuring him to offer for her was excruciating.

Selina would not forgive Lord Victor for this.

Lord Shaftsbury did not make her wait. "You are right, my lady: word always gets out. But we could head off scandal if we were to marry."

Selina stared hard at his face, but she couldn't see even a hint of how he felt at being trapped into making a proposal.

"I understand the notion is repugnant to you," he said, clearly misunderstanding the reason behind her pause. "You needn't worry that—"

"I didn't hesitate because your offer repelled me, my lord. I—I would have thought my reaction to you in that gamekeeper shack should have told you that." Selina was embarrassed by her immodest declaration, but she couldn't bring herself to regret it. Not if it disabused him of the notion that she was in any way repelled by him. Lord Victor had been right about his brother's pride. The marquess would be miserable if he ever suspected that she was marrying him out of pity or fear.

He chuckled. "I believe you just made me blush, my lady. Something I don't recall doing for quite some time."

"If it is any consolation to you, my lord, I've been blushing since well before I sat down."

He smiled, but again it was fleeting. "You are right: there is attraction between us—I feel it, too. However, I'm not sure that is enough reason to marry a man like me. Any woman who consents to be my wife will take on a considerable burden. That is something you should—"

"I beg your pardon, my lord, but you are talking poppycock."

His eyebrows shot up. "Indeed?"

"Yes. I've been the recipient of"—she counted in her head— "seven proposals of marriage—yours is number eight—and not once before did I feel like accepting. And that is after I've lived with you for weeks. I think it is safe to say you've not been on your best behavior for at least half of that time, my lord."

He laughed. "No, that is true. Thank you, that is a very kind thing to say—not the bit about my bad behavior, but the other." His expression became serious. "But... are you *sure*, my lady?"

Was she? She had nervous flutters in her stomach, but contemplating a step this important *should* cause flutters, shouldn't it? And they weren't bad flutters—not like the feeling she got when she thought about leaving Courtland—leaving the marquess—and never seeing him again.

Selina looked at his patient, but tense, face and said, "I'm sure, my lord. I am making this decision with my eyes open, so to speak."

He nodded and an almost shy expression settled on his handsome face. "I must admit that the thought of marriage—to you—makes me feel more optimistic than I thought possible." He suddenly grinned. "And I think my proposal went a great deal better than poor Mr. Darcy's did."

Selina laughed. "It certainly did."

His lordship stood, came around the desk, and then held out a hand. "Perhaps we might seal our agreement with a kiss?"

"Yes, of course," she said, her face scalding as she stood and took his hand.

He slid his hand up her arm and shoulder, his fingers trailing lightly as they found their way to her face. "Ah, here you are," he murmured, taking her chin, and tilting her upward for his kiss. It was a tender brushing of lips—a mere whisper of what they'd shared that day in the gamekeeper shack. And it was over far too quickly.

He released her and smiled. "Thank you for agreeing to be my wife, Lady Selina."

The flutters inside her seemed to multiply, until Selina felt so full of emotion—so excited about the future—that it didn't matter to her if their marriage was commencing to avoid scandal. They liked each other, desired each other, and were compatible in half-a-dozen ways. Most *ton* marriages couldn't even claim one of those things.

It was a shame Lord Victor had felt the need to use such a nasty threat to blackmail her, but none of that mattered now.

They already respected and liked each other; love would come, Selina just knew it would.

Chapter 25

Events moved with dizzying speed once Selina and Lord Shaftsbury, or Caius as he had insisted Selina call him, agreed to marry.

The first thing Selina had to do was write to her sisters and brother—and yes, even her parents—and explain why, yet again, there would be a Bellamy wedding without any family in attendance. It hurt to write those letters, at least the ones to her sisters, but a large wedding was simply not possible.

Her siblings, naturally, sent lovely letters that expressed regret that they would miss her wedding, but they all understood.

The Countess of Addiscombe sent an entirely different sort of letter.

Selina,

I am sure you can imagine my horror over your appalling behavior these last two months. Of all my children, I'd never believed you would be the one to disappoint and shame me most deeply.

And now you are wasting all your beauty—and all my time and effort—and marrying a cripple.

I suppose I should be grateful there is <u>somebody</u> willing to take you off our hands after the trail of scandal you've left in your wake.

A small, unobtrusive wedding is best for both you and a man with Lord Shaftsbury's affliction. I daresay he is too fragile to travel and so we shall not be burdened with your presence at Wych House this Christmas.

Perhaps after a few years have passed and the furor has died down you will be able to impose on Chatham to allow you to accompany him and Her Grace to London as I'm sure your husband will be unable to make such a journey. Until that time, <u>do</u> make an effort to rehabilitate what remains of your reputation. If not for your own sake, then for Katherine, who will be forced to make her debut while laboring under the pall you cast on the Bellamy name.

Your mother

P. S. If you have any influence <u>at all</u> with your sister Hyacinth, and <u>any</u> desire to work yourself back into my good graces, you will write to her immediately and insist that she persuade Chatham to re-purchase Addiscombe House for our family's use. It really is <u>too</u> shameful that the mother and father of a duchess must take rooms at Claridge's if they wish to visit London.

Her mother's ability to surprise her—and never in a good way—was truly impressive. Selina put the letter into the fire immediately after reading it and did not justify the missive with a response.

The second matter that needed to be addressed was, of course, telling the servants at Courtland who Selina really was.

"I have only told Mr. Morris who I am, my lord—I'm sorry, *Caius*," she amended when he cocked an eyebrow at her.

"I imagine Morris was delighted."

"He seemed quite satisfied." She laughed. "At least after he overcame his shock. I think his first words were, *Lady Selina Bellamy? Sister to the Duchess of Chatham?*"

Caius chuckled. "Well, I'm pleased the old snob is happy. Will any of the other servants cause any problems? I shouldn't like to replace any of our staff, but if you are uncomfortable—"

"No, I don't think that will be necessary. But… perhaps if we make the announcement together?"

"Of course, that is an excellent idea. We might as well get that out of the way."

It was impressive to see all the servants assembled—well over sixty with both indoor and outside employees—and it was clear that making the announcement together was the wise thing to do.

Not only did it help to cement Selina's change in status to be seen standing beside his lordship, but it was the first time many of the servants had had a good look at the marquess—or heard him speak—since his accident, so the announcement served the dual purpose of assuring his people that he was well.

Once the various announcements had been made to employees, friends, and family, it was time to plan the ceremony.

All her life Selina had expected to have a grand wedding at St. George's with her sisters in attendance and most of the *ton* looking on. She hadn't realized just how much of that dream was her mother's until it was time to plan her wedding and—instead of feeling sad or deprived—she was delighted that the day would not be turned into a spectacle for the society pages.

Indeed, there would only be five people in attendance: Caius, Selina, Lord Victor, Reverend Sayers—the vicar of the small church in Much Deeping—and his daughter Mrs. Sarah Cooper, who had offered to stand as witness.

Selina had been delighted to hear the kind woman from her first day in Much Deeping was to attend the intimate wedding and she immediately invited Mrs. Cooper to call at Courtland to discuss a few details.

She had worried their meeting might be awkward given Selina's unconventional status in the marquess's household these past months, not to mention that she was now living under her bridegroom's roof, but Mrs. Cooper was too kind to say anything judgmental.

"I daresay the rumors about me that are flying around the village right now are… interesting," Selina said, when the two of them sat down for tea in the coziest of Courtland's sitting rooms, a soothing dusty rose chamber with delicate gilt furniture and a lovely view of the parterre garden.

Mrs. Cooper laughed. "I think everyone in the area is so thrilled that his lordship is getting married—and to a young woman whom many in the village have already met and like—that you will find yourself welcomed with open arms, Lady Selina."

"That is very kind of you to say. Indeed, you have been kind to me even before you knew who I was."

Mrs. Cooper's friendly hazel eyes twinkled. "I hope I will always have kindness to spare for anyone who looks a bit… lost, my lady."

Selina laughed. "That is an excellent description of how I felt that day, ma'am."

Because there wasn't much to plan for such a small wedding, Mrs. Cooper and Selina mainly spent the hour getting to know one another. It reminded Selina of how much she missed her sisters.

While Selina was making arrangements with Mrs. Cooper, Caius and Lord Victor were making preparations to leave for London the next day to procure a special license.

"I'm afraid this trip will take the better part of a week," Caius said. "Shall I send for my maiden aunt, Lady Elinor, to keep you company while I am away?"

"I'm going to be so busy with other matters that I shan't have any time to feel lonely. And if you are concerned about providing a chaperone"—she laughed—"it's rather too late for that, isn't it?"

"Yes, I suppose it is," he admitted with a wry look. "So, you will be fine without any feminine companionship? I feel terrible that none of your sisters can come."

"To be honest, I would simply like to get through the wedding ceremony and let the scandal die down before I turn my mind to friends and family."

"I understand."

"If I do feel the need for female companionship Mrs. Cooper has offered her services."

A strange look passed over his face.

"Is that not acceptable?" she asked. "I thought since she was to be one of our witnesses that—"

He smiled. "Mrs. Cooper is eminently acceptable.

Selina thought he was concealing something, but it was clear that he didn't wish to talk about whatever it was, so she changed the subject. "After you leave tomorrow, I will busy myself readying the mistress chambers for occupation." She was grateful that he couldn't see how red her face was at introducing such an indelicate subject.

He winced. "Lord. You shouldn't have to do that, Selina."

She was pleasantly distracted by her name on his tongue. Why did it sound so much more intimate than *Lady Selina*. After all, it was just the matter of the honorific in front of her name. So why—

"Selina?"

"Hmm?"

"I said why don't you let Morris take care of that."

"Mr. Morris is... I'm afraid there is no other way to put this: he is flagging, my lord."

It was a sign of how much the assessment upset him that he didn't correct her for not using his name. "Is he really that bad?"

"He is just tired. I don't think he wants to retire, but I do think we should engage a housekeeper to share the burden."

Caius looked relieved. "I would hate to see him go"—he grimaced and shook his head. "You know what I mean."

"Yes. I don't want him to leave, either. He just needs a bit of assistance. I shall ask him to contact the employment agency."

"Please do. But that still leaves you cleaning out my, er, dead wife's chambers."

"It makes sense for me to do it. That way I can set up the rooms exactly how I like."

"Well, if you are certain—"

"I am. But I need to know what should be done with her things?"

"Her father was her only real family and he died shortly after we married."

"I see. May I give her clothing, brushes, combs, and that sort of thing to the maids?"

"Yes, of course you may." He gave her a rueful look. "I'm terribly sorry you are left with this."

"I would much rather be busy until you return from London."

"Ah, that reminds me of something else. I will need to talk to your father."

"Oh. You mean about settlements and such?"

He smiled. "Yes, about settlements and such."

"Do you really need to talk to him?"

His eyebrows rose. "It is customary."

"It's just"—she bit her lip, searching for the right words, and then just decided to say what she meant. "I would rather you didn't speak to my father."

"But… there must be somebody to represent your interests."

"You cannot do it?"

He laughed. When she didn't join him, he said, "You are serious?"

"Yes."

"Why don't you want me to speak to the earl?"

"He is the reason all of us—his children—have lived in anxiety for years. I already know he will be hanging on Chatham and Needham's sleeves. I don't want him getting even more money from you."

"Ah."

"I know my father has a solicitor—can't he meet with you on my behalf? I am of age and don't need my father's approval, after all."

"If that is what you want."

"It is. I trust you… Caius."

His eyelids lowered slightly, and he held out a hand. "Come here for a moment."

Selina, who'd been sitting across from him while reading out loud, put a marker in the book and went to him.

Once she'd laid her much smaller hand in his palm, his warm, strong fingers closed around hers and he spread his knees, drawing her closer, until her legs rested against his inner thighs.

Selina suddenly found it hard to breathe and think at the same time.

"It pleases me to hear you trust me." He smiled. "Are you sure, though?"

"Yes, I am sure," she said in a slightly giddy voice.

"Perhaps I will be stingy with your pin money?"

She laughed. "You wouldn't be so cruel."

"Hmm." He moved his legs closer together, trapping her. "Are you looking forward to our wedding? Or are you nervous about getting married? I know that normally a maiden would have the benefit of her mother's wisdom before commencing her new life. Is my haste to marry depriving you of that, Selina?"

Selina gave a very unladylike squawk of laughter. "I'm sorry—I'm not laughing at you," she said when he gave her a look of surprise. "If you knew my mother then you would understand why I laughed."

"Tell me about her."

"My parents do not have a happy marriage. It is no exaggeration to say they hate each other."

He winced. "A marriage of convenience?"

"Yes, but that does not necessarily mean it cannot become a union marked by affection, respect, or even l-love," she cursed herself for stumbling over that word.

Caius smiled and lightly stroked the back of her hand with his thumb. "No, it certainly does not."

Selina bit her lip to stop the hiss of pleasure that tried to escape. Sitting across from him and reading had been difficult enough. Standing between his long, muscular legs with his hand gently rubbing hers... *Urgh*. She was so hot and inexplicably *needy* that she felt like melting into a puddle between his feet.

"Are you still there?" he teased.

"I'm sorry, I was just thinking." *About you*, she could have said, but didn't. "It is kind of you to worry, but I don't need my mother's advice before my wedding night. My sister Aurelia knows all about such matters and saw to my education years ago."

His eyes widened. "Did she?"

Selina laughed. "Shame on you, my lord. She did not come by her knowledge the way you are thinking."

"Oh, what was I thinking... Selina?"

"*You* know," she retorted.

He chuckled. "Tell me then, just how did she become so, er, knowledgeable?"

"She is an illustrator and often does anatomical drawings. And she used that knowledge to our benefit."

"I see."

She narrowed her eyes. "Why are you smirking that way?"

"Was I?"

"Yes. And you *still* are. Why?"

"I'm just thinking that medical journals and scientific drawings have very little to do with what happens between a man and woman in the bedchamber."

Selina made a mortifying gulping sound. Judging by the way his smirk grew broader, Caius heard it. She gently pulled her hand from his light grasp so that she could put both her palms up to her flaming cheeks. "My face could serve as a torch right now."

He laughed, and then stood, their bodies close enough to touch "I wish more than anything I could see you," he murmured quietly, his fingers carefully finding their way from her elbows up to her wrists. He lifted her hands from her face and replaced them with his own palms. "Ah, yes—I can *feel* this blush." His smile slowly slid away and the hunger that replaced it released an entire flock of butterflies in her stomach. "It is a good thing I am leaving tomorrow, Selina," he said in a roughened voice, caressing her cheeks with his thumbs.

"Wh-why is that?"

"Because it would be very difficult for me to behave like a gentleman if I were here for the next week. In fact, it would be impossible not to open the door to my gymnasium and hope the next time you peeked into my room you came inside to join me."

A mental picture of how he'd looked that night flashed through her mind's eye—as it had done times beyond counting—and Selina's breathing quickened at the memory of him naked and sweaty and aroused.

"Oh, my."

He smiled. "*Oh, my*? Is that all you have to say?"

"Yes."

He lightly dragged one thumb over her lower lip and she opened her mouth, flicking his salty skin with the tip of her tongue.

He hissed in a breath as if he were in physical pain. "You teasing minx," he accused when she laughed. "I will miss you," he said, and then lowered his mouth over hers, kissing her with the leashed passion of a banked fire.

Selina eagerly opened to his invasion, her arms sliding around his waist as if that was where they belonged. If she'd felt anything even half as wonderful before, she couldn't remember it. She filled her lungs with the faint scent of cologne and clean male sweat while her fingers explored the latticed muscles of his back, and then lower… to the intriguingly tight globes beneath his sleek pantaloons.

"Yes," he whispered against her mouth, rocking his hips against her, the hard ridge of his erection grazing her belly.

Selina felt dizzy from too much sensation. He smelled and felt and tasted so *good* and his tongue probed her with taunting flicks that had her all but climbing up the hard wall of his body. If she could only get closer and—

He suddenly pulled away with a groan. "Good God," he muttered, inhaling a long, unsteady breath before gently, but firmly, putting her at arm's length. "I want you so much—too much. I'll have your skirts up around your waist and bend you over this damned chair if you stay here."

Selina's jaw sagged at his vulgar words and her body thrummed with desire at his crude threat. She opened her mouth to beg him to *do* it.

But then he said, "You'd better go up to bed now, sweetheart. I am not safe for you to be around tonight."

She wanted to argue—to tell him that *she* wasn't safe, either. That she didn't want to be *safe* and didn't he know that?

"Selina?" His face was tilted toward hers and he was giving her a questioning look.

As usual, a lifetime of doing what she was told had her obeying without question, rather than demanding what she wanted. "Of course, my lord. Good night," she said, and then turned away and trudged up to her lonely room.

But just because she'd left him in the library did not mean that either her mind or body could forget that only a flight of stairs and several corridors separated her from Lord Shaftsbury's chambers. She decided it was better to think of him in formal terms as it was probably the only thing that kept her from flinging caution to the wind and going to him.

As a result of her mental turmoil, she didn't fall asleep until the wee hours of the morning, which meant she had to say goodbye to Caius while smothering yawns. It was only a small consolation that the marquess looked just as heavy-eyed and tired.

As the coach rolled away down the drive, Selina thought about what he'd asked her the night before—the question she had never answered: Was she looking forward to their marriage?

The answer was not as simple and straightforward as she'd formerly believed.

Yes, she found him attractive and desirable and there was no denying that she was looking forward to their wedding night.

Yes, she enjoyed the challenge of managing his household and was delighted that she would be permitted to exercise even more control as his wife.

No, she wasn't concerned about his blindness or how it would affect their lives or future. Maybe that was careless of her, but Selina simply could not bring herself to worry, no matter that Lord Victor seemed to view Caius as a helpless cripple who would need to be hand fed for the rest of his days.

Selina had only ever known Shaftsbury blind, so—unlike his awful brother—she had no sighted memory of the man to mourn. To Selina, he was fascinating, vibrant, devastatingly handsome, and appeared to like her because of the things she said and did, not because she had lips like roses or any other claptrap.

She hadn't known it the day Lord Victor had blackmailed her, but Selina now realized that she would have accepted the marquess's offer of marriage regardless of what his brother had threatened.

But she also had to admit that she probably wouldn't be marrying Caius if Lord Victor hadn't meddled and discovered her identity.

So, in a sense, she had to be grateful to Lord Victor for that one thing, at least.

She would have been overjoyed at her good fortune if not for the knowledge that Victor had likely pressured—if not blackmailed—Caius to marry her as well.

The only thing Selina had to offer a man—her pretty face—meant nothing to somebody who could not see. What if Caius had wanted some other woman for a wife? Or what if he'd not wanted to remarry? After all, his first marriage had obviously not been a happy one.

None of that mattered because Selina had taken any choice in the matter from him the day she'd lied her way into his home and life.

Oh, she knew that he liked her and they got along well enough, but she also knew what it felt like to have her choices taken away. All her life her future had been directed by others, her own preferences of no account to anyone.

And now she had done the same thing to the very man she would be spending the rest of her life with.

***

Caius was surprised by how much he enjoyed the journey to London with his brother.

While Victor was rigid, stern, and far too somber for his age, he was also intelligent, observant, and witty when he let down his guard and forgot that he hated Caius.

But just because he enjoyed Victor's company didn't mean he agreed with everything his brother suggested.

"Once we've changed and rested for a bit we should go to White's." Victor said as Caius's coach pulled up in front of his town house. "You have been gone from London too long," he added, even though Caius hadn't argued. "It is time you made an appearance. There will not be many people in town, so it will be a good way to make, er, to make—"

"To make myself known and show that I am blind without being mobbed," Caius finished for him. "*Blind* is not a vulgar word, you know."

Victor sighed. "Will you go with me?

It was the last thing Caius wanted to do, but his brother was right. The time for hoping he would suddenly wake up one morning having regained his sight was over. He'd resigned himself to being blind, he might as well get on with letting the world know.

By the time Victor was ready to go out that evening Caius had walked the house twice and felt some degree of familiarity with the layout. He wouldn't be able to navigate it with ease, as he did Courtland, but he wouldn't be lost at sea if he were to be left to his own devices.

It was a very short hackney ride to his club and far too soon Caius found himself walking up the familiar five steps as he'd done a thousand nights before, albeit on his brother's arm this time.

Victor kept up a low, running commentary—informing Caius of the members they passed, which allowed him to nod and call out greetings—as they made their way to the back dining room.

They ate their meal while the people he knew stopped by to pay their respects. It was awkward, but at least it was a first step toward dispelling the rumors and mystery that had surrounded his accident for a year. And Victor had been correct about the club being sparsely peopled at this time of the summer.

"Shall we walk back?" Victor suggested once Caius had endured all the socializing he could bear for one night.

"If you don't mind going at my more leisurely pace."

"Indeed, no. It is a lovely evening."

They walked for a while in silence before Caius spoke. "How long will you stay at Courtland?"

"I thought I would leave shortly after the wedding."

"Why so soon?"

"I think we both know the less time I spend at Courtland the better."

"That is how it used to be, Victor. But we are both older now. Surely you are interested in the life you left behind. Do you really wish to live in a foreign country where you know nobody and have no connections?"

"I've been at the monastery for over eight years, Caius. It is my home now and it is England that feels foreign."

Caius considered what he was about to say very, very carefully before he spoke. "Mrs. Cooper has been a widow for years, Victor."

His brother's arm tightened under Caius's hand. "I know that. What is your point?"

"I want to apologize for what I did eight years ago—for what I said. I regret it and I want you to know I feel differently. I am deeply sorry. I cannot change the past, but if I could do things over again, I would listen to you this time. I wouldn't assume that I know best and plan your future as if you don't deserve a say."

Not until they'd reached the house and handed off their hats and gloves, did his brother finally speak.

"Thank you for saying that, Caius."

"I should have said it a long time ago."

He heard his brother take a breath, as if he were going to speak, but then he paused.

"Say what you want, Victor. Let us clear the air and start afresh, shall we?"

Victor still hesitated before saying, "Are you happy with this marriage, Caius?"

It wasn't what Caius had expected at all.

Victor hurried on, perhaps ascribing Caius's silence to something other than surprise. "I'm sorry about how vehement I was that you needed to marry her. If you aren't sure this is—"

Caius reached out, relieved when his hand landed on his brother's shoulder, rather than his face. "I'm glad you were vehement or I might never have raised the issue with Lady Selina. You pressed me, Victor, but it was the right thing to do." He smiled. "I'm just happy Lady Selina did not require any convincing. It was an enormous relief that she didn't find the idea of marriage with me repellent. In any case, I should be thanking you."

"That—that is very generous of you," his brother said stiffly, as if he were uncomfortable with Caius's praise. "I'll, erm, bid you good night, then. I'm going to the library for a bit. Do you need my help getting—"

"No, I can find my room just fine. Good night, Victor."

As Caius tapped his way to his chambers he was assailed by a sharp pang of guilt. His brother had received so few positive words from him over the years that he was obviously rendered speechless when Caius finally *did* say something kind.

He really would try to do better by Victor from now on. Perhaps his brother might even be convinced to delay his return to Morrocco indefinitely if Caius were persuasive enough.

Chapter 26

Selina had been calm—almost serene—all morning, even during the brief wedding ceremony.

And she'd been calm during the wedding breakfast with Caius, Victor, Reverend Sayers, and Mrs. Cooper.

She had even been calm when Caius had insisted that she entertain their guests with a few songs on the piano after they'd finished eating.

But now the vicar and his daughter had gone home and Lord Victor—or simply *Victor*, as he'd asked her to call him—had retired to his chambers and it was only Selina and her new husband.

"You are very quiet, my dear. Are you tired?"

Was that his way of asking if she wanted to go to bed? Surely not. It was scarcely five o'clock in the afternoon. He couldn't be thinking they should—

Caius chuckled. "I can almost *hear* your mind racing."

Selina gave a weak laugh. "Oh, am I being terribly obvious?"

He laid a hand over hers, which was resting on his forearm. "I think it is understandable for a bride to be nervous about her wedding night... Selina."

She noticed that he wasn't leading her up the stairs. "Where are we going, my lord, er, I mean *Caius*."

"I thought we might sit out on the terrace, perhaps share some of the wine I brought back from London. We could even play a game of chess—it is a beautiful afternoon."

Mr. Bascum had delivered the chess set when Caius was in London so they'd not had a chance to play a game yet.

"Oh, yes, that sounds lovely. Shall I ring for Morris and ask him to—"

He squeezed her hand lightly. "It is already done... Lady Shaftsbury."

Selina gave a breathless laugh. "That will take some getting used to." She paused and then blurted, "I outrank my mother, now."

He gave her that look—the one that always made her feel as if he was *seeing* her—and then he laughed.

Selina groaned. "That was a terribly petty thing to say. Wasn't it?"

"Perhaps, but I found it amusing—and endearing." He led her right up to the French doors that opened onto the terrace, barely needing to feel around before finding the handle and opening it for her.

Selina

"I see you've been practicing. Very impressive, Caius," she said as she preceded him outside.

"I have a very impressive teacher."

Selina stopped and stared at the pretty striped tent that hadn't been there this morning.

"Oh, my goodness!" There was a table laden with food, wine, and a profusion of cut flowers. Nearby was the chess table, which was already set up. The two chairs were draped with gauzy material that was the same dark rose as the gown she was wearing.

She turned to her husband. "It is so beautiful. Did you do all this?"

"I was the architect, but Morris put my plans into action."

"How did you know that pink is my favorite color and dahlias my favorite flower?" she asked, unable to resist cupping one of the large, colorful blooms.

"I wrote to Chatham. I thought I owed him a bit of an explanation for using his sister-in-law as my housekeeper and then stealing her for my wife. I'd also hoped his duchess could give me some information about you."

Selina laughed. "Hy wouldn't know what my favorite color or flower was if one bit her on the nose."

"I wasn't aware how unnatural your sister was until Chatham explained it to me," he said, chuckling. "Luckily Lady Needham was able to give me all sorts of information."

"You wrote to Phoebe, too—or the viscount, I suppose?"

"Yes, I did."

Selina was deeply touched. "How thoughtful of you. It is all beautiful, Caius." She brushed a happy tear off her cheek. "Thank you."

"You are welcome."

"I see the wine is here and decanted, shall I pour us both a glass?"

"Please."

"Are you hungry?" she asked. "There is a veritable feast laid—oh! You've got lobster patties, apple tarts, and marzipan." She laughed. "I shall have to write to Phoebe and thank her for giving you such good information," she said, bringing him his glass. "Thank you again for being so thoughtful."

Caius took the wine, and also took her hand, lifting it to his lips. "You are welcome, Selina. It was nice to learn a few things about you." He turned her hand palm up and pressed a kiss on the sensitive skin, holding it to his lips for a long moment before releasing her. "If Morris has done his job right—and I know he has—there should be something for you on the table."

There was indeed a lovely box sitting amid the food and wine.

"Oh, you didn't have—"

"I wanted to get you something. Hopefully it is something you will like." He smiled. "If you don't, then you shall have to scold Lady Needham for the suggestion or perhaps Victor, as he was my eyes for the purchase."

"The box itself is very beautiful," she said, sliding a finger over the cool enamel. "It has floral designs in pastel shades with gold chasing."

"Open it," he urged.

She lifted the lid and hissed in a breath. "Oh, Caius! They are so… pink," she whispered.

He chuckled. "So I've been told. I hope I haven't over done it."

"No, I love them. But… what kind of stones are they? I've never seen the like." Selina picked up the gold filigreed ring with the large cushion cut stone and slid it onto her finger. It fit perfectly.

"They are pink sapphires, but people often call them Ceylon rubies."

There was a necklace, earrings, and bracelet along with the ring.

"I'm putting them on," she told him, fastening the bracelet before removing the slender gold chain and cross that had been her only jewelry for the wedding. "It is a bit extravagant for the dress I am wearing," she admitted, clasping the necklace.

"I think you can be forgiven," he teased. "It is your wedding day, after all."

"There," she said, once she'd screwed in the second earring.

He carefully set down his glass on the table and said, "Come closer. I want to feel them."

Selina went near enough that her breast brushed against his chest. Even that slight contact was enough to send pleasure arrowing through her body. Her breathing—which hadn't been all that regular before—turned positively wheezy when Caius carefully traced the necklace with warm fingers.

"It certainly *feels* beautiful." His lips curled up slowly into a sensual smile that whipped her heart into a gallop.

The expression also created a faint dimple in his right cheek. Selina had dimples—two big ones—and people were always commenting on them. Older ladies and gentlemen often felt free to pinch her cheeks. She had never understood the appeal of divots in one's cheeks.

Until now.

"You have a dimple," she said, reaching for his face.

His smile deepened. "You like that?"

"I do." The words were so breathy they were barely a whisper.

"Are you nervous, Selina?"

"A little."

"Me, too."

"You are?"

"Why are you so surprised at that?"

"You are not a…" Cowardice struck before she could articulate the word *virgin*.

"A virgin? No, I am not. That doesn't mean I can't be nervous… and excited." His fingers lingered on her clavicle, his light touch sending shivers through her. His nostrils flared at her reaction and he didn't ask her if she was cold. His hands, large and warm, stroked up her throat, his grip tightening slightly, making her feel small and delicate and powerless.

He gave a low rumble of pleasure deep in his chest and then loosened his fingers and moved on to her jaw and then ears.

Selina was startled by how sensitive her ears felt beneath his exploratory touch.

He paused and cocked his head as he felt the screws that held the heavy dangles on her earlobes. "I've always wondered, do these become sore?"

"After several hours they do if they are heavy."

He smiled, the expression not sweet, but predatory. "I don't think you will have them on that long tonight."

Selina caught her breath at the wicked look on his face.

His thumb grazed her lower lip and then came back for another swipe, pressing against the sensitive skin until the pad of his finger rested against her teeth.

And then his mouth lowered over hers and she closed her eyes and sagged against him.

"Mmmm," he murmured, drawing her body closer, until they were pressed together from thighs to chest.

His lips parted and his tongue probed and enticed. Selina followed eagerly into the hot velvet of his mouth. The kiss deepened, growing hungry and demanding.

She slid her hands around his hips, which were every bit as muscular as she recalled, the thin weave of his gray pantaloons warm from the hot, hard body beneath them. Her fingers itched to explore and she caressed up his waist, sliding her hand beneath the silver silk of his waistcoat.

He groaned and pulled away just enough to say, "Yes, touch me, Selina. I want lots and lots of touches," he whispered. The raw need in his voice pierced the sensual fog that clouded her head.

Of course he needed to be touched. Just as his hands were now his eyes, his skin was his connection to the world around him. To her.

Selina dug her fingers into the corded muscles of his sides and he growled with pleasure.

"Mmm, strong hands. I like that." His own hands brazenly splayed over her bottom and he cupped a cheek in each palm, squeezing and kneading her in a way that made her very aware of how wet and swollen she'd become. "I don't want to play chess right now," he murmured into her ear, before nipping her hard enough to make her squeak. "I want to go upstairs, Selina."

She swallowed and nodded, her heart hammering against her ribs.

He caressed her kiss-swollen lower lip with his thumb. "Is that a *yes*, Lady Shaftsbury?"

"Yes, my lord. Yes, please."

***

Caius knew it was unseemly to want to bed his new wife so badly that he couldn't even wait for the sun to set.

But he didn't care.

He walked her to the door of her chambers. "I will come to you in half an hour."

"Yes... Caius."

His cock, which was already straining at his placket like a racehorse pawing the starting line, throbbed at the sound of his name on her lips.

But as eager as he was, he walked slowly and carefully to his own chambers. It wouldn't do to hurry, trip over his own bloody feet, and stab himself in the chest with his walking stick and die on his wedding night, would it?

"James," he barked once he entered his bedroom.

"Yes, my lord, I'm right here."

He ran a palm over his jaw, wincing at the bristles. "I need a shave." He'd had one that morning, but his whiskers grew as quickly as they were cut so he'd probably already scraped her delicate skin.

A maid appeared with steaming water so quickly that Caius knew it must have already been on the boil when James rang for it.

Every servant in the house probably knew how eager the master was for his new bride. Caius didn't care; a mere month ago he never would have believed that any woman would want him, not to mention such a vibrant, clever, and caring creature as his new wife. He'd thought his life was all but over, but Selina made him believe it had only just begun.

Selina

As James shaved off his whiskers Caius thought back on the simple wedding ceremony. It had been the opposite of his first wedding, which had been a grand affair in St. George's. The spectacle hadn't been for Caius or Louisa, but for her father, who'd finally achieved his lifetime dream of marrying his daughter to an aristocrat. And if Caius hadn't been the duke that Mr. Corbett had hoped for, the old man had seemed satisfied with the next best thing.

Today's ceremony had been intimate, warm, and comfortable. At least it had been for Caius, Selina, and the vicar.

He'd felt a pang of guilt when he'd heard the stiff, stilted way Victor and Mrs. Cooper had greeted each other, but their behavior toward each other had markedly eased over the course of the afternoon. He might be blind, but it didn't take eyes to know that Victor and Mrs. Cooper still loved each other.

It had been Caius's idea to draw out the wedding breakfast by inviting the vicar and his daughter to stay and enjoy Selina's exquisite performance on the piano. By the time he and Selina had said goodbye to their guests, Caius was quite optimistic for his brother.

It was his fondest wish that he be called upon to serve as Victor's groomsman before the summer was over. He had come to enjoy his younger brother's company greatly and didn't want him to move hundreds of miles away. If Victor married his childhood sweetheart perhaps it might be possible to bridge the gap between them and become friends.

James removed the steaming cloth he'd placed around Caius's neck and face and lightly patted him dry.

"No nightshirt, James. Just my robe—the gray one."

Going without a nightshirt might shock his new bride, but Caius refused to be cheated of feeling every inch of her skin against his. Besides, he could just imagine himself bumbling and tripping if he were to try to remove a nightshirt in a suave, erotic fashion.

Once he'd slipped on his robe, he grabbed his walking stick and tapped his way to the connecting door, using it for the first time in a year and a half.

Hopefully this visit would be more enjoyable than the last ones had been.

***

Selina stared into the mirror as her new maid brushed out her hair.

The day had passed in a blur. The cozy ceremony, the small but enjoyable breakfast, and those scant few minutes in the pavilion Caius had erected for her had all led to *this*.

How could a person be eager and anxious at the same time.

Fanny laid down the brush. "Is there anything else, my lady?"

"No, thank you, Fanny," she said, smiling at the younger woman. "You may go."

The girl—for Fanny was only sixteen—curtsied low enough to please a queen, her face even pinker than Selina's. "Good night, my lady."

Fanny had been one of his lordship's parlor maids. She'd confided to Selina, when she'd been housekeeper, that her dream was to be a lady's maid. It had made Selina feel like a fairy godmother to grant the sweet girl's wish.

Selina sighed and looked around her new room, willing herself to be calm. Yes, it was her wedding night, but her new husband was kind and thoughtful and patient. She knew that she had nothing to fear from him even though her mother had constantly warned her of the perfidy and lust of men.

Lady Addiscombe hated her husband with the sort of vehemence that one usually only witnessed in Shakespeare's plays. And Selina's father hated his wife right back, albeit with more aristocratic sangfroid.

Selina jolted at the sound of the connecting door opening and turned to find Caius on the threshold, garbed in a banyan that was the same shade of antique silver as his eyes.

"It is so quiet in here," he said. "Please tell me this the correct room?"

Selina chuckled. "Yes, you have come to the right place, my lord." She stood, her legs shaky in the presence of such male beauty. And so much bare skin.

"Are you back to *my lording* me, Selina?"

"I'm sorry, I'm just—well, I am nervous."

He made his way toward the dressing table, his steps confident.

"You have been practicing, haven't you?" she said when he stopped only about a foot away from her.

"Yes. I'm learning to listen more closely, which certainly helps me guess a person's location more accurately. As for this room"—he leaned his walking stick against her dressing table and closed the distance between them before sliding his hands around her waist— "I came in here several times already and practiced that smooth, confident saunter you just witnessed."

Selina grinned and set her hands on his shoulders, craning her neck to look up at his face. "You did very well, I am quite impressed."

"I deserve a reward for good behavior, don't I?"

She bit her lower lip to keep from laughing. "I don't know. Do you?"

"Mmm-hmm." He nuzzled her temple and trailed kisses down her jaw and then across to her mouth. Instead of kissing her, he rested his forehead against hers. "A reward would encourage continued good behavior."

"What sort of a reward would you like? Money?"

"Hmmm, how much were you thinking?"

"You would need to speak with my husband; he is the one with the fat purse. All I have is my paltry pin money."

He laughed. "Oh no! Is he clutch-fisted? Well, no need to drag *him* into this."

"No. Especially not when he is prone to throwing books when he is vexed."

"*Ooof!* That was a low blow, my lady. Who knew you were such a dirty fighter?"

Emboldened by his amusement, she cupped his face in her hands. "I don't have any money, but how about a kiss as reward? Will that do?"

"Just one?" he murmured, and then lowered his mouth to hers.

He groaned when her tongue slid into his mouth and she explored him, releasing all the pent-up excitement of the past few weeks.

"Look who is a fast learner," he murmured, tilting his head to give her better access.

"I had a good teacher," she said, her words an echo of his.

His hands roamed her body as if he sought to commit every part of her to memory, his touch confident and possessive.

By the time he released her, Selina had forgotten her own name.

He cupped her cheek with one hand and plucked at her nightrail with the other, his pale cheeks darkly flushed. "Tell me what you are wearing—it is soft but quite… voluminous."

She gave a rueful chuckle. "It is not elegant or pretty, just a simple white nightgown without so much as a scrap of lace."

"I suspect you do not require much adornment, Selina." His smile was soft and his eyes almost black as he traced the line of her jaw with his knuckles. His nostrils flared and he said, "In fact, why don't you take it off."

Selina could not look away, entranced by the desire on his face.

"Do you want me to close my eyes again?" he teased when she hesitated. "Or shall I draw the drapes?"

"They are already drawn," she admitted.

He laughed. "Is there even a candle burning? Or are we *both* in the dark?"

"N-no, there is a candle—there are two of them, actually."

"Would it make you feel more comfortable to snuff them?"

"No," she lied. As ridiculous as it was, taking her clothing off in front of him made her shy. She would have loved to snuff the candles for her own comfort, but she desperately wanted to see Caius—even more than she wanted to hide.

She took a step back, pushed the loose gown from her shoulders, and then brazenly returned to him, standing close enough that her nipples grazed the silk brocade of his robe.

He lifted his hands to her bare hips and his eyelids fluttered as he sucked in a breath. "My God," he groaned. "I have been dreaming of touching you."

So had Selina, but she was too much of a coward to admit it.

"You feel like warm silk." He slid his hands higher, moving with agonizing slowness, making her shiver with anticipation.

His lips parted slightly and his breathing quickened when his fingers flexed around her waist. "Good Lord, you're so small I can almost span you." His thumbs reverently stroked the sensitive skin of her belly before moving up and up, coming to a stop beneath her breasts.

If there was one part of her body that she truly disliked, it was her ridiculously large breasts.

Caius, on the other hand, looked positively enthralled as he cupped them in his palms. "Selina," he whispered.

She shuddered and bit her lower lip when his thumbs circled her nipples.

"You feel divine. I'll wager you taste even better," he said, his voice husky as he lowered his mouth.

It was her turn to groan as he suckled first one and then the other nipple with his hot mouth, nibbling and suckling until her breasts were heavy with need.

"Touch me, Selina."

His words shook her from her pleasure-soaked fugue, and she tunneled her fingers into his hair, which was thick, silky, and fine.

"Yes," he murmured when she tightened her hands into fists, gently pulling.

He sucked her nipples harder, until the pleasure edged on pain. And yet she wanted—no, she *needed*—more.

"Yes, more," Caius said, which is when Selina realized she'd spoken out loud and was wantonly thrusting herself against him, all but shoving her breast in his mouth.

"No, don't stop," he ordered, sliding a hand down to her buttock and pulling her closer, holding her in a firm, unbreakable grasp as he tormented her with pleasure.

"Please, Caius," she begged, not sure what she wanted but certain that he was the only one who could give it to her.

Rather than ease her need, his lips disappeared entirely from her breast and he began walking her backward. "Please tell me that I am guiding you in the direction of the bed and not into the fireplace, darling."

Selina laughed and adjusted their direction slightly.

"Have I told you how much I adore your laughter?" he asked.

"You do? My mother said it was horrid—like the squawking of a startled hen."

"The more I hear about your mother—" he broke off when they bumped against the mattress. "Ah, here we are at last. Get up onto the bed, darling."

Selina scrambled to do his bidding and he followed her up with more grace.

"I need to touch you—all over," he said, shooting her a questioning look as he caressed her feet and calves. "Do you understand what I mean? Did your sister's, er, expertise extend to some of the other things men like to do to women?"

"I know about the act of c-coitus."

He smiled and his hands caressed from her feet up her legs. "This is something else—something that will give us both a great deal of pleasure. Bend your knees for me, darling—yes, just like that," he praised when she obeyed. "Now, let your legs fall open."

A gasp slipped out of her and she clenched her thighs tightly together.

He paused. "That sounded like a shocked noise—was it?"

"Perhaps a little."

He caressed her knees with his thumbs. "I want us to be lovers, Selina, not just a man and woman doing their duty. Yes, I want to put a child in your belly, but I also want us to enjoy ourselves. Of all the activities that are lost to me, pleasing a lover—thank God—is not one of them. I do wish I could look at you." He smiled, exposing that tempting dimple again. "But I'd much rather be able to touch than see when it comes to making love." He leaned close and kissed the inside of one knee, and then the other. "I daresay you've heard the first time is unpleasant?"

Her mother's words echoed in her mind: *It is a repulsive, animal experience, Selina. If you are fortunate, you will only need to do it a handful of times before your duty is fulfilled. Not like me.* The countess had been referring to the fact that she'd endured five daughters and three miscarriages before she gave the earl his heir.

"My mother said it would be sh-shockingly painful," Selina admitted.

"It can be uncomfortable, but there are things—exceedingly enjoyable things—that I can do that will relax you and prepare your body to take me."

"Th-things?"

"Do you trust me, Selina?"

"Yes, I trust you," she said without hesitation. A great deal more than she trusted her own mother.

He stroked her cheek. "You honor me with your trust. I will endeavor to always be worthy of it. Now, if you are shy, you can close your eyes. If you are curious, you can put a few pillows behind your back and watch."

Selina stared at his face and knew in that moment that he would have given a great deal to be able to see her and what they were doing together. She would be a coward to hide away from this experience.

"I will watch."

Chapter 27

Was Caius a bastard to engage in such an earthy, erotic activity with his innocent wife? Perhaps, but he would not live with another woman who hated him and told him to take his physical needs elsewhere. The best way to ensure that Selina always welcomed him into her bed was to seduce her with so much pleasure that she looked forward to his visits.

Caius took his time caressing up her shapely calves to her knees and then firmly stroked the long muscles of her thighs. He didn't need eyes to know that the body beneath his hands was every man's dream. She was curvy and luxuriously feminine, her full breasts as soft as clouds, her hips wide and generously padded, with the tiniest waist he'd ever felt.

He kissed his way up her inner leg, the twitching of her muscles below his lips communicating her nervousness.

Caius hesitated over the silky skin of her thigh and looked up, hoping he was meeting her eyes and not staring at the nightstand behind her. "You can tell me to stop or ask questions any time you like, Selina. Never do anything in bed with me that doesn't please you. In fact, never do anything at all for me, or with me, that doesn't please you."

"I would ask you to do the same," she said.

"I think you already know I have no reservations about complaining when I don't want to do something."

She laughed. "And I've certainly shown no hesitancy when it comes to nagging you."

"How lucky for both of us that I've grown to crave being nagged by you."

"Of course you have, my lord," she mocked, but some of the tautness had eased out of her body, which is what he'd intended.

"Relax and let me give you pleasure." He kissed her inner thigh, closing his eyes and dragging his tongue over the faintly salty skin, allowing the scent and taste of her to invade his senses.

He stroked up her legs and over her pelvis, avoiding her sex for the moment, caressing the gentle rise of her belly and continuing up to the luscious breasts he'd barely sampled earlier. He teased and licked and sucked her nipples until they were once again tight little buds, until her hips were lifting, back arching.

Only then did he make his way down and down, until her private curls tickled his chin.

He could feel the moment she realized where he'd gone because her entire body tightened like a newly strung bow.

"Shhh," he murmured, kissing the thin, sensitive skin of her pelvis while he gently parted her lips with his thumbs and lowered his mouth over her.

"Caius," she gasped as he ran his tongue from her opening to the erect little bud at the apex. "Oh!" Her hips bucked off the bed to chase his tongue when he pulled away.

"Do you want me to stop?" he asked, unable to keep from smirking.

"No! Er, that is, I wasn't aware people could, um, do this sort of thing."

"Ah, your sister has been withholding information from you."

"I don't think Aurelia—*ah*! Knows about this."

He licked the silky petals of her sex but purposely avoided touching the bundle of nerves that would drive her toward bliss. "Does this feel good?"

He heard her swallow. "It—yes, er, but perhaps—" her hips moved to make his tongue or finger go where she wanted. She gave a grunt of frustration when he again missed the spot. "No, that's not it."

He bit his lip, beyond amused and aroused to hear the forthright Mrs. Lanyon babble and stumble.

"Caius—"

He leaned forward and captured her peak between his lips, sucking gently while massaging her with his tongue.

The next sounds she made weren't words, at least no words that Caius had ever heard and her hips ground against his face in a motion as old as mankind. When her fingers found their way into his hair Caius knew she'd lost at least a few of her inhibitions.

He closed his eyes and gave himself up to pure sensation, reveling in her delicate musk and thrilling to the series of increasingly desperate whimpers falling from her lips.

By the time he'd worked the first orgasm from her body—and listened with smug pride as his prim, respectable Mrs. Lanyon shouted out his name—Caius knew that he'd made a convert to at least one *unnatural* bedroom act.

She was still shuddering from her climax when Caius eased a finger inside her tight sheath. He groaned. "My God, but you're tight," he said, his cock throbbing at the thought of thrusting inside her.

Although she was considerably more relaxed than she had been, Caius knew she'd still feel pain when he penetrated her. The more he could work the tension from her body, the better things would be when the time came. What she needed was another orgasm, several if he had his way. And he intended to.

Her hips twitched as he fucked her with slow, gentle thrusts of his finger, carefully avoiding the too-sensitive bead of flesh.

"Yes," he praised as she began to undulate beneath him, spreading her thighs, digging her heels into the mattress, and lifting her hips to take his finger deeper. His new wife might be a novice in the bedroom, but her body already knew what it wanted.

"Is this too sensitive?" he asked lowering his mouth to tongue her peak while he eased a second finger inside her. She whimpered but didn't pull away or stop grinding against his hand, so Caius decided to take that as a *no*.

His bride was a vocal little thing and he suspected that Victor—who was at the far end of the hall—was likely getting an earful. It was a sign of how immature Caius was that he enjoyed the thought of his brother having to listen to Selina scream out her pleasure—over and over again.

Her climax built faster this time and she wrapped her thighs around his head and held him down with both hands, roughly using his mouth for her pleasure.

Not until her legs went slack and fell open did Caius ease out of her tight passage.

Her body was still jerking with contractions as he knelt between her legs. He carefully leaned forward until his lips found her cheek. He kissed her and then asked, "How are you, darling?"

"I'm—that was nice."

He grinned. "Just nice?"

"It was lovely," she retorted, sounding mortified.

He chuckled. "Good. I'm going to play with you a bit more. Is that alright?"

"Uh, ye-yes," she said, her raspy voice breaking.

He kissed her again and took his aching cock in his fist. "Spread your thighs for me, Selina."

He felt her body jolt and then her legs opened wider.

"Mmm," he murmured as he stroked the head of his prick up and down her soaking slit, rubbing the crown over her engorged bud with each pass. "Does that feel good? Do you want more?"

"Yes."

Caius could practically *hear* her squirming. "*Yes* it feels good, or *yes* you want more?" he asked, feigning confusion.

"*Urgh.* Both—*yes* to both," she said, sounding deliciously shy and amusingly irritated at the same time.

Caius decided right then and there that getting his normally forthright—yet suddenly bashful—wife to talk during sex was his new favorite pastime.

He was tempted to make her beg, but he'd already tormented her enough for one night—especially her very first time—so instead he gave her what she needed, using the head of his shaft to stroke her, until her fingers were digging into his shoulders and her body was shaking.

"Come for me once more, Selina," he said, giving her friction exactly where she needed it to push her over the edge.

She shouted something that sounded like his name, her body spasming as waves of pleasure rolled through her.

Caius slid his crown to her opening and then entered her in one smooth thrust.

She gasped, her sheath squeezing him almost painfully tight as another contraction rippled through her body.

"Selina?" he said when she stilled.

"Yes?"

"I'm sorry, darling." Caius leaned down to kiss her. He was aiming for her mouth but found her nose, instead, so he kissed the tip. "I thought it would be better to have done with the uncomfortable part quickly," he explained. "Are you in pain?"

***

Selina blinked at him, intensely aware that he was inside her.

The echoes of her climax were fading now and her thoughts weren't so foggy. It had hurt when he'd entered her—the pain sharp and unlike any other she'd ever felt—but having his hard length inside her had also seemed to intensify the pleasure.

"Sweetheart?" he asked, his voice strained. "You need to talk to me—tell me if you are in pain because I can't see your face."

"It hurt, but only for a few seconds. I didn't think you would feel so big."

He gave a breathless laugh. "Thank you; that is very kind. You feel—well, there are no words to express how good you feel."

"Yes, words seem inadequate for this," Selina agreed.

"How do you feel now?"

"Now it's, um—" she paused, struggling to express the feeling of incredible fullness and the intimacy and—

She finally shook her head. "Never mind."

Selina

He smiled down at her. "Tell me. Please."

"You will think it's silly."

"I didn't think you were the sort of woman who cared what other people thought?"

Selina felt strangely flattered by his words, no matter that she knew she hardly deserved such praise.

He leaned down and kissed her, missing her lips and hitting her chin, instead.

That small action—his own fearlessness—made her bold. "It is so strange to think that a part of your body is actually inside me."

His expression shifted from anxious to bemused. After a moment, he cocked his head. "Hmm."

"See? I told you that you would think it silly."

"I don't think it is silly. You are right, it *is* strange. And wonderful." His lips curved into a slow, sensual smile as he stared down at her, his eyes darker than usual. "And I am the only one who gets to experience such a marvelous phenomenon with you." He punctuated his words by withdrawing slowly.

Selina hissed at the loss of him, missing him already.

"More?" he whispered.

"Yes, please."

Their faces were mere inches apart as he stroked in and out of her, his powerful body maintaining an easy, measured rhythm, his shaft sinking into her deeper with each thrust, until the uncomfortable stretching sensation disappeared completely, replaced by a fierce sense of *rightness*.

His jaw flexed and his thrusts grew harder, less controlled. "You feel so good, Selina—I don't ever want it to end, but I'm afraid it will soon." He grunted and shifted his weight to one arm, sliding a hand between their bodies. "I want to feel you come when I spend in you."

Selina felt a raw shock of arousal, not just at his touch, but at his wicked, erotic words. His clever fingers were already strumming that part of her that seemed magical. She felt the now-familiar sensation of every nerve in her body tightening, as if they were expanding and would soon grow beyond her skin.

Just when she thought it was too much to bear, when she began to ache, he pressed his thumb against her throbbing flesh and she exploded.

Selina was vaguely aware of his hoarse shout and then wild, almost violent thrusts. And then he drove himself deep—so deep it hurt—and she felt him thicken just as a heat flooded her. His big body jerked, the spasms lessening with each successive one, the same way that her contractions had gradually ebbed.

When he shuddered and lowered his weight on top of her it should have been uncomfortable. Instead, Selina felt safer and more cherished than she'd ever felt in her life.

She slid her arms around his hot, sweaty body and sighed with utter contentment. She had been worried about tonight for nothing. Naturally, her mother had been wrong—she was always wrong. Lying with her husband—making love with him, as he'd called it—was delicious.

She smiled and then yawned. Her first day of married life was almost over. Selina decided she was very pleased with her choice of husband.

Her eyelids drifted closed, sleep tugging at her consciousness.

Very pleased, indeed.

***

Caius knew he couldn't have slept for long because his skin was still hot with exertion when he lifted his weight off Selina.

There was a certain stillness to her that told him that she, too, had fallen asleep.

"Selina?" he whispered.

When she didn't so much as twitch Caius smiled smugly to himself and rolled onto his back beside her. As far as wedding nights went, this one was leagues more pleasurable than his last had been.

Really, there was no comparing the two. Louisa had only married him out of duty to her father and his reason had been even less admirable: money.

Caius hadn't guessed that his wife actually *disliked* him until their wedding night, when she'd taken vindictive pleasure in confessing that she was not a virgin.

Caius had been furious with her. Not because she wasn't a maiden—he'd been relieved to avoid a painful sexual encounter with a wife who already despised him—but because she adamantly refused to accommodate herself to having him as a husband.

"I will accept you into my bed because I must," she'd retorted after he'd suggested that they learn to live harmoniously rather than always be at loggerheads. "Never think to defile me with your lustful ways." Her eyes had glittered with actual hatred. "Keep your mistress, Shaftsbury, because I will never willingly welcome you to my bed."

Caius had been bloody relieved when she'd become pregnant the third month of their marriage. He'd also been grateful that it hadn't happened sooner, or he would have always wondered if the child belonged to another man.

Who knows, if she hadn't died perhaps they might have learned to rub along once they'd had children to draw them together, but Caius somehow doubted it.

Not that any of that mattered anymore; he'd been given a second chance. Not only had Selina single-handedly wrenched him from his self-absorbed, self-pitying *Slough of Despond*, but she'd also given him something to live for.

One of the lessons that Caius had learned from being trapped in a coach for four days with his dying wife was just how quickly things could change for the worse.

Life was precious. Plenty of people *said* those words, but it was different when one truly understood what they meant.

Until Lady Selina blew into his life like a brisk, cleansing breeze, he'd thought there was nothing left to live for. Now he knew he'd been a frightened child. Rather than forget how badly—and weakly—he'd behaved after the accident, he vowed to always remember how he'd wasted almost a year of his life. He had survived that horrible wreck and the best way to honor those who hadn't done so was to make something of himself.

And the woman beside him was proof that a person never knew what life would offer up next. He was a very, very fortunate man and he planned to make sure his new wife was a very, very happy woman.

But he would not pursue that plan tonight. One time with his virgin bride on their wedding night was all he could demand of her—no matter how much he might hunger for more.

He sighed, felt for the edge of the bed, and smiled when he realized he'd been too eager for her to even slip off his robe, which was still hanging from his shoulders.

"My lord?"

Caius turned back to Selina. "I thought you were sleeping. I'd hoped to slip away without disturbing you."

There was a pause, and then he felt the touch of her hand on his shoulder.

"Yes?" he prodded when she did not speak.

"Thank you."

His eyebrows shot up. "For what, sweetheart?"

"For—for being kind."

"I hope I am always kind to you, Selina." His mouth twitched into a smile. "I know you have the wit and will to bring me up short if I should ever slip up."

She gave a low chuckle that went directly to his balls, and lightly squeezed his shoulder. "Good night, my lord."

Caius followed the sound of her voice and leaned down to kiss her, his lips encountering the soft, fragrant skin of her temple. "Good night, my lady."

Chapter 28

The room was pitch black when Selina woke and it took her a moment to realize that somebody had closed the bed curtains. Had it been Caius? She had a hazy memory of him leaving the night before. Did he wander the corridors of the house last night? Or was he able to sleep?

As curious as she was, Selina wasn't sure that she was up to asking him such personal questions yet.

She pulled aside the heavy brocade drapery, blinking at the shaft of light that came through the east facing window. The clock said it was half-past nine. Goodness! She'd not slept so late in weeks, not since she'd been in London, where it wasn't unusual to sleep until noon or later after a busy night.

She was about to swing her feet off the bed when she realized she was naked.

The night came back to her in a rush and she pulled the sheet up to her chest, catching her bottom lip with her teeth as she remembered the wicked, wonderful things they had done. Well, *Caius* had done them, she'd merely been the fortunate recipient.

Selina set a hand on her hot face. *Everyone in the house knows what had happened in this room.*

A snort broke out of her at the thought. She sincerely doubted people would know *exactly* what had happened.

"My lady?"

She looked up to find her maid holding up her dressing gown.

"Thank you, Fanny," Selina murmured, slipping into it. She fastened the ties while Fanny pulled back the curtains.

"My lord has ordered breakfast in your room for you, ma'am."

As if on cue, there was a knock on the door and not one, but *four* servants: one maid bearing a loaded tray and three footmen with chairs and a small table.

She stared at the numerous chafing dishes. "Goodness, I shall never eat all this."

"I thought I would join you."

She whipped around at the sound of Caius's voice, momentarily robbed of breath at the sight of him. He wore buckskins and boots with a black clawhammer today, rather than his usual blue. The dark superfine was a stark but attractive contrast to his pale skin and light eyes. "You are up and dressed already," she said stupidly.

He grinned, a disarming expression that seemed to come more easily with every day that passed. As he came toward her, she felt an odd, almost painful, squeezing in her chest. He was so very handsome. The candlelight last night had flattered him, but the bright rays that fell on his face this morning exposed those faint signs of age that somehow made him even more desirable. The crow's feet at the corners of his eyes and deep grooves that bracketed his mouth looked more like smile lines than frown lines today.

He came to a halt in front of her and held out his hand. Selina took it and smiled up into his winter gray eyes. "You are getting very good at judging distance."

"A wise woman once told me that practice will make perfect." He lifted her hand to his lips and kissed the palm, the raw intensity on his face reminding her of last night—of the moment when he'd entered her. "How are you this morning, my lady?" he asked, the faintly smug curve to his lips telling her exactly what he was asking.

She squirmed, uncomfortably aware of the presence of not only her maid, but Carrie, the maid setting out the food. "Hungry, my lord," she answered primly.

Humor glinted in his gaze—how was that possible? He could not see and yet his eyes showed so much.

"Selina?"

She noticed that he'd pulled out the chair and was waiting to seat her. "Oh, thank you." Selina sat and waited until the door had closed behind the last servant to ask, "What may I serve you, Caius?"

"Coffee, black, please, and a coddled egg."

The coddled egg came in its own ramekin, and she suspected that was why he'd chosen it, because chasing items of food around a plate was doubtless irksome.

She positioned his food and said, "Coffee at two and eggs in the center of the clock face."

"Thank you," he said, carefully locating his coffee and taking a sip before saying, "I thought we might go out to the lake today and take a basket with us."

"A picnic? That sounds lovely."

"There is a rowboat—just a small thing, for two. Do you know how to swim?"

"Yes, we swam every summer, so I am quite skilled." She hesitated and said, "I've seen your rowing cup in the library—the one from Eton."

"Ah yes, winner of the Monarch Boat Club competition. I'm a bit rusty, but I suspect even a blind man can manage a rowboat. You can leave the oars to me, but don't think you'll get off lightly. I can only row with a coxswain shouting in my face."

She laughed. "I will try to motivate you in a more civil manner. Is that really what happens?"

His eyebrows lifted. "You've never seen any rowing?"

"No, but my little brother Doddy is starting at Eton and I suspect that is the sort of activity he will adore." She hesitated, and then asked, "He is older than most students—soon to be fifteen—do you think he will have a more difficult time adjusting?"

Caius dabbed his lips with his napkin before saying, "I think *everyone* has a difficult time adjusting. Boys are savages."

She laughed.

"I'm quite serious. He might have to endure a bit more, er, rigorous testing than a younger boy might, but he will find friends and they will make all the rest of it easier to bear."

Selina looked at the sizeable pile of bacon and then glanced at his single egg dish and the empty plate beneath it. "Caius?"

"Yes?"

"Would it offend you if I offered to cut you some meat?"

He stilled and she feared the worst.

But he exhaled and smiled. "It offends me that I need to have my meat cut, Selina, but I am grateful to you for offering. I would love some bacon." He reached a hand across the table slowly, carefully navigating the crockery.

Selina set her hand in his and he gave it a gentle squeeze. "I appreciate that you want to make my life easier and more pleasurable. You are very good at doing both those things, and—if I know you, at all—you're already thinking up meals that don't require me to brandish a knife and hunt for bits of food on a plate."

Selina gave a self-conscious chuckle. "Are you a mind reader, my lord?"

"You may call me Caius when we are alone together, my dear."

She flushed at his gentle reminder. Her mother never called her father anything but *Addiscombe, sir,* or *my lord,* so she was not accustomed to such intimacy, but she liked it.

"Are you a mind reader, *Caius.*"

He smiled. "Not in general. Indeed, if you were to ask my brother, he would tell you that historically I've not only been unable to guess what other people were thinking or feeling, but I didn't care to learn, either." He pulled a face. "Unfortunately, he would have been right. I say *would have been* because you've had a beneficial influence on me."

Selina

Selina took his words—his praise—and hugged it close. It astounded her how much more rewarding what he'd just said was than all the empty flattery she'd heard all Season long.

"What are you thinking? You've suddenly gone quiet, Selina."

"I'm thinking that I'm happy, my lord. Very happy."

And then she had the pleasure of seeing Caius blush.

***

"Am I wrong in thinking there is… something… between Lord Victor and Mrs. Cooper?" Selina asked her husband.

Caius had rowed them back and forth across the lake a half-dozen times until the heat of the sun drove them into the shade.

Selina had unpacked the hamper Cook sent and laid it all out the large blanket. They'd ended up ignoring the sandwiches and eating the slices of wedding cake, instead. It amused her to discover that she and her husband shared a love of sweets.

Now they were lying on their backs under the monstrous chestnut tree, too languid to move.

When Caius didn't immediately answer her, Selina wondered if he'd dropped off to sleep. But when she turned, she saw his eyes were open. He turned when he heard her move, something that looked like guilt on his face.

"They were in love a long time ago—I suppose it is almost nine years, now. Our father had died, leaving me in charge of Victor's inheritance. I told him I didn't condone the match and that I'd withhold his money." He closed his eyes. "When he defied me, I went to the parsonage and confronted the vicar. I didn't threaten him, but I made my displeasure clear." He gave an unamused laugh. "To give Sayers his due, he came as close as a man can come to telling me to go to hell, while still remaining polite."

He sighed and shook his head. "Had it been up to Victor, they would have married. But Miss Sayers—now Mrs. Cooper—knew why I'd gone to talk to her father. She begged me not to take away his living. I never would have done that, but I let her think that I would."

Selina felt an unpleasant jolt in her belly at his admission. "What happened?"

"She told Victor she would not marry him—I don't know what reason she gave, but I'm sure he guessed the truth. Shortly afterward, Victor left. I think he wandered for a while, but I didn't hear from him until he turned twenty-five, which is when the money was his." His eyes opened.

"Ah," Selina said, because… what else could one possibly say?

"*Ah*, indeed. Miss Sayers eventually married and moved away. She had a child and shortly afterward her husband died. She has been taking care of her father ever since." He shifted his head, turning his face toward her. "I sensed something—some emotion—between her and Victor yesterday, but I cannot tell if there is anything left to salvage."

Selina thought back to the bitter man who'd blackmailed her into marrying his brother—using a threat every bit as vicious as the one Caius had wielded against the vicar all those years ago. Although Victor had quickly hidden it, he'd been visibly flustered when Mrs. Cooper had met them at the church yesterday.

"I don't know if there is anything to salvage," Selina finally admitted. "It might have just been simple awkwardness we noticed yesterday, or it might have been more. Neither of them is the sort of person to show their emotions."

"Not the passionate sort who hurl books at servants."

She smiled. "No, not that sort at all, my lord."

He held out his hand. When she took it, he pulled her closer, putting his hands on her hips and positioning her until her knees were on the outsides of his hips, the narrow skirt of her gown bunched up around her thighs.

"What are you—"

"Are you sore, darling?"

"Uh."

"*Uh?*" He smiled up at her, his dark hair charmingly messy, his carefully tied cravat now crushed.

"I'm a little sore," she admitted, mortified to be speaking of such a subject in broad daylight, although why that should matter, she did not know.

"Too sore?" He raised his eyebrows suggestively.

Her jaw sagged. "You mean—you want to do it *here?*"

He laughed. "Why do you sound so appalled?"

"Because we are outside."

"Doing *it*—as you so charmingly put it—is natural, Selina. What better place to do *it* than amid nature itself. There is no shame in the act even though plenty of people—men and women—like to claim that."

"But…"

"But?"

"But anyone might see us." She looked around, half expecting to see heads popping out of the hedges right now.

Selina

"Selina... we are a newly married couple who have gone on a picnic. None of my servants—nor my brother—would dare wander near."

"You mean they think"—she bit her lip.

He drew her lower with both hands, until she was forced to either lie on his chest or crouch over him on all fours. Lying on his chest seemed the more dignified option.

Caius gave a pleased grunt when she laid on him and propped herself up on her elbows.

He cupped her face, kissing her far more gently than last night—not just one kiss, but dozens, until he'd coaxed her lips apart and slid his tongue inside her.

She groaned and leaned closer, the kiss rapidly becoming more heated and less controlled.

He took her by the waist and Selina suddenly found herself on her back, looking up at Caius who was now kneeling between her thighs, pinning her to the ground by the skirt of her gown.

"You never answered my question," he murmured, tracing the neckline of her simple day dress with one finger, the light, almost innocent, touch reminding her of last night and other touches that had not been nearly so innocent.

"Qu-question?" she stuttered when he palmed her breast over her dress, his hand warm and heavy.

He smirked and his hand slid down her body in answer, until he was cupping her mound.

Selina whimpered when one of his fingers rubbed the sensitive nub of flesh that seemed to have swelled.

"Are you too sore to take me today?"

Selina shook her head, too embarrassed to speak, and then remembered he couldn't see her and forced herself to say, "No."

He lightly stroked the seam of her lips. "Are you sure." He applied just enough pressure to send a sharp bolt of pleasure arcing from her sex to her belly to her breasts.

"Yes—yes, I'm sure."

"Hmmm." He released her and began to back down her body.

Selina frowned. "Where are you going?"

"I'm not sure I believe you."

"What don't you believe?"

"That you are not too sore. I will have to verify your claim for myself." He found the hem of her gown and began to lift it.

"Caius!"

"Yes?"

"What are you doing?"

"I'm going to make sure you aren't too sore," he said, not pausing. "Lift your bottom for me, love."

Her body—already primed and eager for what he was about to do—had no shame and obeyed him without hesitation. He raised her skirt, petticoat, and chemise until the fabric was all gathered around her waist.

Selina pushed up onto her elbows and looked from side to side; there didn't appear to be anyone watching and they were on a slight rise—she would see if somebody approached, she would be able to—

"Caius," she gasped when she felt the now familiar sensation of his slick tongue.

"Spread wider, darling," he ordered, gently nudging her thighs apart.

Selina complied, unable to look away from his dark curly head. She'd watched him last night too, but that hadn't been the middle of the day.

The heat of his mouth was a delicious contrast to the breeze that kissed her body—especially noticeable on a part of her that had never seen sunlight.

"God, you're sweet," he muttered, engulfing her in silky heat, tongue thrusting, lips suckling.

Selina spread wider without being asked, the gesture earning her a smug laugh that vibrated up her body. "Such a good, greedy girl."

She blushed and preened at his words, as if behaving like a wanton was somehow deserving of praise.

His finger, when it slid inside her, burned slightly, but her body seemed to be producing a mortifying amount of moisture to ease his entry.

"You're so wet for me, darling—even more so than last night. Does it excite you to do this out of doors?" he asked, his tongue suddenly dropping lower, until he was breaching the entrance to her body alongside his finger.

She cried out and then slapped a hand over her mouth.

Caius stopped. "Don't smother your cries, Selina. I want them—all of them. I *need* to hear it. Tell me what you want—soft, like this"—he demonstrated, his wicked tongue barely caressing her hot, needy flesh—"or harder, like this"—he covered her sex with his mouth and bathed her in pleasure.

Selina

And then he just stopped.

When she looked down, he was facing her, his red, slick lips curved into a smirk. "Well? The first one? Or the—"

"The second."

He laughed and then lowered his head.

They both groaned at the same time, the sounds drowned out by the mad thumping of her pulse, the irresistible pleasure building fast—too fast—she wanted to make it last, but when he took her tight, pulsing bundle of nerves between his lips and sucked, her back arched off the blanket and she cried out his name, not caring who heard.

He proceeded to drive her over the edge again and again, until she'd forgotten to worry about where she was, until she could scarcely recall *who* she was.

Selina was only vaguely aware when he positioned his hot length at her entrance and thrust himself inside her to the hilt. This time, the stretch was pure bliss, the pain of the night before a distant memory.

"My God, you're so tight, Selina. This is heaven," he whispered, and then his hips began to move. The wet sound of their coupling should have embarrassed her, but it only made her want him more.

"Wrap your legs around me darling," he urged in a breathless voice, his hips drumming. "I'm going to fill you so full."

Selina clenched at his vulgar words and he hissed, his thrusts faster and less controlled.

"Again," he ordered.

She flexed her inner muscles and tilted her hips, taking him even deeper.

He groaned, his strokes savage. And then he buried himself, sheathing every inch inside her, pulsing as he filled her, his heart beating so hard against her chest that it might have been her own.

"You make me feel so alive," Caius murmured.

Selina squeezed her eyes shut, but happy tears still escaped. It might not be love that she felt for the man in her arms, but it was becoming harder and harder to tell the difference.

Chapter 29

Several days later Selina was practicing in the music room when Caius entered. It wasn't their usual time to meet, so she asked, "Is aught amiss, my lord?"

He strolled toward her, barely needing his walking stick in such a familiar place. "Not unless you consider me wanting to learn how to play the piano amiss?"

Selina's jaw dropped. "Truly?"

He smiled at the enthusiasm she didn't bother to hide. "Truly. If you don't mind a pupil with ten thumbs."

"Surely not *all* ten?"

He laughed. "Well, maybe nine."

"I am undaunted," she said, and reached out when he was near the bench and took his hand.

He lowered himself beside her and kissed each of her knuckles before looking up. "I don't want you to feel terrible when I am not any good, Selina."

"Am I allowed to feel wonderful when you *are* good?"

He chuckled. "I suppose that is acceptable."

"What changed your mind?" she asked, curious.

"Lately I feel unencumbered with other matters and have enough time to concentrate on something new."

She suspected he meant that he no longer had to work so hard when it came to doing for himself and getting around—certainly not inside the house—and he'd even become more comfortable walking in the garden.

"I'm glad," she said, laying her head on his shoulder. "So glad."

"Let's hope you're still saying that in a month or two."

Selina laughed, for no reason other than happiness.

***

Caius loved the sound of her laughter. He kissed the top of her head as she rested against his shoulder, entirely content in that moment. It was true that he wanted to learn to play the piano, but the real reason he'd asked her to teach him was because he got such pleasure from her company. Even if he never was any good, at least he would get to spend more time with her—and listen to more of her playing, which was superb.

"I've been haunting the stables these past few days and talking to Herrick, discussing some… possibilities."

She lifted her head and he knew she'd be looking at him. "Oh? What sort of possibilities?"

He smiled at the interest he heard in her voice. How had he been so lucky to find a woman who looked for ways to help him do what he *wanted* to do instead of finding fault with him for what he *couldn't* do?

His throat tightened with a sudden, almost overwhelming wave of emotion and his voice was rough when he said, "There is a sort of saddle—it originated in New Spain—and it could accommodate two riders on the right sort of mount."

Her body shifted, until she was fully facing him. "Two on one horse? When we were girls, Hy and I did that on one occasion and were scolded for it."

"And probably rightly so on an ordinary horse," Caius said. "The mount would need to be large enough to comfortably bear both our weight. Also, the saddle is something the horse would need to become accustomed to." He leaned close and whispered in her ear, "And Herrick thinks that it would only be safe if my riding partner rode astride."

Her laughter filled the room. "Oh, how delightfully scandalous. But—and I hate to shock you, Caius—it wouldn't be the first time I've ridden astride."

"You saucy minx—I knew it. Did that breeches-wearing sister of yours corrupt you?"

"You mean Her Grace?"

Caius laughed. "Lord, Chatham must have his hands full," he muttered. "I know the feeling."

She bumped his shoulder. "But you like having full hands, don't you?"

Caius's jaw sagged. "You *dirty* thing."

"I think you like that, too," she whispered.

He did indeed. His new wife was proving to be quite adaptable and adventurous in the bedchamber.

"So, was wearing breeches your sister's idea?" he asked.

"It *was* Hy's idea. We were children then, sneaking into the stables and riding my father's horses. I was only nine and a mere slip of lass. I had to tie the breeches on with a rope to keep them up. I dare say they will fit me quite differently now.

Caius growled. "I will need to feel every inch of you when you put them on—it is only fair as I don't get to look at you." He nipped her ear and she squeaked.

He sighed. "I instructed Herrick to look out for the correct mount and he is going to speak to the saddler about making the tack, but it will likely take some time." He kissed her throat, sucking gently on the sensitive skin. "Of course, we can practice before then."

"Practice?" she asked, exposing her neck to him, shivering as he made his way down, not stopping until his lips were on her breast.

"Yes. I will have to see how skilled a rider you are. You can start practicing tonight… in bed," his voice dropped even lower and he seized her by the waist and lifted her onto his lap. "When you ride me."

There was no more talk of learning to play the piano for quite some time after that.

***

Selina stared at the stack of invitations and then looked at her husband.

"Caius, are you *sure* you wish to go through with this?"

"You sound so worried, my dear. It is just a country ball, and I have attended hundreds in my life."

"Yes, but this will be different. You *know* it will."

He held out a hand. "Come here, Selina."

She stood up from the secretaire that she'd claimed as her own and went to him.

He took her hand and tugged gently.

She gave a startled gasp when he pulled her onto his lap.

Caius slid an arm around her waist, snugging her closer, his other hand sliding behind her neck and positioning her for a kiss.

As she always did, Selina melted beneath his sensual assault, until she forgot where she was. Only when he finally pulled away did she recall that she was perched on his lap like a brazen hussy and the tea tray could arrive at any moment.

But when she squirmed, his arm tightened. "Somebody will see us, Caius."

He caressed her neck and ignored her concern. "Is your only objection to this ball that you think it will be difficult or awkward for me? Or do you not feel like facing our neighbors *en masse* right now?"

"I don't think it will be difficult for you, but I do wonder if you will derive any enjoyment from it."

"For the first time ever, I won't be forced to dance with a great many women I don't wish to dance with." He pulled a face. "I *would* like to dance with you, but there is no time before this ball to practice. I think that with the right dance mistress"—he gave her a suggestive look— "we might attempt it at our next ball."

"You do?" she asked, stunned that he would say such a thing.

"We can certainly try it on our own and see what we think. Perhaps a waltz…"

"That is my favorite dance."

"Is it? That will give me motivation to practice. But you never answered my question—should we delay this a month?"

"Given my rather unconventional start here, I had better establish myself on the proper footing with your neighbors."

"*Our* neighbors now, my dear. And I agree with you. The function will serve dual purposes: introducing you to local society and letting everyone get a look at me. And now that I don't have to worry about falling on my face while crossing a room—thanks to my clever wife—I do not dread it, Selina." He traced her lower lip with a light touch. "You met me when I was at my very worst—no, hush," he murmured when she would have argued and excused his behavior because of what he'd endured. "While it's true that I was at my worst after the accident, I was selfish and willful and reckless long before I was trapped in that carriage. I never shied away from behaving exactly as I wished, regardless of the damage I might do. The accident and my injury did one good thing: they forced me to mature."

His expression turned pensive, and Selina knew he must be thinking about those awful four days.

"Will—will you tell me what happened, Caius?"

She didn't need to explain what she meant.

He sighed, but nodded, his arm tightening around her. "It is not a pretty story, but it is one you deserve to know."

Chapter 30

Caius held her close, for once glad that he couldn't see his wife. It would be hard enough to tell his pitiful, painful story without having to face her.

"Louisa and I married for two reasons: I needed her money and her father wanted my status. I had no idea how unhappy she was about the marriage until after we were married. Evidently her father pressured her quite strongly. In any case, I'm certain she was in love with somebody else." He stroked Selina's shoulder thoughtfully. "Even if she didn't have a lover, we were doomed to begin with. Our characters could not have been more different. She was quiet—almost painfully reserved—and loathed society. She didn't just dislike it; she froze in groups of more than ten people."

Caius took a moment, not sure how much he needed to share with her. He already knew how much he *wanted* to tell: none of it. But she deserved the truth.

"I used our differences as an excuse to behave badly. Or to *continue* behaving badly, rather. She didn't want me to touch her—other than what was strictly necessary—and blamed me for the marriage. She told me to confine my lusts to my mistress. And so I did. By the time she was with child we barely saw each other most months."

He heaved a sigh. "At first, I was delighted that she was pregnant. I thought—well, I foolishly thought that might give us common ground."

"It didn't?" Selina guessed.

"No. If anything, she had even less interest in me and rebuffed my suggestion that we try to rub along better." Caius could remember the row that discussion had spawned too clearly for comfort. He had lashed out and said cruel, vindictive things to her.

"Last August I received an invitation to a shooting party at Lord Mixon's country house. Louisa hated hunting and dreaded house parties. I told her that I didn't care what she wanted, that for once she would accompany me and play the part of my wife for my friends. It was a spiteful thing to do," he admitted, forcing himself to confess the whole of his transgression. "Louisa knew that Lord and Lady Dowden would be there. And she also knew that Lady Dowden was my current lover."

Selina didn't speak, but her shoulders stiffened under his arm.

"I ignored her begging and told her she was going," he said, every word like acid on his lips. "There are some dangerous roads through the mountains—you might have heard of the infamous Hardknot Pass?" Caius felt her nod. "It wasn't that road, but one that turned out to be equally treacherous, especially in the rain."

His palms were sweating and his skin prickled beneath his clothing. He swallowed down the terror that threatened to choke him.

"Oh, Caius," she murmured, snuggling closer and wrapping her soft body around him.

He gave a shuddering sigh and pulled her tighter. "It was late summer and the storm should not have been so dangerous. But there was a lethal combination of factors. Heavy rain, a collapsed section of road, and it wasn't Gamble driving that day. He'd gone to be with his daughter, who'd just given birth, and so I allowed the under coachman to drive us. Perhaps if we'd had a postillion it might have been different, but the lad took ill on some bad food and there was nobody at the posting inn to replace him. I ordered the coachman to continue without him. We could have taken a different route, of course, but it would have been more than half a day longer." He sighed. "But much, much safer. I—well, needless to say I will always regret that decision because if I'd done things differently—"

"You can't change the past, Caius," she murmured. "And who was to know your decision would have such catastrophic consequences? Blaming yourself is not fair to you."

"Thank you, darling." He rested his chin on top of her head, his mind going back to the last few moments in the coach before everything in his life went dark.

"I don't know what happened and there is nobody left alive to tell that story. All I remember was the screaming of horses, the shriek of metal and wood twisting, and the oddest sensation of being weightless. And when I came to, everything was black. At first, I thought it was nighttime, but…" He took a deep breath. "Louisa was still alive—barely. She told me that we'd been trapped for hours and that none of the servants had answered her calls. It was a miracle that she'd lived that long. She'd been impaled by part of the coach door."

"Oh, my God, Caius."

"She was in a great deal of pain." He cleared his throat. "She—she begged me to end her suffering, but I could not do it. Not because I thought she had a chance of surviving, but because I was selfish." He clenched his jaws and forced out the admission that shamed him every day. "I knew that when she died, I would be alone and blind and powerless. And so I let her suffer."

"You couldn't know that you'd be trapped there so long, Caius. You might have been rescued any time and she could have been saved."

He didn't bother to correct her. *He* knew the truth. Louisa had suffered for no reason other than his fear. Caius had never felt so isolated in his entire life as those hours right after her death. He might have been on the moon rather than a ravine in Cumberland.

"After she was gone, I tried to get out of the coach, but one door was crushed against the ground and the other had some sort of obstruction blocking it. I called for help until my voice was gone."

Her hand came up to rest over his heart, making him aware that it was pounding and he was sweating.

"Caius, you don't have to—"

"I will finish," he said, squeezing the words through his tight throat. "The third day was the worst."

"Oh, God," she moaned shaking her head, a choked sob slipped from her. "It must have been a nightmare."

"By the fourth day I was delirious from a lack of water when the rescuers found me. I don't remember any of that. All I know is what I was told afterward. It was a miracle the coach got wedged where it did. Had it not, I would have joined the others—Louisa, Elton, Jonathan, my coachman, and Ben, my footman." He let out a sigh, weak with relief that the story was over.

Her body shook and he heard soft sobbing.

His own eyes were dry. Indeed, he'd not shed a tear about those four days since being rescued. The physician said there was nothing wrong with his eyes—at least nothing physical—to prevent him from weeping. But even when he woke in the middle of the night, his voice raw and ragged, his eyes were still as arid as any desert.

"So, you see, because I wanted to punish my wife by forcing her to go to a house party I ended up killing four people and my unborn child."

Selina pulled away from him and grabbed his upper arms, squeezing until it hurt. "You cannot think that sort of thing. I forbid it. If all of us drew down such wrath when we were cruel or selfish or indifferent, we would all be trapped in smashed coaches. All of us, Caius. It was an accident. A horrible accident, but still an accident." She shook him until his teeth rattled, the strength in her small body shocking. "You are not an angel, but you are not a monster, either. You are just a human being, like the rest of us." Her grip loosened and she pulled him into a tight embrace. "I forbid you to punish yourself any longer," she repeated. "Promise me."

"I can't promise to stop, sweetheart, but I promise to *try*. Will that serve?"

"For now." She sighed loudly and then sat back again. "Those days still plague you—and disturb your sleep at night. That is why you don't fall asleep in the same room with me after we, er—"

"Make love?" he suggested, amused that his fierce wife couldn't say the simple words.

"You have nightmares, don't you?"

Selina

"Yes, I have nightmares." He refused to tell her about the thrashing, shaking, and screaming that woke him up and kept him awake for hours afterward.

"My sister Katie had nightmares for years—nothing as horrible as yours probably are, but still terrifying to her—and she used to come and sleep in my bed. I won't say the dreams went away because of that, but I could comfort her and she could fall sleep afterward. You—you can't sleep, can you? That is why you roam?"

Caius ignored her question and cupped her cheek. "I appreciate what you are offering me, Selina. But it is not a pretty sight—nor am I quiet. Trust me when I tell you this is something I don't want you to see."

"You'd let your pride—"

"Yes. I am excessively prideful." He gave her a wry look. "I've relinquished more of my pride in the last year than I ever thought possible. Leave me this much, darling. It is for the best."

Her sigh told him that she wasn't happy with his answer. "Very well. But the offer stands."

"Thank you. Now," he said, becoming brisk. "Read me the guest list and I shall see if we've neglected to add any names. And then I will frank the invitations and we will prepare to have our house invaded."

Chapter 31

The three weeks before the ball sped by in a blur of activity. Selina had believed that she knew how much work planning a large function would take.

She had been wrong.

Courtland had not hosted such a large party in years and Selina and Morris—and their new housekeeper, Mrs. Shore—all worked feverishly to have everything ready by the night of the ball.

Because it would be the first dinner party that Caius would attend after his accident, Selina had kept the dinner before the ball to just twenty-two people, including the two of them.

Most of the guests were from the neighborhood, but a few—Baron Crawford and Mr. Christopher Newel—were coming from some distance away. The three men had been friends since they were schoolboys and had hunted together before Caius's accident.

Selina had met Crawford during the Season. Indeed, she'd had a rather unpleasant exchange with the baron after he'd proposed to her.

Caius deserved to know the truth about her dealings with a man who'd be a guest in their home, but it seemed cruel to alienate him from a friend he'd known longer than Selina had been alive. Just how much should she tell her husband?

By the evening of the ball Selina *still* hadn't said anything to Caius.

The dilemma was uppermost in her mind as she sat in her chambers and watched Fanny put the finishing touches on her hair.

The best thing to do, she finally decided, was to tell him about the proposal and leave out the less than polite way Crawford had reacted to her rejection. That is how Selina would like to be treated if the shoe were on the other foot.

Just as she'd settled the matter in her mind the connecting door opened and her husband entered.

Selina's jaw sagged. Because she was still staring in the mirror, she had the misfortune of seeing what a dunce she looked like with her mouth hanging open. She quickly closed it and smiled at her maid. "Thank you, Fanny, that looks very nice. You may go," she said, turning to face her husband.

Goodness. She had never seen him in evening blacks before. With his fair coloring, dark hair, and silver eyes he was a striking combination of black, white, and gray.

Only his beautiful lips added any color to the picture.

And right now, they were curved upward, his dimple peeping out. "Hello darling—you are very quiet."

"Hello, Caius," she said after a moment of speechlessness.

"You sound a bit breathless." He held his arms out to his side. "Did James dress me in motley? He was miffed because I refused to wear a white waistcoat, so I wouldn't be surprised if he took his revenge by dressing me up like a harlequin."

Selina stood and closed the distance between them. "You look very elegant. And handsome. And masculine."

It was his turn to look startled. "Why, thank you."

Selina gave a delighted laugh. "I love it when you blush."

He pursed his lips, his color flaring even higher. "You, madam, are a menace."

"Nobody has ever called me that before."

"You shouldn't sound so proud of yourself." He lifted his hand and she noticed he held a box. "This is for you—even though you are a naughty menace."

She took the box and blinked rapidly to clear away the pesky tears that seemed to gather at the drop of a hat lately.

"*Please* don't say, *Oh Caius! You shouldn't have*," he chided when she was silent for too long.

"I would never say such a ridiculous thing," Selina said, swiping an escaped tear from her cheek. "I adore jewels."

"How do you know it is jewelry? Perhaps it is a miniature shovel or a very small goose."

"I *do* love geese."

"I think that might be the first time in the history of the English language the words *I, love,* and *geese* found themselves in the same sentence."

Selina laughed. "Does that mean you won't be buying me any geese?"

"Absolutely not. The beasts terrify me. Now, go on, open it."

She lifted the lid of the beautiful leather box and sucked in a breath. "How did you know I was wearing blue tonight?" she asked, unable to resist stroking the blazing blue stones.

"My vast network of spies informed me of your radical defection from pink." He raised a hand and lightly grazed it up her throat, cheek, and then stopped on her brow. "No pink? Are you feverish?"

She chuckled. "No. I just thought pink seemed like a color for a girl and tonight I must be a marchioness."

His lips pulled down at the corners and he slid a hand around the back of her neck, his fingers gentle with her coiffure. "You should *always* wear whatever you like, darling. I don't want you to change a thing about yourself." He paused and frowned. "Well, maybe your opinion about geese."

Selina gave a watery laugh. "Oh, shame on you. You've made me cry."

"I meant to be nice, not insulting."

"It was a very nice thing to say. I will wear pink again, but for tonight, this more serious blue gives me a bit of confidence."

"You must do whatever you need to do. I know entertaining can be stressful, especially if you are the one in charge of it all."

"You are not angry that I'm not wearing the pink jewels you gave me?" Selina had felt terrible about that decision, but she'd wanted to look mature at her first function and something about pink… Well, her mother had always told her it was a girl's color.

"Of course I am not angry. There will be many other occasions to wear them. Now put on your jewels so I have an excuse to shamelessly fondle your, erm, bits."

"*Bits?*" She laughed and picked up an earring. "Wait—you mean we must have an excuse to do that?"

"*You* never need an excuse to fondle my bits," he said. "In fact, it is one of your most important duties as my wife."

"What a harsh task master you are."

"Mmm, just you wait until later tonight."

Selina shivered with anticipation, suddenly wishing they could leave the guests to their own devices.

Guests. Ugh. She needed to tell him now.

"Caius?"

"Yes, darling?"

"I've been meaning to tell you that I've met one of your friends before."

"Oh?" he asked, his voice distracted as he caressed her hips.

"Lord Crawford."

"Indeed? I didn't think he still went to respectable functions during the Season."

"He went to at least a few. Um, he asked me to marry him."

Caius's fingers tightened and his nostrils flared. "Did he?"

"Yes, he proposed quite early in the Season."

"Well, who knew old Crawford had such good sense." He resumed his casual stroking. "Is anyone else on the guest list a former suitor?" he asked in a carefully modulated tone.

Was he... *jealous?*

"No, he is the only one."

"Hmm." He kissed her. "Thank you for telling me, sweetheart. I appreciate you not sending me to dinner... er, blind."

***

Crawford was a buffoon. Caius had known that for many years. But never before had the man's buffoonery been aimed at *him.*

Although Crawford had been seated on the other side of Viscountess Norland, he had no qualms bellowing past the woman to talk to Caius. "Markham told me you still have your string of hunters, Shaftsbury."

Caius, who'd been conversing quietly with the viscountess, paused. He could hear the other man chewing from six feet away and knew, from long experience, that Crawford didn't always wait to finish a mouthful of food before speaking, no matter how often all his friends had chastised him for the revolting habit.

"That is true," Caius answered, but only because he knew Crawford would just repeat himself if he ignored him.

"I'll take them off your hands."

"They aren't for sale."

"Why the devil not?"

Conversation stuttered to a halt.

Crawford's nervous guffaw told Caius that even *he* must have realized how loudly he'd been speaking. "Er, I just meant you could have no use for 'em." He laughed again. "After all, you can barely cut your own meat; surely you don't expect to hunt ever again?"

The room was positively tomblike. Before Caius could answer the other man, a voice came from all the way down at the other end of the table.

"I haven't seen you hunt in years, Crawford," Victor's normally quiet voice rang out, carrying to everyone in the room. "But I recall you winning the Stirrup Cup at least twice."

Male and female laughter rippled up and down the table at Victor's reference to Crawford's dismal skill in the saddle. It was impolite to tell everyone present that the baron was prone to an excessive number of *unintentional dismounts* during a hunting season, but Crawford had earned the rudeness.

And Victor wasn't finished yet. "I should think my brother's hunters are a bit above your touch in more ways than one, Crawford."

That was a reference to Crawford's financial difficulties, which were a perpetual source of embarrassment to him.

Caius heard cutlery clanking violently against a plate and suspected that was Crawford. For a moment he wondered if he'd be seconding his brother against his friend—his *erstwhile* friend—come morning.

But then Crawford forced a braying laugh. "Quite right, Victor, quite right."

Caius suddenly remembered that Crawford had always backed down like a cornered cur when confronted by a stronger man and he smiled in his brother's direction, flattered that Victor had stood up for him.

Selina's clear, firm voice penetrated the stunned silence that hung over the room like an unpleasant fog, "I am a friend of your daughter Lily, Lord Mortimer. Tell me, did she go to Brighton this summer? I know she was undecided."

Thanks to his wife, conversation gradually resumed up and down the table.

Caius realized that he was smiling and the expression was not forced. He was disappointed that an old friend would scent weakness and attack him like an injured animal, but he was delighted that his small family—Selina and Victor—had risen to his defense without hesitation.

Perhaps he and Victor might repair their relationship, after all. Maybe even build something stronger and more enduring.

As for Selina and their future together? Well, Caius had known for weeks that his marriage of convenience was the best thing that had ever happened to him. Not until that moment, however, did he realize just how totally, irrevocably, and heart wrenchingly in love he was with her.

It wasn't an emotion he'd ever felt for a woman. Indeed, up until a few weeks ago he would have denied the existence of love entirely. And now he adored his wife and couldn't imagine his life without her.

But beneath the elation that suffused him, a worrisome niggle of fear reared its ugly head. Caius had believed that his sight was the most painful loss he could endure in his life.

Now that he was in love, he knew there were even worst things a man could lose.

***

Selina *hated* that Crawford had caught her in a moment of distraction before dinner and she'd consented to a dance with him—and a waltz no less.

The man was a loathsome toad and his behavior during dinner had proved what she had always suspected: he was a bully and a coward.

Lord Victor, on the other hand, had risen to the occasion and exceeded her expectations and she'd felt a rush of affection toward him for his defense of his brother.

She would have liked to tell Crawford to go to the devil, but a hostess could not give in to that sort of impulse, so she would have to dance with him. It was only one set, after all, and one of her skills was the ability to socialize and keep her mask firmly in place, no matter how much turmoil roiled inside her.

And so she smiled and chattered with her current partner—Sir Henley Graves—while inside she was dreading the next set with Crawford.

Sir Henley had scarcely escorted her off the floor when Crawford swooped down on her.

"I believe this dance belongs to me, my lady."

It took him less than one clumsy turn around the dance floor to say something offensive.

"It looks as if you didn't need to settle for a mere barony after all, *Lady Shaftsbury*." He gave a laugh that sounded anything but amused. "Thought you were too good for the likes of me, eh? I suppose your sort is more interested in a cripple who cannot stop her from ruling the roost."

"Is this why you asked me to dance, Lord Crawford? To vent your spleen because I denied your suit all those months ago? I would have thought you'd be well-used to the feeling of rejection," she said sweetly.

"I know what you are," he hissed, lowering his voice but not controlling his expression, which had become vicious. "You look like butter wouldn't melt in your mouth—but you always reeked of desperation to me."

"One more word in that vein and I will see that you are kicked down the front steps of this house, my lord." She smiled up at him and fluttered her eyelashes.

He sneered, his hands gripping her painfully tightly. "And who will do the kicking, eh? Even if Shaftsbury could lay hands on me, he couldn't find the bloody door to throw me out of, could he?"

Selina had never faked a stumble before, but she'd had enough of this oaf. On the next step she raked the heel of her dancing slipper down his shin before pretending to turn her foot.

"Oh dear, how clumsy of me," she said loudly enough to be heard over his pained yelp. "I do believe I've torn the ribbon on my slipper, Lord Crawford." She yanked her hand from his grasp and stepped off the dancefloor.

Within seconds, several people came to her assistance, one of them Victor, whose gaze was positively frosty as it raked over Crawford. "Let me escort you to the retiring room, my lady."

Crawford could scarcely argue with an audience of concerned guests and the host's own brother. He bowed stiffly. "Perhaps we might resume our chat later—after supper, my lady."

"I look forward to it," she lied.

"Was he insulting you?" Victor whispered as Crawford limped away.

Selina smiled reassuringly at the curious guests as her brother-in-law led her out of the ballroom. "Crawford's buffoonery is nothing I could not manage, Victor. But thank you for—"

"My lady."

She turned to find Morris hurrying toward her.

"Yes, Mr. Morris?"

"Peter and Joseph moved the crates of champagne without paying attention to the markings. I'm afraid I don't know which ones we are to use next. If you just tell me, I will go down and see to it."

"I don't recall the names either," she lied. "I'll need to look at the crates."

Victor frowned. "But what about your slipper?"

Selina cocked an eyebrow at him.

"Ah," he said, his mouth curving into a rueful smile. "I see."

She smiled at him and patted his arm. "Thank you for coming to my assistance in. Go back to the ball—enjoy yourself. I will return shortly." Selina turned and left before he could offer any resistance. She needed some time—just a few minutes—to collect herself.

When she reached the cellar, she saw the servants had lit the sconces on either side of the door but there was no hand candle on the table where one usually sat.

"Well, drat," she muttered, entering the gloomy room. She didn't want to walk all the way back upstairs so she leaned down low and squinted to get a look at the—

"Did your slipper repair itself?"

She spun around to find Crawford filling the doorway. "What are you doing here?" she demanded, furious at the fear she heard in her voice.

Crawford heard it, too, and he grinned and stalked toward her. "We weren't finished with our conversation."

"Yes, we were," she retorted, holding her ground.

Selina

The baron didn't stop until their toes were almost touching. He leered down at her. "Look at you! Squaring up against me just like one of those little hens that thinks it's a cock. Is that what you think, my lady? That because you can lead a blind man around by the prick you can browbeat a real man?"

"And who would that real man be? You, Crawford?"

Selina yelped and Crawford spun around at the sound of Caius's voice.

Her husband strode toward them, holding his cane almost negligently—so casually that a stranger wouldn't realize he was carefully pacing off his steps while checking for obstacles.

The baron gave an ugly laugh. "Well, we both know it isn't you, Shaftsbury. You're not cock of the walk anymore, but I'm guessing you still think you are, don't you?"

Caius ignored his question. "Did he put his hands on you, Selina?" Even when he'd been at his most furious and hurling things, he'd not exuded such predatory menace.

"No, my lord."

He smiled faintly. "Will you oblige me by stepping out into the hall, my dear."

Chapter 32

Selina barely hesitated before Caius heard her footsteps move past him. He counted them until he knew she would be close to the door. "Are the sconces the only light?"

"Yes, my lord. I didn't bring a hand candle and neither did the baron," she said right away, her clever brain marching alongside his as if they were a perfectly matched pair.

"Please extinguish the candles before you go."

"Of course, my lord.".

Crawford gave an angry squawk and then further accommodated Caius by shouting and disclosing his location, "I say—what the devil, Shaftsbury. You might not need any light to move about, but I—*argh*!"

The first in Caius's one-two combination—a jab—only glanced off Crawford's shoulder rather than smash his face, but it helped him aim his second punch.

If there was anything more gratifying than the *crunch* of cartilage exploding beneath his knuckles it was the rasping noise Crawford made immediately afterward as he struggled to breathe through his shattered nose.

Caius took a chance that the other man would be bending over and clutching his face—a natural reaction—and was lucky enough to land a third punch, burying his fist in Crawford's gut so perfectly that it was like a hand slipping into a glove.

Crawford gave a pained "*Oof*," and Caius heard feet skittering right before something heavy fell to the floor.

The baron, graceless lummox that he was, took a crate of wine down with him and the sound of shattering bottles was deafening in the stone-walled room.

Caius didn't wait for the glass to settle before poking around at the floor with the toe of his shoe. He encountered something soft that had a lot of give—Crawford's belly—and planted his heel *hard*, earning a pained yelp.

"I've considered you my friend for years, a fact that not only stuns and shames me, but also makes me realize how poorly I used to see things." He pushed down with all his weight. "Get out of my house, Crawford. The next time I have to tolerate your presence it will be at twenty paces and I think we both know that I'm a better shot than you, even with my eyes closed."

His brother's voice interrupted the sound of Crawford's breathy whimpering. "Good Lord! What happened here?" Victor demanded.

Caius removed his foot from Crawford's body. "Do you see my stick, Victor?"

"Er, yes. Fortunately, I brought a hand candle with me because it's as dark as well in here." Glass crunched and something that sounded like a piece of wood clattered to the ancient flagstone floor. Cool metal nudged Caius's fingers and he grasped the head of the cane, only realizing as he did so that his hand was shaking.

"Are you the only one here, Victor?"

"Yes. Selina is at the end of the corridor to make sure nobody else interrupts."

He grinned. "Such a clever woman, my wife."

Victor snorted. "If you both go back upstairs right now you can probably avoid generating too much talk. I will see to the removal of this rubbish—*all* the rubbish," Victor said. "I just hope he offers some resistance."

Caius chuckled. Who knew that his gentle, monastic brother had such a bloodthirsty streak?

***

It was after three o'clock when the last of the revelers rolled off down the drive and Caius shut the door with a relieved sigh. "So, that is over."

Selina laughed as he strode toward her and swept her into a fierce embrace. They had sent Morris and most of the other servants to bed earlier, so there were no witnesses to their scandalous kissing and groping.

"Do you think anyone knew about what happened in the cellar?" Selina asked him when Caius reluctantly released her lips so that she might breathe.

"Victor said a few of the men knew something was going on, but they won't say anything."

"And I doubt Crawford will want the episode noised about either," Selina said.

"No, probably not. Although—"

"Although what?"

"Although I doubt anyone would believe that matters transpired the way they really did," he admitted. "I almost don't believe it myself."

Her body went stiff in his embrace. "Don't do that, Caius."

"Do what?"

"Don't belittle rescuing me."

He snorted. "Rescuing you? I daresay you would have rescued yourself if I'd not bumbled in and—"

"Stop it."

She no longer sounded annoyed, she sounded… angry.

Caius was angry, as well—at himself. "Listen to me, Selina," he said, gripping her shoulders. "I was fortunate tonight—*very* fortunate—that conditions conspired to aid me. But you cannot count on me for help. Like it or not, I am a fragile reed when it comes to being your champion. My spirit is willing, by my body has betrayed me. If you hadn't known to snuff the candles, I wouldn't have—"

"But I *did* know what you meant—shouldn't that matter? You spend hours of your life in that gymnasium of yours. I might know nothing of mills and pugilism, but I can see the grace and power in your body, Caius. All things being equal, you knocked that man—much bigger than you—down to the floor in less than a minute." She paused and then said in a husky voice. "I only wish it hadn't been dark so that I might have *seen* you pummel him."

Caius laughed, but her words caused warmth to spread through his body. "Pummel? Hardly. All I did was take the wind out of him."

"*And* knock him down. If Victor hadn't interrupted you could have sewed up his sees—"

"*Sewed up his sees?*" Caius repeated, his own *sees* wide open. "Where in the world did you learn that dreadful cant?"

"I do have a little brother you, know. And he is positively mad for boxing. One cannot live in the same house with Doddy without hearing such things."

Caius yanked her to his chest. "How is it possible that you get more adorable every day?"

She gave one of her charming laughs and wrapped her arms around his waist. "I'm so glad you find boxing cant adorable because I've loads more to share with you."

Caius kissed her because he couldn't resist. What started as a light peck turned into a deep, passionate melding of mouths and jousting of tongues. Visions of taking his wife right then and there in the foyer—of sinking deep into her soft curvy body and fucking her until she screamed his name—romped through his head. It took a brutal amount of control to call a halt to his erotic desires before he put them into action.

"Tired?" he murmured, once he could make himself pull away.

"A little."

"*Too* tired?"

"I don't know. What do you have in mind?" she teased as they strolled toward the stairs.

"I thought you might come visit me in my room."

"*Your* room? Do you realize this is the first time you have invited me to your chambers?"

"No. That's impossible."

"It's true."

"To be honest, I didn't know you required an invitation, darling. Indeed, I seem to recall you just barging in on one memorable occasion."

Her body shook with laughter. "You behaved very badly that day."

"Admit that you looked at me, Selina—long and hard," he added with the suggestive leer of a pantomime villain.

"I am a lady, my lord. I would never do such a thing."

"Never?" he asked as they reached the landing and turned toward their apartments.

"Well, maybe I peeked just a little."

He opened the door to his bedchamber. "Why don't you come inside and I'll give you a bigger, longer look."

She laughed as he led her into his room. "You are shameless."

"Always, where you are concerned." Caius set aside his cane before taking her hips in his hands and claiming her mouth while pushing her against the door he'd just closed.

"Mmm," she hummed, pressing her body against him and lowering her hands to his buttocks and squeezing hard.

He groaned. "That feels wonderful, but right now I want you to lift your skirts for me, darling."

Caius felt her moving to comply and opened his fall and shoved down his drawers before taking his cock in hand. He quickly found her mound with his free hand and grunted as he slid a finger between her slick, swollen lips. "Spread your thighs wider for me. Yes… that's a good girl," he purred, circling her bud until she was shaking and thrusting against his hand.

He replaced his fingers with his cock, dragging the sensitive head through her silky heat over and over. "You're so wet, Selina—is that for me?"

"Only for you, Caius." she whispered.

He growled, released his prick, and hooked his hands beneath her thighs, lifting her.

Selina didn't need to be told what to do and quickly positioned his crown at her opening.

Caius entered her while standing and she whimpered as he kept her stretched and filled, her sheath squeezing his shaft so tightly that it was difficult to think straight.

"Does that feel good, my beautiful lover?" he hissed in her ear while gently pulsing his hips.

"Yes, Caius… but I need more, please."

Her words were like a bolt of lightning setting every sinew and nerve in his body on fire. He withdrew with teasing slowness and then entered her with a savage thrust that made her cry out.

"Is this what you need?" he demanded, snapping his hips and working her with hard, driving strokes that slammed her into the door.

"Yes," she gasped. "Yes, yes, yes," she chanted between each thrust, her body so hot and tight around his cock that Caius knew he'd not last long.

"There is nothing on earth that feels as good as you do right now, Selina," he growled against her throat as he slid his hands to her buttocks, tilting her in such a way that his thrusts gave her the friction she needed.

Whether it was some primitive effect of fighting for her honor, or the admission to himself earlier that he loved her, Caius didn't know, but his climax struck him with almost knee-buckling force.

And when her body convulsed around his a mere second later it felt like the most perfect moment in his life. Never before had Caius wanted to say the words *I love you* to a woman.

Fortunately, he was not so lost to passion that he didn't know the first time he told his wife those words should *not* be while he was balls deep inside her, when a man was apt to say anything to a woman.

No, Caius vowed he would not act impetuously or without thought when it came to something so important and precious.

This time—and with this glorious, generous, wonderful woman who now held his heart—he would do *everything* right.

Chapter 33

Selina moaned and clenched her inner muscles, chasing the exquisite sensation between her thighs and desperate for the wits-obliterating moment that was just out of reach.

"Yes," a low, masculine voice urged, pulling her from her slumber. "Take what you want, darling."

She blinked into the darkness, suddenly aware that she'd not been dreaming, at all. Broad shoulders pressed her thighs wide and a hot, skilled tongue rhythmically licked and thrusted while soft, silky curls tickled her belly.

Selina tunneled her fingers into his hair and pulled on it the way she'd learned Caius loved.

He groaned and his soft lips ceased their magical sucking.

"Ah, you are awake," he murmured in between leisurely licks.

"*Ungh.*"

"I'll take that as a *yes*. That's too bad, I'd hoped to make you come while you slept."

Even though it was dark and he could not see her, Selina blushed at his vulgar words.

Caius chuckled. "That embarrassed you, didn't it."

It wasn't a question, which was just as well because she was too limp and boneless to answer.

She did, however, wonder how he knew…

"You're probably wondering how I knew that?" he murmured, employing that worrying mind-reading ability she'd noticed once or twice before. "It's because I could feel your little pussy tighten beneath my tongue when I said the word *come*."

Selina gasped at this new word—whose application she could readily guess, although she'd never heard it used that way before—and Caius laughed.

"My prim little Puritan," he whispered, and circled his thumb around the little bead of flesh, applying the perfect amount of pressure as his mouth and tongue slid lower.

Did it make her a wanton strumpet that she adored it when her husband used his mouth on her? Or uttered such filthy words?

Did her sisters' husbands do such things to them? It was difficult to imagine Hy even allowing anyone to kiss her cheek—her sister did not care for physical affection—and Phoebe was such a practical and no-nonsense sort of person that

Selina could not stretch her imagination far enough to picture her modest sister ever allowing such shocking behavior as Caius was engaged in at that moment.

Selina decided she didn't care that she was so depraved she would clutch at her husband's hair and pulse her hips into his face to take her pleasure.

"Caius," she cried out, the force of her orgasm arching her off the bed.

She was still floating on a cloud of bliss when Caius entered her, needing only a half a dozen strokes before he stiffened and flooded her with warmth.

"Oh God," he muttered, his body lowering over hers while he lost himself to passion.

Selina slid her arms around him and then tightened them when he tried to lift his weight off her. "No," she said, the word distorted by a yawn. "I want you to stay."

His body tensed but then relaxed. Soft lips brushed against her ear and he rolled them both onto their sides, so that her head was resting on his biceps. "I'll stay for a while. Go to sleep, Selina darling."

But the thought of him leaving suddenly made her feel wide awake.

"Caius?"

"Hmm?"

"You know how you, er, do that thing to me?"

He'd been toying with a lock of her hair but stopped. "Er, what thing is that?"

Selina gave an exasperated huff. "*You* know." She felt his body tremble. "Are you laughing?"

"I'm sorry, I can't help it. It's just so amusing to hear you come up with new ways *not* to say certain things."

"You beast!" Selina reached between their bodies and pinched him. She'd only meant to grab skin but pinched a nipple instead.

His body went rigid. "Oh, Christ!"

"I'm sorry."

He exhaled slowly and said, "Don't be."

"You mean... you liked it?"

"Mmm."

Interesting.

He took her wrist and placed her hand over his nipple. "Play with it," he ordered in a gruff voice.

The next few moments were exceptionally educational and Selina's body hummed with smug satisfaction as she made her big strong husband squirm and beg.

"So, my lord—the thing I mentioned"—she pinched him extra hard for emphasis. "What is it called?"

"*Argh*," he cried out, adding in a hasty voice, "it's called cunnilingus."

Selina paused her erotic tormenting. "Huh."

"*Huh* what?" he asked.

"That just *sounds* naughty."

He laughed. "What did you want to ask about it?" he said, and then whimpered when she pinched *and* tugged on a nipple.

Very interesting.

Selina pulled her attention back to his question. "Is it—can a woman do it with a man?" she asked.

His body went every bit as rigid as it had moments earlier, when she'd first pinched him.

"Er, yes, as a matter of fact. But then it is called fellatio."

She tried the words out: "Cunnilingus. Fellatio."

"Oh, bloody hell," he moaned. "How come those words sound so damned filthy on that sweet little tongue of yours?"

Selina smirked and pinched his nipple. "Your language is becoming quite crude, my lord."

He grunted, grabbed her wrist and brought her hand to his hardening organ and closed her fingers around his girth. "God, yes," he muttered, and then moved their hands up and down together.

"Is this fellatio, too?"

He groaned. "No, this is—er, Lord. I don't know what it's called when somebody else does it for you. When one does it to oneself it is of course—"

"Masturbation," she finished for him. "I *know* that." Selina said, tightening her grip.

"Are you trying to kill me?" he asked in a choked voice.

Selina was quite enjoying herself, but the angle was too awkward to get a really good grip so she pushed up onto her knees. "That is better," she said.

"Uh, that is actually quite"—he grunted when she stroked him faster and harder. "Oh, Lord. Yes."

She grinned and took the next few minutes to explore, learning the shape and texture of him, only noticing that he was getting slicker after she'd been caressing him for a while.

"Oh. You get wet just like I do," she said.

"Ungh." His body jolted and more liquid seemed to appear as if by magic.

Selina stared down at his ruddy shaft and slick crown, wishing that there was more than just the one candle all the way on the other side of the room. He felt so different than anything else she could think of. The skin was tight yet it moved over the hard muscle beneath in a sliding fashion. He'd begun to lift his hips, to pump into her fist the way he thrust into her body.

When Selina tightened her grip, he moaned. "Yes, just like that—nice and tight."

His words sent a bolt of heat directly to her sex, which was once again swollen and sensitive. Who could have imagined that rendering a man speechless could be so physically satisfying?

But she didn't want to think about her own pleasure—this was for Caius. Every single night he brought her to bliss at least once or twice before entering her and taking his own release.

She wanted to do the same for him.

Selina screwed up her courage and said, "May I kiss it, Caius."

"Oh, fucking hell!" he shouted. His hips lifted off the bed and his shaft swelled and then pulsed, covering her hand with jet after jet of warm liquid.

Selina stared, enrapt, squeezing him harder when no more seemed to be coming out.

Caius hissed in a breath and settled a hand over hers to stop her stroking. "Sensitive," he hissed, his body still clenching with small contractions. "C'mere," he muttered, pulling her down beside him, but tucking the sheet between his stomach and her back. "Don't want to get you wet," he said when she stiffened.

Oh, she'd forgotten about that. Well, the bedding would have needed to be changed in any event.

His arm curled around her and pulled her tighter to his chest. "Mmm," he moaned as she burrowed back against him, tucking her bottom as close as it could go.

He had never been so relaxed with her before.

Selina yawned. Maybe tonight he would stay with her...

***

The next time Selina woke up it was morning.

Her hand went to the other side of the bed and she wasn't surprised to find it cold and empty.

Rather than get up immediately, she stared up at the canopy, her thoughts on her husband.

She'd thought that last night—the way they had joined together to vanquish Crawford and then the things they'd done afterward—had brought them closer. He'd felt so relaxed that she'd hoped he might stay with her. Oh, she knew it wasn't done among their class, but she *liked* having him near her.

Not to mention you like making love with him and would like to do more of it.

She blushed, even though she was alone.

But it was true that she could not get enough of him—not during the day, nor at night. And last night she hadn't got the chance to put her mouth on him.

Selina chewed her lip, suddenly pensive. Was she turning into one of those horrid women who were needy and clingy?

If so, she needed to curb that tendency.

"*Men don't like women hanging around their necks every hour of the day, Selina. It is vulgar and common,*" her mother had said more than a few times. "*They will want to go to their clubs—their women—and you will have your own concerns.*"

Would Caius take a mistress? He'd had one when he was married to his first wife.

The thought of him doing the things they did with another woman sent anger rolling though her body.

Selina already knew that she would *hate* that.

Then don't let it happen.

Somehow, Selina suspected things wouldn't be that easy or straightforward. This was a marriage of convenience, after all. True, it was extremely pleasant and—

—and you're in love with him.

Selina wanted to deny it, but the realization had been nibbling away at the edges of her mind for some time now—maybe even as far back as that day in the rainstorm.

Love. She shook her head, stunned. All her life she'd imagined what it must feel like to fall in love. Never had she expected it to be so gradual, or so… complex. She'd thought it would be *romantic,* like pretty flowers, beautiful gowns, or sparkling jewels. But those things did not even factor into the feelings she had for Caius. She had seen him at his worst and yet that did not make her care for him any less.

When Crawford had tried to humiliate him at dinner last night her reaction had been visceral and fierce, every bit as savagely protective as if somebody had attacked her sisters or brother.

Caius was *hers*. Indeed, she felt an almost physical connection to him even when they weren't in the same room. It was a powerfully intoxicating sensation knowing that such a magnificent man was her husband and that she was in love with him.

And it was also the scariest feeling she'd ever had.

Because what would happen to her if Caius never grew to love her back?

Chapter 34

A week later Selina and Caius were in the breakfast room and Selina was reading the newspaper, her attention only partly on her task.

The rest of her mind was harkening back to the night before. Caius had been insatiable, taking her four times before he'd finally left for his bed in the early hours of the morning. Selina had love bites on her neck and the side of her breast as proof of his passion.

There had been no hiding the marks from Fanny this morning, but then why should she? They were man and wife, and her virile, handsome husband loved her body.

At least he loved some part of her.

"Selina?"

"Hmm? I'm sorry, what did you say?"

"I asked if you could you read me the story on the ship that sank off the coast of—"

The door opened and Victor entered. "Good morning, Caius. Selina."

"Why, hello, Brother," Caius said, looking genuinely pleased.

It was unusual to see Victor in the mornings as he normally chose to eat breakfast in his own chambers.

Even though Victor had defended Caius the night of the ball Selina still hadn't forgiven him for his blackmail. Not because she regretted her marriage—quite the opposite—but because his threat had been so very cruel and cold. She simply could not imagine even thinking such horrible thoughts about one of her own siblings, even if it was the only way to make them do what was best.

To be honest, Selina was no longer sure that Victor would have followed through with his threat. But it would be a long, long time before she could forget the paralyzing fear she'd felt when he'd said the words *marquess* and *sanitorium* in the same breath.

Victor must have sensed her reserve, because she had seen very little of him since she and Caius had married. But although he avoided Selina, he still spent an hour or so most afternoons with Caius, the two of them quickly getting through any remaining estate business, until Caius had confessed to her that he was largely caught up.

She never saw Victor between noon and dinner, which they ate at seven-thirty. Selina occasionally wondered how he spent his time. Was he lonely? Was he making plans to go back to his monastery?

"It's unusual for you to break your fast with us laggards, Victor," Caius said, his words pulling her from her thoughts. "Did you sleep in this morning?"

Victor gave a perfunctory smile at his brother's teasing. "No, I've just been busy. And now... Well, I have an announcement to make. I am getting married."

Selina saw her own surprise mirrored in her husband's face.

"To Mrs. Cooper," Victor added, rather unnecessarily.

Selina had caught a glimpse of the pair dancing the night of the ball and their mutual affection had been plain to see—at least to her—and she had said as much to Caius, who'd been overjoyed.

Caius grinned and stood. "Come here," he ordered, holding out his arms.

Victor sidled close enough that his elder brother could pull him into an embrace. "Congratulations, old man. I am very happy for you both."

"Er, thank you, Caius," Victor said, visibly eager to extricate himself from Caius's arms.

"Congratulations, Victor," Selina said, amused when Victor's face darkened. Was he remembering his role in her own betrothal?

"Mrs. Cooper is a wonderful woman," Caius said.

"She is," Selina agreed. Personally, she thought the gregarious widow was too good for Caius's taciturn, glum brother.

"Thank you both," Victor said. "We want to have same sort of ceremony the two of you had."

"Do you need to appeal to the Archbishop for a special license?" Caius asked.

"No, I've already obtained a common license to avoid delay. We've planned the ceremony for Tuesday."

Caius's eyebrows lifted. "*This* Tuesday—as in two days away?"

"Yes. We feel we have waited long enough."

There was an awkward silence as Victor stared at his brother and it was Caius's turn to look uncomfortable.

"May we host the breakfast for you here?" Selina asked, cutting the unpleasant moment short with her question. She refused to allow Victor to make her husband feel guiltier than he already did about what had happened all those years ago. Especially since Victor was not exactly blameless himself.

Victor looked startled by the offer. "Oh, that would be nice—just... very simple."

"Of course. I hope you will give our congratulations to Mrs. Cooper."

Selina

"Yes, I will. And... thank you both," he said. "I will leave you now. I'm going to tell Sarah that I've made the announcement."

When he was gone, Selina stood and went to her husband, who was still standing and facing the door. She felt him sag slightly when she took his arm.

"Well," he said.

She laid her head against his shoulder. "Don't feel guilty, Caius."

He huffed a laugh. "Is it that obvious?"

She ignored the question and said, "He has almost forgiven you and will do so completely once they are married."

"He has been so alone for so long. I—well, I'm glad he is finally getting what he wants."

Selina wished she could tell Caius that his brother was no saint—that he, too, had flexed his power in a cruel and selfish way. But the one thing she knew for certain about her new husband was that he jealously guarded his pride. If he ever learned that Victor had blackmailed her into marriage, he would never forgive his brother.

Or her.

***

Two days later Caius and Selina were waving farewell to the Shaftsbury coach while it bore Victor and Sarah away from Courtland. The newlyweds were off to London for a bridal holiday while the vicar kept Sarah's daughter Cora so the couple could enjoy a few days alone before they settled at Victor's estate, Beckworth.

Beckworth was a scant five miles away from Courtland so Caius would be able to visit with his brother often—provided Victor was interested in continuing their re-acquaintance.

Caius wasn't sure if that was really what his brother wanted. Victor had been solitary and secretive as a child, two characteristics that seemed to have become more ingrained during his eight years in a monastery. Caius could only hope that Sarah, who was a cheerful and sociable person, would help pull his brother out of his shell.

Selina lightly squeezed his arm. "Shall we go and see what happens to Marianne and Colonel Brandon now that Willoughby has been exposed for the feckless villain he is?"

Caius pulled a face. "Not today."

"I don't think you like *Sense and Sensibility* as much as the first book. You don't like Marianne, do you?"

"No."

She laughed. "You wretched man! She is the heroine; you cannot dislike her."

"All those die-away airs and that ridiculous obsession with poetry. She's not good enough for Colonel Brandon. He would get bored of her within a week."

"She is pretty and fragile and feminine. My mother always told me those are the only things that men want in a wife."

"I think we can both agree on just how much your mother knows about men and what they want." He grabbed her by the waist and jerked her against his body, and whispered into her ear, "Remember that wonderful thing you did last night with my—"

"Caius!"

He grinned. "Well, let me tell you my dear, that is far more appealing to the average man than prattling on about poetry or fainting at the sight of a garden snake."

"You are very impressed that I rescued poor Fanny from that tiny little snake that managed to slither into the conservatory, aren't you?"

"Serpents terrify me." He gave a dramatic shiver. "I am a fortunate man to have you to protect me."

Selina laughed. "You are absurd."

He nibbled on her lower lip. "Not only are you fearless when it comes to vanquishing reptiles, but you also taste good and smell good and you can *almost* beat me at chess."

"I *did* beat you… once."

"No? Did you? I don't remember."

"Clearly I need to make it more painful the next time, so that you remember it better."

He laughed.

"If you don't want to read, then what—"

"I thought we might go to the music room early today as I missed my lesson yesterday."

"Ah, and whose fault was that?"

Caius smirked fondly at the memory of yesterday afternoon, when they'd made love on his desk in the library after playing a game of chess.

"That was my prize for beating you in only six moves."

"You were supposed to wait until bedtime to take your *prize*," she accused him.

"I can hear you blushing," he said, kissing her hot cheek. "And I can taste it, too. Perhaps we should—"

"No. You need your lesson—two, today."

"Are you sure you want to continue trying to teach me, Selina?" he asked, only partly in jest. Although it had only been a few weeks of lessons it was already clear that he would never make much of a musician.

"You just need more practice," she insisted.

"I'm afraid I don't have the dexterity for it."

She yanked him close—just as he had done with her—and whispered. "You seemed to have plenty of dexterity last night, my lord."

Caius gave a delighted crow at her risqué teasing. "Then perhaps we should forget the piano lesson and go upstairs and—"

"No, you promised to learn—you must keep your word."

And so, for the next week, Caius took at least one lesson every day and then practiced on his own for an hour. He would never be a virtuoso on the instrument, but Selina had been correct when she'd insisted that he would enjoy playing the more proficient he became.

"I find myself hearing these scales when I am doing something else," he confessed to his wife as they finished up his sixth day in a row of lessons.

She laughed. "Just wait until you are learning your first piece of music. You will *dream* of playing the song. It used to make my mother furious if any of us practiced our fingering while sitting at the dinner table."

It was through vignettes like that one that Caius had begun to put together a picture of the Countess of Addiscombe and what it was like to be her daughter. As sunny and optimistic as his wife seemed, he did not think that her childhood had been a terribly happy one.

One night, after they'd made love but before Caius had returned to his chambers, he'd asked her about her parents and had felt the shift in her mood—from ebullient and replete to wary and guarded.

"You don't need to tell me if you don't wish to," he'd said, stroking her body in a way that was comforting, rather than sexual—although that could always change quickly around his sensual, giving wife.

Caius found that he could not keep his hands off her—and she did not want him to. He'd never been so physically demonstrative with a lover and didn't know if it was a result of being blind—that he needed more sensory stimulation—or if it was just because of Selina, herself.

Whatever the reason, he adored that aspect of their relationship.

"I don't mind talking about them," Selina had insisted, although she'd sounded less than convincing.

"I already know you don't believe your father is financially responsible. But is that the only reason you did not want me to contact him to discuss matters?"

"That was the main reason. I just *knew* that he would have his hand out."

Caius snorted.

"I'm sorry, that is disrespectful toward my father, but if you knew—well, never mind about that."

"No, tell me, darling. I want to know you."

"My father is a charming man—very charming—but I'm not sure I've met another person who is more selfish. Except for my mother, perhaps. He lost—or I should say *threw away*—everything over the years, until my sisters and I thought we'd be tossed out of our home. I just don't know how somebody could do that to people they loved."

"I've seen some men—and a few women, too—who get an almost entranced expression when they play cards. It is a compulsion for them. That doesn't excuse your father, of course, but perhaps it might explain it."

Her dismissive grunt had said it didn't do either. "As for my mother? I should probably warn you about her."

He laughed. "Warn me?"

"You laugh *now*, Caius, but trust me: the Countess of Addiscombe is no laughing matter. My father at least possesses charm to cover up his failings. My mother has none. Part of that is understandable—a lifetime spent with such a feckless spouse would likely sour anyone. And I can almost understand why she dislikes all her daughters—after all, we are the reason she had to keep having children year after year—but she doesn't even like her son and heir. And I have to tell you, Caius, that my little brother is possibly the most loveable person I know."

Some childish part of him felt a twinge of jealousy—or perhaps envy—to hear that.

"We are all nothing but tools to her. I was the tool she would use to get out of poverty. And I failed her. Her only letter to me since I've lived at Courtland was brief and insulting. She made it perfectly clear what she thinks of me now that I am no longer a useful tool."

There had been a great deal of pain beneath her words.

"My own mother was not the most affectionate of parents," he'd admitted.

"Mine goes beyond that." She'd hesitated and then said, "I will not treat my own children that way, Caius—as pieces on a chessboard to be moved and sacrificed for my own purposes. Be they female or male, clever or silly, plain or pretty, I plan to love them all and make sure they know it."

Selina

What about me? he'd wanted to ask. *Do you think you could ever love me?*

But of course he'd said nothing of the sort.

***

"Do you miss Victor," Selina suddenly asked Caius.

They had just finished a game of chess—Caius had won, but it had been close—and they were both replacing the pieces on the board.

"Yes, I do. But I've also been glad to have you all to myself this past week."

She scoffed. "Victor hardly took up any of my time."

"No, but he took up mine. Speaking of Victor, now that he is gone, I've considered engaging a new secretary, but concluded I'd have better luck finding somebody when we go to London next year. Do you mind taking on that burden until then? Or should I hire somebody now?"

"I would love to help. Truth be told, I felt a bit hurt when Victor displaced me. Although I know he is a man and has better sense when it comes to matters of business."

"No, he doesn't, my practical, clever, pragmatic wife—you have one of the sharpest most intuitive minds I've encountered. Never doubt your abilities. I welcomed Victor's help because I hoped for some rapprochement with him and that seemed a good way"—he snorted— "the only way, really, to spend time with him. After all, I can no longer hunt or ride or do those things that men typically enjoy together. But I never meant for you to feel displaced. Indeed, I thought that mucking about in account books was something tedious you'd be glad to leave behind."

"I liked it," she said. "Not just being able to help you, but it made me understand the estate and the people and how everything functions. Phoebe handled all the tasks typically managed by the mistress of the house, and I helped her from time to time, but she was too efficient to really need me." She paused and Caius waited patiently, certain that there was something she wanted to say. "To be honest, I was never of much use." She gave a brittle laugh. "My mother told me that I didn't need to be useful or clever—she said men didn't like those qualities in a woman and that my purpose was to be decorative, attentive, flattering, and… quiet."

Caius wanted to pick her up, hold her in his arms, and tell her that her mother was an idiot, but he held his peace because he sensed she was not finished.

"Despite her insistence that I be useless, I found that I was good at mending things—just small things like stitching up a rip or tear so that it can't be seen or salvaging a broken necklace or repairing the spine of a book, or—*ugh*—it sounds like such an inconsequential existence when I say it aloud."

"You do yourself a great disservice, Selina. No—" he said, speaking over her demurral, "you do. Not only have you put my house in order, but the servants and our tenants adore you. Don't think I'm not aware of all you do. I've heard Morris and Mrs. Shore come to you to settle squabbles among the staff and I know they both rely on you for a multitude of reasons. And you are especially good at putting yourself into another's shoes—or boots." He held out a hand, pleased when she immediately laced her fingers with his. "Many of us struggle with the matters that you find so simple and that you settle with such grace."

Clasps and torn clothing aren't the only things you mend so easily, he wanted to say. *There are also the people you have put back together. Like me.*

Tell her, Elton ordered.

"I am thankful for you every day, Selina." A rush of emotion caused Caius's throat to thicken and he could barely squeeze the words out.

She gasped softly. "Oh, Caius. What a lovely, *lovely* thing to say."

Just tell her you love her. You are man enough to survive if she doesn't feel the same. Aren't you?

Caius squeezed her hand and said, "Selina. I—"

There was a knock on the door and Caius heard it open. He scowled. "Yes, what is it?"

"I'm terribly sorry to interrupt," Morris said. "But Lord and Lady Victor and Miss Cora have just arrived."

"Oh," Selina said, her hand slipping away from Caius's as she stood. "Goodness, how delightful! I didn't expect them until tomorrow."

"Lady Victor missed Miss Cora, so they came back a day early."

Selina laughed. "Of course, she missed her. Will you please tell Cook—"

"I've already spoken to her, my lady. Lord and Lady Victor asked if it would be acceptable for Miss Cora to join the adults for dinner tonight."

"Yes, it is silly to make her eat alone in that grim schoolroom." Selina laid a hand on Caius's arm. "You don't mind, do you?"

"No, of course not. She is a charming child."

Morris left and Selina turned and laid her hands on his shoulders. "You were saying something when Morris interrupted."

Caius smiled at her and felt for his walking stick. "It was nothing we can't talk about later."

Coward, Elton chided.

Selina

Caius didn't deny the charge. He got to his feet and said, "Let's go welcome the newlyweds, shall we?"

Chapter 35

Dinner that night was a merry affair. Although it was only the five of them, Selina and Cora provided amusement enough for a dozen guests. Selina took such obvious delight in the little girl's company that it was a joy just to be around her. If there had been any doubt lingering in Caius's mind that he loved his wife, then listening to how good she was with Victor's stepdaughter put paid to it.

By the time the meal was over Caius had serious doubts that he could last another two hours—the minimum amount of time he owed their guests—before whisking Selina upstairs as fast as a blind man with a cane could whisk, and saying what he should have had the courage to say weeks ago.

Luckily, Victor rarely wanted to linger too long over port and cigars after dinner.

Caius had hoped that marriage would relax his brother, but—if anything—Victor had been quieter than ever during dinner, leaving Caius and the women to keep the conversation going.

After Victor had given him a glass of port Caius did something the members of their family had always avoided: he asked his brother a personal question.

"You seem preoccupied tonight, Tor. Is something bothering you?" he asked, using the name he'd given his brother when he'd been a little boy, tagging along after Caius and his friends whenever he came home from Eton, always wanting to be included.

"Er, no. There is nothing wrong," Victor said hastily, but not very convincingly.

When had Victor stopped being that adoring little brother? Why had he suddenly stopped being Caius's shadow? He honestly could not recall, but certainly it had happened a long time before their final schism.

A long-buried snatch of conversation rose up like a specter in Caius's head and he set down his glass. "Remember the year I came home for Christmas and took you to watch that mill?"

"Of course I remember."

"I'd let you have too much ale and you were a little worse for wear"—Caius chuckled at the memory. "Mother caught us coming home. She was angry because you were only thirteen and she said something to you, something I've never forgotten: *you know there is no reason that you have to be like him.* What did she mean by that, Victor? I should have asked you then, but she and I had a terrible row after you went to bed and I never had a chance."

His mother had accused him of corrupting Victor and had told him to stay away from his little brother. Caius had been hurt and angry and had left without saying goodbye to either his father or his brother.

"You didn't come home to Courtland for almost a year afterward," Victor said, his voice almost… accusing.

"Yes. I was… angry. Very angry at her."

"Why are you asking me about all that now?" Victor asked.

Caius shrugged. "I don't know. I was just trying to recall when things changed for us. While we weren't exactly close before, at least we were friendly. What did she mean by that, Victor?" He smiled ruefully. "You needn't worry about offending me, I know mother disapproved of me. She made no secret of it, after all. I'd even go so far as to say she *disliked* me and viewed me as a replica of our father."

Victor didn't dispute his words. He didn't say anything at all.

"Victor? What—"

"Mother told me that I am not our father's son and that I—"

Caius lowered his glass to the table with a clatter. "*What?*" he shouted.

"I—I thought you knew."

It was difficult to breathe. "Knew? Knew what?" Caius demanded.

"Are you sure you—"

"Tell me, goddammit!"

"She told me that she'd taken a lover to stop father from coming to her bed. She said that he kept a mistress in London, a woman who'd already given him five or six children. She didn't want him to have any others. He didn't deserve them, she said."

Caius knew the part about his father's mistress and other children was true because he was still supporting several of his half-brothers and sisters.

"Who was mother's lover?" he asked, not believing that part for even a second. Their mother had been so sanctimonious and prudish that it simply did not ring true.

"She didn't say."

"Did father know?"

"She said he didn't and that I wasn't ever to tell him. Or you. She said that he would cut off my inheritance and send me away if he knew."

"That fucking *bitch!*"

"Caius! That is our mother you are—"

265

"I don't give a damn! What sort of mother would say such a thing to her own son? And when you were little more than a child." Caius shook his head. "Why would she tell you that, Victor?"

"She said I didn't need to be like you or father because I didn't bear the stain of his blood. She said I was good, that my real father was a decent man"—Caius barked a laugh at that— "She said that she wanted me to become a priest—"

"Bloody hell, Victor. Why didn't you tell me any of this? Never mind," he quickly added. "I'm sure you were terrified that I would tell Father or confront her." He scowled. "I think she lied to you, Victor. We are a great deal alike in appearance, after all. Have you ever considered that she might have lied to manipulate you into doing what she wanted—to drive a wedge between us?"

Victor gasped. "You don't really think she would have lied about something like that?"

"Who knows? Their marriage was so poisonous that I wouldn't put it past her. Father was careless, selfish, and cruel and she was rigid, moralizing, and unforgiving. It was a lethal combination that they both tried their damnedest to pass down to us. But we don't have to let them win. We have broken the cycle—true, it took almost a decade to mend what I almost destroyed, but you are now married to a woman who you love, and who obviously loves—"

"There is something I have to tell you, Caius," Victor said, his voice unnaturally high and agitated. "It has been eating at me for weeks. I—I can't bear to keep it inside."

Caius had heard about chills running down a person's spine, but he'd never felt it until that moment.

"There is no confessional here, brother. You don't have to say anything else. We can have a fresh start; we don't need to unearth the past and—"

"I threatened Selina."

Caius's hand tightened painfully on the cut glass tumbler. "I beg your pardon?"

"I told her that I would have you declared incompetent, take control of the marquessate, and have you locked away in an asylum if she didn't marry you."

Caius felt like somebody was standing on his chest. It was all he could do to force even one word out. "*What?*"

"I—I just wanted to be gone from here and I knew I couldn't leave without making sure you were, erm—"

"Taken care of, like a toddler who needed a nurserymaid?" Caius supplied, the cold, sick feeling in his belly beginning to boil.

"I was wrong to think you were incapable of managing your own affairs. I was—"

Caius lunged to his feet, his entire body shaking, as if he'd been invaded by some dire influenza. "You were bloody wrong to blackmail a powerless, gentle, and caring young woman into marrying the human equivalent of a fucking anchor, Victor."

"I am *sorry*," Victor wailed. "I know it was a terrible way to begin a marriage, but I can see the way she is with you, Caius. She is happy here, she is—"

At the very last second Caius changed his aim and flung the port at the fireplace instead of his brother's head. The pop of glass on stone was like the report of a pistol in the cavernous room.

"Don't you *dare* talk to me about my wife," he hissed, striding toward Victor without his cane and immediately colliding with a chair. He flung it out of the way with a roar and launched himself in the direction of his brother. By some miracle, he collided with a human chest instead of a candelabrum or firedog.

"You fucking bastard!" he shouted, his fingers scrabbling until he grabbed hold of the lapels of his brother's dinner coat. He shook him and shouted, "Selina doesn't have a selfish or petty bone in her entire body. You don't think she would hide the pain she felt at being trapped into this marriage? You don't think she would sacrifice her hopes and dreams to keep me out of a bloody lunatic asylum and do it with a fucking smile on her face? Of course she pretends that she is happy!" Spittle flew from his lips but Caius didn't care how deranged he looked or sounded. "The woman has had duty bred into her bones since the day she was born. And thanks to you, Brother, I've just become one more goddamned duty in a long line of many."

Victor's hands closed around his wrists. "I never would have done that to you, Caius. It was a hollow threat. I was still so angry at you that—"

"It doesn't matter if you would have done it or not. The threat served its purpose, didn't it? She bloody married me." He flung Victor aside and staggered backward. He was only stopped from tumbling onto his arse by the hard wood of the table that bit into his lower back. "Give me my walking stick."

A moment later he felt cool silver in his palm.

"Caius, I—"

"Straighten my clothing."

"Wh-what?"

"Straighten my fucking clothing so I don't look like I was just in a brawl."

Victor tweaked his coat and neckcloth with shaking fingers. "There," he muttered a moment later.

"Ring the bell and have somebody clean up the mess I just made. It is time to go to the ladies. It has been thirty minutes." Caius turned away without waiting for a reply and left the room, not caring whether Victor was behind him or not.

When he reached the staircase, he was tempted to turn left and head to the foyer. He could trip and tap his way out of the house and off the property. If he was lucky, he could tap his way to a cliff and fling himself off the edge, finishing the job that had begun a year before.

Or maybe he could just go and fetch that pistol he'd forgotten all about—the one that was still nestled in his nightstand like a lurking cobra, the one he'd been too cowardly to use.

But no, putting a period to himself *now* would devastate Selina because she would believe that it was a failure on her part. That was no longer an option.

No, he needed to do the honorable thing. He needed to cut her loose—free her to be something other than nursemaid to a blind man for the rest of her life. She deserved it.

Caius might be new to love, but he already knew that he'd do anything to make her happy.

Even let her go.

***

"I will brush my hair tonight. Why don't you go to bed, Fanny," Selina said, taking up the brush.

"Good night, my lady."

Normally Selina enjoyed her maid's company, but she was feeling restless. Would Caius come to her? She wasn't sure. He had been so odd after dinner and she wondered whether he'd argued with Victor, who'd looked positively ghastly when the two men had entered the drawing room after their port.

But Caius had immediately asked for music and so both Sarah and Selina had taken turns on the piano and even little Cora had played a few songs.

Selina had been disappointed when Caius had begged off a game of chess, unable to recall a time when he had passed up an opportunity to play. But he'd claimed a headache, which was also something he had never done before. And then he'd been abrupt with her when she had offered to mix him one of Nanny Fletcher's poultices.

"Don't fuss over me, Selina," he'd snapped. "I just need a bit of rest."

Did *rest* mean all night? Or just a few hours?

Would he come to her?

Look at you! Selfishly wanting your nightly bed sport when your husband is suffering a headache in his room.

Selina

Her face heated at the accusation and she paused her brushing. Perhaps she should knock on his door and offer—but no, he'd already said he didn't want a draught.

Selina sighed and put down her brush. What she should do was go to bed. It was only one night without him, after all. She could survive that much, even though she would miss him.

***

Not only did Caius not come to her chambers, but—for the first time in weeks—he did not come down to breakfast the following morning.

She'd not heard any sounds coming from beyond the connecting door, so she'd not wanted to knock in case she woke him. Her brother Doddy was plagued by headaches—terrible ones that caused him to vomit and gave him chills—and often stayed in bed for several days after one struck.

If that was what Caius was suffering from, he would not welcome her company.

But perhaps he wasn't in his room. Perhaps he'd gone out to the stables. He and Victor had drawn up a plan for a riding arena—one that was much larger and where Caius could practice riding—maybe they were out in the stables with Mr. Herrick going over the recent work.

Or maybe they had just gone for a walk. Selina knew that Caius looked forward to his rambles with his brother.

And yet… something just didn't feel right.

She'd had the strangest feeling yesterday afternoon that Caius had been on the verge of saying something important before Morris had interrupted.

Her heart thumped faster at the thought; not that she really believed he'd been about to declare his love for her or anything so momentous.

Well, Victor and Sarah would be leaving today and they would have the house to themselves. Perhaps he was just waiting for privacy to talk to her?

Buoyed by that thought, Selina looked up from her empty teacup. "Do you know where his lordship is?" she asked Timothy, the footman who was on breakfast duty that morning.

"He is in his gymnasium, my lady."

"Ah, thank you."

Well, that was interesting. He still spent time boxing, but usually that was something he did if he could not sleep.

Selina was tempted to look in on him but decided to respect his need for privacy.

Whatever had happened between him and Victor last night after dinner—and she felt sure that something had occurred—he obviously needed time to work it out of his system.

***

Caius's knuckles ached and he flexed his hands, making them hurt worse but relishing the pain. It was better than the agony in his head, after all.

"Ah, there you are," Selina said to him as he entered the foyer. "My goodness! Are you bleeding," she asked quietly, taking his hand.

"It is nothing," he said, gently extricating his fingers just as footsteps came from the marble steps behind him. "That sounds like our guests," he said, grateful for the distraction.

"Thank you so much for having us," Sarah said as the footsteps came to a halt in front of him. "I'm sorry we have to leave so soon."

"I asked Victor to stay longer," Caius lied. "But he is itching to get home and I daresay you are, too, Sarah."

"Me, too," Cora piped up, making everyone chuckle.

Sarah took Caius's outstretched hand and gave it a gentle squeeze. "Indeed, I am... Caius."

His new sister-in-law sounded shy using his Christian name.

"Selina promises me that you will both visit in another month or two, once there are not boxes and crates littering every room," she said.

"I look forward to it," Caius said, leaning close enough to brush a kiss on her cheek before turning to the sound of scuffling feet he heard beside her and crouching down. "Cora, won't you give your new uncle a kiss before you go?" A touch like butterfly wings landed on his cheek and he smiled. "Thank you. Now, I want you to make sure that your father buys you a pony—that should be the first thing he does when you reach Beckworth."

Everyone laughed except Cora, whom he could hear leaping up and down. "Oh, please, Papa, will you? A gray pony?"

Victor chuckled and the sound was forced. "I daresay something can be arranged."

Caius stood back as Selina embraced them, evidently giving Cora a second and third hug for good measure. He heard a watery sniff or two that told him his soft-hearted wife was crying.

They went outside and waited until the trio were tucked into the coach.

Yet more teary goodbyes were exchanged through the open window and then, finally, the sound of horse hooves and carriage wheels filled the air.

Selina

Selina slid an arm around his waist and leaned against him as they stood and waved the carriage off, until the only sound was that of distant birdsong and summer insects. "Oh, Caius. I *will* miss Cora. And Victor and Sarah, too, of course."

He smiled. "You are a goddess to that little girl."

"I adore them when they are that age," she admitted as they walked slowly back toward the house, still arm in arm. "But I must say I am glad to have you to myself again."

Caius smiled tightly as their feet led them to their favorite room. "Shall we have a game of chess?" she asked. "Or do you wish to read another chapter or two of *Emma*? I know you are not liking it nearly as much as *Pride and Prejudice*, but perhaps it will grow on you?"

He opened the door for her and then closed it behind her.

"Caius?"

"Have a seat, my dear."

He sat behind his desk rather than beside her; he needed distance for this conversation.

"What is wrong, Caius? You are worrying me."

"You needn't be worried, Selina. It's just time we had a talk."

"A talk?"

"Yes, I was waiting until Victor was all settled and it was just the two of us."

"Very well," she said, sounding wary. "What do you want to talk about?"

"Don't sound so worried," he soothed, keeping his tone light and pleasant while he was hemorrhaging inside. "I just wanted to tell you that I know you only married me because Victor threatened to have me put away, Selina. You needn't pretend any longer."

Deny it! Deny it! Please, God—say it never mattered.

But her silence told him all he needed to know.

"You—you knew that is what he'd planned?" she finally said. "He told me that you weren't aware of what he would do."

Caius gave a hearty chuckle he wasn't feeling. "Oh yes, he threw all sorts of threats at me to get his way—rescuing your reputation, my reputation, the dignity of the family name, and so forth. A declaration of incompetence was just one of many."

Say you never believed him! Say you married me because you wanted to—not because you sacrificed your future to keep me safe! Say it!

He heard her swallow. "He did the same with me," she admitted slowly. "Except first he used the story of my scandalous liaison with Shelton and that dreadful fight at the inn to try and coerce me to do his bidding." She gave an unhappy laugh. "He was speechless when he realized I really didn't care about rescuing my reputation."

"And so he tried a more serious threat," Caius murmured.

"Yes. He said it would be easy to have you declared incompetent. When I pointed out, quite rightly, that a lack of vision was in no way a lack of wits he said the fact that you'd lost your sight from trauma to your head would influence the court. He even told me that a judge could force me to testify." She stopped, her breathing heavier. "But he *lied* to me—he told me that you didn't know. I had no idea that he'd threatened you to your face, that is even worse. Did—did he use the threat of my ruined reputation to pressure you? He did, didn't he?" she went on, oblivious to his turmoil and apparently unable to hear the sound of hope collapsing inside him.

"I know you love him, and he's your brother, but I'm afraid it will take a long time until I forgive him, Caius."

"Yes," he said hoarsely, "I can see how you would find that difficult to forgive."

"

"Don't you?" she demanded. "Although I suppose the threats, he used for you were a bit different—unless… were you really afraid he would win if he went to a magistrate?"

Caius turned toward her and lied yet again. "Yes, he might have prevailed."

She gave a sigh that sounded like relief. "I am glad we stopped him. I hope he has apologized to you, Caius?"

"Yes, he apologized." He cleared his throat and forced himself to go on. "I just want to discuss our arrangements."

"Arrangements?"

"Yes. I was going to mention it before Victor and Sarah arrived, but they arrived early and I never got the chance."

"That is what you wanted to say when Morris interrupted us in the music room?"

He hesitated and then said, "Yes."

"What do you mean by arrangements?"

"I will always be grateful to you for pulling me from my *trough of despond*, but I think it is time we got on with our own lives."

"I—I don't understand what you mean, Caius."

Selina

He heard the confusion in her voice—was there something else? Sadness?

No, that was just his wishful thinking.

Caius steeled himself and said, "You don't need to stay here and tend to me, Selina. You've already done what you set out to do—Victor cannot hurt me anymore; you made sure of that by becoming my wife. We needn't continue this... farce any longer."

"Farce?"

"I have already instructed Morris to contact the employment agency and engage not only a steward, but a secretary. All those chores—reading the newspapers and managing my correspondence and what-have-you—can be taken from your shoulders."

"I thought you were going to wait until we went to London to do that?" she asked, a quaver in her voice.

"I never really meant to go to London, my dear," Caius lied with a faint, rueful smile on his face. "It would be too... hectic for me there. But I want *you* to go. There is no reason to bury yourself with me in the country."

"I don't understand, Caius," she said, her voice louder and higher.

He smiled while his chest caved in on itself, obliviousness beckoning him. "Surely you understood that you only needed to remain here until Victor's concerns were allayed, Selina? You are free now, at liberty to visit your family or begin your life in London or—"

"What are you saying?"

"I'm saying we no longer need to pretend that our marriage was ever anything but a convenient arrangement."

Silence greeted his words.

"You are a very young woman, Selina. There is much of life that still awaits you. I—well, my path leads in another direction."

"Another direction? You mean one that doesn't include me? Have you known all along you would say these things to me?" she asked, her voice so sharp and brittle that he scarcely recognized her.

"Well, not *exactly* these words, but I knew this was a temporary agreement, one that would yield benefits for both of us."

When she didn't answer, he said, "You need to experience life, Selina."

"And this—what we have? That is not *life*?"

"It was an agreement—a contract, if you will—and we have both satisfied our parts and are now free to move on."

Silence met his words.

And then footsteps and the sound of a door opening and then closing.

Chapter 36

Selina walked out of the library, down the stairs, and out of the foyer, not stopping for a hat or cloak. She was vaguely aware of passing servants and them speaking to her, but she had no words left inside her.

Her thoughts refused to be corralled and tamed. Over and over she heard Caius's dismissal.

One thought pushed its way through all the others, like an especially vigorous salmon fighting against the flow of an unstoppable river: Selina had stupidly believed that Caius had wanted her for herself. As things turned out—and just as her mother had always warned her—without her face, she would never be enough for anyone.

Selina laughed and was startled by the sound. She looked around her and saw that she was headed toward the lake—toward the same place where she and Caius had spent an idyllic afternoon. An afternoon during which he must have already been thinking of how soon he might be rid of her.

Or perhaps it had begun even earlier? Maybe as far back as the first time he'd left his room and begun to take control of his life. Had her role in his recovery ever been anything beyond the simple act of forcing him to leave his bed?

Mrs. Nelson—her predecessor—would probably have effected the same result had she not fled.

Instead, it had been Selina's task.

And now that it was over, he saw her for what she was: an entirely average woman who happened to possess exceptional beauty. And beauty was the one attribute Caius could never again have any use for.

Selina came to the edge of the lake and slumped to the ground. The noise in her head was simply too much.

Too much.

She lay back in the grass and closed her eyes.

***

Selina woke up remarkably rested and refreshed.

Until she remembered why she was lying in the grass at the edge of the lake. It was like a nightmare, but with her eyes open. Caius had asked her to leave—had all but ordered her to go.

Selina sighed, suddenly tired again. But the sky had darkened, telling her she'd already been gone from the house a long time. A glance at the watch pinned to her bodice told her it was after seven-thirty; she had missed dinner and would owe Cook an apology.

She knew she should get up and go home—*home*, ha!—but her body was too leaden.

Instead of getting up, Selina lowered her head in her hands and squeezed her eyes shut against the tears that threatened. It was just too humiliating to think of going back to Queen's Bower—even if Mama and Papa weren't there. And she couldn't go to either of her married sisters. Nor did she especially want to go to London and tolerate the sly looks and comments her presence—without her husband of barely a month—would elicit.

You have money—you have jewels you could sell. Go into Much Deeping and get on the first coach leaving the inn. And just ride and ride and ride until you are far away.

She could do that—she knew how to do it better, now. She could keep going until she was in Paris.

Her hand reflexively went to her midriff.

No. She couldn't run away. Because she was almost certain that she was carrying Caius's child. It had only been a week since her missed courses, but she knew her body.

Even if she could run away from her husband and deprive him of his child—a thought that had more appeal than it should right then—she could not steal a child away from its own father.

Like it or not, she was now tethered to him and yet he'd rejected her.

Selina couldn't just collapse and give in; she was a mother already. Parenting didn't begin at birth. There was groundwork to lay. A nest to build.

You can't run away from this any more than you can run away from yourself.

The thought should have been frightening, but it actually calmed her.

She breathed deeply, her racing thoughts gradually slowing.

If Caius wanted her to go, she would go. But she didn't need to go where he told her, did she?

She had made her own way once; she could do it again.

It would be both better and worse this time. Better, because she had a baby to look forward to—a person of her own. And worse because she would be forced to leave behind the man she loved.

***

Caius didn't think Selina would really leave Courtland.

You're a fool if you believe that, Elton said, the certainty in his phantom voice chilling Caius to his bones.

No, she likes our life together; she will stay. She will fight for us, like she once fought for me.

Go to her and apologize.

I'm doing this for her! She gave up her freedom to save me. The least I can do is give that back to her.

Elton had no response for that.

Selina didn't come to him—she didn't fight. She didn't speak to him at all.

It took five long, frosty days before her bags were packed and the traveling coach was ready to depart.

Caius suspected she would have left without a word if he'd not instructed Morris to keep him informed of her plans.

"Please send word when you arrive safely in London," Caius said, his hand on the window of the traveling coach, as if that would somehow keep the carriage from leaving.

"Of course, my lord. Thank you for your concern."

The cool staccato words were like a series of sharp slaps.

"Are you sure you have enough—"

"I have enough of everything, my lord. Thank you." She raised her voice. "I am ready, Gamble."

Gamble, who'd been Caius's coachman for fifteen years, cleared his throat.

Caius nodded. "Keep her safe, Gamble."

"Aye, my lord."

"Drive on," he ordered.

Caius waited until he could no longer hear the hooves and wheels. Even after those sounds had dissipated, he still stood, his mind, for the moment, blissfully empty.

"My lord?" Morris said. "It has begun to rain, sir."

Caius blinked and shook himself out of his fugue, grateful that the moisture on his cheeks wasn't tears. If he broke down sobbing his poor butler would probably suffer a nervous collapse.

"What time is it?" he asked, because he had nothing else to say.

"Ten o'clock, my lord."

"Ah." He tapped his way back inside the house and then paused in the foyer, suddenly confused.

It was ten o'clock, normally the time he and Selina went through the day's correspondence and caught up on bills. But Selina was gone, and Caius's new secretary would not arrive until the following week.

"My lord?" Morris prodded again, clearly befuddled as to why his master was standing in the middle of the foyer like a human stalagmite, an accretion of bone and sinew and misery rather than rock.

Caius swallowed down the emotions that threatened to choke him and said, "I'll be in the gymnasium."

***

"Caius? *Caius*?"

Caius jolted as a hand grabbed his wrist and spun him around.

"Victor?" he gasped, his lungs aching with each breath. "What are you doing here?"

Another hand landed on his bare shoulder and he heard a gasp. "Good Lord, Caius—your skin is on fire. Morris says you've been in here since Selina left."

"Why? What time is it?"

"Eleven o'clock."

"What of it? I usually spend more than an hour. This is noth—"

"It is eleven o'clock at *night*, Caius. You've been in here all day and most of the night. Here, drink this." Cool glass pressed against his lips and Caius seized the container with both hands and drained it.

"Let me refill it," Victor said. "I suspect the only reason you aren't lying on the floor right now is that Morris said he's sent a footman up every hour with water. Although you snarled at the poor man."

"I did?" Caius had no recollection of either footmen or water. "What are you doing here?" he asked after he'd drained the second glass, wiping his mouth with the back of his hand.

"Morris sent for me this morning."

"Why?" Caius gasped. "Good God! Has something happened to Selina? The coach is it—"

"Calm yourself, Brother. Selina is *fine*. At least as far as I know. No, Morris sent to tell me that she'd packed up all her things. He said the two of you had been... well, nonexistent from the day Sarah and I left. I wish to God that Morris had contacted me sooner, but he didn't believe she would really go."

"She went," Caius said, suddenly angry. "What of it?" he snapped, furious with Morris for contacting Victor and with Victor for rushing to Courtland as if Caius could not take care of himself.

Victor's hands closed around his shoulders and this time his fingers dug into the fatigued muscles until they hurt. "This is about what I told you, isn't it? You fool," he hissed before Caius could answer. "You sent her away, didn't you?"

"I gave her her freedom."

"Did she *ask* for her freedom, Caius?"

"No, she is too self-sacrificing to ever ask for such a thing."

"I don't suppose you've considered any other possible reasons that she never asked to be set free," Victor retorted with altogether too sarcastic a tone.

"What are you getting at, Victor?"

"She doesn't *want* to leave, Caius." He made an exasperated noise. "I blame myself for all this—if I'd just kept my damned mouth shut the two of you would have been just as happy and deeply in love as—"

"She doesn't love me."

"Caius, I truly hope you will forgive me for what I'm about to say."

"What?"

"You must be truly blind—soul blind—not to realize that woman is in love with you. I don't know if she ever said the words, but she declared herself in every look and action. It is my dearest wish that my own wife will one day regard me with the same adoration that Selina shows you every minute of the damned day."

"I—no. That can't be true. You must be wrong." Caius's heart was beating so loudly his voice sounded as if it were coming from a long way off.

"Why must I be wrong? Because I'm the idiot who threatened a woman to marry you when she was already half-way in love with you and would have married you *without* me behaving like a beast? Bloody hell, man! If you don't believe me, then ask somebody you trust." He raised his voice and shouted, "Thomas—go fetch Morris."

The door opened and a familiar voice said, "Er, I'm right here, Lord Victor."

Victor snorted. "Listening at the door, Morris?"

"No, I would never—"

"Shame on you, Morris," Victor chided, talking over the old man. "But since you already heard, then you can tell my brother that what I just said is true."

Morris cleared his throat. "Her ladyship is exceedingly fond"—Victor cleared his throat—"Her ladyship loves you, my lord," Morris amended. "And I can honestly say that it has broken her heart to leave you." The last words were garbled and Caius heard a watery gulping sound. "I know you cannot see, but... Surely you could hear it in her voice—or feel it in your heart, my lord?"

Caius was afraid of the hope in his chest. "If what either of you believe is true, then why did she leave me?"

"If you love her, then why would you make her go?" Morris retorted, angry for once.

Caius opened his mouth, and then closed it. And then opened it again, "I... this is—"

"This is mendable," Victor interrupted in a hurried voice. "But—like a broken bone—a broken heart will heal best if it is quickly treated. Don't wait almost nine years like I did, Caius."

"How—"

"I came here in my curricle. It is a clear evening, and the moon is waxing gibbous. Gamble will stop at the Greedy Vicar for the night, as he always does. If we ride through the night, we can catch her tomorrow."

Caius nodded, his body already moving toward the door. But then he stopped and turned to his brother. "Victor—thank you for this. I—"

"You are my brother, Caius, and I love you. Of course, I came. Now," he grabbed Caius's arm. "There is no time for talk. Let us go and get your lady."

Chapter 37

Traveling as a marchioness had distinct advantages, and not just the best suite of rooms at the Greedy Vicar Inn, but the best horses and fastest service.

"His lordship is well-known and well-liked on this stretch of road, my lady," Gamble, the old coachman, boasted when she remarked on the speedy, gracious treatment they received.

Selina had eaten a meal she didn't taste, taken a bath she didn't remember, and then dismissed her maid early so that she could cry herself to sleep.

She'd woken up to a face in her mirror that looked a decade older. She had never used cosmetics in her life. But when Fanny had—diffidently—asked about applying a *bit of color* to my lady's cheeks Selina had taken the offer without hesitation.

Now they were on the road for another long day. One more night at an inn and then she would be in London.

After several days of consideration, she had changed her mind about visiting either of her two sisters. Not because she didn't think they would both accept her with open arms, but because she wasn't ready to tell anyone about the collapse of her marriage. Besides, she needed to carve something out for herself, not bring her problems to somebody else to solve.

These past five days had convinced her that she was pregnant, which meant she would have to go back to Courtland at some point, but not for several months. Before that happened, she would scour Caius out of her heart so when she did return, it would be as a cool, mature woman who could live with her husband the way her mother had always insisted *ton* marriages should be conducted: separately.

Before leaving she had answered all the letters that she'd received from her siblings, addressing their questions with vague generalities. She was as uninterested in dissecting her disastrous marriage on paper as she was in person.

Luckily, Hy and Phoebe were so busy with their new lives that they probably wouldn't notice anything amiss.

Only Aurelia might wonder, but her wise, loving, supportive older sister was hundreds of miles away, living her own life.

Selina wasn't surprised when a tear streaked down her cheek. Lately it seemed like anything was enough to make her cry, although she reserved a special reservoir of tears just for Caius.

She surreptitiously wiped them away, not wanting to upset poor Fanny.

Selina sighed, staring at the same page of her book that she'd been looking at since they left the inn an hour and a half earlier. Usually journeys by carriage seemed to drag, but this one was flying by, as if the fates couldn't wait to deliver her to her new, empty life in London.

Quit complaining. It could be much, much worse. Instead of a wealthy, independent woman of means you could be headed back to Queen's Bower and your mother's oppressive expectations and your father's frivolous dissipation. That was Nanny.

Or, even worse, you could be married to Shelton, Hy chimed in. *Marriage to Fowler might have been slightly better than Shelton. After a year or two the baron might have got up the nerve to actually speak to you.*

That thought was enough to make even Selina's lips twitch. It also calmed her nerves enough to read. She'd just turned her first page in ages when the big coach suddenly jolted.

Selina yelped when she bumped against the window, her book sliding to the floor.

"What in the world was that?" she asked her maid, who'd bent to fetch the book. "Thank you, Fanny."

Fanny pressed her face to the glass. "I can't see—but I think Timothy just shouted something," she said, referring to the footman riding on the box.

Selina scowled when she saw the spine of her book was cracked. It wasn't like her to be so careless. This book had come from—

"May I uncover the back window, my lady?"

"Yes, of course." Selina moved over on the seat so that her maid could reach the coverings they'd closed to block out the early morning glare.

"Do you think it is highwaymen, my lady?" Fanny asked, her sixteen-year-old eyes filled with a concerning amount of excitement at the thought of being robbed at gunpoint.

"In broad daylight? Unlikely. Unless they are the stupidest highway men ever to—"

"Oh look, my lady—it is the master in a curricle."

"*What?* He's driving a curricle?" Selina spun around and knelt on the seat beside her maid. It *was* Caius—but with Victor driving, thank the Lord.

"You must have forgotten something at home," Fanny said, her smooth brow bunching up with wrinkles. "I don't *think* we left anything important behind."

Selina snorted. As if her husband and brother would come rushing after them in a curricle because Fanny had forgotten to pack her curling tongs.

There must be something wrong.

Selina

Please, God, don't let something have happened to any of my sisters or Doddy.

Selina immediately felt like a beast for not including her parents in that prayer.

She barely waited until the ponderous coach rolled to a stop before flinging open the door and stumbling out. "What is it?" Selina cried. "Is it my sisters? Doddy? Is one of them—"

"Your siblings are all fine," Caius assured her, disembarking far more gracefully from the stylish curricle.

"Is it my mother or father?"

"Nothing is wrong with anyone, Selina." His face creased into a smile that was both relieved and overjoyed. "It is good to hear your voice."

Selina blinked, confused. "What—? Caius, I don't understand. What is going on."

"I lied," he said, not stopping until he was right in front of her.

"You mean something *is* wrong?"

"Yes, your husband is an idiot."

Selina greedily gorged on the sight of said idiot, but forced herself to be stern. "Please tell me you did not come all this way to tell me something I already know, my lord."

He laughed and said, "I deserved that."

Selina crossed her arms and stared.

Victor, who'd dismounted in a more leisured fashion, came up beside his brother. "Er, she is not smiling, Caius. She has crossed her arms and looks... angry."

Selina shifted just enough to include Victor in her glare. "You have a great deal of nerve showing your face, Lord Victor."

"I know."

She lifted one eyebrow.

"I've been as big a fool as Caius"—her husband cleared his throat and Victor sighed and said, "A *bigger* fool, actually."

Selina waited.

"I apologize for threatening you all those weeks ago, my lady. I should have begged your pardon long before now."

"You shouldn't have made such a loathsome threat to begin with."

"No, I shouldn't have."

It was difficult—not to mention unrewarding—to argue with somebody who capitulated so quickly and humbly.

"I regret what I did because it was cruel, but also because it was unnecessary. You would have married my brother without any coercion on my part, isn't that true?"

She slid her gaze to Caius, whose expression was anxious and adorably hopeful.

No! she mentally scolded herself. *Do not give in to him just because he is adorable.*

"What difference does that make?" she retorted, forcing her gaze back to her brother-in-law.

"None," Caius replied before Victor could open his mouth. "I was an idiot to let you go for any reason—whether I'd gained you in my life by coercion or not. I should have locked you in the cellar, not let you go."

"You didn't *let* me go. You all but kicked me down the front steps of Courtland."

He winced at her accusation. "You are correct. I am worse than an idiot. I don't know what word to use."

"Idiot works well enough for now," Selina said.

Caius choked on something that sounded suspiciously like a laugh and held out his walking stick to his brother before dropping to one knee.

"Caius, what are you—"

"I am not a humble man, Selina, but I will not hesitate to beg for your forgiveness. If you don't feel like forgiving me now, I will follow you to London. I will knock on the door of Shaftsbury House every single day until you forgive me and come home."

"What if I never forgive you?"

He swallowed. "Being rejected by you every day for the rest of my life is better than never getting to see you at all, Selina."

She stared down at him, mesmerized as always by his dazzling silvery gaze. "You have ruined those pantaloons, Caius."

He caught his lower lip with his teeth. If he was trying to bite back his smile then he failed miserably. "I love you so much, darling. I am a proud, hotheaded fool—"

"An idiot," she corrected.

He laughed. "A dunderhead."

"Dunce."

"A numbskull and more," he agreed. "But I promise to do better if you give me another chance. Please."

Selina's throat tightened and her eyes got that itchy feeling that heralded tears. She cupped his beloved face in her hands. "You threw me away so easily, Caius. What is to stop you the next time you have doubts?"

"It wasn't easy at all, sweetheart—it almost killed me."

"Why didn't you just *ask* me why I married you?"

He swallowed and blinked, his own eyes getting a little glassy. "Because I'm an idiot?"

Selina gave a watery laugh. "I married you because I wanted you—*you*, the man, not because of some charitable impulse to save you. I wanted you the way you are, not the way you were." A wretched tear slid down her cheek. "Although I didn't recognize the feeling when we were betrothed, I now know that I loved you even then, Caius."

He closed his eyes and leaned his forehead against her belly. "You have no idea how badly I wanted to hear that."

"Oh, trust me, I have a very good idea. Now, get up before you hurt your knees."

He laughed and Selina reached down and took his hand, waiting until he'd he was back on his feet before she leaned close and said, loud enough so only Caius could hear, "I have one condition before I agree to go home with you."

"Anything," he said without hesitation.

"I want you to stay with me some nights—I want to wake up beside you some mornings."

"But you know—"

"I don't care—or rather, I care very much and want to be with you. *For better or for worse,* Caius."

"As you wish, Selina." He laid his forehead against hers. "Do you forgive me?"

"I think you might need to grovel a bit more."

He grinned. "You will need to come back with me to enjoy my groveling," he pointed out with a hopeful look.

Selina brushed her lips against his, her face scalding at her own boldness.

"Will you come home with me, Selina?"

She took his hand and led him toward the coach. "I thought you'd never ask."

Epilogue

Three Months Later...

Caius struggled against the huge hand crushing his chest but his arms and legs refused to obey him and move. He was paralyzed, trapped in the dark. He wanted to shout—to scream for help—but his lips and tongue were numb.

He was suffocating while Death hovered over him, laughing and mocking Caius for being so utterly useless and powerless.

Help us! A voice shouted, but it was only in Caius's mind because his mouth refused to move. *Please! Anyone, help us! Pleeeeeeeee—*

"Caius. Darling—you are dreaming. Wake up Caius," a sweet voice whispered, gentle hands stroking his immobilized shoulders and arms. "It is only a dream, my love. Come back to me, Caius."

This time, when he tried to force his eyes to open, his eyelids obeyed him.

And yet nothing had changed; the same muffling darkness hung over him. He was awake—he'd left the nightmare behind—but he was still blind.

A cool hand stroked his brow and he sagged against it, the tension draining from his body. His life came back to him slowly at first, and then in a rush. He might be blind, but he was married to the most wonderful woman in the world. And she loved him—just as he was.

"I'm sorry," he croaked, his throat parched and sore. "Was I shouting again?"

"Yes, but just for a moment this time, you seemed to come about more quickly."

He didn't tell her that the dream felt as endless as it always had. Having her beside him when he woke made his nights bearable for the first time in over a year. He had fewer nightmares now. Sometimes several weeks would pass without him having any when they slept together in the same bed. And when he did have the awful dream, she gently brought him back to himself.

Caius exhaled, relieved and overjoyed to wake up beside her. "Thank you," he said.

"For what?" she asked.

"For being here when I wake up. For not minding that I keep you awake with my thrashing and shouting. For loving me. For a hundred other things."

"Just a hundred?"

Selina

He laughed and rolled over onto his hands and knees, straddling her luscious body. She was naked from their earlier lovemaking and her generous curves were soft and welcoming.

He caressed a hand over the gentle swell of her belly and lowered his lips to kiss where their child was growing. "I'm sorry for keeping you awake. Especially now that you are sleeping for two."

She chuckled. "Oh, I've been getting enough sleep for four. I think I took at least that many naps yesterday."

Selina was not shy at all about sharing the changes she was experiencing. Nor did she try to hide herself away from him. If anything, she had become more relaxed about her body and welcomed his touches. That was a relief to him, because touching her was so important to him; he needed it like air or water. It amazed him that he'd lived most of his thirty-seven years not even considering how much information he received through his skin.

And there was nothing he liked touching more than his wife's delicious body.

"How do you feel?" he asked, sliding a hand down to cup her sex.

She gave that squawky chuckle that never failed to charm him. "If that is your way of asking if we might have another go—"

"Have another go? *Have another go?*" he repeated in disbelief. "Just who is teaching you these vulgar phrases?"

"I think that was something you said, Caius."

"I would never," he said, moving up her belly to her breasts. "Your nipples are hard—are you cold?"

"Well, you did kick all the blankets off us." She lifted her arms to embrace him. "I think it is now your responsibility to keep me warm."

He growled with approval and lowered his torso over hers, reaching between them to guide his erection into the tight clasp of her body. They both groaned when he pushed inside her.

"I love it in here," he murmured, his hips thrusting languidly, giving her his full length with each stroke.

"You certainly spend enough time in there."

"Selina!"

She laughed.

"You brazen hussy you." He nipped her ear. "Have I told you how much I love it when you are naughty?"

"You might have mentioned it a time or twenty," she said, bending her knees until they bracketed his hips, her pelvis tilting to take him deeper.

"Yes, you take me so good—so deep and tight," he murmured. The way she clenched told Caius that he wasn't the only one who appreciated a bit of innuendo and filthy language. He adjusted the angle of his hips so that he rubbed her sensitive little nub with each stroke. "I want you to come with me, Selina." He pumped into her fast and hard, driving her up the bed with the force of his thrusts.

She clenched her inner muscles, her fingers digging into his buttocks as she rolled her hips to meet his thrusts.

"Now," he hissed, driving himself as deeply as he could go before relinquishing control and flooding her with his seed.

She convulsed around him, calling out his name as she surrendered to her passion, milking every drop from him with fierce, delicious contractions that left him boneless and blissfully sated.

As much as Caius wanted to collapse on top of her, he rolled to the side, instead. Selina claimed that she liked being crushed beneath him, but lately—as her belly had swelled—he worried he would hurt her.

After his harsh breathing had settled into a more natural rhythm Selina turned to him and laid a hand on his stomach.

"What time is it?" he asked.

"Just after five o'clock."

"Hmph. Not really worth going to sleep again since we need to be up and off in a few hours." He slid a hand over until he found her mound and idly stroked his fingers through her swollen petals. She was soaking wet with both their juices and Caius couldn't wait to fill her with even more. He loved to think of her going about her day with slick, slippery thighs.

"Mmm." She caressed his abdomen, her fingers tracing the grooves between the muscles. "Who said anything about going back to sleep?"

Caius laughed. "You are insatiable. I love it." He turned onto his side, so they were facing each other. "And I love you."

She cupped his face and kissed the tip of his nose. "And I love *you*." She stroked his jaw. "Are you sure you want to do this?"

"By *this* you mean go to Wych House for the holiday?"

"Yes. You know that my mother and father will be there. And Wych House is old and rickety and confusing and—"

"Yes, I'm sure." He slid a hand around her waist and pulled her closer, until her sweet little belly was pressing against him. "I already told you that I will be fine."

"I know you will. It's just that it might be a bit… much. I would understand if you changed your mind and decided to stay. We could have Victor, Sarah, and Cora over and—"

"I want to meet your family, Selina. Don't you want me to?"

"I do—more than anything I want you to meet my sisters. And Doddy is wild to meet you. You know you're his hero? He will pester you for stories that he can tell his new school friends. And you already know Chatham, so that will be nice…"

"But?"

"I am so sorry that Shelton and Fowler will be there, Caius!" she wailed.

Caius grinned; so that's what all her nervousness was about. "It's hardly your fault that they're going to be there. And you can't do anything about it." He shrugged. "So long as neither of them tries to elope with you then I shan't have any reason to administer a drubbing or call them out."

Selina laughed. "Thank you for being so understanding about this. Lots of husbands would be jealous and difficult."

Oh, he was plenty jealous. But, at the end of the day, Caius had Selina, while those other two men would likely regret the loss of her for the rest of their lives.

"But really, I could just throttle Katie for asking those wretched men along to a family gathering."

Caius was more surprised the two fools had accepted. Why in the world would they want to spend Christmas with the family of a woman who had robbed them and then run away?

Selina's hand slid lower, until her dexterous little fingers lightly stroked his balls. She'd become increasingly bold over the past few months when it came to exploring his body. Caius subtly spread his thighs wider to encourage her adventurous spirit.

"I don't think I've ever heard Hy as incensed as she was in that last letter," Selina went on. "She absolutely *loathes* Shelton. And Phoebe is beside herself at being forced to play hostess to Shelton."

"Have I told you lately how much I like your sisters?" Caius murmured, palming one of her luscious breasts.

His wife didn't seem to hear him. "Fowler and Shelton will be bad enough, but I just know my mother will be rude and thoughtless to you. And I'm sure my father will—"

"None of that will matter if I'm with you." He kissed her. "But I appreciate you being concerned about my comfort. You are very good to me." He knew she'd be squirming at his praise. "Besides," he said, thumbing her nipple, "it will be good practice for when we go to London, where I will be forced to confront countless rude, thoughtless people, not to mention hundreds of your ex-suitors."

She laughed again, but it sounded distracted and breathy as he was pinching and tugging on her nipple until it was a tight pebble.

"I'm so sad that Aurelia won't be able to go to Wych House. It won't be the same without her."

"Yes, I'm sad, too," Caius agreed, giving her other nipple the same treatment. "I was looking forward to meeting her—and thanking her for training you up so well in the erotic arts."

She gave him a light shove. "Promise me right now that you won't say any such thing."

"I won't say it this time, seeing how she won't be there," he murmured, rolling her onto her back as she chuckled and kneeling between her thighs.

"I wonder what made her change her mind about coming at the last minute," Selina mused, considerately opening her legs nice and wide to accommodate him.

Caius grinned; God, he loved her.

"I'm worried about her, Caius. Her employer sounds like an odd sort of man."

"Does he?" Caius asked as he braced his forearms against her thighs and then gently parted her lower lips with his thumbs.

"Yes, he does. And I can't help wondering if there is something—*ah, good Lord,*" she moaned, as he flicked her engorged little bud with the tip of his tongue. "Oh, my goodness." She gave a sensual little shiver. "That's—mmm—I love that, Caius."

He lifted off her just enough to say, "Oh? What else do you love?" And then he lowered his mouth and sucked her sensitive bundle of nerves between his lips.

"*Unghh,*" she groaned, clutching a handful of his hair, and pushing his head down.

"What?" he asked, smiling against her tender flesh. "I didn't quite catch that?"

"Catch *what?*" she demanded, sounding more than a little frustrated.

"I asked what else you loved, darling."

"*You!* I love you." She pushed his head down, or at least tried to. "Now... why don't you just—"

"But you were in the middle of telling me something about your sister? I should hate to distract you from your stor—"

"*Arrgh!* You already distracted me."

"I did?" he asked in an innocent tone. "How about this?" he asked, sliding two fingers inside her and working her with languid thrusts. "Is that distracting?"

She groaned. "No, no, not completely," she said tightly. "Perhaps you should stop talking and apply yourself if you are *truly* trying to distract me."

He laughed. "I love you, darling."

And then Caius applied his not inconsiderable skills and commenced to distract his demanding wife utterly and completely.

The End

Dearest Reader:

I hope you loved Selina and Caius's slow burn romance and weren't too shocked or disappointed that she passed over poor, tongue-tied Fowler to look for a man who loved her for herself.

I found it challenging to write Selina's character. Why? Mainly because I'm not so beautiful that I scramble men's brains, lol. That sort of beauty has always intrigued me, but it is a foreign landscape and I was an eager tourist. I've known one person in my life who had Selina's type of beauty. She was also extremely sweet and kind and very much wanted to be liked/admired/respected for something other than her appearance. She was definitely my inspiration for this character.

I think, if I'd written this book at 25, I would have had an entirely different perspective about Selina and her problems. From the vantage point of an older (hopefully wiser!) woman, I know that looks are not all they are cracked up to be. Beauty fades, a sexy body ages, and what is left needs to carry a person through the second half of their life.

On some level, Selina knows that. She's not brilliant like her sister Hy or a talented artist like Aurelia. And the one thing she was supposed to do well—marry—she's completely screwed up. In fact, she went one step further than just dropping the ball, she scored against her own team when she left a trail of scandal in her wake.

Lately in historical romance there has been a trend to make every single heroine a kick-ass, ninja-style, outspoken, tough chick who won't take *no* for an answer.

Um, yeah... I don't think that was as prevalent as we like to think.

I think there were a lot of women like Selina, who struggled to find their way within the confines of the patriarchy, not "smashing" it, but undermining it by using the means available to them.

Selina keeps trudging along to get what she wants, even though she's been repeatedly put in her place by men (and her mother) and groomed to be subservient. She might be a kitten in a lot of ways, but she's a resilient one who knows how to get up after being knocked down and who is so accustomed to being underestimated that she doesn't let her pride get in the way.

So, what about Caius?

Before his accident he was your basic hot jock party boy. In his own words, he was a *man* before his accident. And afterward... Well, he has some serious adjusting to do. Is he angry and unreasonable and difficult? Yes, very. Behind all that bluster is a dump truck load of fear.

I didn't want his blindness to be a gimmick. I didn't want it to be a way to teach him how to be humble and then *hey presto* he'd get his vision back after another knock on the head. I wanted Selina to fall in love with who he is *now* rather than who he used to be.

It was challenging to write a character who is blind. I did what I usually do when I write: I tried to put myself in his place and take into consideration the era, gender, social class, etc., as best as I am able.

As twenty-first century people it is hard to understand just how isolating blindness would have been in the early 1800s. No radio, TV, audiobooks. It was also before Braille, so no reading or writing.

Just *think* about what Caius could do to entertain himself—or just keep occupied. Almost *everything* would have involved another person. Over time he might learn to do new things that wouldn't require assistance—maybe sculpt or carve or play an instrument—but the learning curve would be a steep one.

Also, blindness was regarded very differently during the period. It is not inconceivable that somebody (as Victor threatens to do) might argue that Caius suffered mental as well as physical damage and have him put away.

When I was an undergrad, one of my many jobs was working as a reader for the blind. All the people I read for were in graduate school, and the books I read were textbooks in a variety of subjects—from law to chemistry It was the first time I'd been around people who'd either been born without sight or who'd lost and—in one memorable instance—were in the process of losing their vision.

I read for one woman who was going through law school part-time (as well as raising two kids and working for the IRS). I've kept in touch with her over the years and she was kind enough to answer some questions and direct me to some excellent source material. She has Stargardt Disease, which is a rare, hereditary type of macular degeneration that starts in younger people.

In talking with her—and in reading about blindness in general—one of the most significant factors in how people adjust to being blind is whether they were born blind or become blind later in life.

For example, if you were born blind, you'd not be in the habit of making eye contact and you might not bother opening your eyes as often. People who lose their sight as adults would have those behaviors ingrained. Those are just a few of the differences. Obviously, there are many factors at play and blind people come in as many types as sighted people.

I decided to save my research about chess, card playing, and other hobbies until after I wrote the sections of the book that mention those activities. I wanted to see what solutions *I*—and by extension, Selina—might have come up with before I saw what was available.

Minerva Spencer & S.M. LaViolette

Chess was easy. My husband and I play (it's what we did on our very first date!) so I could imagine what would need to happen to make the game possible for Caius.

Playing cards was likewise intuitive. I know card sharps mark the cards with almost invisible markings, so I figured there would be some way to mark playing cards that would be both visible to the player and not visible to their opponent. I made a set by gluing millet to the cards. They were a disaster, LOL, and I decided to leave card games out of the story.

So, what's next for the Bellamy Sisters? Well, you might be disappointed that I didn't give you a Christmas house party in this book, but it was already too long to do that. And I didn't want to give a party short shrift, so I'm thinking about writing a holiday novella, but we'll see… I still have a few books on my plate this year. AURELIA is already up for preorder, and that will be out March 2024.

Up next on my publishing schedule are my two science fiction romance/post-apocalyptic novels in THE TIME CONTROL trilogy. These aren't hard science and are more focused on the characters and their journeys. AND THEY HAVE THE DUKE OF WELLINGTON AS A CHARACTER!! (Sorry to shout, I'm just very excited to give the Iron Duke the romance he needed…)

I'd love it if you decided to check them out. Here's the title for the first in the series, AMIRA'S GAMBIT. Incidentally, this story won 1st prize in the Rocky Mountain Fiction Writer's Contest!

In October, I've got the second book in that sci-fi series, THE IRON DUKE, and also the final book in my WILD WOMAN OF WHITECHAPEL series, THE CUTTHROAT COUNTESS. If you liked the knife throwing Jo Brown and her mischievous raven, Angus, then here is your chance to read more.

In December is book 6 in THE ACADEMY OF LOVE. This is THE STORY OF LOVE and features feisty heroine Lorelei and a man who is her match, Stand Fast Severn (gotta love those Puritan names!).

So, that's a lot for only a few more months of 2023, right?!

As always, if you've enjoyed the book, I'd love a review. I don't pay people to write reviews for me, so I rely on actual readers. Even if you see reviews already there, add your own because Amazon bumps up the most recent reviews.

If you have something (nice, lol) you'd like to share with me I'd love to hear from you! Drop me a line at: minerva@minervaspencer.com or check out my website at https://minervaspencer.com

Until next month, dear reader, happy reading!

Xo

Minerva/S.M.

Made in United States
Cleveland, OH
04 January 2025